MW00860515

THE COLOR OF COURAGE

CODENAME ODILE

TIMELESS AGENTS SERIES
BOOK 1

HANNAH BYRON

Copyright © 2024 by Hannah Byron

All rights reserved.

No part of this book may be reproduced in any form or by any electronic or mechanical means, including information storage and retrieval systems, without written permission from the author, except for the use of brief quotations in a book review.

This book is a work of fiction, inspired by real events and individuals from World War II. Names, characters, businesses, places, events, and incidents are used in a fictional manner, even when based on actual historical facts and figures. While the narrative may incorporate real names and locations to enhance the authenticity of the setting, the portrayal of characters and events is purely fictional. Any resemblance to actual persons, living or dead, or actual events is coincidental and should be interpreted within the context of a fictional story. For more information, please see the Author's Note.

ISBN eBook: 978-90-833027-5-1
ISBN Paperback: 978-90-833027-6-8
Book Cover Design by Ebooklaunch
Editor: Amber Fritz-Hewer
Website: Hannah Byron

IN HONOR OF CAPT. LISE MARIE JEANNETTE DE BAISSAC MBE CDEG

CUREPIPE, MAURITIUS, 11 MAY 1905 – MARSEILLE, FRANCE, 29 MARCH 2004

"I needed cold-blooded efficiency for long weary months more than heroism".

Lise de Baissac

PREFACE

Welcome to *Timeless Agents,* a dual-narrative historical fiction series that delves into the groundbreaking missions of the British female secret agents of the Special Operations Executive (SOE) French Section during World War II.

With Book 1, *The Color of Courage*, we embark on a journey through time with Captain Lise de Baissac and graffiti artist Sil Anderson. In the forthcoming books, I will intertwine the missions and lives of each featured agent with the struggles and triumphs of a contemporary woman.

As a historical fiction author, my goal is to present a diverse and inclusive portrayal of history. In my books, courageous women take the lead in a war that was initiated and predominantly fought by men. The *Timeless Agents* series honors the crucial, yet often overlooked, role of the women in the Resistance.

The SOE's female and male agents were among the bravest individuals to have ever graced the earth, yet their stories are frequently overshadowed by the grand battles of WW II and the heroic victory of the Allied Forces over Nazi Germany.

During the recent 80th Anniversary of D-Day in 2024, the speeches lauding the heroism of the soldiers seldom referenced these 'ordinary civilians'. However, the SOE agents were instrumental in delaying the German advance to the Normandy beaches, thereby saving countless Allied lives.

And in the years leading up to D-Day, the largest military operation in human history, the SOE agents courageously and selflessly armed, organized, and galvanized the French resistance from within occupied France.

It continues to awe and inspire me that a few hundred shopgirls, typists, lawyers, journalists and socialites took a few weeks of intense combat training and Morse code training before jumping from a plane over occupied France to face an unknown fate. Their only requirements: a British passport and fluency in French.

Armed with patriotism, a large dose of pluck, and a sense of adventure, they pursued the Germans with relentless energy and courage, built vast networks of resisters, and provided the Allies with indispensable information from the field. Of the 470 SOE men and women sent into France, 91 men and 13 women did not survive.

In my humble opinion, the willingness to give one's life for their country as a non-military person represents heroism in its purest form, and I am honored to share their stories once more.

In *Timeless Agents*, each of these 39 heroines will be given the spotlight they deserve as their stories are unearthed by remarkable contemporary women. I will begin with the lesser-known women, and as 14 (one of whom died of illness) of them sadly did not return, one in every three books will focus on an agent whose short, well-lived life ended in captivity and death. The main reason for using the dual timeline is to tell their stories without leaving, you reader, too saddened by their fate.

Please note that, while this series is rooted in historical events and about real secret agents, *The Color of Courage* is a work of fiction and not a history book. I have taken some liberties with historical details for the sake of storytelling, but I have strived to portray the missions and lives of these women as authentically as possible.

For historians and SOE experts in particular, I invite you to read my Author's Note at the end of the book, where I disclose any deviations from recorded history. Please also note that the portrayal of all the historical protagonists reflects *my* interpretation of their character and behavior.

Given the mention of numerous agents, networks, and their codenames and aliases in this book, I provide an overview of the agents and a map indicating the approximate locations of the networks on the next page for your reference. I hope this helps clarify who's who and who's where.

Voilá *The Color of Courage*! I hope you will enjoy Sil's & Lise's story.

Happy reading,
Hannah Byron

P.S. for an overview of the SOE agents Section F appearing in *The Color of Courage* see the next page. They are alphabetically on codename. Also a map of France with the SOE Networks during WW2.

Please sign up for my Newsletter here to get exclusive bonus material on this book.

CODE NAME	NETWORK	ROLE	ALIAS	LAST NAME	FIRST NAMES	FATE
Adolphe	ADOLPHE (subnetwork PHYSICIAN)	organiser	Pierre Leclair	Culioli	Pierre	Survived capture
Alcide	WIZARD	organiser	Michel Richou	Savy	William Jean	Returned
Alphonse	PIMENTO	organiser	Antoine Brevin, André Bonal	Brooks	Anthony Morris	Returned
Aristide	SCIENTIST I	W/T operator	René Pol	Landes	Roger Arthur	Returned
Athos	BRICKLAYER	organiser	Joseph Marie Fernand Dumontet	Antelme	Joseph France Antoine	Executed
Claudine	SCIENTIST I	courier	Marie Louise Vernier	Herbert	Mary Catherine	Returned
David	SCIENTIST I	organiser	Clément Bastable	De Baissac	Claude Denis	Returned
Denis	SCIENTIST II	organiser	Michel Rouault, Claude Marc Boucher	De Baissac	Claude Denis	Returned
Denise	PHYSICIAN	courier	Denise Urbain	Borrel	Andrée Raymonde	Executed
Geneviève	SCIENTIST II	W/T operator	Paulette Janine Latour	Latour	Phyllis Ada (Pippa)	Returned
Gilbert	FARRIER	organiser	Marius Faber, Henri Goguenard	Déricourt	Henri Alfred Eugène	Returned
Hector	STATIONER	organiser	Robert Moulin, Maurice Leblanc	Southgate	Maurice	Survived capture
Jacqueline	STATIONER	courier	Josette Norville	Nearne	Jacqueline Françoise Mary	Returned
Léopold	BARBER	W/T operator	Roger Francois Marcel Doucet	Rousset	Marcel Joseph Louis	Escaped
Lise	SPINDLE	courier	Odette Metayer	Sansom	Odette Marie Céline	Survived capture
Louise	SEAMSTRESS	courier	Corinne Reine Leroy	Szabo	Violette Reine Elizabeth	Executed
Marcel	PHYSICIAN	W/T operator	Jacques Chevalier	Agazarian	Jack Charles Stanmore	Executed
Marguerite	PHYSICIAN	courier	Francine Fabre	Agazarian	Francine Isabella	Returned
Marguerite	SCIENTIST II	courier, second-in-command	Jeanette Bouville	De Baissac	Lise Marie Jeanette	Returned
Max	BUTLER	organiser	Francis Le Gwen	Bouguennec	Jean	Executed
Odette	SCHOLAR	W/T operator	Yvonne Jeanne Bernier	Baseden	Yvonne Jeanne Thérèse	Survived capture
Odile	ARTIST	organiser	Irène Brisse	De Baissac	Lise Marie Jeanene	Returned
Olive	STATIONER, SHIPWRIGHT	W/T operator	Alexander Shaw	Schwatschko	Alexandre	Suicide in capture
Prosper	PHYSICIAN	organiser	François Despree	Suttill	Francis Alfred	Executed
Renaud	BRICKLAYER	organiser	Antoine Ratier	Antelme	Joseph France Antoine	Executed
René	SCIENTIST II, VERGER	W/T operator	Jean Marie Demiremont	Renaud-Dandicolle	Jean-Marie	Died from wounds
Stanislas	ACTOR	organiser	Roger Lalande	Landes	Roger Arthur	Returned
Suzanne	MONKEYPUZZLE, ADOLPHE	courier	Jacqueline Gautier	Rudellat	Yvonne Claire	Died in captivity
Urbain	PRUNUS, WHEELWRIGHT	W/T operator	Michel Blount	Bloom	Marcus Reginald	Executed
Vladimir	SCIENTIST II, VERGER	W/T operator	Maurice Louis Langlade	Larcher	Maurice Lous Marie Aristide	Killed
Yves	VENTRILOQUIST, SCIENTIST I	second-in-command	Victor Charles	Hayes	Victor Charles	Executed

AREA OF OPERATIONS FOR MAIN CIRCUITS

~ SIL ~

Marseille, France
August 2004

1

THE PHOCAEAN CITY

Marseille, August 2004

The TGV from Paris to Marseille slid into Gare Saint-Charles train station without a hitch and came to a standstill with little more than a snake's hiss. The brakes released a sigh of compressed air, mingling with the hum of the cooling engines.

Sil hoisted her yellow Nomad backpack onto her shoulders, the familiar weight settling against her back, and clasped the straps around her jean-clad hips. Brushing past a pram with a wailing toddler, she inhaled the faint scent of baby powder mixed with the tang of sweat and train exhaust.

Next, Sil bumped into a man in a dark suit, his forehead glistening under the harsh station lights as he scrambled to get his luggage. The scent of his expensive cologne provided another attack on her nostrils. His dark hair was neatly combed, and a pair of wire-rimmed glasses perched on his nose, giving him an air of serious determination.

"*Mademoiselle, vous n'avez pas de manières?* Can you not wait a moment?" he snapped, his voice a sharp contrast to the background chatter.

"Watch your own manners, man!" Sil grumbled under her breath, meeting the brown gaze behind his spectacles for a brief, charged moment. She saw the eyes widened in surprise. He'd probably never seen a girl with rainbow hair and a nose ring before in his life.

She noticed a flicker of recognition, the mixture of irritation and intrigue she mirrored unconsciously. As she turned to leave, her backpack brushed against his hand, causing him to drop a leather-bound notebook, which she caught with a quick movement before it could hit the floor.

"Here, try not to lose your precious notes," she said, as she handed him back the notebook.

"*Merci,*" he replied, a reluctant smile tugging at the corner of his lips.

"It's *all* in the manners," Sil answered with one distinctive eyebrow raised.

"*Bienvenue à Marseille,*" the stranger replied, his tone a tad kinder. Sil shrugged as she firmly directed her army boots to the exit. The clomp of her boots on the tiled floor through Halle Honnorat echoed against the high ceiling of the station, a rhythm that matched her heartbeat.

Sil had no eyes for the shops with billboards for Chanel No1 or Hermès Jane Birkin bags, but kept her Kohl smudged eyes, narrowed like a cat on the prowl, fixed on the glass-paneled front of the hall.

Bienvenue à Marseille. Welcome to Marseille. She repeated the grumpy, suited man's words as she exited through the front doors. A wave of Mediterranean heat hit her and made her almost scramble back for cover in the cool of the station.

Sil searched her pockets for her sunglasses and fished out a pair she'd got at the Oxfam charity shop for two pounds. She peered around the large pedestrian square with the outdoor terraces and the impressive stairs that led down to the center.

Surrounded by buildings and pavements of natural yellow stone, a cloudless azure sky, the rippling Delft blue sea, and red parasols like the skirts of can-can dancers, she let out a deep breath.

This is it, girlie! You're free now!

At that moment her Motorola started vibrating in the back pocket of her jeans. What now? It was not a call she wanted to take, so she swiped to ignore and folded open her map to find her way to the apartment. Then the caller tried again, Sil blocked him.

I should have done that weeks ago, she thought angrily.

The salty tang of the sea breeze mingled with the aroma of grilled seafood and freshly brewed coffee from the street terraces, creating a unique blend of scents. The Mediterranean air carried a warm, sun-soaked saltiness, quite unlike the sharp, cold brine of the Bristol Channel where she grew up, and what she now firmly had left behind.

Overhead, seagulls squawked, their cries cutting through the ambient noise of the Metropole at her feet. Hungry, tired, and in need of the bathroom, her human needs would have to wait. Vieux Port first. Check out the apartment.

The thought of an air-conditioned taxi zooming through these sweltering streets and her heavy backpack resting comfortably in the boot was tempting. But no.

"God gave you feet to march, my dear. One foot in front of the other."

Oh Grandpa, you with your stories of trekking towards Arnhem in wintertime with frozen toes and too little booze. Grandpa Jack's Band of Brothers were his chaps from the Royal Welsh Fusiliers. All dead now.

So was Grandpa Jack. But he taught her not to be afraid to use her legs. And to leave a place when it didn't suit her anymore. Pointing his walking stick over the edge of the Blue Lagoon in Pembrokeshire on a sunny day in August, he'd instruct her eight-year-old, angry little soul, "the sea and a good pair of legs is all you need to escape from the past, Silver. I did it a few times and it always held water. So, stop moping and get walking."

Map in hand, Sil left the station behind her and descended the grand staircase of Gare Saint-Charles, each step taking her closer to the heart of Marseille. According to the directions it would take her about 15 minutes to reach her destination, Vieux Port.

As she made her way down the stairs, she greeted the view like a new friend. The panorama of the ancient city sprawled out below her, the brilliant blue of the Mediterranean glistening in the distance.

This, Sil, this!

The heat was intense, and the air was filled with the scent of street food—kebabs sizzling on grills and the fragrant aroma of herbs from nearby stalls. Sil navigated the bustling Boulevard d'Athènes when a stray cat meandered through the crowd, its thin body weaving between legs. Sil reached into her bag and broke off a piece of her granola bar, crouching to offer it. The cat sniffed cautiously before accepting the morsel, purring in gratitude.

"There you go, little one," she murmured, giving it a gentle pat.

Despite the heat and the mid-afternoon repose, the boulevard was abuzz with activity. Vendors shouting in French and Arabic, tourists snapping photos, and stoic Marseillaises going about their business as usual.

Turning right onto Rue de la République, she was greeted by the grand Haussmannian buildings with their elegant façades and wrought-iron balconies. The street was shaded by plane trees, providing a welcome respite from the tropical sun.

Sil passed charming cafés with outdoor seating, where patrons sipped espresso and white wine, chatting with that southern animation, gestures and all. The hum of conversation, the clinking of glasses, and the occasional burst of laughter *"Ahhh oui, Ahhh non!"* created a welcoming atmosphere.

Her artist's eye caught flashes of color on the side streets. Even though she wasn't passing by Cours Julien – a place she was dying to visit on the earliest occasion – she still spotted several impressive pieces of graffiti.

On one wall, a vibrant mural depicted a phoenix rising from the ashes, its fiery wings spread across the brick canvas. Another alleyway revealed a series of abstract faces, their exaggerated features and bold lines reflecting the diversity of the city's street artists.

Yes! Oh, she couldn't wait to meet them all. Leave behind the Bristol scene and embrace vibrant Marseille.

Sil paused briefly to take in the street art, shifting the weight of the heavy pack on her back and taking a gulp of water from her eco-friendly bottle. The colorful murals were a feast for her weary eyes, adding an edgy touch to the historic surroundings. Bristol had those streets too, she had to admit, but there was just something about Marseille...

She took a quick photo of the phoenix mural with her phone. She'd explore it in detail later. As she reached the end of Rue de la République, she caught her first glimpse of Vieux Port, its azure waters dotted with sailboats and yachts, surrounded by a mix of old and new buildings. She had no idea it was going to be so big.

Expecting a cozy little harbor, she was surprised to see that the Greeks who founded this Phocaean City had clearly dreamed big. With renewed energy and ignoring the heat that made her clothes stick to her body like flypaper, Sil continued her trek, her thoughts buzzing with the adventures lying ahead. The most prominent being the Ecole Supérieure des Beaux-Arts de Marseille in September.

Nobody back home had thought she'd take the plunge, let alone have the money for such a prestigious education. But there was nothing that could stop Sil Anderson now. Nothing.

The red pin on the map on her map told her she'd arrived at her destination: 32 Rue Sainte. Sil gasped. It was an I-need-to-pinch-myself-to-see-if-I'm-not-dreaming moment. A real, classic Haussmannian house, complete with elegant wrought-iron balconies and tall, shuttered windows, directly in view of the port with the bustling street below.

From the outside, 32 Rue Sainte looked like a stately old mansion, a far cry from modern, student accommodation. Sil checked the address on the email she'd received from the art school. It was correct.

She rang the third-floor bell, half expecting a Marseillaise to open the window and shoo her away. No one answered and she tried again. Re-reading the email, she buzzed the first floor for the landlord. Finally, through the intercom, a French-accented voice asked, "Miss Anderson?"

"Yes, that's me," Sil replied.

"Come on up to the third floor," the male voice invited.

The door buzzed open, and Sil found herself enveloped by a cool, tiled hall. The entrance was grand, with intricate mosaic floors and high ceilings with ornate moldings. A large, gilded, many-armed chandelier hung overhead.

To her left, a sweeping staircase with a polished wooden banister led up to the upper floors. The walls were lined with period artwork —portraits of stern-looking men and women in oval frames, and rectangular landscapes that captured the beauty of the Provence.

Quel boring art, Sil thought as she ran her hand along the smooth, cool banister as she climbed the stairs. Reaching the third floor, she found herself in front of a sturdy wooden door with a brass knocker shaped like a lion's head. Her floor? *Quel bonheur!*

Before she could knock, the door opened to reveal the same man from the station.

"You again?" Sil blurted out, her irritation clear.

"So, you must be Miss Anderson? It seems we were destined to meet again. I'm Justin Bellamare, your landlord," he said, a hint of amusement in his voice. "Let me show you to your apartment."

Sil followed him down a narrow hallway, the floors creaking slightly underfoot.

They stopped at a door at the end of the corridor. Justin Bellamare pushed it open to reveal a surprisingly spacious and airy apartment. Tall windows with delicate lace curtains let in plenty of light, and the room was furnished with a blend of modern and antique pieces that gave it a practical yet stylish feel.

"The apartment was recently renovated," Justin explained. "It has a lot of character, don't you think?"

Sil nodded, eyeing her new abode with a mixture of astonishment and glee. High ceilings, polished hardwood floors, and a marble fireplace. Clearly no longer in use, but it would have gotten the stamp of approval from Grandpa Jack, who used to judge a house by its fireplace.

"Here's the kitchen, the bedroom and the bathroom. I hope you find everything to your liking," Justin said, speeding through the apartment, as if he was on his way to an important meeting. But he still seemed to notice her hesitation.

"It's fine," Sil replied curtly, suddenly tired and confused. Justin Bellamare was an attractive man but very French and proper.

He handed her the keys. "If you need anything, I'm on the first floor. Welcome to Marseille, Mademoiselle Anderson."

With that, Sil was left alone in her new space. Really alone. It seemed like ages since she had been... alone.

Downing the last of the lukewarm water from her bottle, she walked over to the window and looked out over the port and the busy street below. The double glazing, a modern feature clearly recently put in, muted most of the noise.

I am home. I am safe. I am alive.

Sil pressed her hot forehead against the cool glass. The heat, the sleepless night of travel, and the walk made her blood pulse at her temples like the throbbing of an engine.

I need to lie down, was all she could think when the doorbell buzzed. Thinking it was Justin Bellamare who'd forgotten to give her some instruction, she pressed the button without asking who was there.

A few minutes later, someone pounded on her front door. All excitement faded on seeing the familiar figure of Felix Quirk appearing in the doorway. She pushed against the door to shut him out, but his foot was between it.

"Sil, no!" The voice was rough, strained, and filled with desperation.

"Go!"

Sil's pulse quickened, the fatigue momentarily forgotten. Why was Felix here? What did he want?

As she braced herself against the door, her mind raced with questions while the sinking feeling in her stomach told her this confrontation was far from over.

2

THE CONFRONTATION

Before she knew it, Felix Quirk stood in her apartment, his eyes bloodshot and his hands trembling. His once vibrant, sandy hair was now matted and unkempt, and a faint trace of paint still lingered under his fingernails. His clothes hung loosely on his gaunt frame, as if he had lost even more weight since she last saw him. He smelled foul as well, a cocktail of unbrushed teeth and stale alcohol.

"What the hell are you doing here, Felix? Go away! Leave me alone!" Sil's voice was shrill, but she kept it down, afraid her landlord or one of the other tenants would hear their argument. She was so done with drama, with him, with the Bristol scene. Her practiced artist's eye took in all the details of his disheveled appearance.

Felix had always been tall and lean, but now he looked almost skeletal. The dark circles under his eyes told the story of sleepless nights, and his cheeks were hollow, a very different expression to the vibrant and rebellious boy she'd met in the Bristol graffiti scene when they were both fourteen.

They had shared everything—art, dreams, even the wild experimentation with drugs that had nearly cost her life. He'd followed her. Just as he'd said he would do. *Pshaw!*

"What do you want, Felix?" she demanded again, trying to keep her voice steady.

"I needed to see you, Sil," Felix replied, his voice hoarse. "You can't just leave like that. We've been through too much together. We belong together."

Sil's heart clenched at his words, but she forced herself to stay resolute. She had sworn off drugs after that near-fatal overdose, dedicating herself to passing the entry exam for the École Supérieure des Beaux-Arts de Marseille. Leaving Bristol had been her chance to start anew, free from the chaos Felix and the Bristol scene represented.

"Felix, we talked about this," she said, her tone softening slightly. "I can't save you. I had to save myself."

"I know," he whispered, taking a shaky step towards her. "But I need you, Sil. I can't do life without you."

Sil looked away, the weight of his words pressing down on her. She had tried to help him, tried to pull him out of the abyss, but it had been a losing battle.

When she finally passed the entry requirements for the prestigious art school, she'd been overjoyed to leave Bristol and start a new life. Yet, here he was, dragging the past back into her present.

"How did you find me?" she asked, more to buy time than out of real curiosity.

Felix shrugged, a ghost of his old, defiant grin appearing on his face. "I have my ways."

The determination in his eyes was both unsettling and heartbreaking. Sil took a deep breath, steadying herself. "You need to go, Felix. This is my chance to move forward, and I can't have you pulling me back."

"Please, Sil," he pleaded, his voice cracking. "Just give me one more chance. And unblock me on your phone, for heaven's sake. If you don't want to be my lover anymore, I can accept that. But we're friends. We belong together."

Her resolve wavered for a moment, but she knew she couldn't go back to that life. "No, Felix. I can't. You need to find your own path, just like I did."

His face crumpled, and for a moment, she saw the boy she had once loved beneath the wreckage of his current state. But like all addicts, his mood swings were mercurial.

His desperation turned to anger, and he lashed out, his foot stomping against the wall of her freshly painted apartment in a violent kick. Sil watched in horror as the antique wallpaper tore, revealing a gaping hole in the plaster.

"Dammit, Felix!" she exclaimed, her frustration boiling over. "Look what you've done!"

She could feel tears stinging her eyes as she surveyed the damage, knowing that the landlord would be furious. Maybe even kick her out, and she would be at square one.

Felix smirked, an ugly twist to his once handsome features. "I don't care, Sil. You owe me. You're being obnoxious."

"I owe you nothing. Certainly not after this!" she snapped back. She hardly dared to look at the gaping wound in her wall, but her mind was already doing somersaults trying to hide the wreckage. Drag that small cupboard in front, get a handyman to repair it, lie and tell Bellamare she accidentally fell against the wall.

"But you owe me plenty now, don't you?" A sudden resolve hardened inside her. She stepped closer, feeling the heat radiating from Felix's unwashed body mingling with the musty scent of the sudden hole in the old building. "And I'll make sure you get your due if you don't disappear from my life this second!"

Her voice was a low hiss, filled with a cold fury that made Felix blink. The tension crackled in the air like static electricity, and Sil could hear the faint hum of the city outside, very different from the charged silence within the room. The taste of adrenaline was sharp on her tongue, her heartbeat pounding in her ears.

His expression faltered, uncertainty flickering in his eyes. He swallowed hard, the sound audible in the tense quiet. The defiant smirk wavered, replaced by a flash of fear as he realized the gravity of her threat.

"I know about the stash you hid in the old warehouse. Your so-called 'loot for a rainy day'," she continued, her voice cold and steady. "The police would be very interested to know about that, wouldn't they? I didn't want to use this against you, but you leave me no choice."

Felix paled, the color draining from his already gaunt face. "You wouldn't, Silly."

"Don't call me Silly. And try me," she replied, her gaze unwavering. "Get out, Felix. And don't come back. Ever."

For a moment, he seemed on the verge of arguing, but even though his brain was befuddled, Sil could see he grasped she was able and willing to cut his lifeline - his access to his drugs.

The realization flickered in his eyes, a mix of fear, betrayal, and a reluctant acceptance. Their eyes locked, and in that silent exchange, years of shared history, pain, and love flashed between them.

Felix's blue eyes softened for a brief second, a silent plea lingering there. But Sil's gaze remained hard, unyielding. She had to do this. For herself. For her future. She saw the moment he understood, truly understood, that this was the end.

The finality of the understanding seemed to crush him, his shoulders slumping as if the weight of Atlas's globe had finally settled on him.

Would he have the guts to save himself? flashed through Sil's mind. But no, no thinking of that. They had crossed that bridge.

Felix turned and stumbled out of her apartment, each step dragging him farther away from the life they once shared. He glanced back one last time, but Sil turned away, unable to bear the look of defeat in his eyes.

She stood in her new, now blemished apartment, her heart pounding, listening to the echo of his footsteps fade into the hallway. The silence that followed was deafening, filled with unspoken words and lost hopes.

WITH HER HOT forehead pressed against the cool wood of the door, her body felt limp and drained by the confrontation, but it also solidified her determination to move forward. This was goodbye. To Felix. Forever. To Bristol. Perhaps.

She moved to the window, hidden behind the lace curtains, to assure herself he was out of the building, out of her life. She would hand him over to the police if he showed his face one more time. She would not hesitate.

Thank you, Marseille, thank you for my new life. More than ever, I now know I needed to come here.

Little did Sil know, that life was going to be very different from what she envisioned. The remnants of history hidden within her new home were about to pull her into a different kind of adventure altogether.

3

THE VALISE

S il turned away from the window, listening carefully for the landlord coming up the stairs to check what the commotion had been all about. She also listened for signs of life from her other tenants, but the house remained silent.

Knowing she would have to face the remnants of Felix's visit at some point, she reluctantly approached the damaged wall, her fingertips tracing the ragged edges of the torn wallpaper.

Anger and fear from the confrontation ebbed and flowed within her, but curiosity slowly began to take over. The once-elegant fleur-de-lys design now hung in tatters, revealing the real reason Felix's foot had gone through so easily.

It wasn't a solid wall at all. Just a board with a thin layer of plaster and the old-fashioned wallpaper that had been there for decades. Her heart thumped in her chest as she peered through the hole, but the darkness inside prevented her from seeing what was behind the board.

Flicking on the flashlight on her Motorola, Sil directed the beam into the hidden space. Dust particles danced in the light, and the faint scent of mildew and old wood filled her nostrils. As she moved the light around, she saw the board had been put up to hide an extra space. The makeshift construction was full of dust and small bits of gravel, likely undisturbed for years.

Her initial anger at Felix for the damage began to mix with a rising sense of curiosity and wonder. What was this hidden space, and why had it been sealed off? The torchlight finally settled on something unusual—a small, weathered leather valise, reinforced with metal corners. Sil's breath caught in her throat. The valise looked ancient. There was no doubt it had sat there for many years, probably never meant to be discovered. The leather was cracked and worn, its original color faded to a bluish gray under the dust.

She stretched her arm through the hole as far as she could until her fingers brushed against the rough surface of the suitcase. She tried to draw it closer to the opening in the wall, but it seemed stuck. Finally, she managed to close her fingers around the rusty metal handle that groaned from lack of use.

Her mind revved up. This wasn't an ordinary piece of luggage; it looked like a keepsake from a forgotten era. The potential significance of her discovery made the hairs on her arms stand up.

Afraid the old thing would fall apart if she lifted it, she dragged the valise closer to the hole. It was light. Was it empty? As she brushed off the thick layer of dust, Sil's fingers trembled with anticipation. She inspected it from all angles and then saw the letters I.B. embossed next to the handle.

I.B. Clearly initials. A man? A woman? Who did this belong to? And what could be inside? Letters? Documents? Old clothes? The possibilities were endless. As she carefully lifted it from the false wall, she could feel the weight of history in her hands - a tangible link to the past as she placed the old valise on the table.

The clasps were too rusty to obey the pressure of her fingers. No padlock, though, so a bit of rust remover should do the trick. As Sil sat back on her heels, the dust settling around her with the valise in front of her, a smile started forming on her lips.

Sil had come to Marseille to start a new chapter in her life, and now it seemed the very walls of her new home were about to reveal their own story.

A FEW HOURS LATER...

THE SUITCASE LAY open on Sil's desk, the stubborn clasps finally yielding to her careful application of homemade rust remover. She'd worked meticulously, using cotton swabs and the remaining dregs of a warm bottle of Coca-Cola from her backpack to loosen the rust.

And then the supreme moment, the valise lay open, revealing its secrets. It only held letters, neat bundles of letters, tied together with faded ribbons. A collection of maps of France and newspaper clippings in folders.

As far as Sil could gather from the French language, the contents dealt with France in the Second World War. *That old!*

"You'd have liked this, Grandpa Jack," Sil mumbled as she gazed down at the yellowed papers in front of her, wondering what this all meant and why such personal stuff had been hidden here, possibly for decades.

Each bundle seemed part of a last will, a testament to a life lived long ago, fragile and intimate. She hesitated to touch anything, suddenly questioning her right to look inside. Should she bring it to the police station, or a museum, or notify Bellamare about her discovery?

Her fingers hovered over the topmost bundle of letters when a sudden shyness struck Sil. These letters looked so personal, almost sacred. Yet, curiosity gnawed at her, especially when she noticed a painting wrapped in tissue paper tucked at the bottom of the suit-case. Carefully, she unwrapped the tissue paper, revealing a portrait of a young woman.

"How unusual," Sil murmured, "wonder who she is."

The woman in the painting looked straight at her, wearing a navy-colored top with lace trimming. Her eyes were very clear and blue, the eyes of a confident, aristocratic woman with soft, wavy dark hair and a strong chin. Underneath was written, *"Pour Lise, ma très chère amie. Pour toujours, ton Henri."* It was dated 16 July 1939.

Sil stared at the portrait for a long time, her artist's eye recog-nizing the influences of Impressionism and Modern Art that were prevalent at the time the oil painting was made. The brushstrokes were both bold and delicate, capturing the woman's strong essence with striking clarity. But who was Lise? And who was Henri? They didn't match the initials I.B that were engraved on the suitcase.

As she pondered this dissimilarity, the late afternoon light filtered through the lace curtains, casting a sunflower-yellow hue over the room. As the shadows lengthened, the space adopted a quiet, almost reverent atmosphere.

The sounds of the bustling street below, where people returned from work and cafés served Pastis and Vermouth, were muffled. Sil sat there as if in an insulating bubble that swooped her away to another time, another love affair.

Suddenly, she froze. She heard voices in the corridor outside her door. Clearly, people had returned home. Her heart pounded in her chest, fear creeping in. What if someone found out about her discovery before she had a chance to understand it?

She quickly closed the suitcase, shoving it under her bed. But then she heard keys jingle, doors creak open, then close, and quiet returned to the house.

Her stomach rumbled, a sharp reminder she hadn't eaten since lunch. With an absent mind, she reached for the last granola bar from her backpack, still full of questions. She couldn't let this go. Food and unpacking had to wait.

The portrait, the letters—they were a doorway to a story long forgotten. She had to know more about Lise and Henri, and what their connection was to this hidden space.

4

THE LETTER FROM THE PAST

S il took a deep breath and retrieved the suitcase from under the bed. She may have been imagining it, but when she gently reopened the clasps, the valise seemed to give off the sound of a sigh.

More determined now, she untied the first bundle of letters, her fingers brushing against the fragile paper. The blue ink was faded, but the handwriting was strong, even powerful. And neato, it was in English!

She began to read...

"LONDON, *5 January 1947*
  Mon cher Henri,

THANK *you so much for your kind letter. It was so good to hear from you again. Of course, I was saddened to hear about your divorce from Jeanne. I can only imagine how difficult this time must be for you.*

. . .

DESPITE THE YEARS and the distance, you've always been in my thoughts. Our happy pre-war moments together, though fleeting, have left a lasting imprint on my heart. You know that back then you were the love of my life but forces mightier than us tore us apart. The disapproval of our relationship by my family (especially my mother!!) and then that wretched war that forced me to flee Paris as persona-non-grata. Oh, it broke my heart!

IT MAY BE selfish of me to say so, but your letter and the expression of your desire to see me again, has been the most cheerful message I've received in ages. And I laughed out loud at your remembrance of those foolish and carefree days when we were young!

That you remember my horrible (!) lavender-blue chiffon dress and white hat I wore for a stroll through the Tuileries on Whitsun Sunday! I hated that dress with a vengeance though you apparently admired the Schiaparelli little nothing. That dress was a typical Mother de Baissac choice. I felt way too old-womanish in it and was sure everyone was staring at me.

In my opinion, lavender-blue garments should be forbidden for women under fifty, and certainly girls under twenty. But I know you like your pastels, so you're forgiven. And I've almost matured enough for lavender again!

I WRITE to you from my flat in Mayfair where I — like every other Londoner - try hard to forget the war but don't seem able to shake off the memories. We are in strict rations still, and the bombed-out craters make London ugly - all scars from the war. So many of us didn't return. My brother Claude and I were the lucky ones. I'm keenly aware of that now.

. . .

AND THROUGH IT ALL, I miss France so much. It's almost surreal to pick up my post-war life in England when all I did during the war was fight for the liberation of France. It feels as if a part of me is amputated now.

I CAN ALMOST SEE you raise your distinctive eyebrows at my last sentence, my dear. Yes, I fought for France and that's what I want to tell you all about. I didn't stay in Britain after I fled Paris. In fact, I spent most of the war in France as a secret agent.

I'M TAKING both a security risk and a getting-my-heart-broken risk telling you about my secret missions, but it is important to me that you understand the woman I've grown into from that lavender giggle. If we are to be more than friends—which, one day, I truly hope we will be—we can't have any secrets between us. You told me everything about your relationship with Jeanne and how it didn't work out because you couldn't forget me, well I want to make a clean sweep as well."

SIL STOPPED READING ABRUPTLY, a wrinkle in her forehead. The distant drone of the air conditioner and loud laughter from the street below had torn her out of her concentration. Who was this Lise, and what was she getting herself into with a man she'd not seen for almost a decade and who was suddenly wooing her again? Meanwhile, she seemed to have been a kick-ass secret agent during the war.

Don't have any illusions you can handle love better, Sil, she reprimanded herself, thinking back at what had happened earlier in the afternoon between Felix and her. With that vague reassurance, she read on, desperate to hear how Lise would confide her deepest secrets to her Henri.

. . .

"IF I TELL YOU EVERYTHING, especially the parts where you may disagree with the decisions I made, you will better know if you want to continue pursuing our relationship.

LET me begin by telling you how I left Paris after our hasty goodbye on 23 June 1940. A day forever etched in my memory. Being suddenly an enemy to the Reich because of my British passport, was not a scenario that had ever crossed my mind.

The hopeless exodus that followed was probably the worst part of the war for me. I'm not good at being helpless; I prefer to be in charge.

WHEN MY BROTHER Claude and I left my apartment on the Avenue Kléber, the streets were complete chaos, something I've never seen before in my life. Thousands of people, rich and poor, trying to escape from the Nazis. Jewish people, people with the wrong passport like me, families with small children, couples in their eighties. I assume you saw the scenes with your own eyes. I was among them, Henri.

IT WAS SUCH a hot summer day. The air was thick and muggy, the scent of fear and uncertainty awash, a mixture of sweat, diesel, and the permeating odor of burning debris. Families clutched their belongings, panic everywhere as everyone had only one thought: Get out of Paris!

THAT OUR BEAUTIFUL, thriving capital could have become a hell of despair in a matter of days. My brain couldn't grasp it. I felt myself swept up in the panic, which is very unlike me. But there wasn't really a plan Claude *and I could adhere to. Going south as fast as you can on your own two legs isn't really much of a coherent plan. Trains – if they ran at all – were over-full, and the roads were clogged with vehicles. We didn't have a car, so we walked.*

WHAT ELSE COULD WE DO? *News filtered through that British people by the hundreds were put in detention camps as retaliation for the jailing of Germans on the Isle of Man. An eye for an eye was the Nazi policy, as we encountered so bitterly over the next years."*

SIL PAUSED AGAIN, shaking her head at the vivid imagery Lise depicted. This was what her Grandpa Jack had described to her so often, the intense cruelty of the Nazis. Sil shuddered. What had happened to Lise? Well, she was alive and willing to consider courtship again in 1947, so she had survived it all. At least there was that.

In her artist's eye, Sil pictured the chaos around Paris and Lise with her small suitcase and her brother walking mile after mile in the blistering sun. She felt a growing admiration for Lise's resilience and courage, much like the qualities her grandfather had always shown. There was one yellowed sheet of paper left in this letter.

"CLAUDE AND I *didn't discuss fighting back then, but I know the seed of resistance was sown in us on that terrible trek south. With hardly any food or water and the constant risk of being caught or bombed from above, one's mind either freezes or starts to fight. De Baissacs have always been resilient and allergic to despotism. We have proud blood and refuse to be victims.*

. . .

BUT I HAD WEAK MOMENTS, *the weakest of all the war! Imagine, we carried the few earthly belongings we still had, while the soles of our shoes wore thin, and our skin blistered from too much exposure to the sun.*

THE ROADS WERE CLOGGED *with cars, bicycles, and people on foot, all moving in a slow, determined march like a huge caterpillar crawling forward under the relentless sky. Children wailed, explosions rumbled, airplanes roared, old men and women fainted, and the oppressive heat sapped the last strength from our bodies. We shared what little we had, a small gesture of humanity in the midst of chaos.*

IN MY GOOD MOMENTS, *I blessed my robust health, our out-of-doors upbringing in Mauritius, my strong will. I drew from my quiet resolve and discovered I possessed a deeper strength within myself, one that eventually would carry me through all the terrifying moments of my life as a secret agent.*

HOW RELIEVED *we were to cross the demarcation line into Vichy and feel as if the Germans weren't breathing down our necks as furiously anymore. Though Pétain and his puppet regime weren't much better, of course. But we didn't know that at the time.*

THEN I FINALLY ARRIVED IN *Cannes, where my dear friends, the Montdidiers, ran me a hot bath, made me the tastiest coq-au-vin I've ever tasted in my life, and let me put my weary limbs between silk sheets. Oh, heaven of heavens!*

.   .   .

BUT MY ARRIVAL in Cannes turned out to be only the beginning of the most adventurous and dangerous episode of my life. I hope to share more of these memories with you in my next letter, mon cher Henri. But I'll first wait for your reply to see if you even want to continue hearing about my life as 'Irène Brisse', codenamed 'Odile.'

JUST KNOW I can't wait for the day when we'll sit together with no more secrets between us. I hope our journey through my war memoir will bring us closer than ever, and we can start anew with just love and understanding between us.

AVEC TOUT MON AMOUR,
   Ta Lise"

SIL's EYES flew over the last words, her surroundings fading as she seemed to be pulled deeper into Lise's world. Her visual eye could see all the details of the young woman's flight from Paris. The helpless cries to the skies, the menacing Messerschmitts overhead – 'Butcher birds' Grandpa Jack called them - and the oppressive heat that seeped into the marrow of her own bones.

But behind the words, Sil tried to form a picture of the lady behind the letter. How could this Lise keep her cool amidst the turmoil her life had become? Pushing forward with the feisty spirit of a modern Joan of Arc?

"You're not that different, Silver! You're a hell of a fighter for fair shakes yourself!"

Grandpa was suddenly so close!

"I hope so, Gramps," Sil said aloud, in an attempt to return to the real reason she found herself in Marseille. That was not Lise de

Baissac. But the École des Beaux-Arts had a rival now in the form of an old suitcase filled with love letters. Sil couldn't wait to learn everything about Lise and her Henri.

"Good gravy, I came here for my future and seem to step right back into a time machine," she mumbled to herself, the flimsy paper still between her fingers, "but I really ought to unpack and get settled."

She folded the letter and stuck it back in its antique envelope, scolding herself for tearing the corner due to its fragility. But Sil's mind was far from unpacking and organizing her overloaded bag. She kept standing still in the middle of unfolding her clothes and arranging her toilet items, lost in thought about Lise's escape.

While she loved art, history was never her thing. And as her recent encounter with Felix made clear as daylight, she wasn't very romantically inclined either. Yet, Lise with her ardent love and war struggles, tugged at Sil's soul like a flag in the wind.

What is happening to me? Now I simply must know it all, she thought.

"You will know," a voice in the room seemed to whisper, jerking Sil out of her bubble. But no, there was no one. It was just the whirring of the air-conditioning.

As past and present blurred, Lise's untold story lay at Sil's feet. Like an introduction, an initiation into what it meant to become independent, to become bigger than yourself.

Sil heard Lise's resistance spirit calling out to her across the decades, drawing her into a life of danger, intrigue, and heroism.

ONE MORE LETTER, she promised herself, knowing it wouldn't end there. Sil read until the last of the night's lights went out over Marseille and she dozed off with a head full of dreams, resting gently on one bare arm.

~ LISE ~

France/England
June 1940 - September 1942

5

CROSSING THE THRESHOLD

Cannes, France, June 28, 1940

Lise Marie Jeannette de Boucherville-Baissac stepped out of the Montdidiers' grand villa on the Avenue des Palmiers, the warm sea breeze gentle on her face.

The azure sky without an airplane in sight formed a sharp contrast to the tumultuous past few weeks of her escape from Northern France, which now was completely under German control.

In the tranquility of Cannes, summer rolled out as if the war took place on another planet. It enveloped Lise's battered body and bruised soul as a welcome reminder of long Paris summers when her troubles consisted of where to dine and what to wear. But those days seemed gone for good and, even in not-a-care-in-the-world Cannes, the first cracks were appearing on the surface, trickles of refugees with haunted faces and dusty suitcases.

As Lise descended the marble steps of the grand villa, the heels of her polished shoes clicked rhythmically, a familiar sound that grounded her in this new reality.

She inhaled the scent of blooming jasmine and freshly cut lawns, pushing the dark worries to the back of her mind. She watched the curved waves lapping onto the sandy beach, where early sun worshippers lounged in deckchairs while garçons busied around them with coffee and cocktails.

Cannes, a Mediterranean oasis, untouched by warring Germans, was still a picturesque haven where life continued with an air of obliviousness. But it was a fantasy about to crumble.

Lise straightened her hat, a chic creation by Madame Agnès, ensuring it sat perfectly atop her coiffed dark hair. Her small, slight frame, draped in a freshly pressed elegant Schiaparelli dress, exuded just the right air of aristocratic grace. She was a Parisienne to the core, accustomed to the good life, but her resolve had never been stronger. There was a different person rising inside the neat exterior.

Lise learned fast and what she'd witnessed in the past weeks had shaken her to the core. The flashbacks of the rows and rows of Germans marching into Paris - the chaos and despair their arrival brought in its wake - had ignited a fierce determination within her.

And Pétain, once the hero of the Great War, had sold out France, opening his arms to the enemy with his Armistice and Vichy Government. His betrayal of the French fueled Lise's anger. This was not the France she recognised. The French weren't cowards, and they didn't bow to dictators. She never would. Never! But what could she do about it? A single woman, chased out of her house, on the run, dependent on the charity of friends.

I need to get to England. After all I am a British subject, though I feel more French. Such is the fate of being born in Mauritius.

A vague plan had formed in Lise's mind. The British Consulate was now her hope, though she had no idea if it was still operational.

But Emmeline Montdidier had scribbled the address on a perfumed sheet of paper and pressed it in Lise's hand with a warm grin.

"I'd rather you stayed here with us, my dear, but I see you're languishing and your heart is soaring to other places, so who am I to stop you?"

As Lise walked along Cannes' busy streets, the shoppers happy and carefree, she observed all the bustling with keen, blue eyes. The locals going about their business, shopkeepers arranging their wares under burgundy awnings, children playing by the fountains, and tourists snapping photographs of the picturesque scenery.

Every detail registered in her mind, her instincts already sharpening, missing nothing as she took in the semblance of normalcy around her.

With the British Consulate closed – just a simple sign stating 'no longer operating, the American Consulate will take care of your affairs', Lise started out towards the second address Emmeline had wisely thought to give her.

The American Consulate was housed in a stately building on the Rue d'Antibes, its façade a blend of neoclassical elegance and modern functionality. As Lise approached the entrance, the consulate's bronze doors gleamed in the sunlight, as if radiating a ray of hope and refuge.

Inside, the atmosphere was cool and formal. The scent of polished wood and ink lingered in the air, while the hum of diligent activity behind closed doors reached her ears. Prominent American flags stood everywhere.

"Bonjour, madame. How may I assist you?" the young receptionist with an American accent asked in polite, schoolgirl French.

"Bonjour, I am Lise de Baissac," Lise began, trying to control the emotions that whirled inside her. "I need to arrange travel to Britain. It is of utmost importance."

The receptionist's eyes flicked with recognition. "Of course, madame. I take it you have British citizenship?"

"Yes."

"Please have a seat. Someone will be with you shortly."

Lise took the seat in the waiting area with a flicker of hope. She thought of Claude, her brother, who'd insisted on going to Spain on foot, crossing the Pyrenees. Their separation had been necessary but painful. *Be safe and come out in one-piece, little brother!*

Her gaze wandered around the waiting room. The walls held portraits of American dignitaries, most of whom she couldn't identify. But their stern faces seemed to say, 'Look, we've shaped a great country built on the dream of liberty, now you do your bit.'

Yes, she agreed in silent response. *Et je ne peux pas vivre dans une France qui n'est pas libre! I can't live in a France that isn't free.*

Her thoughts were interrupted by the arrival of a consulate official, a middle-aged man with a kind face and an air of authority.

"Madame de Baissac, please follow me." His American English was a strange comfort, as if her British citizenship suddenly became more of her being, the French part temporarily put on hold. If she went to England, she'd have to switch languages again. Well, it would be fun.

Lise rose and followed him down a corridor lined with doors, each one representing a different facet of American diplomacy. They entered a small office, the official gesturing for her to sit.

"Mademoiselle de Baissac, I understand you wish to travel to Britain?" He sat down across from her and lit a cigar. The smoke was acrid in her nostrils but she tried not to cough. Politeness was everything now.

"Yes, Sir, I need to get there as soon as possible. I have...urgent matters to attend to," Lise replied, choosing her words carefully but they didn't come out as fluently as she'd hoped. She handed him her British passport.

The official briefly inspected the document. "I will do my best to assist you. We get many of such requests these days. All Britons want to leave the country, and who could blame them? But as you must understand, Mademoiselle de Baissac, travel arrangements are complicated due to the war and the number of applicants we get. However, we will manage, if necessary, with some detours on your behalf."

Lise felt a surge of gratitude wash over her. The rescue was neigh. "Thank you so much, Sir. I appreciate any help you can provide."

Next the official detailed the steps they would take while Lise listened carefully.

"So probably from Lisbon? Are trains still operating across the borders?"

"Yes, in essence this part of France is not German. Not yet, one could say." The official looked weary, clearly wishing himself soon back in the States. "But as you undoubtedly know, the Allied ties with Spain are volatile because of Franco's alliance with Hitler."

"I understand I'll have to cross through Spain. But Portugal can still be trusted, right?"

"Absolutely, Ma'am. That's where we'll take you first." He hesitated, suddenly looking rather bashful, "May I ask whether you'll be able to pay for your travel expenses, Mademoiselle De Baissac. And could you cope financially if you encountered a setback and had to stay in a place for a longer period?"

Now it was Lise's turn to feel embarrassed. "I guess, I could ask my friends to loan me the money for the trip?"

"We can loan it to you as well, Ma'am. The British authorities will pay us back as soon as you've arrived on British soil and have reported your arrival to them. We have these agreements with other people too. And my apologies for asking such an impudent question but in these uncertain times I wouldn't want a lady like you to find herself in dire circumstances."

Lise was very grateful for his tact and foresight. The expenses for her travel had been somewhat of a worry to her, though she'd told herself she'd bring it up with the Montdidiers that evening. Now it wasn't necessary to trouble the waters of their friendship with money matters.

"That's very kind of you, sir, I'm ever so happy I came to see you." Lise gave him her ladylike smile. "I can, however, put your mind at rest about traveling as a woman alone. I'm used to traveling and I can fend for myself in all circumstances."

"That is a relief to hear, indeed. Well, I'll start the preparations to expedite your request. Is there an address or telephone number where I can reach you once the formalities are settled?"

Lise gave him the Montdidiers' number. "How long do you think the travel permit will take, sir?"

"I'll do my utmost to have it ready within a week, but alas I can't bend space and time."

"I understand." She bid him a warm farewell, thanking him profusely.

Lise left the consulate with a light heart and a swift step. The sun was higher now, casting shorter shadows, and her path shone clearly. She would reach Britain, and she would make herself useful.

As she walked back through the streets of cloudless Cannes to the villa on the seafront, she was ready to face whatever challenges Spain or Portugal may raise. France was behind her. Until she came back.

6

THE WAITING GAME

4 months later - Lisbon, Portugal, November 1940

The weak November sun had barely risen over Lisbon's rooftops when Lise descended the grand staircase of the Hotel Avenida Palace. The polished marble steps gave off a dull gleam in the morning light, and the hotel lobby was still quiet. Only the muted sounds of conversation and the stacking of tableware could be heard coming from the breakfast room.

In the luxurious room, furnished with thick carpets and colonial-style chairs and tables, and paintings of Portuguese fishing vessels and harbor scenes on the walls, Lise took her usual seat by the window, the white linen tablecloth crisp under her fingers.

She glanced around the room, recognizing the faces of the early guests—presumed British secret agents, war reporters, and weary refugees—mostly absorbed in their own thoughts or underhand conversations.

A waiter approached her table, his uniform and grooming

immaculate. "Good morning, Madame de Baissac. What may I bring you for breakfast? The usual?"

"Bom dia, João. Quero o de sempre, um café com leite, um croissant e algumas frutas frescas, por favor."

The young man made a gracious bow. "I know, Madame, but it is always a pleasure to hear you say that in perfect Portuguese."

A lackluster smile hovered on the corners of Lise's mouth. "It just means I've been here way too long, João."

"I know, Madame, I truly hope you'll get that reassuring telephone call today. Though, personally, I'll miss serving you your breakfast."

"You're too kind."

He left in a trot to give orders for her breakfast. Lise took to staring out of the window into the Rua 1º de Dezembro. The city was waking up, the streets resounding with the rattling of iron shutters opening, vendors arranging their merchandise and the screeching wheels and ringing bells of the trams.

Lisbon's sights and sounds were both comforting and frustrating to Lise; life in Portugal went on, seemingly untouched by the war that raged beyond its borders. No shortages, no throngs of hungry refugees with wild eyes and hearts full of pain.

But she'd been stuck in Portugal's capital for over four months now with no sight of a passage to Britain. With the shortening of the days, the waiting seemed to grow longer. And Lise wasn't good at loitering. She was an active person who needed to see progress. The waiting was becoming beyond irksome for her mental wellbeing.

And yet, looking around her, with money, food, a roof over her head in a friendly country, what was there to complain about? And it wasn't like she was the only one who was unable to find a plane or a ship. 'Stranded in Lisbon' could have been the refrain to a new war song.

Her breakfast arrived promptly. She took a sip from her coffee -

good quality and strong as always - and bit into the soft, flaky croissant. Yet, despite the luxurious surroundings and the delicious food, the sense of restlessness, the futility of a life-in-between in a country that wasn't hers, gnawed on her insides like a burning worm.

Days blurred into each other; each one marked by the same tedious routine. A walk to the post office to see if there was word from the British consulate. Or perhaps from her family, from Claude, or from Jean, her eldest brother, who'd left for England earlier to join the RAF.

After finishing her breakfast, Lise donned her coat and hat to make a fresh attempt at the main post office on Praça dos Restauradores 58c. Stepping out into the cool morning air, she took a deep breath. The sea was near, which was a comfort. Having been surrounded by the Indian Ocean since birth, Lise loved the seaside, any seaside. Mauritian azure blue or dark gray, as Portugal's Atlantic Ocean in the fall, it appeared she could find peace near any ocean.

The streets of Lisbon were a labyrinth of narrow alleys and wide boulevards, each with their own charm. She walked past the Praça do Comércio, where the grand archway stood as a gateway to the city's heart. The square was alive with activity—street performers entertaining passersby, children chasing pigeons, and old men sitting on benches chatting and smoking. The weather was still agreeable though a cold chill drifted in from the Atlantic.

Lise caught snippets of conversations in Portuguese, French, and English, a cacophony of languages that mirrored the city's cosmopolitan nature. As she strolled along the waterfront – what haste was there to get to the post office anyway? - the salty breeze from the Tagus River ruffled her hair.

She paused to watch the ships anchored in the harbor, their flags fluttering in the wind. Among them were vessels from neutral countries, lifelines for those fleeing the horrors of war. Why could *she* not just board one and be gone?

Arriving at the post office, she pushed the revolving door with her gloved hand. She listened, how many times already, to how her heels clicked on the tiled floor fifty times before arriving at the counter. The young female clerk already shook her head when she saw Lise.

"I'm sorry, Madame de Baissac, nothing for you today."

"*Está tudo bem. Volto amanhã.*" It is alright. I'll be back tomorrow.

But the silence was harder to take every day.

Slowly, Lise made her way back to the hotel, trying not to let her shoulders hang. It would be almost time for lunch when she got back. Another distraction. But Lise's mind churned with thoughts of the past and worries for the future.

It was hard not to wonder what would happen to her if she was stuck here for years. Germany's power was still on the rise. This war was going to last a lot longer than was initially expected. Should she return to Cannes? Perhaps cross the Mediterranean to North Africa instead of wasting her time in Lisbon?

One more day! She promised herself.

Back in her room, the telephone rang, startling her from her reverie. It was reception.

"Madame, I have a call for you from Madame Montdidier in Cannes. Shall I put her through?"

"Yes, please." Lise's heart sprang up as she waited for the connection. Would this be it? Finally progress?

"Lise, darling, how are you?" Emmeline's posh voice chirped in her ears but for once Lise wasn't capable of small talk.

"What's the matter, Emmeline? Have you had word from the Ameri...?"

"Non, non, ma chérie, I wish I had," Emmeline purred, "but I do have news for you. You know Jacques got this business associate in Barcelona and he got word Claude is there."

"Claude?!" Lise exploded. "What is Claude doing in Barcelona?"

"Ah chérie, don't get all worked up. Apparently, he's in prison. He was caught by Spanish guards while descending the Col des Poiriers."

"Heavens, what now?" Lise thought aloud. Claude in jail in Barcelona and she stuck in Lisbon. What a bad joke. Her heart sank, but she quickly gathered her resolve.

"Can Jacques arrange a visit to the prison for me? I need to see how my brother is doing. We're not equipped for prison life, Emmeline. He's not a criminal. What are they thinking?"

"I'll see what Jacques can do, chérie, and then I'll phone you again. I'm so sorry about this whole mess."

"Oh, I just hope I can go and see him. It's not like I'll get a lift to London tomorrow so I might as well travel back through Spain to lift his spirit."

"I'll get back to you when Jacques has spoken to his business associate, chérie. But please, just travel on from Barcelona and come to stay with us in Cannes. I don't understand that desperate urge of yours to reach England. We're safe here. Really safe."

"I'm not desperate, Emmeline. I just hate being useless. I promise I'll visit as soon as I can. And thank you for your help. I can't wait to see Claude."

THREE DAYS *later*

THE TWO-DAY TRAIN journey was arduous, but Lise was determined to cross the breadth of Portugal and Spain to visit her brother. First, she boarded a train bound for Madrid that went at a snail's pace and was packed with passengers.

Apart from an overnight suitcase, she brought a basket filled with Portuguese delicacies she was sure would lift her gourmand brother's spirits. Presunto ham, Pastéis de Nata, which were a sort of custard tarts, and dried figs.

Traversing Spain was marked by long hours of staring out the window at the changing landscape, her thoughts oscillating between her happy past and uncertain present.

Once in Madrid, she boarded the train to Barcelona. Halfway down, while she'd finally dozed off, she was gruffly awakened by a Spanish ticket conductor who eyed her with suspicion, perhaps even scorn, his black eyes squinting. After a long inspection, he found Lise's papers in order and moved on to the next compartment. Lise let out a long breath of relief.

As she placed her papers back in her handbag, she noticed a white envelope she'd forgotten all about. Henri had pressed it in her hands on the day they said goodbye. On that sunny day in June in Paris when the Germans marched in. It seemed lifetimes away now. In all the chaos she'd totally forgotten about his token of love, but it was a welcome surprise from her drudgery now.

MA CHÈRE LISE,

MY HEART IS *in so much pain knowing you had to leave Paris so suddenly and there's no way to know how long we will be separated. I'm so worried about you and I wander the streets feeling a big emptiness. I can't even paint and I have to deliver the portrait of the Comtesse de Artois next week. I've never hated painting, not even for a commission like this, but I can't even stare at her photograph without seeing your distraught face before me.*

·   ·   ·

PLEASE, *my darling, know that my thoughts and prayers go with you wherever you are. Please stay safe and do nothing foolish. I know how passionately you believe in justice but there is no way we can get the Germans out but to sit and wait. I would be devastated to hear you'd tried to stop them in any way and were caught. I heard you and Claude talk often and you are such freedom-loving people, even stauncher French patriots than people born in this country.*

Don't get burned on your passion. Your life and safety are worth more to me.

WHILE YOU ARE GONE, *I'll try to work as hard as I can, finishing my degree in Architecture and earn more money. That way I hope your family will see I'm not the penniless Quartier Latin artist they take me for. I want to be worthy of you, Lise.*

Just make sure you return to me! Do you promise?

TIL THEN, *remember our walks through the Tuileries, the laughter we shared, and the dreams we spoke of. Hold those memories close, as I will, until we can create new ones together. Though the war may separate us now, my love for you goes where you go.*

TRY *to write if you can!*

AVEC TOUT MON AMOUR,

HENRI

. . .

As Lise read Henri's outpouring of love, she almost drowned in the emotions that engulfed her. How was she going to survive without him? The tenderness and sincerity of his words wrenched on her heart. And yet, she knew she couldn't afford to dwell on her feelings for Henri Villameur for too long. They wouldn't sustain her through the war. They would only serve to weaken her resolve.

"I have to fight, Henri, it's who I am," she whispered, more to herself than to him.

She folded the letter carefully and tucked it away, making a promise to herself to bury Henri deep within her heart. The luxury of heartbreak wasn't hers to court. There was too much at stake, too much to be done.

With her head held high, tears in her eyes, Lise vowed not to contact Henri Villameur again until the war was over. No matter how much she loved him, she had a battle to fight first. A battle he couldn't understand.

7

THE JOURNEY CONTINUES

T he Spanish Civil War had left a heavy mark on Barcelona, physical scars evident in the buildings and emotional scars visible on the faces of the people. Lise hurried through the streets with her basket and her suitcase, feeling as if she'd once again entered a war zone. Though the war in Spain had ended on 1 April 1939, the evidence of that brutal clash between Franco's fascist supporters and an alliance of international and Spanish brigades was evident in the pockmarked Catalonian capital. And the outcome had not been what the world and millions of Spaniards had hoped for. Franco presided over Spain, as Hitler did in Germany, and Mussolini in Italy.

It made Lise hurry on to the prison, thinking how her beloved France at that very moment was being crushed under the Nazi boot. Was Europe in for a new world order in which the freedom of the people existed no longer? *Liberté, Égality, Fraternité* - the hard-earned results of the blood-drenched French revolution - no more? Would they need another revolution, blood and all, but on a larger scale this time? Lise almost wished she was back in unscathed

Lisbon where she wasn't forced to helplessly witness the wreckage mankind inflicted on one another.

La Model Prison, officially known as *Centro Penitenciario de Hombres de Barcelona*, was one of Barcelona's prominent prisons. Finished in 1904, it had a panopticon-style layout, featuring a central tower from which grim guards observed all the wings radiating outward.

As Lise approached La Model, the high stone walls topped with barbed wire loomed over her, austere and foreboding. The heavy iron gates and watchtowers added to the sense of confinement. It was architecture that reflected both grand design and grim reality. Lise felt her heart pounding. Visiting a prison had not been part of her upbringing, but a De Baissac never shied away from what had to be done.

After announcing the reason for her visit and showing her papers, she was seen into a large waiting area. Two guards, suspicious of all visitors, meticulously searched her basket and suitcase, examining every item for hidden contraband or weapons. The process was thorough, with the guards poking through the contents and checking for anything that might conceal a weapon or escape tool. They opened jars, inspected bread loaves, and probed the lining of the basket itself. Her suitcase had to undergo the same treatment, while Lise blushed as her underwear was held up in the air and shaken out.

The inspection completed, Lise was led through a series of heavy, metal doors that clanged shut behind her. She was escorted to a visitation room, where she was told in gruff Spanish to wait at the small wooden table and not to get up or move around. The room was stark, with whitewashed walls and barred windows allowing in sparse day light. One lightbulb over the table. Two chairs, and two guards flanking the door.

It was silent apart from a fly buzzing around her basket. The sausage inside smelled strongly of garlic, which upset Lise's stomach. In her hurry to get to La Model, she'd forgotten to have lunch.

Claude was brought in, his broad stature slightly stooped by the weight of his imprisonment, but his spirit not beaten. Lise almost jumped up at the joy of seeing his familiar figure, but a growl next to the doorpost froze her in her seat.

"Oh Claude! Oh brother!" Her throat was tight, but his name came out strong. She saw how his blue gaze, so much like hers, lit up at recognizing his visitor, a smile breaking over his weary, unshaven face.

"Lise? How did you get here?" he inquired, the surprise fighting with the delight. His voice was rough and gravelly, as if he'd not spoken in a while.

"Oh Claude!" Lise repeated, loving the sound of his name. "Dear me, how did you end up here and how are you holding up?" They fell back into speaking French, as always.

Claude hesitated before he answered, his eyes flicking over to the guards. "It's been far from fun. But seeing you here... it helps."

Lise reached across the table, taking his hand in hers.

"No physical contact!" was barked from the door. Lise pulled her fingers back as if stung.

"I've brought you some goodies. I hope that will perk you up." She quickly said, pushing down the tears. "They let me keep it after a thorough inspection, so I guess it's okay for you to have."

As soon as she pushed the basket over the table, Claude attacked the food.

"Are you that hungry, mon frère? Are they starving you?"

"No, silly, but this tastes so good. It tastes of freedom," he laughed with his mouth full of sausage and figs.

"So, what happened? How did you end up here? Has there been a trial of any sort?" Lise fired question after question at him, while Claude shook his head, eating, half grinning now despite his circumstances. He looked so much like the small blond boy that had always been by her side in their freewheeling years in Curepipe. Always eating, always grinning.

"I got caught while descending the Col des Poiriers. Stupid in fact, but it is what it is. I guess it's fortunate the Spanish border patrol didn't turn me over to the Germans in nearby Gascony. That would've been the end of me, no doubt."

"But why are they keeping you here in La Model? They have no reason." Lise was at a loss as to what Claude's threat to Franco's government could be.

"I have no clue either and I think neither do the Spanish authorities. I've been here for six gruesome months now. The British Consulate in Madrid is trying to do what they can. Which is very little so far. It's all just useless red tape. But, what about you? Are you still in Cannes with the Montdidiers?"

"No!" Lise suddenly realized her brother didn't even know she was almost as stuck as he was, but in Portugal.

"I left Cannes after a couple of weeks. I've been in Lisbon waiting for a plane or boat to England since the end of July. No luck so far. The war seems to have stagnated all travel abroad."

"Well, go back to Lisbon, Lise. I'll be a free man soon. I'm sure of it. And we'll get to England together."

"If only that would be possible." Lise tried not to sound too dejected. At least, she had the luxury of waiting in freedom.

"I know, ma soeur, it's hard, but we'll get there. De Baissacs always do."

"I know," Lise replied softly, "we will find a way to get out of here. We will be in England soon. Together."

The conversation, though brief and overheard by guards, was enough to lift the spirits of the siblings. They'd always cheered each other up and would continue to do so.

Lise left the prison feeling a renewed sense of hope. She had to get to England, not just for herself but for Claude as well. In case they didn't let him go.

UPON RETURNING to the Hotel Avenida Palace in Lisbon, wonderful news awaited Lise. João, the loyal waiter, was standing in the hotel lobby, waving a letter.

"I think I'm going to miss you!" he said, his face showing mock disappointment.

It was true. Lise had in her hand an officially-stamped letter from the British consulate approving her to travel to Gibraltar and from there aboard a liner to Glasgow. The news made her sink down in a chair and cry with joy.

AFTER FIVE LONG months of waiting Lise could hardly believe she was nearing Gibraltar. As the gateway to the Mediterranean, the British overseas territory was a bustling hub of military activity. The strategic importance of this rocky outpost meant there were British soldiers and sailors everywhere.

The Rock of Gibraltar loomed overhead, its sheer limestone cliffs standing as a reminder of the strength and unconquerability needed in trying times. The harbor was filled with ships, from destroyers and submarines to supply vessels.

Lise marveled at the sight of the aircraft carrier, the HMS Ark Royal, as it sailed past, its majestic hull cutting through the water with ease, while RAF planes stood parked side by side on the massive deck. She simply loved the sight of so much military muscle.

The Ark Royal's presence in the Mediterranean was an important symbol of the Royal Navy's might. Maybe her brother Jean was on there, just about to take off or land his plane.

Lise also caught a glimpse of Gibraltar itself from aboard the small boat taking her and other passengers to the harbor. The town was alive with the sounds of war preparations—soldiers drilling, vehicles rumbling, and the distant hum of aircraft.

Civilians and military personnel alike filled the cafés and shops, their conversations a blend of English, Spanish, and other tongues she couldn't decipher. Despite the war, life continued here with a certain vibrancy, a determination to endure. A southern European spirit of liveliness and spunk.

Lise made her way to the docks, her valise in-hand - her only earthly belongings at this point - but filled with enough cash to make sure she could reach her destination.

Approaching the HMS Britannia, the ship that would take her to Glasgow, she took her place in the line of passengers -refugees, military personnel, and civilians -all eager to make the journey to safer shores. The ship, a weary old lady of a liner but firmly equipped with anti-aircraft artillery and even a cannon, was now her lifeline, representing hope and a new beginning.

As she stepped onto the gangway, she glanced back at the Rock of Gibraltar, the massive fortress standing guard over the entrance to the Mediterranean.

Leaving the Continent behind was emotionally complicated, a relief and a challenge. Ahead lay the open sea, with all its dangers, and an unsure future.

I will be back. Some voice inside her whispered. *This is not adieu. It's à tantôt.*

Once on deck, the wind whipped through her hair as she watched the activity in the harbor recede into the distance. Two British planes flew overhead to protect them. Lost in reverie, Lise startled when she suddenly heard a familiar voice behind her.

"Ma soeur!"

"Claude!" For a moment Lise lost all her usual composure and coolness and threw herself in her brother's arms.

"How? How did you manage this?" Her eyes shone with delight, and he grinned widely under his now neatly-trimmed moustache.

"Keeping an eye on you, lady!" he joked.

Arm in arm, they watched the mainland become smaller and smaller while the HMS Britannia ploughed through the waves.

With Claude free and securely by her side, Lise was more than ready to cross the threshold into the next chapter of her life.

8

TEA AND TRANSITIONS

Fifteen months later - London, March 1942

L ise mounted the stone steps of Lady Edith Kemsley's townhouse in Belgravia, the lingering chill of an English spring nipping at her cheeks. Despite the usual rationing and wartime austerity, the door opened to a warm, inviting atmosphere, with the scent of Earl Grey tea and freshly baked scones wafting through the hallway.

"*Ah, Lise, ma chère amie!*" Edith greeted her with a kiss on each cheek, her elegant figure draped in a rich velvet gown that defied the wartime fashion constraints.

"Edith, it's always a pleasure," Lise replied, her eyes reflecting a rare moment of relaxation.

The portrait of Edith, by Philip Alexius de László, hung proudly in the drawing room into which Lise was ushered. Despite being past fifty, Marie Edith Merandon du Plessis, as Lise had known her in Mauritius, possessed eternal grace and enduring poise. But the Lady was also equipped with a sharp mind and a quick tongue.

The two women settled into plush armchairs, while a fire crackled in the hearth, enveloping the large room in an enjoyable warmth. A tray of delicate china teacups, a teapot, and an array of treats sat on a low table, inviting them to have a leisurely afternoon in each other's company.

While Edith poured the tea with practiced elegance, she asked, "pray tell me, Lise, how is working for my husband at the Daily Sketch? And don't spare either him or me!"

Lise sighed, her fingers tracing the rim of her teacup. "It's... interesting. But not quite what I had envisioned. Reporting on society events and the latest fashion trends feels somewhat trivial given the circumstances. I want to do more, Edith. I *need* to do more."

Her friend's eyes filled with understanding. "Oh, I know, chérie. We all want to contribute in a meaningful way. I feel my hands are tied as well. It's a challenging time with the war raging on. So frustrating. I miss my travels, as well."

"But you at least have your Daily Sketch War Relief Fund," Lise observed. "You're sending millions of pounds worth of clothes and comforts to troops in all parts of the world. That's being of use to the war effort."

"You're also doing more than you realize. You're bringing some semblance of normalcy and hope to people's lives through your writing." Edith looked at her friend sternly.

Lise smiled weakly. "Perhaps. But I can't shake the feeling I'm wasting precious time."

The conversation turned to memories of their shared past in Mauritius, reminiscing about the grand parties on Edith's father's sugar plantation. The laughter and the carefree days were a distant dream now, but revisiting a time when life was good was a welcome respite from the harsh realities that surrounded them now, the war news, and the perpetual London rain.

Edith, seventeen years Lise's senior, had always been a figure of admiration and guidance for the young De Baissac girl. Those days, filled with sunshine and the sweet scent of sugarcane, took place decades ago and yet were still so vibrant and real. Lise was fourteen when her family moved to Paris, and the close relationships between De Baissac and the Merandon du Plessis families had withered.

As the afternoon light began to fade and the tea turned cold, sherry was announced and a knock interrupted their pleasant reveries. Edith's butler entered, holding a letter.

"For you, Madame," he said, handing it to Lise. "It was delivered to the Daily Sketch office, but the bellboy ran down here."

Lise immediately recognized the handwriting as Claude's. Though excited to know what his hurried message entailed, she put the envelope in her handbag. She'd read its contents when back in her rented accommodation in Mayfair.

"You so want to open that letter now, ma chère. I can see it. And I too want to know what Claude is writing. It must be important!" Edith uttered with a tinkling laugh, and turning to her butler added, "Mr. Barry, please get Madame de Baissac my letter opener. It's on the desk in my study."

The letter was brief but to the point: Churchill had given his permission for women to join a hush-hush secret training that Claude had been involved in for a while now. He couldn't exactly reveal what it entailed but it had to do with France, and he thought Lise would like to know. He believed the organisation useful. He'd put her name forward, just in case, and they were interested in her!

Lise's heart made a small jump in her chest. This was her chance, the opportunity she'd been waiting for. She was sure of it. Glancing up at Edith, her eyes twinkled.

"What is it, chérie? Is he getting married, or what? Don't keep it from me!" Edith cried.

"I think my path has just become clear to me, Edith dear. Claude's put my name forward for a secret organisation that has to do with France. Maybe I'll become a secret agent," Lise replied with a giggle. "I'm sorry, I'll have to tell Gomer I may not be coming back to the Daily Sketch."

Edith smiled, a knowing look in her eyes. "Gomer will survive. Oh girl, I always knew you were destined for something extraordinary. The first time I saw what a killer shot you were in my father's backyard, and you always were so athletic and outdoorsy. I'll miss you though. But whatever you decide, I'm here for you."

"Thank you, Edith. You and Gomer have truly helped me through these glum months. I'll never forget that."

Lise's mind was already racing with possibilities. The thought of joining a secret organisation that Claude also was part of, filled her with fear and wonder. He'd written they called themselves the Inter-services Research Bureau, but that was just a cover-up. If the Prime Minister was involved in it, it was something big. Really big.

As she made her way to her brother's place to hear him out about this new assignment, Lise thought about how enigmatic Claude had become since living in London. She'd often tried to pick his brain about what he was doing for a living, but his answers had been annoyingly vague, "yeah, yeah, office work, nothing important, keeping my options open, nothing real yet." But he'd probably been involved in dangerous underground work ever since he arrived. And now it was her turn.

Two weeks later

LISE GOT out of the taxi in front of the Victoria Hotel on Northumberland Avenue for her interview with the Special Operations Executive, the real organisation behind the Interservices Research Bureau. The London air was damp, with a hint of rain that had yet to fall, a typical British spring. The war and the weather cast a grey pall over the city, but inside the hotel, a different kind of anticipation permeated the air.

She was directed to a small, austere room on the second floor, where an unknown and non-descript, middle-aged man sat smoking a pipe. He didn't introduce himself, just nodded in her direction through a whirl of blue smoke. But Lise, intelligent and thoroughly prepared, had extracted from Claude that his name was Selwyn Jepson and that he wasn't an army man but in fact a crime writer, who spoke excellent French.

The room had bare walls, except for one wall with metal filing cabinets, and minimal furnishings—a wooden desk, two chairs, and two windows with the shutters closed. A single lightbulb shone directly onto the wooden desk.

In the distance, the hum of the only other occupant of the Victoria Hotel, the Quartermaster-General's directorate, sounded through the hallway. Here, the larger machinery of war was at work.

Selwyn Jepson, who called himself Captain Jepson, was a man in his mid-forties with thinning black hair and very dark eyes that radiated his sharp intellect. His tongue was even sharper. Claude had told Lise that Jepson could be charming and caustic in equal measure.

Looking up from his notes, the coal-black eyes assessed the newcomer with keen, clinical interest. "Aha, Miss de Baissac, I presume?" he began, his voice carrying a trace of sarcasm. "Do take a seat and make yourself comfortable." His French was very good, intonation and all, Lise had to admit. But she didn't like him one bit.

There was nothing comfortable about the hard wooden chair he pointed to, but Lise wasn't one to be intimidated and certainly not by an author of fictional novels, even if his books had been turned into films by Hitchcock.

"Thank you, Sir." Lise's tone was stony as she arranged her skirt on the hard chair opposite him. Claude had pressed her she wasn't supposed to know his real name.

Jepson studied her for a moment before speaking again. "I understand your brother Claude recommended you now that we're recruiting women. But family connections only go so far. Can you tell me, dear Madame, why you, as a woman of a certain position in society, would want to join a clandestine organization like ours?"

Lise met his gaze without hesitation. "I believe I can be of service to both my countries. France and England. As a Mauritian, I support both and my family has always opposed the type of tyranny Hitler stands for, and fascism in general. We believe in a free Europe. I also have the skills and the determination needed for working as a secret agent."

Jepson's eyebrows lifted slightly. "A secret agent? Oh-la-la. And skills, you say? And what skills might those be?"

"Fluent in French, a British passport, some understanding of the German occupation in France, and experience in handling firearms," Lise stated plainly.

Her interrogator leaned back in his chair, thin fingers steepled under his chin. "Aha, yes. But this work requires more than just skills. It requires a certain... resilience. Tell me, Miss de Baissac, if we sent you into France, would you be prepared to die for this type of work?"

Lise's gaze didn't waver though her heart stopped for a few beats. "Go into France? Well yes, in that case I'd be prepared to die." She quickly added with more conviction. "But I won't die. I'll take every precaution necessary not to."

Jepson's eyes narrowed. "Do you fully grasp what you're getting yourself into should you return to France? Betrayal, arrest, interrogation, torture and ultimately death at the hands of the Germans? You, a small slip of a woman, will be betraying others to save your skin before you know it. These Gestapo hounds will tell you Hitler issued a special warrant, secret British agents are now enemies of the highest rank and will not receive any of the rights of prisoners of war. If you're captured, they will not show you mercy. Not even to a small slip of a woman. The Gestapo has orders from the highest man to break the strongest spirits. Do you understand?" He was almost shouting at her.

"I understand," Lise replied. "I've seen what the Nazis are capable of with my own eyes. I am prepared to face whatever comes."

The novelist-turned-interrogator leaned forward, his tone growing more intense as if visualizing a scene for his next book. "Picture this, Miss de Baissac: you're in a dark, dank cell. The walls are closing in, the air is thick with the scent of blood and fear. You hear the screams of your comrades echoing through the halls. The Gestapo officer approaches, his tools of torture gleaming in the dim light. You are alone, no hope of rescue. Can you still hold your resolve?"

Lise took a deep breath, the image now also vivid in her own mind. "I can, Sir. My resolve will not break."

His expression remained stern. "What about names, places? Can you withstand the pain and not betray your fellow agents? Your friends, your family?"

"I will not give up anyone," Lise said firmly. "I would rather die than betray those I love."

"And how about killing another human, dear Madame, not a wild boar or a pheasant in sunny Mauritius but an SS officer in a dark alley in Lyon? Can you take his life if it's yours against his? Could you look him in the eye and still pull the trigger?"

"If it means protecting my mission, my comrades, or myself, then yes, I can and I will." Lise's voice was still steady, though her heart pounded in her chest. She wished the interview was over, but her present torturer went on and on, his questions only growing harsher.

"Can you go without food, without shelter, endure endless physical exertion to reach your goal? Can you stand the loneliness, keep up an alias always, perform demolition work without lifting an eyebrow?"

Lise nodded again. "I have the physical and mental fortitude for it. I am ready to endure whatever it takes."

The captain's eyes flashed with sudden ferocity. "You will not be Lise anymore! No Lise, no Lise!" he shouted, his voice echoing off the bare walls. "You will be your alias, and you must live it every moment. One slip, one tiny mistake, and you could doom us all. Are you truly ready for that?"

Outwardly Lise remained calm, though she was about to start screaming back at him. The man and his manners were intolerable.

"I am ready. I will be whatever is needed for the liberation of France."

Jepson leaned back, a slow smile spreading across his face lifting his black moustache in a funny way. "Very well. I will recommend you for training. But understand this, Miss de Baissac, your training will be grueling. You will be pushed to your physical and mental limits. You will endure everything I have described and more. This is not a game, and you must be prepared to face the worst."

"I understand, Sir. I won't let SOE down. Ever."

As Lise got up from the unyielding chair, her legs were shaky, but her gaze and handshake were firm. The path ahead may be highly uncertain, fraught with all the dangers Jepson had so vividly painted for her, but it was a path she was ready to walk.

. . .

OUTSIDE, the rain had begun to fall, but Lise hardly noticed the weather. This new chapter in her life was one that would demand every ounce of her courage and resilience. Jepson had made his point crystal-clear. A bit of rain was a matter of no importance.

9

THE TRAINING

Three months later - The New Forest, England, July 1942

Beaulieu Estate, nestled in the heart of the New Forest, served as one of the major Special Operations Executive's training grounds. With its lush greenery, ancient trees, and grand villas - now confiscated for the war effort - the sprawling estate provided the necessary privacy to train agents in what Churchill had dubbed 'irregular warfare.'

The serenity of the surroundings and the aristocratic appearance that marked Lord Montagu's barony exuded peace and harmony, a very different landscape from war-scarred London. But the peace and serenity were only superficial. Hard-core training in combat and guerrilla tactics took place among well-tended rose gardens and Victorian gazebos.

As all agents before her, Lise was struck by the beauty of the Beaulieu Estate. The main house particularly, Palace House, was an elegant manor with immaculately manicured gardens, quite similar to the large country house she had grown up in in Mauritius.

The July air was fresh with the scent of pine and blooming gardenias, a deceptive tranquility masking the grueling regimen she knew awaited her.

A young, silent, male agent escorted her to the women's training facility, The House in the Woods, lying in the middle of a large plot of woodlands, invisible to possible prying eyes.

THE NEXT MORNING Lise was introduced to the three other women in her class, all four of them dressed in the same new, stiff, khaki uniforms of the First Aid Nursing Yeomanry, the so called FANY.

A tall, stern man with a lined face stood in front of the makeshift classroom and introduced himself as Kim Philby, the black arts instructor. Lise had no clue what 'black arts' entailed but took in her fellow recruits with great interest.

They weren't supposed to know each other's names or nationalities and from the get-go had to invent an alias. Lise decided on Irène Brisse. Irène meant 'peace' in Greek. She liked that.

There was a studious, slim woman with a ready smile, who apparently spoke six languages fluently, and who like Lise was older than the other two. Lise thought she detected an Irish lilt and wondered if that was her nationality. But she knew her as Marie-Louise. The two younger ones were introduced as Odette and Josette.

Lise thought Odette was a bit theatrical and self-absorbed, but she was definitely the liveliest pacesetter. Josette, as pretty as a movie star, seemed nice but kept mostly to herself, fiddling with the manual in front of her.

"Your first job is to sign the Official Secrets Act," Philby handed around a sheet of paper. "Read and sign your real name or be gone," he snapped.

. . .

I DECLARE that I will never disclose to anyone any information which I have acquired or at any future time acquire as a result of my connections with this Department unless such disclosure is necessary for my work for the Department.

LISE READ IT TWICE, trying to make sense of it. It was as vague as it was official. With no way back, she unscrewed the tip of her fountain pen and, with curly letters, signed her full name, Lise Marie Jeannette de Boucherville-Baissac. She assumed it would be one of the last times she'd sign a document with her own name.

PHILBY'S EYES bored into their faces, "and your second job: no real names from now on. Use only your assigned code name, wherever you go. The instructors. The aliases you're going to construct are for blending in with the French and tricking the Germans. All other communication between agents and the Firm, only your codename. Clear?"

Lise nodded. From now on she was 'Odile' and no one in the room other than Kilby would ever know her as anything else.Not a name she'd have chosen herself, but she could live with it. She looked at the woman she knew as Claudine, there was also a Jacqueline, and funnily enough someone had been given the codename Lise, but of course that woman had no idea there was a real Lise in the room. It was all rather confusing, but she'd do what was expected of her.

THE DAYS that followed were both trying and fun. Training began at dawn with all sorts of physical exercises. She joined her fellow recruits - men and women alike - in punishing runs through the forest, their breath visible in the cool morning air.

The instructors, hardened by their own experiences, pushed them to the limits. Lise's small, slight frame belied her strength and stamina, and she kept pace with the best of them.

In the afternoons, they moved onto more specialized skills. She learned the art of sabotage—how to set explosives to derail locomotives, to destroy bridges, to blow up factories.

There was no time to reflect on the oddness of these assignments in the middle of rural England, as one demolition followed the other and each was carried out with great seriousness and full concentration.

She practiced picking locks, cracking safes, and the subtle art of invisible writing—skills the instructors thought would prove invaluable when she was back in enemy territory, but Lise considered it highly unlikely she'd find herself writing a message in invisible ink sitting at some outdoor café in the south of France while spying on Germans around her.

But who knew? She liked the training, useful or not, both the physical expeditions and the skills routines intrigued and challenged her.

As a strong member of the De Baissac lineage, she excelled at everything. A fast learner and highly intelligent, she was determined to come out on top. Even fighting a man almost twice her size, was done with skill and grace.

On the training ground, her eyes focused on the tawny figure before her, the Shanghai police officer, William E. Fairbairn, bespectacled and fierce. Fairbairn's reputation had preceded him. He was known for his unorthodox methods and here to demonstrate how petite Lise could take down a grown man much taller than she with minimal effort. His gruff voice carried over the field.

"Leverage and precision," he barked. "Size doesn't matter two fiddlesticks if you know where to hit your opponent."

Lise stepped forward, her body tense with anticipation. "Like this?" she asked, mimicking his stance.

He nodded approvingly, "yes, but with more force." He struck out, and Lise followed suit, her movements sharp and controlled. She felt a surge of confidence as she executed the maneuver perfectly.

"Try me," he grinned, and the power struggle began with Lise ending in the dust.

"Unfair, Lieutenant Fairbairn," Lise protested, jumping to her feet and brushing the dust from her uniform. "Let me try again with a classmate."

Fairbairn grinned again, enjoying her spunk. "Choose one, Madame, but make it a real challenge."

Lise scanned the semi-circle of agents around her, wondering who she'd dare to kick in the groin. Because that was what was expected from her. It was her time to grin, her natural confidence shining through.

"Let me turn this around. Who's game?" she asked, adopting Fairbairn's attitude by standing firmly on her legs, not budging one inch. A tall, sturdy man with very light hair and Nordic eyes stepped into the ring. Lise recognised him as one of the Norwegians, known for their bravery and cunning in the secret war.

"I'm your victim, Madame, with pleasu..." Before he could say anymore, he doubled at the waist and lay in the same dust Lise had just risen from. "Ouch," he cried but with a glint of amusement, "don't get in her way, lads, she's deadly."

THE CLASSROOM SESSIONS were equally intense. One day, Lise found herself seated across from the enigmatic Philby, who was tasked with teaching the students the black arts of foreign propaganda. His eyes twinkled with a mix of mischief and intelligence as he addressed the group.

"Propaganda is a weapon, just like a gun," Philby instructed, "but it's more insidious. It infiltrates minds, changes perceptions. You must learn to craft your messages with precision."

Lise listened intently, absorbing every word. She practiced creating subversive leaflets, writing fake radio scripts, and crafting subtle messages that could turn the tide of war by confusing the Germans. Philby's lessons were invaluable, giving her the tools to manipulate information to her advantage.

On the shooting range, Lise met her match in the form of a grizzled veteran who had seen more battles than he cared to remember. His piercing blue eyes assessed her with a critical gaze as he handed her a rifle, a .45 Liberator, which he insisted on calling one of his 'sweets and toys.'

"Let's see what you've got," he challenged.

Though Lise was unaccustomed to rifles of this caliber, her hands were steady. She aimed at the target and fired, the shot ringing out in the crisp air. The bullet hit the outer ring, not quite what she wanted.

"Again," the instructor commanded. "Focus. Breathe. Become one with the weapon."

Lise took a deep breath, her focus narrowing. She fired again, this time hitting the bullseye. A happy grin spreading over her face.

Thank you, Papa, for letting me practice with guns from a young age! Not all the girls were that fortunate, as became obvious around her.

"Well done," the instructor said with a tinge of admiration. "Keep practicing, Odile. You've got potential."

Exactly what Lise wanted to hear. Or was it Odile?

10

THE GRADUATION

Three weeks later - Beaulieu, New Forest, August 1942

More than anything, Lise looked forward to tackling the final challenge of the SOE training—parachute jumping. Everything about the 'graduation assignment' thrilled her: the moment of the jump, the adrenaline rush that would follow, the tumbling down at high speed, then the glorious snapping open of the parachute, followed by almost weightless floating in the air, and ultimately steering herself and the equipment to the ground for the most perfect landing of all time.

Lise had envisioned every detail of the jump long before it took place. The constant mental and physical stress of the training over, she could now indulge in her dream. This was going to be her moment. If she couldn't fly a plane, at least she could jump from one. Planes had been her thing ever since her pilot friends had offered her a seat in the cockpit, as early as in her Curepipe days.

Finally, the sunny August morning arrived that Lise and her

classmates were driven to the Parachute Training School at Ringway Airfield near Manchester. As soon as they left the Jeep, the roar of engines and the smell of aviation fuel filled the air. Lise inhaled deeply, while the other girls wrinkled their noses.

The instructor, a seasoned paratrooper with a no-nonsense demeanor, greeted them with a curt nod. "Before you can jump from a moving airplane, we practice from a static balloon. Baby steps first."

Lise eyed the static balloon that loomed ahead, tethered to the ground but rising high into the sky. The instructor continued, "this first exercise is about mastering your fear and ensuring you can land safely."

Fear? Lise thought. *What fear? Let's get cracking!* But the instructor wasn't done with the recruits yet.

"Same system applies to the balloon jump as to the plane jump. If you aren't smart enough to remember these nine steps, you'll hurt yourself. And it can end badly." He paused for effect. There was some shuffling around Lise, and she even heard a small moan. Was it Odette?

The instructor raised one finger at a time and Lise was already memorizing, "1. Chin on chest, 2. Back rounded, 3. Hands on risers, elbows forward, 4. Feet and knees together, 5. Knees slightly bent, 6. Turn off at a 45-degree angle, 7. Present the balls of your feet to the ground, 8. Go into a roll, and 9. Spill your chute by running around it or by pulling in two or three of the lines which are closest to the ground."

The nine steps were drilled into them until every trainee knew them by heart. Lise was almost trembling with excitement as she hoisted the parachute over her slim, overall-clad body. The harness was tight, the weight of the equipment unfamiliar but as she knew it was her survival kit, she trusted it. She lined up with her fellow trainees, but the instructor called her to the front.

"Odile, you seem eager. Eagerness may not be a good trait in a secret agent, but it helps with the jumping exercise. Do you want to go first?"

"Oh yes, Sir."

She got into the balloon's basket.

"You know the routine, Odile?"

"I do, Sir."

"Alright, Odile. Make sure you remember your training and trust your equipment. And for God's sake, keep your wits about you. I'll give you the sign."

As the ground receded, Lise took in the world around and below her, overseeing the patchwork of green fields and the runway. The instructor's voice cut through the noise of the wind.

"Ready, Madame?"

Lise approached the edge of the basket, the wind whipping through her hair. She took a deep breath, her pulse racing.

"Jump, Odile!" At the instructor's command, she jumped. The initial rush of freefall was exhilarating, the world blurring around her. Chin on chest...back rounded... she commanded herself, while counting the seconds until she felt the reassuring tug as her parachute deployed.

The descent was rapid, the ground rushing up to meet her. She focused on the steps, in quick succession, preparing for the landing. With a controlled roll, she hit the ground, the impact jarring but manageable.

"Well done, Madame! Next."

The show went on while Lise recovered from one of the fastest and most exhilarating experiences of her life. The thrill of the jump, the mastery over fear, and the success of the landing filled her with a new-found confidence. She knew this was just the beginning, and the next step was a jump from the C-47 Dakota, which she was sure would be everything she'd ever dreamed of and more.

BACK IN BEAULIEU THAT EVENING, Lise was almost nostalgic. It was her last evening at the training facility before returning to London and waiting for the instructions on when and where she'd be dropped into France.

That she'd passed the training with sufficient results, she was sure, but the whole adventure that awaited her after these intense weeks was a bit of an unknown. So, she cherished the last moments in Claudine's company.

Among her fellow trainees, Lise had quickly formed a warm bond with the woman codenamed Claudine. Her quick wit and infectious laughter had made the Irish woman an instant friend. Sometimes they were joined by Jacqueline, who had also warmed to the two 'nestors' in her class. The young woman codenamed Lise preferred to hang out with the male agents.

"I still can't believe we're actually doing this," Claudine whispered as they shared a final pint at the Royal Oak, the local pub on the Beaulieu Estate where trainee agents would unwind.

Lise agreed. "I know. Doesn't it feel surreal? But it's also empowering. I feel so much stronger after these weeks of training. And my head is still spinning with all the instructions. I'm not sure I'll need any of it, but it was sure fun to learn being a bit of a rascal. If we're selected would you actually go to France, Claudine?"

Claudine looked thoughtful, not answering the big question straight away. Then she nodded, still hesitant. "I think so. I have no idea what it will be like to arrive in France right now, you know, how dangerous it is going to be for us, but I think my conscience tells me to go, you know make the difference we can."

Lise raised her glass. "Here's to us making a difference, Claudine. And to staying friends."

"To us," Claudine echoed, "and to eternal friendship. As long as we may last."

They clinked glasses. The warmth of the pub, the hum of conversations around her, and the camaraderie of her fellow agents made it a difficult moment for Lise to leave Beaulieu. To be on her own again. To now probably return to occupied France she'd left with so much difficulty two years earlier. Was that madness or courage?

"...final time we'll encounter Philby." Claudine cut through her reverie, her bright eyes twinkling with amusement. "He's a character, isn't he?"

Glad to be drawn back into the now, Lise laughed. "He certainly is. But he knows his stuff. I've learned so much from him."

Claudine nodded, her expression growing serious. "Do you think we'll pass, Odile?"

"Maybe not everyone on the course, but about us two I have no doubt. The Firm needs tough girls like us." Lise finished the last of her lager and wiped the foam from her lips. It felt good to call SOE the "Firm". Something she was a part of now.

The moment Lise mentioned the Firm, the door of the Royal Oak opened and Philby marched in. She nudged Claudine's elbow. "Something about speaking of..." she mumbled. Philby came straight for their table.

"I can already tell you you've both done well, Odile and Claudine," he announced, "You're ready for the field. Remember, your greatest weapon is your mind. Stay sharp, stay focused, and you will succeed."

"Thank you, Sir." The girls saluted at the same time. As their black arts' instructor turned his back on the newly graduated secret agents to swagger to the bar, Lise and Claudine fell into each other's arms.

"We did it!"

Though passing the training felt like the ultimate triumph, Lise knew this was only the beginning. The most treacherous part of her life was about to begin.

11

PREPARATION FOR FRANCE

Two weeks later - London, Early September 1942

Lise sat rereading her Beaulieu instructors' final report, while she waited for Vera Atkins to join her at Manetta's Bar, the conspirational cocktail lounge and sophisticated hangout in Mayfair, and Vera's favorite place to meet agents ready for the field.

"MISS DE BAISSAC IS INTELLIGENT, extremely conscientious, reliable and sound in every way. Is quite imperturbable and would remain cool and collected in any situation.

IN BOTH PRACTICAL exercises and theoretical problems, she has shown a capacity to sum up a situation, make a decision and stick to it without becoming flustered.

· · ·

A CONSIDERABLE EXPERIENCE of the world has built up for her a very high degree of self-confidence. A pleasant and quiet personality.

SHE IS VERY MUCH AHEAD of her fellow trainees and, had she been with others as mentally mature as herself, she would have shown herself even more capable.

WE WOULD CERTAINLY RECOMMEND her for employment in the field."

LISE LOOKED up from the paper full of praise as the buzz of conversations around her filled the air, blending with the clinking of cocktail glasses and the hum of the gramophone playing a soft jazz tune. Manetta's was busy and glitzy as always, the perfect cover for a clandestine meeting.

She spotted Vera Atkins entering the restaurant, her sharp eyes scanning the room before settling on Lise in her FANY uniform. Vera herself was wearing civilian clothes, a navy suit, pearls and pumps, radiating an air of quiet authority as she made her way to the table in the corner.

"Miss de Baissac," Vera greeted, taking the seat opposite Lise, smoothing her wrinkle-free skirt. It surprised Lise that Vera still used her real name but that was probably for the formalities. "I trust you're well?"

"Yes, quite well, Miss Atkins." Her voice was neutral.

"Can I call you Lise?"

"Please do, Miss Atkins. I like my name and I'm not sure I'll hear it much in the coming time."

"Correct!" Vera proffered a tiny smile, lighting one of her

beloved Craven A cigarettes. "Care for one?" she offered Lise the packet.

"No thank you."

Vera glanced at the report in Lise's hands. "I see you've been reviewing your final assessment. Quite impressive."

"Thank you," Lise said, folding the paper neatly and placing it on the table.

"Let's get straight to the point," Vera's tone was still kind but businesslike. But before she could continue, they were interrupted by one of the waiters who knew well not to waste Miss Atkins' time.

"What are you having?"

"A Scotch Tape for me," Lise answered.

Vera raised a pronounced eyebrow. "You like Scotch?"

"Just this time." The answer was calm and collected. Vera ordered a ginger beer for herself and smoked her cigarette. Through the smoke she said in her typical husky voice, "You're scheduled to go to France as a courier for the PHYSICIAN Network in Paris, Lise. You'll be parachuted in near the Loire Valley on the next full moon, 24 September. Are you ready?"

Lise fixed her blue gaze on the spymistress through her smoke curtain. "Miss Atkins, I appreciate your preparation, but I must be frank with you. I do not want to go as a courier to a specific network. I'm willing to do everything you ask from me and more, but please let me operate on my own. That way I can guarantee my own safety and that of everyone I meet."

Vera was clearly taken off guard, looking puzzled. "What do you mean? Operate on your own?"

"I'm well aware of the risks we British agents run over there. I also know I'm one of the first women to go into France for SOE, and I know what it's like in Paris, which is swarming with Gestapo officers. I'd much rather operate from a rural area, get a feel for the

French sentiment in, say, Poitiers. Set up a small network, help other networks from my own small hub."

Vera said nothing, just sipped her ginger beer and smoked, so Lise continued, "I've thought it all through. If I need a W/T Operator I will contact the networks around me, if you give me the details. I can scout landing grounds, receive new agents, help them acclimatise. I truly see myself more as a helper to a variety of networks and groups than attached to one particular one. I promise to send all my reconnaissance without delay by traveling through the country by train, or by bicycle. I'll be fast and swift, so I reduce the risk of getting caught. I truly believe central France will be an excellent base for SOE to grow its activities."

Vera's eyes narrowed slightly. "What about your alias? It's based on a Parisian widow. Your accent is Parisian. It will make you suspect. And without a dedicated W/T operator, fast communication with London will be difficult. It's highly unconventional. You were trained to become a courier, Lise."

"I *will* be a courier, Miss Atkins." The words came out with force. "And my life story is a widow who escaped the hard life in Paris, fleeing to the countryside to feel less stressed. And I've read everything about the Crusades and Eleanor of Aquitane, who was from the Poitiers area. I have a real interest in history, so that is not fake. My hobby will be a perfect cover-up for cycling around the countryside on so called archaeological expeditions when I'm really looking for drop zones." She saw she was slowly winning over hard-nosed Vera Atkins.

"I'll blend perfectly into Poitiers society, draw no attention to myself. I'll have much more leeway to operate and I promise I will not let you down. I will make sure you get all the information you need when you need it."

Vera studied Lise for a long moment, her expression unreadable.

"You realize that if something goes wrong, you'll have no support network. You'll be entirely on your own."

"I know," Lise's voice was firm. "I am fully prepared for that. I am willing to operate alone and I am confident in my abilities."

Vera took a moment to stir the melting ice cubes in her glass and light another cigarette. Her movements were precise and controlled.

"Very well," she concluded. "I will convey your wishes to Colonel Buckmaster, Lise. See what he says, and I'll come back to you."

"Thank you." Lise took a firm sip from her strong drink, enjoying the warmth that spread through her body. "I am still prepared to go on the next full moon."

"I can only hope you're not underestimating the challenges you'll have to face, Lise. Going in without a network is an uncommon request, but your maturity and your excellent graduation report, make me think you might actually be right to go it alone."

"Thank you, Miss Atkins."

"Please call me Vera." A glimmer of a smile played around the spymistress's well-formed mouth.

"Thank you, Vera."

The smile widened, the expression softened. "You remind me of myself when I first joined SOE, Lise. Determined, unyielding. Please just be careful. We don't want to lose you."

Lise met Vera's gaze, feeling a rare moment of camaraderie between them. "I will be careful, Vera. I promise."

"I'll get in touch with you when Buckmaster's given his consent. I'll let you know about the final arrangements but jot down the 24th on your calendar. Now, take these weeks to say goodbye to friends and family. And just have a good time."

As they prepared to leave, Vera placed a hand on Lise's arm. "I hope to see you off at the airfield but if not, good luck, 'Odile.' Make us proud."

"I will, Vera. I can't wait to go back to France on a mission."

~SIL~

Marseille, August 2004

12

A CLASH OF WORLDS

Marseille, August 2004

S il Anderson sat cross-legged on the floor of her apartment in Vieux Port, Lise's "Preparation for France" letter to Henri Villameur resting in her lap. The twilight of the summer evening cast willowy shadows across the high-ceilinged room, the heat of the day lingered in the air while the air-conditioning purred like a lion ready for a meal.

Boxes of Thai take-away and empty Pepsi bottles lay scattered around her. Her cell phone beeped twice but she ignored it. Sil wasn't in the room. She was miles and decades away in a world she hadn't even known existed—a world where women were tough as nails, adept at wielding handguns, and ready to blow up bridges. She had no idea such women even existed outside of movies like Tomb Raider or Kill Bill.

But Sil was in trouble. When wasn't she? She'd neglected her life outside the old suitcase embossed with I.B. She'd already missed the first introduction day at École des Beaux-Arts, though she'd continued to work on her portfolio in between reading. Sil wasn't good at doing two things at once. She was a total-focus person who could paint for hours in the blink of an eye, and now she had been dreaming for days over stacks of old letters.

"I'll get a shower and an early night so I can show my face at school tomorrow. No more Lise de Baissac until the weekend," she mumbled, her slender fingers wrapping the ribbon around the set of letters.

She'd just put everything back in the suitcase and shoved it under her bed when a sharp knock on the door jolted her back to the present.

Before she could even reach the door or call "Entrez!", her landlord, Justin Bellamare, marched in.

"I've sent you at least a dozen messages, but you never reply. What is this stink, Mademoiselle? I can't stand it any..." His eyes behind the Tom Ford spectacles narrowed as they fixed on the gaping hole in the wall.

"What the hell happened there?" he demanded, his voice tight with anger. He was dressed in his usual suit, looking dashingly overdressed in the hot summer evening—ever the appearance of a gentleman, albeit an angry one.

Sil rose to her feet, squaring her shoulders and pushing a curl of rainbow-colored hair from her eyes.

"It's not what it looks like," she began, but Bellamare cut her off.

"It looks like someone took a sledgehammer to the wall of a historic building!" He glared at her, his eyes drifting to her hair and her Sex Pistols tank top. "Explain."

"Okay, okay. Take a breath and give me a sec." She waved her hands defiantly. "My ex-boyfriend did it, but it wasn't intentional. He got angry and—"

"Angry?" Bellamare's voice rose. "Do you even realize this is an ancient, monumental building I've just acquired and am in the process of restoring to its original glory? How do you plan to fix this with your meager student loan? Oh, and don't you dare to let that boyfriend of yours anywhere near my house again, or you're out as well."

Sil bristled at his condescension. "I said ex-boyfriend. And I said I'd take care of it."

"And how exactly do you intend to do that?" Bellamare's gaze was icy, his frustration palpable. The tension between them crackled in the hot, sticky air of the summer evening.

Sil met his glare with equal intensity. "Look, I know it's a mess." She hesitated, then added with a sigh, "I am a mess, as usual."

For a moment, she thought she saw a flicker of concern in Bellamare's eyes, but his voice remained far from sympathetic. "What are you doing here in Marseille, Mademoiselle Anderson? The École des Beaux-Arts assured me you were an international student with great qualifications, but you make a mess of your room, have an aggressive boyfriend, and you hardly go out. Are you a recluse?"

"Felix is not my boyfriend anymore. I told you so twice. He won't dare show his face here again. I've taken care of that. And I'm not a recluse. Why would you think so?" She stealthily kicked the Thai boxes and Pepsi bottles under her bed with her bare toes.

"Well, for one, term has started and all you do is stay in this pigsty. It doesn't seem very healthy."

Sil sighed. "I know. I've been busy. Are you spying on me, or what?"

"Well, I suppose it's none of my business how you spend your time, as long as you pay your rent and keep the place a bit cleaner. I'm not here to judge your cutting classes. You make your own decisions."

"Why did you come here then?" Sil retorted.

"Because...I felt... it is my duty to see if you're alright."

"Who told you?" Sil's suspicion flared.

"No one told me. But I'll be away for the next two weeks, and..."

"... you just wanted to make sure I wouldn't set the house on fire?" Sil grimaced.

"Considering you've already managed to break down a wall, it might be just as well I checked on you." Bellamare walked over to inspect the damage, peering behind the board.

"How strange," he mumbled, "it seems like a fake wall. Was there anything in that space?"

Not ready to share her secret yet, Sil quickly shook her head. "Not that I know of."

"Apparently, this was Monsieur Villameur's room. At least that is what the realtor told me. He passed long ago, and the wife, Madame Villameur, only used it as a storage room. The house came on the market when she passed this spring."

Sil gasped at his mention of their names. Her eyes darted to the suitcase under the bed, relieved Bellamare only had eyes for the space behind the wall.

"Oh, I see," she managed to say.

Bellamare turned to her. "I'll send a repairman over, but I'll ask him to make it a fair price."

"Thank you, and I'm sorry for the damage. I'll go to school and be a good girl from now on," she said, half to herself and half in jest.

He smiled, suddenly looking way too handsome. Sil fought the urge to offer him tea.

"Now go!" she said instead. "I need to prepare for becoming a good girl."

"You do that, Miss Anderson, and I'll check on you when I'm back."

Sil didn't know if it was a promise or a threat. But she cleaned the room, took her shower, and spent the next four days getting to know students and teachers at École des Beaux-Arts de Marseille.

UNTIL FRIDAY NIGHT, and the suitcase was retrieved....

~LISE~

France
September 1942 - August 1943

13

THE JUMP INTO THE UNKNOWN

Mer-sur-Loire, France, 25 September 1942

I t was a perfect night for a parachute jump. No clouds, no low-hanging mist, a full moon that rose into the sky like a giant snowball, casting an ethereal glow over the dense woodlands below. Just enough light for the pilot to maneuver the plane without headlights. The meandering Loire River glimmered beneath them like a glowing worm, the surface rippling gently in the reflection of the moonlight.

As Lise peered through the window of the Whitley bomber, her hopes soared. If the reception team got their act together tonight, the agent codenamed Denise and she would be able to jump. The weather wouldn't be the problem.

Yesterday had been such a disappointment. The pilot had refused to drop them because the flashlights at the landing site weren't as agreed. Only two lamps instead of three. He'd turned the Whitley around and flew them straight back to RAF Tempsford.

All Lise could think was, *why?* But they'd had to sit through another arduous flight with the relentless drone of the engines vibrating through their bones. Lise's behind was still sore from sitting on that hard aircraft floor all those hours with her parachute clinging to her back and the straps pressing into her skin.

But this was a new night and a fresh chance, and she'd likely laugh at herself for complaining about a minor discomfort like this. There'd be plenty of times she would be a lot less comfortable on French soil, with Germans waiting to skin her alive if they could get their hands on her.

The cold night air seeped through the fuselage, carrying the scent of engine oil and the metallic tang of the aircraft. Denise and she were the first "Janes" to be parachuted into France. So far, the pilots had only escorted "Joes."

Suzanne, who'd been with Denise in the first batch of female recruits trained for SOE, had arrived before them, traveling by felucca via Gibraltar. If all went well this night, Suzanne would be waiting for them with the reception team down below.

They sat squashed in the small space with their legs drawn up, listening over the drone of the aircraft's engines for the sound of German anti-aircraft artillery. So far, so good.

To distract herself, Lise stared at the moon. It was as bright and lemony pale over France as it used to be during her childhood summers, watching it float up over the Trou aux Cerfs in Mauritius while sitting snugly between her brothers, Jean and Claude.

But no thinking of them right now. No thinking of the past, nor the future. She would only think of the moon, that benign beacon guiding their pilot to the right landing ground.

The night stretched before her like an endless expanse of ebony velvet, punctuated by the distant glimmer of millions of stars. The roar of the plane's engine had reduced conversation with Denise to shouting short sentences in each other's ears. It became so exhausting they'd given up. Now Denise was probably as huddled up in her own thoughts as Lise herself was.

The light of the moon followed the landscape below, illuminating the patchwork of fields and forests that blurred into indistinct shapes as they hurtled through the darkness.

Another flashback took her to the fields behind their house in Curepipe. Zigzagging through the tropical evening in a linen dress and sandals, occasionally blipping her flashlight to let her brothers know her position.

They'd left Mauritius twenty-three years ago, and since then she'd lived in Paris and in London. Why did she find herself going back to her wild, early years on the island in the Indian Ocean right now?

Because, after the long-drawn, boring years in the newsroom office, she was finally embarking on a real adventure again. The flashbacks reminded her of who she once was. Bold, confident, strong-minded.

Still, being a secret agent in occupied France would be far from child's play. Lise was very aware of the gravity of her situation, yet she found herself oddly detached, her emotions veiled beneath a veneer of icy composure.

She knew all the risks of this mission, not just because of Jepson's intense interview and her recent Beaulieu training, but also because she was that kind of person. She calculated and dissected every outcome of her actions like a skilled surgeon considers the steps of the surgery.

There was no room for sentimentality, for heroism, for fear. The world of espionage needed only cold, hard logic and a steely resolve to see the mission through to its conclusion.

As the Whitley Bomber of the Special Duties Squadron rumbled on, she glanced through the dusk at Denise, who sat with her hands clasped around her knees, making herself as comfortable as possible by resting against her parachute.

Lise didn't know much about her as Denise had been in the first SOE training for women and Lise in the second. Her companion looked tense, forlorn. She was very pretty with dark hair and regular features, at least fifteen years younger than Lise. She appeared to be a very charming, uncomplicated sort of girl.

Of course, Denise was tense. Why wouldn't she be? She was heading for the hub of Nazi-occupied France: Paris. Lise was bound for sleepy Poitiers. But the young agent looked like a tough cookie, and apparently, she was a hell of a wireless operator, much better at sending messages than Lise was.

Lise double-checked her equipment in the dark, fingers tracing the familiar contours of the parachute buckles, ensuring each strap was securely fastened. Her overalls felt constricting, a second skin clinging to her like a shield over her fashionable French dress, but not warm enough to protect her from the biting cold.

The Colt in the holster outside her overalls felt like an out-of-place yet necessary accessory, but it was needed in case their reception team didn't have the tea ready. After her shooting drills, she'd probably be capable of taking down a German or two even in a pitch-black forest.

Ugh, no thinking of that. She continued with her check, just to keep busy. The adrenaline kept her wide awake, though she usually wasn't a night owl. The folded switchblade sewn into her sleeve was another layer of security, though she hoped she wouldn't have to cut it loose from its hidden compartment on arrival. The torch was in her leg pocket. All there.

Then her fingers touched a smooth flat case in another pocket. For a moment she hesitated. What was it? Oh, she'd forgotten. It was the golden cigarette case that Buck, nickname of the head of Section F, had pressed into her hand at the airport. A gift to remind them of home. Well, she wasn't much of a smoker, but it was a kind gesture.

Tracing her finger over the embossed relief, she wondered what was imprinted there. She was too preoccupied when they finally took off, so she'd shoved the case in her pocket without a proper look. It was probably worth quite a bit.

At her side was her valise, strapped to its own parachute and containing the essential supplies for the widow Madame Irène Brisse, her alias. There was no room for error here, no margin for hesitation; every action must be executed with flawless precision if she was to evade capture by the Germans.

Apart from the agents and their luggage, there was also a parachuted crate with supplies for the French Resistance. Revolvers, ammunition, detonators, those sorts of things. The reception team would take care of the crate when it landed. Lise and Denise just had to get out of these harnesses as quickly as they could and hide the parachutes.

"Orléans!" She pointed to Denise, who nodded, staring unblinkingly out of her own window. The Whitley nosed down and headed towards Blois. The descent created a certain giddiness, but Lise breathed through it.

Let the flare paths be in place tonight. I can't stomach another return to England.

Her watch showed 12:50 a.m. Almost there. She peered and peered, but it was inky black down below apart from the moon and the glistening river.

After only one parachute jump in the dark and on safe British soil, this was it. As the moment of truth drew near, Lise prepared herself to hurl her body into the abyss, in the knowledge that the fate of a free France was determined by the success or failure of missions like hers.

In the seconds that remained before the jump, she steeled her body and mind, knowing she must be ready for every possible outcome. This was the ultimate test of her courage and commitment, a matter of life and death. Once she plunged into the darkness below, she knew she must face her fate, as expected from a trained agent.

"Remember I jump first," Denise shouted in her ear. Lise gave her the thumbs up. She'd preferred to go first, as it was harder to follow and land near the first jumper, but they drew straws and Denise had won.

The moments now stretched into an eternity. Lise felt a surge of adrenaline pulsing through her veins, heightening her senses to the highest degree. The deafening roar of the Whitley's engines faded into the background, replaced by the pounding of her heart, steady and rhythmic like a drumbeat in her ears.

She stole a last glance at Denise, her features illuminated by the dim glow of the full moon, her eyes reflecting a mixture of trepidation and determination, mirroring Lise's own.

AND THEN, without further warning, the moment arrived.

Dot. Dot. Dash. Dot. F!

THE CORRECT MORSE signals flashed up. Like the first tones of Beethoven's 5th.
Thank God!

"Jane 1 and Jane 2, ready yourselves." The crackling voice of the pilot sounded through his microphone, and Lise felt the plane dipping even lower.

The dispatcher emerged from the cockpit and opened a hole in the bottom of the aircraft. An icy wind whistled through the open floor of the low-flying Whitley.

As the aircraft roared between the trees, she felt turbulent vibrations beneath her feet. Denise sat on the edge of the hole, her feet dangling down. She gave Lise a final glance, her chin up defiantly. Then she was gone. Lise followed immediately, swift and soundless.

With a prayer on her lips and a resolve like tempered steel, she tumbled down, the rushing wind tearing at her senses as she plummeted toward the earth below.

Time seemed to blur, each passing second stretched thin like taut wire, as the ground rushed up to meet her with terrifying speed. The sensation of weightlessness enveloped her, a fleeting moment of surreal tranquility amid the chaos of the jump. Her senses reeled as the world spun around her, the roar of the wind drowning out all other sound, leaving only the deafening thud of her heartbeat echoing in her ears.

With a sudden jolt the parachute snapped open above her, billowing outwards in a triumphant flourish of silk and cord. She gasped in awe as the world slowed to a standstill, the earth below stretching out before her like a vast canvas of shadows and light.

With practiced ease, she guided the parachute towards the ground where flashlights flickered at regular intervals, her hands steady as she navigated the swirling currents of air with precision born of earlier training. And then, with a soft thud, her boots made contact with the earth below. She'd done it.

In an equal puff of white cloth, she saw Denise landed only a yard away. Thud, thud, thud. Their valises and the crate. As she scrambled to her feet, she saw three figures racing towards them. Their reception team, she hoped.

The Whitley took off over their heads, pointing its propeller upwards back to the bright moon. It was gone over the trees in seconds, leaving the moon for them. The only sign of its momentary presence was the distant thrum of its engine. Back to England. Back to safety.

"*Je suis Adolphe*," a French voice whispered in the dark. "Welcome to the Resistance, mesdames. Let me escort you to your safe house."

Relief flooded through Lise's whole body on being greeted by friendly Frenchmen and not a German sentry. Fluid and silent as night animals, the women buried their parachutes and collected their luggage. All was done within seconds. But there was no sight of Suzanne and no time for questions.

Lise's legs were wobbly, and her stomach churned, but her head was calm, happy almost. Well, now she was back on French soil! Who'd have thought that a few months ago?

As Denise and she followed their guides, Lise felt a sense of accomplishment mixed with an eager appetite for what lay ahead.

14

MERDE ALORS!

The next day - Mer-sur-Loire, 26 September 1942

Adolphe took Lise and Denise to a shed in the woods where they'd have to wait for daylight when curfew lifted.

"Good night, *mesdames*. I'll come back to take you to your safehouse in the morning."

"Good night," they replied and that was about all they shared as conversation after the French Resister left. Too exhausted for anything more, they lay down on the makeshift wooden bunks to rest their weary bodies after two nights of air travel and all the tension of arriving in France.

Still dressed in her overalls over her dress, chilled to the bone by the night damp, Lise quickly scanned her surroundings before falling into a light slumber, her Colt by her side. She had no energy left to process where she was.

In the morning, she told herself. *Now, try to sleep.*

She dreamed of a camping adventure with her brothers near

Curepipe. Claude, the youngest, teased her because she'd pegged up her skirts to make them look like pants.

He chuckled and slapped his thighs, comparing them to harem pants. "You'd better start training your chubby tummy, Lise, if you want to be sold as a belly dancer to a Turkish harem."

"I don't want to be sold!" she cried, when a hand clamped firmly over her mouth.

"You're sold alright," Jean hollered, dragging her along.

Lise struggled, kicking her older brother's shins while uttering a muffled, "let me go, you scamp!"

She woke with a start, noticing she held her own hand over her mouth. Her breaths came in gasps as she'd been suffocating herself. *Am I this scared?* flitted through her mind, realizing the dream reflected her unconscious mind. She listened in the dark. It was still inside the hut, but it felt as if the night outside was teeming with unseen life.

The distant hoot of an owl, the rustle of leaves as some creature scurried past the other side of the wall, the wind creaking the roof planks. The forest smelled of damp and earth making her aware of her rural surroundings. They were in the middle of nowhere, on their own. In occupied France.

Listening to Denise's regular breathing, with a soft snore at the end of every inhale, Lise was glad her companion seemed to be enjoying the sleep of the innocent. Lise, however, was wide awake now and, as whenever she couldn't sleep, drilled her alias through her head to push her real identity back. It was Irène Brisse who was in France, Lise de Baissac had been left behind in England.

I am Madame Irène Brisse, a Parisian widow of modest means. I have no children. I seek refuge in Poitiers to escape the tension of life in the capital. I am an amateur archaeologist with a great interest in Eleanor of Aquitane. That's why I'm cycling around the provinces looking for interesting sites.

The minutes crawled by; each one marked by the steady tick of her watch. Her own watch, as it was a Cartier and thus French and fit her alias. Aside from her underwear, which she'd bought at Galeries Lafayette before the war, and her watch, nothing else had ever belonged to Lise.

In that shoddy shed, she fully embraced the identity of Madame Brisse. A woman who'd once been married. Something Lise never had experienced. *Oh, Henri!*

The cold of the night seeped through her overalls and thin wool dress. Lise pulled her trench coat tighter around her. Her stomach growled softly. Aldophe had left them some bread and cheese, which she and Denise had wolfed down. It hadn't been enough, but the bottle of red wine he'd left on the table had been a kind, welcome gesture.

As dawn broke, the first light filtered through the cracks in the wooden walls. Lise could now orient herself better. The shed was no more than a hunter's hut with two elevations that served as bunk beds. No fireplace, no sink.

She peered through a crack next to her. The world outside was shrouded in late September mist, the trees around the shed standing like hazy sentinels, dripping wet leaves in the windless morning. Something stirred and she instantly withdrew her eye from the crack, her hand on the Colt.

Someone was coming! She listened with all her might when seconds later Aldophe entered the shed, quiet as a church mouse. Relaxing, Lise smiled, eagerly taking in the French Resister in daylight. Aldophe was known in London by his real name, Pierre Culioli; though French with no British ties, he was connected to the Firm. Buck trusted him and used him many times for reception committees. He'd told Lise that much.

Adolphe, as she must remember to think of him for both of their safety, was a small, slight, and wiry man with a nervous manner, horn-rimmed spectacles, and a toothbrush mustache. Anyone could see he was a proud Frenchman, who was fiercely anti-German. His arrival in that gloomy hut on that cold morning was a pleasant reassurance to Lise that she knew at least one trustworthy person in France.

"Time to move," he whispered, his voice barely audible over the soft stirrings of the forest awakening.

Denise blinked the sleep from her eyes and shot up to a sitting position. They quickly gathered their few belongings with as little noise as they could make. Stepping outside into the crisp morning, Lise marveled at the gradient of dark-blue and pale-pink sky waiting for the sun to break above the treetops. Going from the New Forest in England to the Loire woodlands in France seemed a flawless transition. So far. She'd have loved to go for a jog.

Adolphe held the horse, as they clambered onto the back of an old cart with their suitcases. The sturdy brown mare snored softly as Pierre patted her neck. Denise and Lise settled themselves among sacks of grain and hay. The cart creaked under their weight, as it jerkily set into motion.

They trundled through the misty countryside, the rhythmic clip-clop of the horse's hooves and the creak of the cart sounding way too loudly for Lise to feel comfortable. But they met no oncoming traffic and Aldophe seemed relaxed, humming under his breath. Denise sat silently beside her, her eyes wide open, breathing small white plumes in the air.

Turning towards them, Adolphe said," "I'm taking you to Monsieur and Madame Brossard. They'll take care of you for two days. They're good folk."

"Thank you," Lise answered. Denise nodded in agreement. They arrived at the Brossards' farmhouse just as the sun broke free from the morning mist. The house was a typical, yellow-stone structure with small windows and a slate roof. A large, wooden barn stood next to the house and a red tractor was parked in the yard. Smoke curled lazily from one of the chimneys.

An elderly couple came to the gate to greet them. Adolphe exchanged a few words with them, dropped them off, tapped his cap and rode off again. Lise thought their new hosts were a picture of rustic charm. Monsieur Brossard, with his weathered face and twinkling eyes, wore a woolen cap and sturdy boots, while Madame Brossard, round and rosy-cheeked, sported a floral apron over her dress.

"*Bienvenue, mesdames*," Monsieur Brossard said warmly, shaking their hands. His hands were rough after a long life of toil. Madame Brossard followed suit, but her hands were soft and gentle.

"Thank you for taking us in," Lise smiled. She was truly grateful for their hospitality and so glad to be able to speak French in France again.

Denise's smile was even wider, "You have such a lovely house! Thank you for having us."

"Come inside, *mes filles*, you must be cold and hungry." Madame Brossard ushered them into the warm kitchen where the scent of freshly baked bread and herbs filled the air. Another surprise awaited them. The agent codenamed Suzanne operating under the alias Jacqueline Gautier, which is how the Brossards knew her, stood by the hearth, stirring a pot of soup. She turned and smiled as they entered.

Suzanne had been in France for two months already, traveling by felucca from Gibraltar to the south French coast. Lise didn't know Suzanne, but Denise hugged her like an old friend. They knew each other from their training period in the spring. Lise received a handshake and a hearty "welcome, Odile. It's good to see you have both landed safely." Her heavily accented English marked her as a true Frenchwoman.

Suzanne was older than them, well into her forties. Lise thought she looked tired. Life as a secret agent was clearly wearing her slight frame down. Lines furrowed her forehead, and her shoulders were hunched, but her smile was bright. "It's good to have more female agents now! Though we won't be seeing much of each other, the idea I'm not alone helps."

"Make yourselves at home," Madame Brossard interrupted, pointing to a wooden bench in an alcove surrounding an oak table on three sides.

The well-stocked, French kitchen with its delicious scents of food preparation and the feeling of being surrounded by safe people was a welcome relief after the cold night in the shed. Lise looked around her, feeling more at ease. The ceiling had wood-stained beams, and Madame Brossard's copper pots and pans glinted in the firelight. It felt homely and safe.

Lise looked forward to two days with the Brossards, learning the latest news on French terrain, the distribution of ration coupons, travel papers, and the general lay of the land. Any tidbits to better prepare her for what lay ahead.

Suzanne grabbed her coat and headed for the door. "I'll send the Firm a radio message that 'Agents Odile and Denise' have safely arrived. Good luck, girls. *Bon courage!*" And out the door she went, and with her another connection to a life once led in England.

Denise looked lost. She'd clearly wanted to chat with Suzanne a little longer, but this was the reality they now faced. The less contact they had with other agents, the less they could betray each other if caught. Suzanne already fully understood that. Friendship would have to wait until after the war. If she and Denise survived.

Madame Brossard knew all these subtleties and placed a friendly hand on Denise's hunched shoulders.

"Here, dearie, you get that inside you and you'll be right as rain."

The real ground coffee and the warm buns exuding the aroma of plump raisins and melted sugar brought a tiny smile to the corners of the young agent's lips, "Thank you, Madame. I think I'm just a bit tired."

"You two have a quick nap before we get to work." Madame Brossard gave them a wink, "a bed with lavender-scented linen, I think that'll do the trick."

Lise and Denise attacked the delicious breakfast. Their first glimpse of French life was tranquil and delicious.

...

The next morning, they rose early to help with chores around the farm, milking the cows and cleaning the cowshed. Then they assisted Madame Brossard with preserving peas and tomatoes. All the while they got the information they needed to get on their way the next day.

Lise liked the simple manual work; it gave her hands something to do while she kept her ears and eyes open for what she could learn.

In the evening, they sat around the kitchen table enjoying omelettes and wine. Monsieur Brossard turned to Lise. "*La vie n'est pas vraiment libre encore, n'est-ce pas?*" he observed, his eyes sad. Life isn't really free anymore, is it?

"No, it isn't," Lise admitted, "but here at your farm it's very doable. I haven't seen a German yet."

"Oh, but you will. They are everywhere. And if you can't see them, they still control us with all their laws and restrictions. I'll never learn to live with them."

Thinking of the curfews, the rationing, and the ever-present threat of arrest, Lise sighed, looking over at Madame Brossard, who was always so chirpy and upbeat.

This elderly couple faced immense danger by hiding British agents. They'd be shot without mercy if the Germans found out. But it was not a topic she could bring up. The Brossards had chosen their side in this war and may God protect them for their bravery.

"I understand you know where to go in Paris tomorrow, Denise?" Monsieur Brossard continued in his raspy voice. Denise nodded.

"But for you Irène, you make sure you contact Monsieur et Madame Gâteau in Poitiers. I'll give you the address. They will help you settle."

"Thank you!" Lise's gratitude swelled in her heart.

WHEN THEY WERE ABOUT to take leave of their hosts the next morning, Madame Brossard took two loaves of bread, still warm from the oven. "Take one each, for the journey," she said, her voice thick with emotion.

"Merci," Denise replied with shining eyes. "We will not forget your kindness."

"Never," Lise agreed, feeling a tear well. How much kindness would they meet from here?

After a hasty goodbye, they headed for the station carrying their suitcases filled with their alias lives. On the platform, a quiet local track in the middle of nowhere, where Lise would go one way and Denise the other, they said goodbye. They didn't hug and they didn't shake hands.

"I might see you in Paris if we're lucky," Lise offered in an under-tone, "as I haven't got a W/T operator with me, I'll need to travel to Paris or to Bordeaux to send my information to the Firm."

"You know the contact place in Paris? The café in the Rue de Caumartin? Go there." Denise's voice was thin but even. The same struggle was in her eyes that Lise had seen after Suzanne left the Brossard farm. They were on their own after this.

"I know the place. Thank you, Denise. Merde Alors!"

A delicate smile broke over Denise's pretty face as she replied,

"Merde Alors!" It was the Firm's slogan to galvanize agents ready to go into "the field".

And then she was gone. A pretty, young, and a talented wireless operator with the codename Denise. May God save her!

The train rattled along the tracks, carrying Lise towards her uncertain future. She gazed out the window, the landscape passing by in a blur of green and gold. Her heart was heavy and light at the same time with the anticipation of what lay ahead.

But after meeting Adolphe, the Brossards, Denise, and Suzanne, she somehow felt less alone. And her brother Claude, who'd been in the Bordeaux region since July organizing the SCIENTIST Network —maybe she would get a glimpse of him in the coming months.

They all carried in them the spirit of resistance, the hope to free France from the yoke of Nazi oppression. That hope and knowing she was not alone in her fight kept Lise alive. And on her toes.

15

MADAME BRISSE ARRIVES IN POITIERS

Poitiers, France, 30 September 1942

Madame Irène Brisse, whose suitcase Lise was carrying, had never been to Poitiers. Lise had researched the surroundings on maps during her training in England and concluded that the city in west-central France would be an excellent base for her new ARTIST network.

Arriving on the fourth day of her arrival back in France, she found Poitiers to be a quiet town on a hill with a church on almost every street corner, nestled between Paris and Bordeaux, roughly at the same distance from both big cities Lise would use to send her messages to London. The perfect place to settle for a Parisian widow who didn't want to draw attention to herself. And one who loved history and churches.

A sharp September wind swept through the steep, deserted streets. At first sight, the chill and the tense silence didn't appeal to Lise at all. After the hospitality she'd enjoyed at the Brossards',

Poitiers seemed a cold place, though its picturesque charm was undeniable.

Mind you, it's exactly what I need for my undercover operations, she reminded herself. *I haven't come here for cream teas and chatter.*

With a resolved step, she began the steep climb from the station to the address the Brossards had given her. At Beaulieu, she'd heard agents argue it was best to blend in and take cover in huge cities like Paris and Lyon, but from the start of her training Lise had wanted to gauge the willingness of rural, French people to resist the Germans.

That's where she could receive agents and arms, not on the Place de la Concorde. Here in Poitiers and surroundings, Lise would be most helpful to the Firm. She was sure of it. Whether she liked it or not. Whether she was with an existing network or on her own.

Romanesque churches and cobblestoned squares spread out before her like a postcard come to life. In the distance, she spotted the remnants of an ancient aqueduct.

Make note, Irène! Take that in as well, because that's what you are supposed to be interested in!

Shards of French history lessons received on an island in the middle of the Indian Ocean as a primary school pupil flooded back to Lise—Poitiers, a city that dated back to the times of Charlemagne, the Crusades, and the Holy Roman Empire.

Well, Irène was here on a crusade of her own, but Lise could certainly have done with some of the tropical, Mauritian sunshine. She pulled her coat tighter around her and walked at a brisk pace, as fast as the uneven cobblestones allowed the heels of her Charles Jourdan pumps.

There was something about these dainty, French shoes that gave Lise extra confidence, a connection to her fabricated identity. Everything around her may be new and unknown and surrounded by war, but she cared how she looked. Modest, but well-bred. Even when there was no one obviously watching her, as at this quiet mid-afternoon hour the shops were closed and people had withdrawn inside.

Lise's highly-tuned senses felt the unseen attention of eyes peering through half-closed shutters and lace curtains. It was as if she could hear the whispers: "Must be another refugee arriving in Poitiers! What are they all fleeing from?"

Lise was fully prepared for their stares and their eventual questions. Irène, though a war widow, wasn't a pushover but a proud Parisian. She had every right to walk these streets to her rented accommodation. She was just one of the many who sought respite in the provinces.

Her ears caught every sound—the tolling of a church bell, the thumping of German boots, the occasional clatter of a bicycle on the bumpy streets.

Germans were everywhere, but to Lise's amazement they seemed as subdued as the few Poitevins she passed. These weren't arrogant, loud-mouthed conquerors but bashful young lads, looking as if they would be hardly capable of standing their ground.

Lise observed it all with a calm eye from under her hat, knowing that appearances could be deceiving. Just like hers. These street patrols may be a weak version of their superiors by design.

The narrow alleyways and old buildings created a fascinating, yet disorienting, maze. Shadows played tricks on her eyes, alerting her to every unexpected movement. Every step demanded caution, attention, preparation. To be a solitary secret agent exploring new territory was not a walk for the weak-minded.

Before she arrived at the address the Brossards had given her, she went through her story for the umpteenth time. Madame Irène Brisse-war widow from Paris -seeking accommodation in Poitiers - amateur archaeologist - Eleanor of Aquitane and Richard the Lionheart.

She tapped the knocker lightly with a flutter in her heart. *Is this the right address? Not a trap?* Moments later the door opened to reveal a middle-aged man with thinning, gray hair, a Roman nose, and perceptive, hazel eyes. He glanced up and down the street before ushering her inside with a curt nod.

"Monsieur Gâteau?" she asked softly.

"Yes, come in quickly." Lise slipped inside and he immediately bolted the front door from the inside.

"I've come from the Brossards."

"I know. You must be Madame Brisse. Welcome to Poitiers." His voice was low and measured, carrying the weight of experience. He led her through a dimly lit hallway to his office, cluttered with antiques and artefacts. Lise remembered the Brossards had told her Monsieur Gâteau was an auctioneer. The smell of aged wood and musty books filled the air.

"Please have a seat, Madame." He gestured to a worn leather chair. "I understand you are looking for a place to stay?"

Lise sat down on the edge of the seat, putting her valise at her feet. "Yes, I need something discreet but comfortable. I don't know for how long, maybe six months or more."

Monsieur Gâteau leaned back in his chair, studying her with interest. Lise didn't know how much he knew about her, nor what the Brossards had known; did any of them know she was a British agent? It wouldn't come up for discussion, but that she was of interest to the Poitiers auctioneer, she could see.

"I think I have just the place for you, Madame Brisse. It's a ground-floor apartment on a busy street near the station. No nosy concierge to worry about. The house belongs to a local lady, Madame de Vigny, whom I'm well acquainted with and who has left for North Africa to escape the war. I look after the place for her, and she assured me I could sublet it for her. It's quite spacious and luxurious—ideal for entertaining, which I understand may be part of your...cover."

Lise smiled faintly at his discretion. "Yes, I'm an amateur archaeologist, and I understand there are many people here in Poitiers studying Eleanor of Aquitane, who was from this region. I'd like to acquaint myself with them."

She could see he appreciated her discretion as well. There was no need for truths that were dangerous.

"Excellent. There is only one but. The apartment is one door down from the Gestapo headquarters. Will that be a problem?"

Lise took a moment to reflect on this and then slowly shook her head. "Not at all. It might even be a perfect protection for a widow on her own, n'est-ce pas? May I see it?"

He eyed her for a moment with those perceptive eyes. They held a glint of appreciation. "Well, in that case, please follow me, Madame. May I carry your luggage for you?"

Lise handed him her valise. Playing the modest widow was all part of the cover, no matter she had a Colt under her belt and enough French banknotes and ration coupons in her luggage to provide for half of Poitiers, if she wanted.

"Please come and have tea with my wife soon, Madame. Marguerite would love talking about historic sites with you."

"Thank you. I will as soon as I'm settled in."

His friendliness and the knowledge he was on her side instantly made Lise feel better about Poitiers. Like the Brossards, the Gâteaux were good, French people, people she could rely on in an hour of need.

Gâteau led her through the chilly afternoon to a solid stone building just a short walk away. The streets were livelier now - the shops had reopened after the lunch break. Daily life was almost normal, as vendors advertised their wares, the clatter of carts sounded on cobblestones, and the hum of conversations resounded.

Deceptively normal, as there was a tense veil hanging over the city of which Lise was acutely aware.

As Monsieur Gâteau unlocked the door to the apartment on the Boulevard Solférino, Lise scanned the building next door, a house very similar to the one they were entering, but for the two swastika flags flapping in the stiff breeze and the German cars in front of it.

Strangely enough, being separated from the enemy by one mere wall, left Lise quite cold. It wasn't the same as being forced to leave her comfortable flat on the Avenue Kléber in June 1940 with the little she could carry. Not knowing when or if she ever could return.

In a way, the tables were turned. She was back under their eyes with a new French identity and the assignment to get them out. Cohabitation with the Germans was temporary. The fight back had begun.

Her new abode enveloped her with its warmth and comfort. It was a sumptuous, woman's place. One Madame de Vigny must have reluctantly left. Had it been because of her new neighbors?

The scent of polished wood and lavender still filled the air as if the occupant had recently been there. Subdued sunlight streamed through the gauze curtains in the tall bay windows, casting a honey-gold glow over the living room that was furnished with plush sofas, cocktail tables, and elegant rugs.

The auctioneer and the widow walked from room to room. Lise took in the high ceilings, the walnut paneling, the tasteful furnishings, and the luxurious touches that made her immediately feel at home.

The kitchen was well-equipped, and the dining room boasted a large table perfect for hosting dinner parties. She could already envision the coded conversations taking place here, hidden beneath the veneer of social gatherings.

"It's perfect, Monsieur Gâteau, more than I could have hoped for."

He smiled, a hint of patriotism in his eyes. "I'm glad you like it, Madame Brisse. I hope it serves you well. Just remember to be cautious. The proximity to the Gestapo headquarters could prove both a blessing and a curse."

"I'm fully aware of the danger," she replied with a steady voice. "Thank you for your help. How much do I owe you per month?"

He cleared his throat. "100 Francs, Madame. That covers heating, too. And just one more thing. You'd best line up early at la Mairie tomorrow to obtain your food tickets. The town hall closes for the afternoon and the queues are often long. I left you some bread and meat tickets on the kitchen table for now."

Lise thought fast. This was her chance. "Let me get you your 100 Francs for this month." She was already opening her valise. "And would you care to check if the coupons I brought with me pass your scrutiny? It's my first time using them... uh... here... you see." Lise blushed, having almost blown part of her cover, but Monsieur Gâteau was unperturbed.

"Naturellement! Show them to me, Madame."

Lise got the stack of ration books, forged at Briggens House near Harlow, from the double lining of her suitcase and handed them to Monsieur Gâteau. He walked to the window to have full light and studied them intently.

"Great job, Madame. Nothing to worry about there. Do you mind if I take my own coupons back then? We're not as fortunate as you are."

The smile they exchanged spoke volumes.

"If you're ever short of coupons, you know where to find me," Lise said with a wink.

AFTER HE'D LEFT, Lise stood in the center of her new living room, letting the reality of her new Poitiers life sink in. At least she had one ally, and an apartment that was everything she needed—safe, discreet, and strategically located.

For as long as needed, Irène would make this her headquarters, and from here, she'd embark on her first mission to free France.

You've got your work cut out for you, Madame Irène!

16

THE FIRST CONTACTS

Lise quickly unpacked her suitcase, checking that the Colt, the wads of 100-franc banknotes, and all her forged papers were well hidden in the second lining.

Her clothes and personal items went in one drawer and on one rail in the closet. There was so little of herself. Lise had never felt this empty, this lightweight in her life, not even when she left Paris, because these weren't her own belongings. They were neutral, impersonal. Irène's.

Finished with unpacking, she wandered to the front parlor of her new place on the Boulevard Solférino, where she took up a position behind the sheer curtains, surveying the street. The view revealed just the sort of bustling, provincial street she'd hoped for, people going about their daily lives, heading to or from the station.

Her eyes settled on a German soldier exiting from under the swastika flags next door. This was Lise's first, full, uninterrupted view of the enemy. She could study him without being seen.

At Beaulieu, they'd spent hours distinguishing the different Nazi uniforms on a poster on the wall. From the shoulder straps to the insignia, to the caps. But seeing them for real was nothing like a textbook illustration.

As the man strode past her window in his heavy boots, she identified him as an SS brownshirt, with only one dot on his shoulder and collar. A Schärführer. Not the lowest rank, but not high up either. He didn't really pose a threat to her.

Wrong! she corrected herself. To consider a low-ranked Nazi not to be dangerous was the wrong assumption for a secret agent. His smooth, almost gentle demeanor belied the hawkish, bootlicking ambition in his eyes. He was young, in his early twenties, but his face already showed the ruthless determination of someone eager to climb the ranks.

"Get to know him. And the rest of the staff next door, but from a distance," she mumbled to herself, as she watched the high, black boots and feldgrau back disappear around the corner.

The weight of her mission became clearer now she was 'settled'. This wasn't just a matter of recognizing uniforms and ranks anymore. And even giggle when they got it wrong. It was about understanding the nuances, the hidden dangers that each individual German represented, in uniform or otherwise.

Every encounter, every faulty observation could mean the difference between life and death. And she had to be prepared for it all, every hour of the day and night. The scent of the unknown owner's lavender wafted up her nostrils, as if to calm her high-strung nerves. Lise felt alone, vulnerable, and yet she would have to face this unfriendly world.

"Out with you, and into the thick of it!" she ordered herself.

As she approached the town square, she spotted a small café, Café de le Paix, its windows fogged up from the warmth and busyness inside.

A perfect name to start my investigation, to pick up a sense of which way the winds are blowing in Poitiers.

Poitiers, so close to the Vichy demarcation line, held an important position. Was it pro or con the German occupation? It would make all the difference for her work.

Pushing open the glass-paneled door, Lise was greeted by a wave of cigarette smoke, and the scent of cooked food and liquor. Her stomach rumbled in reply, reminding her she hadn't eaten since Madame Brossard's bread on the train.

The interior was dimly lit, with a few patrons sitting at small round tables, speaking in hushed tones. Faded murals of pastoral scenes covered the walls, adding a touch of 'couleur locale' to the setting. A timbered counter ran along one side, stacked with bottles and glasses. Sand, spread on the floor to collect dirt and grease, crunched under Lise's soles as she walked the length of the establishment.

Without drawing attention to herself, she took a seat at an empty table near the back, so she had a good view of all comings and goings. Her eyes scanned the café and its guests, while she attempted to blend into the interior.

A woman about Lise's age approached, drying her hands on her apron. The expression on her sharp-featured face was weary but kind. Her auburn hair was pulled back in a loose bun and her dark-green eyes conveyed both warmth and a hint of caution. She wore a simple dress, faded from many washes, and the apron had also seen better days, but she carried herself with an air of quiet determination.

"Un café, s'il vous plaît," Lise ordered, making sure her Parisian accent was clear. "And what is the daily?"

The waitress eyed her with a little more interest, and Lise saw her think, *another Parisian refugee. Why on earth do they think life is better in Poitiers?* But she smiled and nodded. "Today we have potage and a potato gratin with minced meat."

"That sounds perfect. A vegetable soup and potato gratin. Thank you."

"It will be with you in a minute, Madame."

Lise continued her eavesdropping as she stirred her coffee and waited for her meal. The conversations around her were mundane: talk of ration lines, whispers of discontent, and the occasional laugh that quickly faded. Despite all the caution she needed to keep her cover, she relished hearing rapid French all around her and being back in what felt like her homeland.

But after listening for a while to the easy chitchat by people who'd known each other all their lives, she suddenly felt a little lost. Where did she even start her mission without knowledge of the area, no landmarks, no other agents?

Had she made a mistake, as Buck and Vera tried to tell her? When she'd declared she wanted to go on her own, it had been more for security reasons than because she knew how to build a network from scratch. The enormity of the task loomed over her, and for a moment, she felt a pang of doubt. Where did she even begin?

But Lise was not a pessimist. She had faced adversity before and emerged stronger. The journey to reach England hadn't exactly been smooth sailing. *And what about giving up Henri?* a small voice whispered in her head.

Pushing doubt and love aside, Lise focused on the practicalities. When the waitress arrived to place the steaming soup in front of her, she seized the opportunity.

"Excusez-moi," she began, infusing her voice with confidence and warmth. "Could you tell me where I might obtain a bicycle? I'm afraid I had to leave mine in Paris. I just arrived here today, you see."

The waitress paused, caution in the expression of her eyes. "Oh, you'd have to ask Renard," she replied, her voice low. "But bicycles are hard to come by these days, Madame. The Germans confiscate whatever they can lay their hands on." She now avoided Lise's eyes, concentrating on wiping the table surface with a wet cloth, as if afraid to say too much.

"And where can I find Monsieur Renard?" Lise asked, leaning in slightly to convey her earnestness.

First glancing around the establishment, her gaze now met Lise's. There was a flicker of understanding, perhaps even sympathy in her eyes. "He usually passes by around this time. You might be lucky if you wait another hour."

"Thank you," Lise said softly, appreciating her subtle assistance. "Can you bring me a glass of red wine in that case?"

"Tout de suite, Madame. Would a local Cabernet do? It's good."

"Absolutely," Lise replied and dropping her voice even lower, added. "My name is Irène Brisse. I've just moved into the house next door to the Gestapo headquarters."

The bartender's eyes lit up. "Ah, so you live in Madame Éléonore de Vigny's house? So, you must have met the wonderful Monsieur and Madame Gâteau?"

Lise nodded enthusiastically. Contrary to her earlier doubts, she now saw the contours of a rudimentary network develop before her eyes.

"I'm Claire Rimbaud, the owner of Café de la Paix," Claire added, "in case you need me."

As Claire moved away, Lise felt a lot better. The potage tasted delicious, and the wine did wonders soothing her anxiety. The Poitivins seemed more interesting. Lise liked how they employed shadow-talk. She would learn to listen to all the nuances of clandestine conversations.

The door opened, and a man in his forties stepped in, his dark eyes flicking around the room before settling on Lise, the stranger in their midst. He wore a dark coat, the collar turned up against the chill. He was dark-haired, handsome in a French way. He vaguely reminded Lise of Henri. But no thinking of him, not even in a café that was called Café de la Paix. There was no place for peace nor love when there was a war going on.

The man walked up to the counter and sat down on a barstool in a corner, facing the door. A cautious man. Claire slid to his side in seconds, and she must have mentioned Lise because he was looking her way once again. She knew then this was the man Claire had called Renard.

Pastis in hand, he came her way, glancing down at her with barely hidden curiosity. "Madame? Claire said you're looking for a bicycle?"

Lise extended her hand, mentally noting everything about him. "Yes, I am. You must be Monsieur Renard? I'm Madame Brisse." That came out without a hitch.

He smiled. "Renard is actually my first name, but everyone insists on adding Monsieur to it, so I let them. What brings you to this region, Madame, if that isn't too impolite a question? I hear a Parisian accent. Most newcomers arriving here in Poitiers hail from the coast."

Irène Brisse recited her story with equal doses of modesty and conviction - the bike was needed, she couldn't wait to find all those interesting archaeological sites. When in reality, she was looking for dropping grounds for arms and agents. Not something she could tell Renard, of course, though she felt a familiarity that pointed in a hopeful direction. But it was too early days to drop even a fraction of her guard.

Renard suspected nothing beyond the Parisian widow in front of him and proved ever so helpful. "I'll bring the bicycle around tomorrow morning if you want. It belonged to Liliane, my grown daughter, but she moved away to Nice. Unoccupied territory, you see." Renard winked, "so she has no use for her bicycle at the moment. I will check the tires and brakes for you."

Thanking Renard, Lise gave him her address and prepared to leave. As she rose from her seat, she caught Claire's eye and offered her a friendly nod. "Merci, Claire. I'll be back soon."

The nod was returned, a hint of a smile playing around the café owner's lips, and Lise felt a flicker of camaraderie. These small gestures of connection were what would sustain her in the days to come. This is the way she would find out where people really stood.

Stepping back into the chilly Poitiers air, she drew her coat tighter around her to walk back to her apartment. The streets were quieter now, dusk already falling. Her belly was full. The bike would arrive. Irene had made her first acquaintances.

But her cheerful mood fell again when she spotted the stone building that would serve as her refuge and base of operations for an unknown period. The mission was daunting, the enemy close. Every step, every conversation, every decision must be executed with precision and care. Failure was not an option.

As she was about to put her key into the lock, she caught sight of movement next door. The door swung open, and a tall, imposing man stepped out. His uniform was immaculate, the black boots shining, the belt tight around his lean waist, and all the insignia that marked him as the leader.

This was the Head of the Gestapo in Poitiers.

17

THE CYCLING WIDOW

The four dots on his collar meant he was an Obersturmbannführer. As by instinct, Lise cast her glance to her Charles Jourdan shoes but then corrected herself. Fear could be as deadly as brashness. So, she leveled her gaze and met the Nazi's eye.

He had sharp, angular features, a high forehead, and piercing blue eyes that seemed to miss nothing. Not what she'd hoped for. His hair was dark under the high black cap. Mid-forties, she guessed, Prussian perhaps.

His attitude exuded authority and an air of menace that made Lise's skin prickle. This man was accustomed to command and being obeyed without question. As their eyes met, she knew this moment was crucial. She couldn't afford to appear anything but a harmless widow who nonetheless stood her ground. Offering him a polite nod, she allowed a small, respectful smile to touch her lips.

He paused, studying her for a moment longer before nodding in return.

"*Bonsoir Madame*, you must be Madame de Vigny's new tenant?"

The Obersturnbannführer's voice was deep and resonant. To Lise's surprise, he spoke French fluently without even much of an accent. And he seemed not without manners.

"I am Madame Brisse," Lise admitted. As the German didn't extend his hand, she kept hers by her side as well.

"*Enchanté Madame, je suis Kommandant Grabowski.* Have a pleasant evening."

Before he continued down the street, his eyes lingered on her. She still felt these piercing eyes on her as she slid the key in the lock, and with an audible breath closed the door behind her. Though shocked, her mind was already analyzing Herr Grabowski. She decided there was something undetermined about him. And the excellent French was a puzzle. Could he be French? But no!

Then she thought some more. What threat did he pose to her? What if he wanted to make her acquaintance? How could she gather more information about him?

Being an agent under Herr Grabowski's scrutiny was going to be even more of a challenge. And yet Lise slept well that night in Madame de Vigny's bed. There was something about the house that made her feel safe.

Two Weeks Later, 15 October 1942

LISE PEDALED through Poitiers narrow streets, the wind biting at her cheeks and the cold seeping through her coat. By now she understood the maze of alleys and streets the city consisted of. She even got as far as mapping the outskirts. Renard's daughter's bike had proved a precious gift, and she gripped the handlebars with more confidence each day, whether she faced headwind or tailwind.

Lise had taken a liking to her new habitat with its rich history, each turn revealing another layer of its storied past. Today, as always, her pretext was Eleanor of Aquitaine, a figure that drew enough interest to explain her presence and veiled her more clandestine purposes.

By now, she was known as 'the widow with an interest in archaeology,' allowing her to roam freely, ask questions, and take notes. While doing so, she scanned faces for cooperation and scouted fields for potential drop zones. Notebook in hand, she jotted down secluded spots, abandoned buildings, and hidden clearings that could serve the Firm.

The cobblestones beneath her wheels rattled her bike, and she gripped the handlebars tightly, her eyes constantly on the alert. Each landmark she passed was a potential part of the ARTIST network she was building—a female-led network of one, though the first helpers were on the way. Lise had her eye on Renard, Claire and, of course, the Gâteaus. But it was too early for further steps.

She cycled past the castle ruins of La Petite Villette, the Roman aqueducts, the city's buttresses, and even the dense thickets on the outskirts of town—they all now had potential uses in Lise's shadow war.

But with every cycle of her wheels, the enemy closed in as well. The tension of the occupation followed her like her own shadow. She spied around her, always on the alert. So far, the country lanes she took were deserted. Crops had been harvested, and life was too chilly and too hostile to stay out of doors for too long. It was just Lise and her bike.

Black clouds gathered overhead, as a prelude to a fall storm approaching from the west. Her eyes narrowed as she spotted a vehicle in the distance. Coming closer she saw it was what she'd been dreading all along. A German patrol.

She slowed her pace, taking steady breaths to appear calm and composed. She was just another local going about her business. The

Kubelwagen stopped in the middle of the narrow road making it impossible for her to pass.

"Papiere, bitte," the driver barked in German, getting out and stepping into her path.

Lise reached into her coat pocket and handed over her Irène papers, keeping her expression neutral. It was the first time the Germans made her stop, and she had to show her false papers.

He scanned the documents, then flicked his eyes to her face. She saw a speck of curiosity - or was it suspicion? - but she held his gaze steadily.

"What are you doing out here on your own?" he asked, his tone sharp.

"I am an amateur archaeologist, Herr Leutnant." Lise adopted a friendly, neutral tone but made sure she stressed his low rank. "I am researching sites associated with Eleanor of Aquitaine. Poitiers has such a rich history, don't you think?" She couldn't help throwing in some righteous French pride.

The Leutnant in his feldgrau uniform studied Lise for a moment longer, then nodded and handed back her papers. She thought the ruddy German had no idea what she was babbling about but thought her harmless.

"Very well. Be on your way, Madame."

"Thank you, Leutnant." Lise let the Kubelwagen pass before hopping back on her bike. The tension in her shoulders eased as she pedaled away from the patrol. She'd passed the first real test as Irène Brisse.

On arriving back in Poitiers Lise was already considering her next move. She'd need to get to Bordeaux or Paris soon, to wire London the details she'd gathered. Time for the first trip to share the good progress she was making. She'd host her first dinner party that night to test the waters.

The storm rolled in faster than expected, so she biked as fast as she could to get home dry, pleased to have added another possible dropping ground to her list. The wind picked up, howling through the narrow alleys and rattling the closed shutters.

By the time she arrived home, rain came down hard and fast, heavy drops pelting against the windows, turning the cobblestones slick and wet.

Lise rushed inside, but not before parking her precious bike safely in the garden shed. The Germans were always stealing French bikes, especially when drunk.

Time to prepare her first dinner as a secret agent host. She closed the curtains in the living room to keep prying eyes at bay and was glad she had enough wood to get a cosy fire going.

The flickering candlelight cast dancing shadows on the walls, and the scent of a simple stew filled the air—a mix of potatoes, carrots, and a small piece of meat stretched thin to serve three.

Claire, the Café de la Paix owner, and Renard, the only obvious Poitiers resister, were her first guests. She'd thought about inviting the Gâteaus as well but decided to keep it very small at first.

With small hints and careful inquiries, Claire and Renard had proved to Lise they were anti-German, with Renard telling her flat out he'd been a resister from the first hour. They had no idea yet, though, on what mission Irène Brisse had landed in their midst, but they were about to find out some of it during the dinner. Not every-thing, of course. The fact she was a British secret agent could never be revealed.

18

THE ARTIST NETWORK IS BORN

A s Lise, Claire, and Renard sat at one end of the long dinner table, the storm provided a constant backdrop of sound, as if their conversation needed to disappear in the background noise. The stew simmered in a pot, the earthy aroma mingling with the scent of the bread she had baked. She poured a modest amount of Bordeaux wine into three glasses, the liquid catching the candlelight.

Claire took a sip, her dark-green eyes reflecting the flickering flames. "This is lovely, Irène. Thank you for having us."

Lise smiled, though her mind was far from the pleasantries of hosting a dinner table. "It's my pleasure. It's good to share a meal with new friends, especially in times like these."

Renard, his dark eyes alert and ever watchful, nodded in agreement. "Yes, we must take what small comforts we can."

As she ladled the stew into bowls, Lise steered the conversation toward the information she needed. "It's been quiet in Poitiers," she remarked casually. "I expected more... activity."

Claire glanced at Renard before answering. "There used to be more... activity, Irène, but the Gestapo crushed all signs of resistance in and around Poitiers. Those who weren't killed are all locked up in jail. The Germans moved swiftly and ruthlessly in the first year of the war. It's dangerous to be associated with the movement now."

Renard added in a low voice. "We're all that's left, really, with the Gateaus. The few of us who remain do so under the radar. It's safer that way."

Lise absorbed the weight of their words. "I understand. But we must find a way to rekindle the spirit of resistance. This quiet acceptance, and in many cases active collaboration with the occupiers, is unnerving. I've also noticed most of the Germans here are young lads who seem more afraid of being skinned by us than the other way around."

Claire looked at her, her expression thoughtful. "Who are you, Irène? I mean, I thought you might be against the Germans because you knew the Gateaus, but were you involved with the Resistance in Paris? You seem not to be completely who you say you are."

"I agree," Renard chimed in, "you're so perceptive. It's – how shall I say it – inspiring? Maybe you came here to bring some hope back to Poitiers."

Lise offered a small smile, thinking *if even you knew*. "Perhaps. But it will mean us working together, carefully and quietly." She hesitated a moment but pushed on now she felt she could. "I might be able to get us some more good people and weapons. But I'll need help hiding them."

"You?" Claire and Renard stared at her open-mouthed.

"Yes. I have some contacts in Paris, you know. Through my late husband. Bless his soul."

Lise took a deep breath. As if really thinking of him. But the words were out. The bond with Claire and Renard was forged.

"It's true, I've not only taken my time to investigate the area around Poitiers for archaeological reasons. I've also checked ... uh...

drop zones and storage places. I promised Roger, you know, that his death wouldn't be in vain." Another sigh, and she hoped no more questions down this fantasy path. "I can't do this alone, though. Will you help?"

"Sure, I'm here to help." Renard didn't hesitate.

"I want to," Claire said softly. "You may always use the café as a meeting place."

"That's very kind, Claire, thank you!"

Claire lit a cigarette and stared at her host through the smoke. There was admiration in her eyes and a hope that made Lise a little emotional. What they had suffered in the past years at the hands of the Germans would be a lifetime wound. And by all appearances, the war was far from over.

"If I manage to get us more people and materials, they will be air-dropped. I'll need a reception team to help hide everything." Her voice was level, almost business-like, to make it sound as if it was just a shopping list that would whirl down on them.

"Ah, bon sang!" Renard exclaimed, gazing at her with renewed admiration. "Of course, I'll get us some new people. What you think, Claire, shall we ask Doctor Giraud?"

"Biensûr! And don't forget the Gateaus, and then there's Bernard the farmer we can ask to store stuff."

Though Lise hadn't revealed her true mission, she could see Renard understood more than her words had said. She would never reveal her identity, and he wouldn't probe, but the awe in his eyes made her almost uncomfortable. It was a matter of keeping her gaze steady, unblinking.

Claire sighed, "we may have another urgent matter on our hands. I'd hoped we could bring it up, but now I certainly know we can. Renard and I sometimes get word of downed airmen—British pilots whose planes have been shot down and who need help getting out of the country via the Pyrenees. We were thinking that the shed in your garden would be an excellent hiding place, temporary of course, as it has an exit into the alley at the back and an entrance into your house from the garden. Now, I dare to ask if you'd be up for that?"

As she spoke, the storm outside grew fiercer. The wind howled like a wounded animal and the rain lashed against the windows as if they were being battered by heavy ropes. Suddenly, there was a loud crash outside, and they all froze, their eyes darting to the door.

They stayed glued to their chairs at first, three pairs of ears listening if the front door was broken down. But after the crash, it remained silent. The storm had wreaked havoc by felling a tree in front of the house.

"We'll see to that later. Hopefully it came down on the building next door," Renard observed. The relaxation that followed was guarded. Their discussions alone were enough to put them in front of a German firing squad.

"Always on edge," Renard muttered, the grip on his cigarette tightening.

"Always," Lise agreed, "but that's the life we've chosen. And to answer your question, Claire, of course, I'll be a safe house. I'll give you a key to the gate."

"Thank you." Claire looked relieved and added hesitantly, "My fifteen-year-old daughter Sophie is also very anti-Nazi. I want to keep her safe, but I know she'd love to help in some minor way. If I help, do you think she could do something too? Oh, I'm hating myself for saying this. It's just that she..."

"...an innocent widow and a young girl would be a perfect cover." Lise's mind worked fast. Putting a young person in danger was not what she wanted, but she saw the advantages—nobody would suspect such a duo. "Having Sophie around would be beneficial. She can help with small tasks and keep watch, accompany me sometimes. We all will have to look out for her."

Claire's face was still clouded but also held relief and determination. "Thank you, Irène. This means a lot to both of us. I lost my husband too, you see. Vive la France!"

"Vive la France!" Lise and Renard replied as one.

Feeling they now had a shared goal, Lise said. "I'll be away for a couple of days to arrange... uh ... matters. So don't worry anything happened to me. Can you manage things here while I'm gone?"

"Of course," Renard replied firmly. "We'll keep everything under control."

"And see if you can find other trustworthy people. We need more. I was thinking perhaps that young priest, Frère Jean. I have a feeling he's got his heart in the right place."

"Frère Jean certainly has," Claire agreed. "I'll have a chat with him after Mass on Sunday."

"Wednesday night dinners at Irène Brisse's," Lise announced, "for all those Poitevins interested in the Crusades and Eleanor of Aquitaine."

"Don't forget Richard Lionheart," Renard chuckled. "He's my favorite."

The storm outside continued to rage, but inside, purpose and solidarity filled the room. By the time she saw off her guests, Lise's heart felt pounds lighter. Standing by the window on the garden side, she watched the rain streak down the glass, her reflection merging with the night outside.

The shadows of the past blended with the present, and she could already imagine the figures of men in blue RAF uniforms walking down her garden path.

This was her own mission now. Her work had begun. This was the ARTIST network. Time to travel to Bordeaux and announce it to London.

19

THE ARRIVAL OF THE FIRST AGENT

F *ive weeks later - Poitiers, 22 November 1942*

THE CAFÉ de la Paix on the Place d'Armes was a haven from the November chill and Lise's lonely apartment. The café's sparse lighting, the clinking of glasses, and the hushed conversations created an atmosphere she looked forward to every day and it proved a perfect location for her covert meetings. And it was always a comfort seeing the familiar and friendly face of Claire, who'd become more than a reliable confidante.

Lise scanned the café to see if her corner table, at the back but facing the door, was available. This table, with its polished wooden surface and its vase of dried wildflowers, had wordlessly become reserved for Irène, whether or not she had a meeting. It was nearly always empty for her.

The locals, aware of this unspoken rule, nodded in greeting but kept their distance, mindful of her proximity to the Gestapo Head-quarters. Claire had told her that much. Nothing escaped the Poitevins, and the widow had been seen exchanging friendly greetings with the feared Head of the Gestapo.

She considered this misinterpretation of her alliances a temporary blessing in disguise. As long as it didn't rub the citizens the wrong way.

Claire's daughter, Sophie, approached the table with a purposeful stride.

"Un café, Madame Brisse?" Sophie asked, her eyes glancing around the room to ensure no one was listening.

"Yes, please, Sophie," Lise replied with a warm smile, knowing her young helper had more than just coffee to deliver.

As Sophie poured the coffee from the pot, she leaned in and whispered, "Renard told me to let you know Renaud's arrival was successful. I guess you know what that means?"

Lise gave her a slight nod, "*Biensûr*. Thank you, Sophie. I expect he'll arrive here soon."

Sophie straightened up, despite her fifteen years, looking all grown-up and important. "Is there anything else you need?"

"No, thank you, Sophie. That will be all for now."

Her young helper disappeared into the café's bustling activity, leaving Lise to sip her coffee and contemplate the successful operation. Moments like these warranted a sigh of relief. She'd done it. London was sending her first agent.

Through the MONKEYPUZZLE network an agent codenamed Renaud had been dropped near Chambord on the full moon of 18 November. It was her task to help her fellow Mauritian acclimatise in France. Like her, he had a British passport and was raised with the French language, but apparently, he'd never been in France. She checked her watch. He should arrive shortly.

Claire was next, approaching her table, a smile softening her worn features. "Sophie tells me you are expecting company?" she bent closer under the pretext of wiping the table.

"Yes, Henri Gâteau is bringing a new guest. Please spread the rumor it's a cousin from Paris."

Claire didn't ask who, just said. "I will. And I'll turn up the music a little."

"Thank you, Claire. You're the best."

As Claire moved back to the counter, Lise settled into her seat, thoughts drifting to the upcoming meeting. The soft strains of Edith Piaf's "La Vie en Rose" played in the background, making even Lise feel a little rosy.

Moments later the door opened, and a man stepped in. Lise knew this was Renaud, though she'd never met him before. His face was tense and pale, betraying a slight nervousness. Intense, dark eyes drifted over the room as if they didn't know where to settle. Lise was glad to see his valise was in order and wouldn't betray anything British. Henri Gateau escorted Renaud to Lise's table, gave her a curt nod and disappeared to the bar to order a drink.

Lise rose and shook the new agent's hand, aware all eyes were on them. What was a widow doing with another outsider in their midst? She could only hope Claire's rumor about her and her cousin would spread soon and the guests would return their attention to the beastly weather and what was available on the black market.

"Welcome, Renaud, I'm Odile but people know me here as Irène Brisse. Please, only call me Irène. I'm here to help you with all things French." She lowered her voice to such a faint whisper she wasn't even sure if she spoke aloud. But she couldn't risk compromising her cover identity with the locals, and Renaud looked so nervous she didn't know if he remembered her codename *and* cover identity. So, even with Piaf's high notes reverberating in their ears, she had to exercise extreme caution in sharing anything in their public locale.

"Bon après midi, Irène, thank you for helping me."

As Renaud took the seat opposite Lise, her heart skipped a beat at his accent. He spoke the French of her youth, of that sun-drenched island where all had been peace.

Her sharp eyes took in everything of his outfit and demeanor. There was still work to do on the new agent. His nervousness, though he'd tried to keep it under control, was too obvious for a secret agent to be effective, and ever more risky for generating suspicion of any resistance activities.

It didn't matter for a fidgeting cousin, but Renaud would need a crash course in blending in without drawing attention to himself. And they only had one day, as she'd escort him to Paris the next day, where his work would start.

The Mauritian agent was an attractive, dark-haired man, probably in his early forties, athletically built, broad-shouldered and wearing a neatly pressed suit. Lise was informed he'd been a successful businessman before the war. So, it was probably the unfamiliarity of his situation that had him so on edge.

As the Firm wanted him to raise funds for the growing SOE networks in France, they obviously had great trust in Agent Renaud.

Henri Gâteau came back with three Pastis and sat down at their table. It was a gesture to reassure the locals all was well. Henri and Marguerite Gâteau were known to be 'chummy' with the widow.

"Santé," Henri toasted, giving Renaud a reassuring smile, that communicated he was in good company. Lise was glad for Henri's easy manners and his ability to bridge their world with that of the Poitivins.

Lise leaned in, her voice still low, but a least audible to the guests at her table. "How was the trip, Renaud?"

Renaud managed a tight smile, and Lise saw his hands trembled slightly as he picked up his glass. "All well, thank you, Irène. It's... good to be here. Though I must admit a little overwhelming at first. You know I've never been to..."

"Yes, yes, I know. Don't mention it. You never know what the walls can hear." Lise quickly interrupted. Plus, she didn't want Henri Gâteau to know too much.

"I've arranged for you to stay with me and my wife tonight, Renaud," Henri chimed in, "as I understand you're both heading back to Paris tomorrow?"

How much does Henri really understand? Lise couldn't help thinking. Renaud's French was certainly not Parisian, and why would Irène's cousin step out of a British plane in the middle of a French field if he hailed from Paris? But Henri Gâteau wouldn't ask the hard questions, he was the epitome of tact and helpfulness.

With his jovial smile that smoothed away all doubt, he said, "My wife is already preparing a traditional dish from the Poitiers area for you. It's called 'Farci Poitevin'.

"Oh, I have not tasted that yet," Lise exclaimed, grateful Gâteau steered the conversation away from difficult topics. "What is it?"

"You're invited too, Irène. You know our door is always open to you. What it is? Let me think. I've had it so often, I could probably make it myself, but Madame la Chef doesn't let me near her kitchen. Farci Poitevin is a kind of terrine made from leafy greens, herbs, pork, and sometimes bacon. The mixture is wrapped in cabbage leaves and then cooked. You can eat it hot or cold cut in slices. I never tire of eating it and Marguerite still manages to get all the ingredients on the black market."

He leaned in and whispered in Renaud's ear. "Wherever you go in France, make friends with someone who knows the nearest underground market and follow him like a dog. That way you won't starve."

They all laughed. Lise knew it was the truth. Marguerite had shown her how to expand their meager rations with the rich produce they could get from the fields around Poitiers. And it confirmed for her that Henri knew Renaud was not a Frenchman.

The new agent's eyes lit up at the idea of a good meal. He relaxed ever so slightly and finally stopped fidgeting with his glass. As they discussed the other rudimentary rules for surviving in occupied France, Lise could see that the warmth of the café and the camaraderie at the table began to ease Renaud's nerves and his good-natured personality began to emerge.

With the initial tension beginning to dissipate, they spent the next hour going over details, ensuring Renaud felt prepared for the tasks ahead. By the time they left the café, Lise felt confident Renaud would be a brilliant agent. Under other circumstances and in another epoque, they could have become friends.

But friendship was a luxury Lise couldn't afford.

20

PARIS IN THE FALL OF '42

The next day - Paris 23 November 1942

Before they set off for Paris, Lise took their few hours together to instruct Renaud on all the things he needed to know about living in occupied France, in particular those things they weren't taught during their training in Britain. How the Germans moved, when to steer clear of them and when to greet them. How to gauge the sentiments of the French. All the things she'd picked up during the months she'd been 'in the field.'

"I feel much better prepared now, Odile." Renaud said.

"Good," Lise replied, closing the door to her apartment and instructing the new agent how to greet Obersturmbannführer Grabowski, who had just gone inside his headquarters.

The train journey to Paris transpired without any difficulties. From Gare Montparnasse, Lise and Renaud took the metro to Neuilly-sur-Seine, where the Firm had leased an apartment from an influential Parisian family. From this apartment in the rue Chartran Antelme could set up his BRICKLAYER network.

Lise stood by one of the tall windows, looking out at the bustle of the Paris street below, a wave of nostalgia hitting her.

"Oh, I didn't know until now how much I missed this city," she said softly, more to herself than to Renaud. "So much has changed, and yet it's still good old Paris to me."

Renaud, rummaging through his valise for hidden articles in the lining, paused and watched her for a moment.

"The cherished places we leave behind," he sighed, "and the uncertain future that awaits us. Will this place be kind to us, or will it be our last?"

"I know that's how you feel now, Renaud, but I still believe that if we're cautious as cragsmen, we can stay out of Gestapo claws. Just never let your guard down."

"You're good at this, Odile!"

"I do worry at times, Renaud. I'm not made of steel. We know darn well not everything is in our power and what we're doing is the highest treason according to the Nazis. But most days I try to think of the future as little as I can."

"Wise words."

To steer the conversation away from her melancholy and the danger they were in, Lise asked. "So, when did you leave Mauritius?"

"In 1932, when I was in my early thirties. I was mostly stationed in Durban. At first, I had to get used to living in Africa, but then I loved the wide landscapes and the freedom. I hope to return there one day. My wife and our sons are still living in South Africa."

Lise offered him a sympathetic smile. "I think this job is even harder for agents with young families."

"We all leave families and friends behind, Odile. It's hard for everyone. But we know why we're here. And I can at least be glad mine are safe where they are."

The room fell silent for a moment, both agents lost in thought. The bond of shared sacrifice and purpose was felt strongly.

"Do you miss Mauritius?" Lise couldn't help asking. Her own longing for the white-beached island in the sun seemed to grow with every day in grim, wintery France.

Renaud's eyes reflected her own longing. "Every day. Curepipe, the island, the warmth, the people... it's a part of me. Hopefully, one day..." his voice trailed off.

Leaving the window and taking a seat on the couch, her hands folded in her lap, Lise said firmly, "I shouldn't have brought up Mauritius, nor my former life in Paris. Let's focus on our next steps. I hope to introduce you to Prosper and Alcide later today, to see if they can help you make contacts to secure more funding for SCIENTIST and PHYSICIAN. SCIENTIST is a huge network around Bordeaux and PHYSICIAN is Prosper's network here in the Paris area. These two are growing exponentially and so do the costs."

"I'll be grateful for the introductions." Renaud took a large swig from a flask he retrieved from his valise.

"Care for some rum too?"

"Not at the moment, thanks." Lise's sharp eyes zeroed in on the drink he was offering her. "And do get rid of that British flask and its contents now. I can't understand why Buck didn't check all your belongings before you left. Vera is so strict with us girls. Here, let me check all your clothes to see if they have French labels, buttons and stitching."

"Hey, what are you doing?" Renaud looked genuinely shocked as Lise started rummaging through his underwear. But she snapped, "Do you want to be caught and instantly branded a British spy? That will be the last breath you take when captured by the Gestapo."

Renaud made a movement indicating she could continue, and put the flask to his mouth.

Lise grumbled on, her hands deftly checking and folding Renaud's clothes. "I've wired the Firm a long list of requirements on what to check for before sending agents over, but do they even read them?"

Renaud settled himself in the windowsill, sipping his rum and observing Lise's foray through his belongings. She created two piles.

"Get rid of this set and buy some other clothes here in Paris. I'll show you the shops."

"They should make you in charge of this whole operation, Odile," he mused. "You're top of your game. Any agent near you has a chance of survival. Thank you."

"You're welcome." And less sternly, Lise added, "It's not your fault, Renaud. You've never been here before. And I guess we can't blame the Firm either. Buck's knowledge of France is like ten years old. None of the office people have been on the ground since the war started.

"True. But I still owe you."

"It's a good thing we're between safe walls and can discuss these things openly. It's tiring to only whisper in cafés or talk in riddles. Let's just be grateful for this moment. Now is there a guzzle left in that flask, or have you polished it off already?"

"I saved some for the Queen of SOE," Renaud joked. When he smiled, she saw how handsome he was and how he finally relaxed under the influence of the Mount Gay rum and her instruction.

"Just be careful with the liquor as well, my friend," Lise said wiping her mouth. "You won't be the first agent who slips back into English or starts saying foolish things when under the influence."

Renaud rose to his full length and stretched. "I won't, Queen, I promise."

"Stop calling me Queen," Lise laughed, "but if the Firm calls me back to England, I wouldn't mind being an instructor for a while. I think I could indeed teach a practical thing or two by now."

After inspecting the collar of Renaud's jacket and coat and

approving the label, they set out in search of Lise's friend from before the war, known as Maître William Savy. Savy, codenamed Alcide, was a busy man with a threefold career: he was a chef, a lawyer and now also a member of the French Resistance. And he had an impressive circle of friends that could help Renaud in his new network.

As they descended into the Paris Métro, the familiar scent of damp stone, garlic and stale cigarettes filled Lise's nostrils, and yet it fitted like an old coat. The underground world, a labyrinthine echo of the city above, had always thrummed with its own rhythms and anxieties, but these were now amplified by the constant presence of SS Officers. The Métro was a crucible of occupied Paris, where allies and enemies brushed shoulders daily.

The station bustled with both Parisians and Germans, but it was the attitude of the citizens that struck Lise most. People whispered and hurried with heads down, unlike the Poitivins who, while subdued, were not completely stripped of their French pride.

The posters on the walls, long-since defaced with German propaganda, served as forceful reminders of the city's subjugation. Lise felt a pang of sorrow seeing the swastika overlaying familiar places, intended to bring the population to their knees.

Lise led Renaud with the practiced ease of someone who had roamed these tunnels countless times. She glanced at him, noting the tension in his shoulders, the way his eyes darted about, absorbing every detail. But he kept his nerves under control. He was getting much better at this.

They reached the Line 1 platform to get to their destination at Rue d'Alger. The approaching train's metallic arrival drowned out the murmurs around them. They boarded swiftly, choosing a spot near the doors for an easy exit if necessary. The car was half-full, mostly French people with tired faces and wary eyes.

Lise and Renaud stood close together, vigilant but with a neutral expression. The Métro was a place to be even more alert. A careless word or a revealing glance could unravel everything very quickly, knowing there were many French traitors willing to snitch in exchange for money. Paris was not sleepy Poitiers. Lise was very aware of that.

The train jolted into motion, the rhythmic clatter of wheels on tracks a sound so familiar to her. Lise allowed herself a fleeting moment of nostalgia. The Métro had been a constant in her Parisian life, a silent witness to her life in pre-war Paris. Now, it was a conduit for her resistance work, fraught with peril instead of transport to a pleasant outing.

Her gaze swept the carriage. A mother cradling a child, a couple speaking softly, an old man with his newspaper. Ordinary scenes, yet each person a potential threat or ally. The presence of German soldiers in their enemy uniforms added a layer of tension among all. They stood in groups, their laughter – only they were laughing – echoing in the confined space.

As the train approached the Marbeuf stop for their transfer, a commotion broke out. What looked like a Jewish family, though they weren't wearing yellow stars, attempted to escape from the clutches of one of the groups of German soldiers.

The father, a man in his forties with a determined set to his jaw, shielded his wife and two young children behind him. The soldiers barked orders first in German, then in broken French, their faces twisted with contempt.

The mother's eyes, wide with fear, met Lise's for a fleeting moment. A silent plea hung in the air, a desperate cry for help. But any intervention was impossible. Lise's heart ached, but she knew the harsh reality: they could do nothing without jeopardizing their mission and their lives.

The father tried to reason with the soldiers in German, his voice trembling but resolute. The children clung to their mother; their innocent faces streaked with tears. The rest of the people in the compartment held their breath, staring at their shoes or out of the dark windows. The scene was a grim illustration of the terror and paralysis that had become routine in occupied Paris.

The soldiers, unmoved by the family's pleading, pushed them out of the train with force. The father's defiant look never wavered, even as they were marched away. The other passengers averted their eyes, the collective shame and fear palpable.

Lise and Renaud stood frozen, the horror of the scene tugging at their heartstrings. But the train moved on, the doors closing on the harrowing tableau as with a serpent's hiss. The mood in the car was somber, the air thick with suppressed despair and rage.

When they reached their stop at Les Tuileries, Lise was still angry with herself for not stepping up. Jews awaited a horrible fate once arrested, of that, she was sure. Over and over, she told herself there was nothing she could've done. Not now. But she would not forget. Never.

Picking up on her dissatisfaction with herself and the situation they found themselves in, Renaud whispered to her, "Let it be, Odile. Our time will come."

"I know. I'm just not good when I see injustice and my hands are tied. Best let me stew for a moment until it passes."

She took a deep breath. The cold underground air was almost a welcome respite from the stifling tension inside the carriage. They ascended the stairs, emerging into the Parisian streets where the familiar sights and sounds greeted her. *Let it be, Odile!* This was Paris too, barren and brutal in the autumn of 1942 but still her City of Light.

As they made their way to Maître Savy's office on the Rue d'Alger, Lise's usual steely resolve returned. She was here for a purpose, and every step along the way brought her closer to her goal.

WELCOME to occupied Paris in 1942. Let's get to work.

21

THE MONEY MAN

Maître William Savy's office was in a stately but unassuming building to ensure the renowned lawyer's official reputation was upheld but didn't show any hints of clandestine activities.

To rule out the chance that she and Renaud had been followed, Lise scanned the surroundings before ringing the bell. They were let in by the concierge.

"I have an appointment with Mâitre Savy."

"Certainly, Madame. Second floor, last door on the left."

On reaching the second floor Lise rapped on the last door, which opened to reveal William Savy, codename Alcide. His sharp, intelligent eyes behind wire-rimmed glasses and his thick, salt-and-pepper hair gave him an air of distinguished authority. He hid his deformed left arm partially beneath a well-tailored jacket.

"Well, well, if it isn't Odile visiting the old fox with a slightly younger fox," he greeted them with a wink, his face lighting up at seeing her again. "Good to see you, my friends. Come in, come in."

Lise and Savy had frequented the same circles before the war, and the international lawyer still held the esteemed role of providing French high society with legal advice.

During their unexpected reunion on a train to Paris the month before, Lise had found out about her friend's alliances.

Jovial and an excellent communicator, Savy had offered to assist in any way he could, should Lise want to make use of his broad network. Even a high-profile citizen like Maître Savy could get away with being a French secret agent.

He led them into his spacious office filled with legal books and documents, showcasing his profession and meticulous nature. Despite his escalating role in the Resistance, he still juggled his other careers, using his position to gather funds and intelligence.

"Alcide, please meet Renaud," Lise introduced them to each other. "The Firm has sent Renaud to establish the BRICKLAYER network, basically to secure funding for our other networks." She decided to cut to the chase, as even meetings like this shouldn't last too long. And in this case, she was only the intermediary.

"Pleased to meet you, Renaud," Savy said warmly, giving the new agent the eagle eye from behind his spectacles. "Odile told me London speaks highly of you, so I'm glad to be of any help I can."

"The pleasure is mine," Renaud replied, a hint of nervousness in his voice at meeting the man who was already somewhat of a legend in the French Resistance. "Your compliment is an extra incentive to do my very best. It's an honor to work with you."

Maître Savy studied him for a moment longer, the sharp gaze assessing him at top speed. "We all play our part, Renaud. Some better than others, but we all play our part. Now, I understand London has asked for funds and connections inside France to keep two of your most important networks operational?"

"Yes," Renaud replied eagerly, "independently from each other, PHYSICIAN and SCIENTIST have both wired London they're in dire need of financial support. They're growing so fast the situation is becoming critical."

"I see," Savy nodded, and Lise was listening with open ears. SCIENTIST, after all was her brother Claude's network.

Renaud continued, "London also urged me to contact the organizers of both networks and tell them to get back in touch with the Firm. Since the requests for more money, there's been radio silence for six weeks, which is alarming. Because of the fear of infiltrations into these crucial networks, I was instructed to personally contact both organisers, David and Prosper, to ascertain their current liquidity and security situation. Do you have any news on them, Alcide?"

Lise's heart skipped a beat. *Why hadn't Renaud told me?* But then she realised he didn't know how deeply she was connected to SCIENTIST; no one did other than London. Six weeks since her brother had been in touch with the Firm! She'd head to Bordeaux as soon as she could to see if Claude was safe.

Putting her worries on hold, she listened to Savy, who said calmly, "nothing has reached my ears about infiltrations, but from my own experiences – and I'm sure Odile agrees – I know the operators can't wire London on the spur of the moment. To stay ahead of the German Funkabwehr, they change houses more frequently than I change my socks and sometimes they simply can't find a safe enough spot to transmit. I understand London's impatience, but they should give the operators some leeway."

"True," Lise agreed, but her thoughts were on her brother anyway.

Savy lit a cigar and puffing small rings of smoke into the air, continued, "to prepare for your announced arrival, Renaud, and knowing we have no time to lose, I've already been securing loans through my contacts. It's been a risky endeavor, but thanks to some credit I have with reliable clients, I've managed to arrange loans of

250,000 francs for each network. I hope that will pull them through at least part of the winter."

"That's great," Renaud exclaimed. "What use do I still have?"

Savy laughed, "it's only the start, Renaud. I'll get you in touch with more contacts, so you can do your work. With your charm and background, you will certainly rake in some more cash."

Lise was impressed both by her friend's capabilities and his easy manner. And she was pleased for her brother.

"Thank you, Alcide. I knew we could rely on you."

Savy waved her compliment away. "Rich clients plus an anti-German sentiment equals loans, my dear. Easy math. The Nazi regime won't last forever, and money is usually the bottleneck in situations like this. We can't have that happen." Then he changed the subject. "Odile, you mentioned earlier you could bring me into direct contact with the SOE Headquarters in London. Does that offer still stand?"

"Yes, of course," Lise confirmed, realizing Savy was already more or less a go-between between the British agents in France and the French Resistance. "I can arrange for a secure line of communication with London. They need to know what you're doing here and how crucial your role is. It will also ensure that any intelligence you gather can be quickly relayed."

Savy's face showed a rare moment of vulnerability as he remained silent, before continuing in a less assured way. "I'd appreciate that, Odile. But there's more. I'd like to be trained as a SOE agent in England. All this lobbying for money, though essential, isn't enough for me. I want to take an active part in this fight as well."

Lise's eyes inadvertently darted to Savy's disfigured arm. He followed her glance. "Don't worry about that. I'm right-handed and a darn good sharpshooter. And I'd probably be more of a courier anyway. So can you arrange my request?"

"Sure," Lise beamed. "With pleasure, Alcide."

"That's settled then. Now about the money. It's here in a safe. Can you take it to Prosper tonight, or should he send a courier to pick it up? I'll take the money to David myself as I have a meeting in Bordeaux next week. I'll also remind him to wire London to check in."

Lise would have preferred to transport the money to Claude herself and see how her brother was faring, but after all Savy had done for SCIENTIST, it was his right to deliver the money and get the praise.

"I hope to introduce Renaud to Prosper tonight. We can take care of the Paris loan, if you want?" Lise suggested.

Savy turned to Lise looking puzzled. "Clarify this for me. Is the network called PHYSICIAN or PROSPER? I hear these interchanged."

"Prosper is the organiser's codename, and the network is officially PHYSICIAN, but it's often referred to by the organiser's name. Hence the confusion."

"Ah, I thought I just wasn't smart enough," Savy grinned, while Lise thought she'd probably never met a more intelligent man in her life.

As they rose to leave with their sack of money, Savy pressed the importance of staying safe. "We have much work to do, friends, and we can't afford to lose anyone."

"True," Lise agreed, shaking his hand warmly. "As soon as I have a reply from the Firm, as we call it, I'll be in touch. And we will win. We must."

"We sure will. Vive la France!"

"Vive la France!" Lise and Renaud replied.

With banknotes worth 250,000 francs tucked in a rucksack, the two Mauritian agents made their cautious way to the café tucked away in the narrow Rue de Caumartin.

22

THE CAFÉ IN THE RUE DE CAUMARTIN

L ight was fading fast as Lise and Renaud stepped out into the chilly Parisian dusk. The streets were already beginning to empty as the city prepared for the nightly curfew. They quickened their pace, a sense of urgency driving them to reach the café in Rue de Caumartin before the streets fell silent and the Gestapo patrols became more frequent.

The heavy weight of the francs in the extra bag was constantly on Lise's mind. The sooner that was in the hands it needed to be in, the less risk they ran. She kept up a brisk pace, all senses on high alert, covertly scanning every corner and alleyway for sudden movements or unwanted checks.

Renaud followed closely, tension evident in his rigid posture and darting eyes. As they neared Rue de Caumartin, Lise breathed a little easier. The café was a known, discreet meeting place for members of the PHYSICIAN network—a small but lively establishment where the busyness and music provided a veneer of normalcy. Despite the war, life went on, and this café offered a semblance of peace amidst the chaos.

Once inside, they were greeted by a warmth and noise that felt like a winter coat. The diffused lighting cast a mellow glow over the wooden tables and faded posters on the walls. The scent of liquor and tobacco, mixed with music and conversation, created an atmosphere that lightened the weight of their mission.

Another smoky café, another secret rendezvous, Lise thought wryly. Her prewar entertainment had centered on ballrooms, shooting parties, and Michelin-starred restaurants. *Look at me now.* But if she were honest, she liked her hands-on life a lot better.

Surveying the café, her eyes landed on Agent Denise, the young W/T Operator she'd arrived with in France two months earlier. Seated at a corner table, Denise looked up in surprise. Her tired eyes, with dark circles underneath, widened in recognition before a smile broke over her pretty face.

"Good to see you, Denise," Lise greeted her warmly. Denise got up, and Lise wrapped her arms around her. The younger agent leaned into Lise's warmth for a lingering moment. As she let go, Lise said, "I'm sorry I couldn't let you know we were coming. That's my fate without a W/T operator, but it's sure good to see you."

In her soft musical voice, Denise replied, "Yes, lovely to see you, Odile. How are you?"

"I'm okay, but I better ask how you're doing. You look pretty worn-out. Are you getting enough sleep and food in Paris?"

"It's been a tough few weeks," Denise admitted, "but Prosper and I keep going strong."

Lise introduced Renaud, who'd been waiting politely for the two female agents to greet each other properly. "This is Renaud, Denise. He's got news for you, but are you sure we can talk freely here?"

Denise looked around her and gave one of the bartenders a signal with her hand. He turned up the music a notch. "Sure, we're okay tonight."

"Renaud has just arrived from London to set up the BRICK-

LAYER network near Troyes. But he's also the go-between with the Firm concerning finances."

"As a matter of fact, Alcide, one of Odile's contacts, already secured some loans for PHYSICIAN," Renaud chimed in.

Denise's eyes brightened at the news. "That's a huge relief! We've been running on fumes lately."

"Alcide also reported that London says you haven't been sending messages for the past six weeks." Lise tried to keep the concern out of her voice.

"As I said, it's been crazy the last couple of weeks," Denise sighed. "Every time I thought I had a safe house and was just about to set up my set, my lookout warned me the Funkabwehr came down the street. I'm afraid they're on my heels, so I have to lay low for a bit."

As they spoke, the door to the café opened, and PHYSICIAN's organiser, codenamed Prosper entered. Prosper was a dashing figure who hid the limp from his war wound well. His tall frame, clad in high-waisted trousers and a suit jacket, had seen better days— perfect cover for blending in.

Even locals couldn't afford new clothes two-and-a-half years into the war, so he didn't stand out. His hair was neatly parted, and his blue eyes sparkled with determination. A brave smile lit up his face between two large ears, exuding a confidence that never failed to reassure his team.

"*Bonsoir, mes amis,*" Prosper greeted them, his French heavily accented. Lise knew he leaned on Denise for doing most of the talking for fear of revealing his British-education background. Their cover as brother and sister salespeople in agricultural products provided the perfect guise for their travels.

"Prosper," Lise said, standing to greet him. "It's good to see you."

Prosper shook hands with Lise and Denise, holding their hands in the grip of a leader. He reminded Lise of Claude. Neither man had a military background, but they slipped into the role as if they were born into it. No matter that Prosper had had a successful career as a barrister before the war.

"I'm glad you made it safely to the France, Renaud. Any word from David, Odile?" Prosper asked, knowing what he shouldn't— that Lise and Claude – codenamed David - were related. Prosper seemed to know everything about everyone. He was that kind of an exceptional agent.

"Alas, not for a couple of weeks, Prosper. I've been busy with my own network in Poitiers, but I heard the Firm is worried about not hearing from both you and David."

Prosper's eyes darted to Denise. "Lately it's not been safe enough for Denise to transmit radio messages to London. The German radio detection vans are ruthless and everywhere."

"Yes, she just told me," Lise affirmed. "I wonder if things are heating up in Bordeaux as well."

"They sure are." Prosper's expression darkened. "Damn Germans, they're not only ruthless, but they're also very well organized. And their detection systems are getting better by the day."

Denise broke in, "Odile and Renaud brought Alcide's funds, Prosper, so we have no choice. I will have to send a message to London tonight. 'Alcide est en bonne santé' as was the promise."

"You just be careful." Prosper's blue eyes rested with an almost fatherly glance on his W/T operator, who was also his trusted courier.

"I'll be her lookout," Lise offered, knowing she'd stay the night over in Paris.

"Thank you." Denise gave her a wan smile as the bag with the banknotes changed hands.

The group settled into a serious discussion, the café's ambiance providing a deceptive shield against the gravity of their conversation. They discussed logistics, the distribution of funds, and the increasing dangers they faced.

Prosper's leadership was evident, his strategic mind working tirelessly to keep the network operational despite the mounting pressure. Renaud was soaking up every single word the experienced agent spoke.

As Prosper, the former barrister, did most of the talking, Lise sat back and observed her fellow agents, her heart heavy with concern for them. But she knew better than to give in to premonitions. She could only hope they'd take the same precautions she was taking and didn't run into moles from within the networks.

With the flurry of messages being sent and accepted by SOE operators, the Germans were busy infiltrating, and it wouldn't be long before the first arrests took place. The struggle for the freedom of France would be bought at a high price for SOE.

In the small, lively café in Rue Caumartin, that realization struck Lise like a battering ram. She was very aware of the alive-ness of her companions—their youth, their courage, their fiery spirits. *Will I ever see them again after tonight?*

The door opened again, and a few more patrons entered, their laughter mingling with the low murmur of the café and the loud music. Lise took a deep breath, allowing the normalcy of the scene to anchor her. For now, they were safe. For now, they could plan and hope.

As curfew approached, the meeting wrapped up, each agent preparing themselves for the journey back through the darkened streets.

The road ahead was fraught with danger, but with allies like Renaud, Prosper and Denise, Lise knew they stood a fighting chance. The café might have been a brief haven, but the war waited for no one.

~SIL~

Marseille, September 2004

23

REVEALING THE SECRET

Marseille, Early September 2004

Sil jolted upright as if the echo of a gunshot still rang in her ears, the tension from Lise's world gripping her chest like a vise. Her artist's mind instantly translated the terror of the nightmare into a vivid, half-formed mural—one side of the room drenched in the bright, sunlit colors of Marseille's early morning, the other awash in the sepia tones of war-torn Rue de Caumartin in Paris.

On one wall, she could almost see the outline of Denise, bleeding and ghostly pale, being dragged away by black-clad men whose boots left a trail of destruction in their wake. The image clung to Sil's mind like a half-finished piece of street art, the harsh lines and dark shadows refusing to fade. Lise's fears and worries from her last letter clearly left a mark on Sil's mind – it filling in the blanks and assuming the worst for the fate of the poor W/T operator. The acrid scent of cigarette smoke from her nightmare was still in her nose, wrapped around her senses like a suffocating shroud and making it hard to shake off the dream and re-enter reality.

The cool, clean air of her room did nothing to dispel the oppressive atmosphere. Denise's scream echoed in her ears, a long-drawn wail that seemed to ripple through the very fabric of the walls, leaving behind smears of despair. Sil blinked, trying to shake off the fog of history, her breaths coming in shallow gasps.

With a sharp intake of breath and an aggressive shake of her head, Sil's present world crashed back in—the hum of the air conditioner, the distant chatter of people in the Rue Sainte, the soft rustle of paper under her fingertips.

It was 2004, not 1942, but the terror of that moment still gripped her heart, the half-painted graffiti of her mind blending the horrors of the past with the sterile reality of the present. She reached for her Apple laptop, her fingers still trembling as she navigated to the search engine, the unfinished mural of fear and uncertainty lingering in the back of her mind.

She typed in names, one by one: *Agent Prosper, Agent Denise, Agent Renaud, WWII SOE secret agents.* Each click brought her closer to the brutal reality Lise had feared, that her own mind created with a cruelly vivid nightmare.

The search results filled the screen, and Sil's heart sank as she began to read:

Francis Alfred Suttill, codenamed Prosper. Executed in March 1944 at Flossenbürg concentration camp. Arrested in Paris, tortured for months before his death.

Andrée Raymonde Borrel, codenamed Denise. Executed in July 1944 at Natzweiler-Struthof concentration camp. One of the first female agents of the SOE to be captured and killed.

Joseph France Antoine Antelme, codenamed Renaud. Executed in March 1945 at Gross-Rosen concentration camp. Endured brutal conditions after being betrayed and captured.

Sil stared at the screen, her vision blurring with the weight of this knowledge. These were not just names from history; they were Lise's comrades, her friends. People she had fought alongside, people she had feared for. Sil felt a pang of pain for Lise. How had she coped with their unknown and likely doomed fates? And how had she mourned them after they didn't return?

With an aching heart, Sil closed her laptop, grateful that at least her Lise had survived. Her life had been spared. How had she done that? Oh, she needed to find out. But not now.

Sil sat back, staring at the ceiling as the events of the past days of reading Lise's letters spun through her mind. That world was jam-packed with danger, loss, and sacrifice. How could Sil even begin to compare her own meager struggles to that?

"But I can't live in the past, I live now!" She said aloud, almost jumping at the sound of her own voice. OMG, the École des Beaux-Arts!

She glanced at her watch and cursed under her breath. She'd almost missed another class. Determined to pull herself out of her historical reverie, Sil gathered her things in her rucksack and bolted out the door, snacking on a cereal bar for breakfast and grabbing a take-out coffee on the way.

I'm a disaster but I'm willing to change. Help me, grandpa. You know I can do it. I'm not always a dreamer, I can be a doer as well.

On approaching the École des Beaux-Arts de Marseille on the Avenue de Luminy, Sil was – as always – in awe of the grandeur of her new school. With its imposing stone façade and ornate detailing, it was a piece of history itself. She felt almost like the illustrious Paul-Auguste Renoir, who'd also been a student there, when walking through the entrance, framed by tall, arched windows and decorative cornices. It gave the school the palatial feel that had dominated most of Marseille's 18th-century architecture.

The heavy wooden doors creaked as she pushed them open, revealing a cool, well-lit interior. The kind of light artists crave. The high ceilings were supported by beautiful masonry, while the marble floors were worn smooth by generations of aspiring artists who'd walked these halls before her. The scent of linseed oil and turpentine spilled even into the corridors, the pungent perfume on which artists thrived.

Moving at high speed through halls adorned with classical sculptures and vintage wooden easels, Sil felt yet another deep connection to the past—a reverence for the countless students who'd honed their craft within these walls. It was as though the very stones of the building whispered stories of artistic struggle and triumph, urging her to add her own chapter to its history.

Her class was already inside but she managed to slip to the back of the room without being noticed. The professor, Madame Fournier, was an elegant woman in her fifties with a sharp eye for detail and an impressive career in modern sculpture. Today, the lesson was on the *use of light and shadow in contemporary sculpture*, a topic that fascinated Sil, though sculpting was not her forte.

As Madame Fournier spoke, demonstrating with slides and examples, Sil tried to focus, but her mind kept drifting back to Lise, to the letters, to the tragic fates of Renaud, Denise, and Prosper. She wondered how they had lived their last moments, whether they had found any peace.

"Mademoiselle Anderson?" Madame Fournier's voice cut through her thoughts.

Sil jolted in her seat, realizing she had been staring blankly at the projector screen.

"Are you with us?" Madame Fournier asked, her tone gentle but with an edge of concern. "I asked you a question."

"Yes, sorry. Could you repeat it please?" Sil replied, forcing herself to pay attention.

Madame Fournier nodded, her gaze sharpening. "I was asking how you would approach the use of light and shadow to convey emotion in a contemporary sculpture. How might these elements change the viewer's experience of the piece, Mademoiselle Anderson?"

Sil thought hard. It wasn't an easy question. Well, it wasn't an easy program.

"I always work from my heart, Madame Fournier," she began cautiously. "I don't plan for light and shadow. I just...feel them. But I guess if a piece moves me, if I see light and dark in it, I can only hope it evokes the same feeling in others."

Madame Fournier smiled a fine smile. "Interesting answer, Mademoiselle Anderson, but I think you're here for a reason and that is to understand *what* you're doing, so a blend of heart and head. Please pay more attention, will you."

Sil blushed, feeling her cheeks go red.

"I will, Madame. I promise."

She made a few notes, determined to pull herself back to the present, but the past had its hooks in her, and it wasn't letting go easily.

As the lesson continued, Sil found herself studying the interplay of light and shadow with a new intensity, perhaps influenced by the darkness she had just uncovered about Lise's comrades. She began sketching ideas for a piece that would reflect the contrasts she felt— between light and dark, past and present, life and death.

· · ·

AFTER CLASS, Sil felt a bit more grounded, but as she returned to her apartment, the weight of the suitcase filled with letters loomed large in her mind. Lise's story was far from done. The events in the classroom had done little to erase the eerie connection she felt to the past.

When she reached her door on the second floor, she was surprised to find a repairman waiting for her, toolbox in hand. And standing next to him was Justin Bellamare, his expression unreadable.

"I didn't know it was planned for today," Sil said, fumbling with her keys as she let them both in. "I had class, but please come in."

The repairman immediately set to work inspecting the damaged wall, while Bellamare's eyes scanned the room, his gaze lingering on the disheveled state of her apartment. Sil felt a flush of embarrassment but quickly pushed it aside.

"So, this is the damage," the repairman muttered, more to himself than to anyone else.

Bellamare, however, was not focused on the wall. His eyes drifted to the open suitcase on the bed, the yellowed letters peeking out from inside.

"What's this?" he asked, his voice soft but laced with curiosity, almost as if he'd stumbled upon a secret he wasn't supposed to find.

Sil frowned, inwardly cursing herself. She hadn't meant for him to see the suitcase, let alone its contents. Hesitating for a moment, she felt a flare of irritation rise up. This was her discovery, not something to be scrutinized by a landlord who was already too involved in her life.

"That was behind the wall," she replied, her tone edged with defensiveness. "I found it after that hole was made. It's filled with letters—old letters from World War II."

Bellamare's eyes widened slightly, his curiosity sharpening like a knife. "You said earlier there was nothing behind the board," he reminded her, his gaze flicking back to hers, a challenge in his eyes.

Sil met his gaze, her irritation simmering just below the surface. "And you weren't supposed to barge into my room uninvited," she shot back. "We've both done things we shouldn't have, so I guess we're even." She crossed her arms, more to steady herself than to block him out. Bellamare had a way of pushing her buttons, making her feel vulnerable in a way she wasn't used to.

A tense silence hung between them; the air thick with unspoken words. Bellamare's gaze lingered on her for a moment longer before he turned his attention back to the suitcase. "These letters... they could be important. You shouldn't just keep them hidden away."

Sil felt her pulse quicken, not just from his words, but from the way he said them—like he cared, but also like he was pushing her boundaries, testing her.

"I'm not hiding them," she retorted, trying to keep her voice steady. "I'm just not ready to share them with someone who doesn't understand."

Bellamare raised an eyebrow, a smirk playing on his lips. The tension crackled between them, electric and undeniable. Sil wasn't sure whether she wanted to push him out the door or pull him closer. "So, you're saying you've been reading someone's letters that aren't yours, that were found in a building you don't own, and you aren't planning to share them...yet?"

Sil bit her lip, it was true. What right did she have to Lise's innermost thoughts? She felt torn, torn by her contradictory feelings for her French landlord and by all the emotions that rattled her life at that moment.

Bellamare interrupted her thoughts. "Maybe you underestimate what I can understand, Mademoiselle Anderson."

Maybe just maybe he, for all his brusque manner, could be

trusted. "They're from a woman named Lise de Baissac. She was an SOE agent during the war."

Bellamare looked at her, his expression thoughtful. "This was Lise de Baissac's house. It came on the market after she passed this spring."

"Yes, I know she lived here," Sil said softly, her eyes flitting to the repairman who seemed oblivious of all that was going on around him and was measuring a new board and getting ready to cut it to size. "I've looked her up on the Internet. It makes the suitcase and the letters extra special."

"So, what are these letters about? And why do they affect you so much?" Was there a tinge of tenderness in his voice?

"They're... intense. They've kind of taken over my life since I found them."

Bellamare was silent for a moment, processing this information. Then he nodded, as if coming to a decision. "We should talk more about this. But first, let's get this wall fixed."

Sil breathed a small sigh of relief, grateful for the reprieve. But she knew that the conversation was far from over. The secret she had uncovered was now out in the open, and there was no turning back.

As the repairman continued his work, Sil couldn't shake the feeling that the open suitcase was like Pandora's box. She had already peeked inside, but what would happen when she—or Bellamare—delved deeper? *Will Bel- Justin really understand, will he join me in reliving Lise's history?*

~LISE~

Poitiers, France
December 1942 - August 1943

24

AN UNWANTED INVITATION

Poitiers, December 1942

The icy wind sliced through Poitiers's narrow streets, turning Lise's daily cycle into a rigorous test of endurance. Each day, she pedaled up and down the steep lanes, the cold seeping through her coat as she kept her head down, focused on the task at hand.

With the Firm's knowledge of her access to safe landing grounds, her responsibilities had doubled. More agents were coming in, and her work was increasing by the day.

Under the guise of archaeology, Lise continued her covert operations, though the chill of winter made the pretense harder to maintain. She had enrolled in typing classes—a practical skill that might prove useful, but more importantly, it provided a perfect cover while she expanded her network.

She kept her eyes and ears open, constantly scanning for any glimmer of resistance against the Germans. Every possible resister, or 'helper' as she liked to call them, was mentally cataloged for future contact.

On Claire's recommendation, Lise had also enlisted the services of Clementine, a middle-aged widow with a reputation for discretion. Clementine was invaluable, stepping in as a housekeeper when Lise needed to host secret dinner parties or when an Allied pilot, downed behind enemy lines, needed a safe place to rest for a night before continuing his journey along the Comet Line and over the Pyrenees.

This December morning life was no different—another day to keep up appearances while the cold stung her cheeks and her hair blew into her face despite her woolen cap.

I need a haircut and a dye as soon as I return from Bordeaux, she told herself, hating how fast she was going prematurely gray. Lise didn't have many feminine vanities, but the gray in her hair was something she found hard to accept. Even a widow like Irène Brisse deserved to look her best wartime or not.

As she cycled briskly to stay warm, Lise's thoughts drifted to the past. Life had become dull and monotonous in Poitiers lately, despite the danger of her work. She missed the days of combat training at Beaulieu—miles of hiking through the woods in the middle of the night with only a torchlight and a compass to find her way back to base.

Crawling on her belly underneath nets, seeing who was the fastest. She'd often won despite being one of the 'oldies.' And her absolute favorite part of the training: parachute jumping. She missed all of that, but what she really missed was the camaraderie with fellow agents. She missed her family. She missed...Henri.

Those days are gone, she sternly reminded herself.

Always on guard, never able to be yourself except the few hours of sleep granted in another woman's bed. It took its toll even on a level-headed woman like Lise. But she never allowed herself to wallow in self-pity. Her mission was clear, and the ARTIST network was making good progress.

Despite her youth, Lise had found a wonderful 'little helper' in Sophie, Claire's daughter, who'd become a dear companion to her. Through Sophie, Lise had come to know other young Poitivins, who now functioned within the ARTIST network.

And of course, there was Renard and the Gâteaus, the auctioneer and his wife, and Claire herself, who was so clever at keeping eyes and ears open in Café de le Paix.

The network was growing, with fifty reliable contacts and more joining every day, even as far as Ruffec. But they needed weapons— badly! Though as a network, ARTIST was still but a pinpoint within the Firm, Lise rebuilt the Poitiers's resistance spirit day by day with her inexhaustible energy and willpower.

She planned to travel to Bordeaux to use one of Claude's operators to communicate her needs to London. It was a risk, but necessary. The train stations and carriages were teeming with aggressive Germans, emboldened by the recent annexation of the Vichy puppet state into the Reich. Each encounter with the SS was a nerve-wracking ordeal, the soldiers' lecherous gazes making her skin crawl.

The soldiers harassed young women relentlessly, their lecherous gazes and inappropriate remarks making Lise's skin crawl. Claire and she had decided never to let Sophie travel alone. The Wehrmacht soldiers might allow an older woman like her to pass with minimal trouble, but she remained constantly on guard, every nerve on edge.

On her way back from Paris the other week, Lise had witnessed a young woman being pulled aside, her papers scrutinized in way too much detail, while the SS men laughed and whispered among themselves.

The woman, hardly more than a girl, looked slightly Jewish and

Lise, who understood enough German, heard that was what most of the jokes were about. The girl's fear was palpable as she stood there, clutching her handbag. The terror in her eyes was haunting, and it appeared as if they would not let her go.

Every part of Lise screamed to intervene, to insert herself between those menacing soldiers and an innocent girl, but she checked herself. Had she been an ordinary French woman, she wouldn't have hesitated one second, but she had herself and her cover, and 50 'helpers' to protect, so she bit her lip.

Lise with her focus on getting rid of these practices rather today than tomorrow, tried to shake the memory of it. She needed to keep her cool and anger, even diluted with time and based on a memory, was a bad advisor when it came to security.

As Lise approached the train station an hour later, she felt the reassuring cold of the Colt nestled against her hip and the invisible weight of the switchblade sewn into the hem of her sleeve. She clutched the handle of her overnight bag, willing herself to remain calm.

Each step through the station felt like a march into the unknown, every German a potential threat. As she reached the ticket counter, she joined the row with a sense of urgency. She simply needed to see her brother Claude this time—she simply needed to. She couldn't live with this tension twenty-four hours a day without seeing a familiar, beloved face.

JUST BE THERE IN THIS, *Claude!*

SHE HADN'T BEEN able to meet with him on her earlier visit. It was deemed too dangerous for them both, so she'd done business with his go-between. Though fully aware the goal of her trip was not a family visit but the use of his operator, she longed so much to see her brother this time.

The moment it was her turn to purchase her train ticket, a voice cut through the cold air. "Madame Brisse?"

Lise didn't need to turn around to know who it was. The last person she needed to see right now. Obersturmbahnführer Grabowski. He loomed up behind her, wide-legged and clad in black, the hawk-like eyes scrutinizing her as if she were his prey. His uniform was immaculate, the SS insignia glinting in the pale morning light, and the sharp scent of his cologne prickled her nose.

Prepared as always for the unexpected, Lise forced a polite smile, hiding the irritation that churned her stomach. All show of discontent or hurry was uncalled for. "Herr Grabowski, how can I assist you?"

"*Bonne journée a vous, Madame!* Are you traveling today?" he inquired, his voice as smooth as silk but with an edge that set her nerves on high alert. Fluent French, hardly a trace of a German accent.

"I am, indeed. I plan on visiting a family member in Bordeaux." She kept her tone neutral, hoping he would lose interest in her and move on. And she wasn't lying.

"Are you pressed to take this train, Madame, or would a later train not inconvenience you too much? I happen to have a window in my busy activities and would appreciate it if you could answer a few questions I have." His tone left no room for refusal.

Lise longingly looked at the ticket office and the board where the trains were announced. She thought fast. A window in his busy activities. This didn't sound like an interrogation. What busyness could a widow have to refuse the head of the Gestapo? It would create bad blood. And this man's French was perfect, what had he picked up in the restaurants and bars he frequented about Irène Brisse?

Seeing no way out of his unwanted invitation, she nodded, a half-smile playing on her lips. "Of course, Herr Grabowski. Lead the way."

With lead in her shoes and her heart pounding, Lise followed Grabowski out of the station, heading for 'the house next door.'

I am trained for this, she reminded herself.

Posture straight, she exuded an air of confidence as she walked next to the German. Feeling Poitiers eyes pricking on her, almost as stinging as the cold wind biting through her coat. But she ignored it, focusing on the task at hand.

Do I need to get discreetly rid of the pistol? In case he searches me? She decided against it. *I'll shoot my way out if needed.*

As they walked, Lise also thought of the L-pill tucked in her coat pocket—the agent's last resort. It would kill her in fifteen seconds. The thought of it never had felt so real as this moment.

25

INTO THE LION'S DEN

Lise shook herself from her morbid thoughts, trying to remember all the lessons of her training should she need them. Irène Brisse carried nothing that pointed to anything out of the ordinary. The only thing Grabowski could hold against her was the Colt nestled against her hip. If it came to that, she'd say it was a present from her late husband—a precaution he'd insisted upon, just in case.

The heavy clunk of the lieutenant colonel's boots jarred her already high-strung nerves, each step reverberating through her like the tolling of a death knell.

"You're quiet, Madame," Grabowski observed, this voice a smooth blend of curiosity and authority.

"Just looking around, Herr Obersturmbannführer. One must always be observant, especially in times like these," she replied, her voice as steady as she could manage. "And considering you've not yet told me the nature of these questions you want to ask, I thought it best to save my words for when they are needed."

Grabowski uttered a dry laugh, a sound devoid of humor. "A wise approach, Madame Brisse. Observation is indeed a valuable skill."

He glanced around, his eyes scanning the empty streets as if ensuring no one else was listening. "I'm as much French as I am German," he confided suddenly, his tone almost conversational. This revelation surprised Lise, but she remained silent, waiting for him to elaborate. Could the uniform be a cover? But no! This man was as Nazi as they came.

As if reading her thoughts, he continued, "Not that I'm not a loyal soldier to my Führer. But I've lived in France since the Great War, first as a prisoner of war and then I decided to stay. I own a farm in this region, but I hail originally from Cracow."

Lise mentally filed away this information, recognizing its potential usefulness. Out loud, she offered the compliment he seemed to be fishing for. "Ah, that explains your excellent French, Herr Grabowski. I take it you like working for Germany in your adopted country?"

"Oh, I do," he replied, his tone laced with unspoken complexities. He paused, as if considering whether to say more, before shifting his focus back to her. "I've seen you cycling around the countryside and often going to the train station. You have an interest in local history, particularly in Eleanor of Aquitaine and the Crusades, yes? A fascinating period, I must say."

His tone was casual, but Lise could sense the underlying scrutiny. He knew enough about her alias, enough to make her wary. She wasn't a nobody to him, which she would have preferred.

"Indeed, Herr Grabowski. History has always been a passion of mine. There is much to learn from the past," she replied, keeping her tone measured.

"Good. Very good. Now, let's continue to my office, shall we?"

The Gestapo headquarters on Boulevard Solférino was outwardly similar to her own home—a gray, stone building with shuttered windows and a small porch over the front door. But unlike her house, this place emanated a grimness that befitted its occupiers. As Grabowski ushered Lise inside, she took in every detail, mentally mapping the corridors and exits in case she needed to make a quick escape.

The dimly lit halls were lined with closed doors, behind which she could hear the muffled sounds of voices—some pleading, others screaming. The air was thick with the smell of leather, cigarette smoke, and Grabowski's sharp cologne, all of it creating an oppressive atmosphere that settled heavily on her chest.

He led her quickly through the building, clearly intending to keep her away from the more unsavory aspects of its function. His office was an austere room dominated by a large desk and an imposing portrait of Hitler, the Führer's blue stare seeming to follow her every movement. Lise forced herself to remain calm as Grabowski gestured for her to sit. She did so with the poise of a queen on her throne, keeping her coat and hat on and holding her bag firmly in her lap.

He offered her a Gitane, a French cigarette. "Sorry, I don't smoke," she declined, her voice tinged with modesty. The less he knew about her preferences, the better.

Grabowski settled into his chair, his boots creaking as he crossed one leg over the other, the butt of his pistol clinking against the armrest. His hawkish eyes locked onto hers, searching for any hint of deception.

"I hope I'm not interrupting your plans, Madame. As I said, I've noticed your frequent travels and heard about your interest in the regional history of this area." His smile was small, a mere twitch of the lips that did nothing to warm his intense gaze.

Lise sensed Grabowski was a complicated man, one who played his part well but had other, more personal motivations lurking beneath the surface. It was her job to uncover those motivations without revealing too much of herself.

"When I moved here, I started to explore the area as well. I've always had a keen interest in history, like you, particularly the medieval period. So, I thought we might have a fascinating conversation."

The topic caught Lise off guard. Was this truly the reason he'd plucked her away from the station? Or was he setting a trap? For now, she decided to play along, feigning interest to find out what he was after.

"Absolutely, Herr Grabowski. I haven't come across many who share my interest in our period of history. I seem to bore everyone when I bring up Eleanor or the Crusades."

"Excellent that we have found one another," he said, leaning forward slightly, his curiosity piqued. "Tell me, Madame, what drew you to Eleanor of Aquitaine in the first place?"

Lise's inner voice screamed at her to end this charade and leave, but the Irène in her politely smiled. "Eleanor was a remarkable woman, a true queen in every sense. Her political acumen, her influence over the Crusades, and her role in shaping the cultural landscape of her time are endlessly fascinating to me. I have a penchant for strong French heroines. Joan of Arc is another of my favorites."

Joan of Arc, with her fight for a free France, was a risky topic, but Grabowski seemed to take it in his stride. His eyes brightened with genuine interest, and Lise, inwardly sighed with relief. Perhaps this conversation really was as innocent as it seemed.

"Indeed, Eleanor was a pivotal figure," Grabowski agreed, "I've always been particularly intrigued by the Crusades and the role of the Teutonic Knights. Their dedication and their impact on European history cannot be overstated."

"Absolutely," Lise replied, casting an unseen glance at her watch.

"The Teutonic Knights played a crucial role in the Northern Crusades, particularly in the Baltic region. Their influence extended far beyond the battlefield, impacting trade, politics, and culture."

A young French woman entered, serving coffee with her eyes cast down. Lise noticed how quickly she disappeared afterward; no doubt eager to avoid any interaction with the Gestapo officers. As Lise sipped her coffee, she racked her brain for more historical tidbits to keep the conversation flowing. Irène's knowledge of medieval history needed to stretch a little further.

Grabowski leaned back in his chair, his fingers steepled as he seemed to savor their exchange. "Madame Brisse, it is refreshing to meet someone with such a deep appreciation for history. In these troubled times, it is a solace to discuss the past and remember what we are fighting for."

Lise nodded, keeping her expression neutral. "The past holds many lessons for us, and it is important to remember them as we navigate the present."

As the conversation wound down, it was Grabowski's time to check his watch. "I must apologize for taking up your time, Madame. But I have truly enjoyed our conversation. Shall we continue our discussions another time?"

"I am always happy to discuss history, Herr Grabowski."

He rose to his full length and offered his hand. "Soon, Madame, soon. I wish you a pleasant stay in Bordeaux."

She shook his hand firmly, the polite smile glued to her face. "Thank you for the stimulating conversation, Herr Grabowski. Until next time." *God save me*, she added silently.

As she stepped outside the Gestapo headquarters, the cold air hit her like a wall, but the surge of relief she felt was greater. She had successfully navigated yet another encounter with the enemy. And the Colt was still in her possession.

. . .

UNTIL NEXT TIME, history-obsessed Obersturmbannführer!

26

A FRIEND TO BEHOLD

The train ride to Bordeaux was uneventful, yet an undercurrent of tension kept Lise on edge. The encounter with Grabowski had left her unsettled. Though the conversation had appeared harmless on the surface, she couldn't shake the suspicion that there was more to it.

Why had he chosen to interrupt her journey? As her network grew, so did the risk of exposure. And the fear that her name might surface in the wrong circles loomed larger with each passing day.

Lise had already resolved to avoid attending her own drops—too many nocturnal outings would raise eyebrows for a solitary woman of her age, especially with the curfew in place.

She was caught in a web of conflicting thoughts: on one hand, the history chats with Grabowski offered an excellent cover; on the other, they brought her uncomfortably close to danger. Grabowski was slick, calculating, and she had no doubt there was more to him than met the eye.

Was he subtly circling her, waiting for the right moment to strike? The whole interaction gnawed at her, and the isolation of not being able to discuss her strategy with anyone weighed her down. The power Grabowski wielded over her made her blood run cold, yet all she could do was maintain the facade of sweet, compliant Irène Brisse.

As the train approached another stop, Lise forced herself out of her dark thoughts. Each halt brought the risk of inspection, and she needed to remain vigilant. With a deep breath, she pushed the unsettling encounter to the back of her mind and refocused on the mission ahead in Bordeaux.

The countryside gradually gave way to the bustling city, the transition marked by an increase in military presence. Bordeaux, a vital port for the German navy, was a far cry from the rural quiet of Poitiers.

As she stepped off the train, Lise smelled the distinctive scent of saltwater mingled with the acrid stench of diesel from the German submarines docked in the port. The imposing structures of the Atlantic Wall loomed in the distance, an undeniable reminder of the city's strategic importance to the invaders.

Large German vessels, behemoths that had slipped through the British blockade, now were moored in the harbor, taking over the once proud French port city.

Lise's watchful eyes took in every detail. Wehrmacht soldiers patroled the streets with a swagger of possessiveness, while the French citizens moved about their business with heads down, weary with cold and repression.

She pushed her hat firmer on her head, held her bag tightly, and set off toward yet another café, another meeting point. Café Bertrand, a small café discreetly tucked away from the main thoroughfare, was a simple establishment that didn't draw much attention from passersby.

Just one of Bordeaux's many seaside bars, Café Bertrand served as one of the most important hubs of the vast SCIENTIST network that stretched from the Spanish border to the south of Brittany. With its staunch Resistance owners protecting agents and French resisters alike, this non-descript place was a household name within Claude's network.

The wooden sign creaked in the sea breeze. Inside, the air was thick with cigarette smoke and baked goods, but the warmth was a welcome respite from the outside cold and tense atmosphere.

She spotted her fellow trainee, codenamed Claudine, at a corner table, her fair hair and tall, slender frame making her easy to identify among the mainly dark-haired, short-built French dockworkers. Claudine, who was her brother's courier, looked up as Lise approached, a warm smile spreading across her sweet, attractive face.

"Odile! It's so good to see you," she exclaimed, standing up to greet her friend with a hug. It crossed Lise's mind that the last time they met it had been at the Royal Oak on the Beaulieu estate. And look at them now. Both secret agents, both settled into France as if they belonged.

Claudine's natural Irish courtesy and generous spirit were evident in her embrace. She held Lise tight, and Lise temporarily felt some of her uptight tenseness melt away. She lingered, savoring closeness to a good and trustworthy human.

"Oh Claudine, it seems like ages ago," Lise replied, letting her go but keeping her eyes fixed on her friend's face. "I think I live for moments like this. I know it sounds weak, but it's just great to see you."

"I know," Claudine echoed her sentiment, "with all we're facing, moments like this remind us we're not alone in this fight. Come, sit, Odile, I've ordered coffee, or would you prefer something stronger in this ghastly weather?" Her French, though a learned language, was impeccable.

"No, coffee's fine. I seem to survive on the stuff these days."

"You're telling me!" Claudine laughed, and with her voice down, "when we can't get a good cuppa, we might as well take un café au lait."

The brew the waitress served was strong and dark, a welcome change from the watered-down versions Lise was used to in Poitiers. She supposed the German dominance demanded better quality coffee, though Café Bertrand didn't seem like a place teeming with enemy spies.

Though it was a place where they could still let their guard down a little, Lise and Claudine remained on guard as they chitchatted about everything and nothing, giving off the impression of two French women who were overjoyed to be in each other's company after not having seen one another for a while..

Lise's ears perked up as she noticed the open anti-German sentiment in the conversations around them. This was very different from Poitiers, where collaboration or silent endurance were the norm. Bordeaux, with its strategic importance and its large working-class community, appeared to harbor a more defiant spirit

Claudine, noticing Lise's keen listening, filled in the blanks. "Bertrand, the owner, is one of David's best couriers."

"Resistance must run in the genes of café owners," Lise remarked with a smile, "I also have so much support from Claire, who owns a café in Poitiers."

"We couldn't do half of what we do without these cafés," Claudine observed. "They're sanctuaries, really. Places where we can meet and blend in, shielded by the everyday noise of life."

"True," Lise agreed, savoring the warmth of the coffee and the momentary reprieve from the cold." She loved talking with Claudine, whose intelligence shone through in all her observations. Lise couldn't help but feel a longing to relax and let go, to just sit and talk with her, pretending they didn't have a job to do. That they weren't persona non grata in a hostile environment where they could be dragged away from a moment like this at any time.

After some time, Lise leaned in, lowering her voice. "Will I be able to see David this time?"

Claudine's voice was even softer despite the noise around them, "I know he is your brother, Odile, and I also know I shouldn't know that, so yes. It took some organizing, but I've arranged a rendezvous for you two later tonight. But for now, you'll stay with me. It's safer that way."

"Thank you so much, Claudine. I can't tell you how much that means to me."

Claudine smiled, her blue eyes twinkling with a lovely warmth. "I think I do understand what it means to you. If I could see my brother, who's fighting with the Irish guards, I'd be over the moon. We're all in this together, my friend."

Lise felt like hugging Claudine again but stayed in her seat. She couldn't become overly emotional. As they continued to talk, Claudine's passion for languages became apparent. She spoke engagingly about her recent studies in Spanish, her enthusiasm infectious.

"You should consider learning it too, Odile," she suggested. "It's a beautiful language, and it might come in handy someday. You know, the trek over the Pyrenees, etc." She waved her slender hands as if sweeping over the mountains.

Lise was intrigued. "You know, that's not a bad idea. It might be a good way to pass the long winter months in Poitiers." And to herself, she thought, it might give her an excuse to steer conversations with Grabowski away from medieval history. *The widow has a new passion. Sorry, Herr Obersturmbannführer!*

～

As evening approached, the tension in the air heightened, even within the relative safety of Café Bertrand. Curfew was strictly enforced, but even so the activities of the shadow fighters increased as darkness fell. Some customers scrambled to get home, some to get ready for action.

Lise and Claudine left the café together, the streets of Bordeaux now cloaked in shadows, each movement a potential threat. With Claudine by her side, who'd only been in Bordeaux for a month but already knew her way, Lise stifled her apprehensions.

The promise of seeing Claude, her little brother who wasn't so little anymore, gave her strength. The mission continued, but family mattered.

The safe house where Claude was hiding was unassuming—a modest stone house with ivy creeping up one side and shutters once painted a vibrant green but now weathered by sea salt, wind, and neglect. The narrow street was deserted, the only sounds an occasional bicycle bell or a distant engine revving up.

It was a house that would easily be overlooked, which made it perfect for clandestine meetings. *How many of these houses are scattered all over France?* Lise thought. *Owned by brave French citizens and opened up to support the Resistance.* She took a deep breath, steeling herself for the reunion and whatever news Claude had to share.

This is the life we chose, she reminded herself. *And we'll see it through, no matter the cost.*

27

DAVID AND ODILE

As Lise and Claudine approached the back door of the modest townhouse where the head of the SCIENTIST network had sought temporary refuge, Lise felt an unexpected wave of doubt wash over her. The prospect of blending her crafted alias with the raw reality of seeing her blood brother again suddenly seemed overwhelming. The idea of stepping out of her role as Irène Brisse or Agent Odile, even for a brief moment, threatened to unravel the carefully maintained composure she'd honed.

"Perhaps this isn't—," she began, as she reached to a stop, gripping her friend's hand. The thought of seeing Claude in the flesh, of facing him while they couldn't be their real self, made her think this wasn't a good idea after all. But Claudine, ever intuitive, cut her off gently but firmly.

"Do this now while you can, Odile. Trust me, it will do both of you a world of good."

Not letting go of Claudine's hand, Lise pushed forward, ascending the creaking wooden steps of the veranda. Taking in a deep breath, she let the scent of damp earth from the garden and the cool night air ground her in the moment.

Despite entering through the back, a precaution in these dangerous times, Claudine knocked three times in a specific pattern, announcing their arrival.

The door swung open to reveal a young French man, his eyes shaded by a cap, who gave Lise a brief nod before stepping aside to let them in.

"*Bonsoir, Yves*," Claudine greeted him in a low voice, "is everything in order?"

"Oui, Claudine. Maman left dinner for you on the kitchen table. I'll be off now," Yves replied slipping out into the night—one of the countless shadow workers whose silent efforts were becoming the backbone of the growing SOE networks across France.

Claudine led Lise through the scullery and kitchen, the smell of cooking lingering in the air, and into a narrow hallway that opened into a modest sitting room.

The room was simple, furnished with a worn but serviceable sofa, a wooden coffee table, and a few mismatched chairs. A chest of drawers stood against the far wall, its surface cluttered with papers and a single, unlit candle. A typical, lower-class French house.

The air was thick with the scent of tobacco and burning wood from the fireplace, a stifling combination that only added to the weight of the emotions pressing on Lise's chest. It wasn't just the room that felt suffocating; it was the impending confrontation between the life she'd been living and the one she'd left behind.

Claude de Baissac stood by the table, his back straight and his presence commanding even in the simple, unassuming surroundings. Tall and broad-shouldered, with an athletic build that spoke of a lifetime of discipline, he was a striking figure. His face, with its set jaw and serious expression, was framed by thick black hair and a well-groomed mustache. Despite their shared, unblemished, pale skin, there was little outward resemblance between the towering Claude and his petite, dark-blonde older sister.

Dressed in a plain brown jacket and trousers, a beret tucked under his arm, Claude might have blended seamlessly into the civilian population, but there was no mistaking the air of authority that clung to him. Even in this safehouse, far from prying eyes, his every movement was deliberate, every glance calculated for potential threats.

He was reading a document with intense concentration when they entered, his eyes flicking up only when he heard them approach. Lise noticed the brief hesitation in his hand as it hovered near his side, where his concealed weapon was ready to be drawn at the first sign of danger. But as his gaze met hers, the steely resolve in his eyes softened, just a fraction, into recognition. Even here, even with family, security was paramount.

"Odile." The way he spoke her code name was formal, almost distant, lacking the warmth she had hoped for. Lise cringed inwardly at how rigidly he clung to his SOE role, but as he stepped forward to embrace her, she caught a fleeting glimpse of the emotions he kept tightly bound—pain, longing, and something that almost resembled vulnerability. His grip was firm, yet measured, as if afraid to let too much of himself show.

"David," she replied, her voice adopting the same formal tone as his. It felt strange to address this familiar figure by his codename, a name that didn't truly fit the man she had known all her life. Doubt crept back in—had it been a mistake to ask Claudine to arrange this meeting? Everything about the situation felt surreal, as if they had been plucked from their childhood island in the Indian Ocean and dropped into this war-torn country that was theirs by birth, yet no longer theirs in any real sense.

"It's good to see you. How have you been?" Claude's voice was clipped, betraying little emotion. Lise wished the embrace had lasted longer, that he had allowed a moment of genuine connection. But he had already pulled back, returning to the table and the document that seemed to demand more attention than she did.

In their childhood in Mauritius, Lise and Claude had been close, but as they grew into adulthood in Paris, their relationship had become more complicated, shaped more by duty than affection. Emotions, never their strong suit, were rarely expressed between them. Lise remembered feeling closest to Claude when he was at his most vulnerable, locked up in La Model Prison in Barcelona in 1940, and how he had seemed truly overjoyed by her unexpected visit.

What they shared now was a deep, unspoken patriotism and a mutual respect for the caution and precision with which they each carried out their missions.

"I've missed you," Lise blurted out before she could stop herself, the words escaping against her better judgment. Claude didn't respond, his focus unyieldingly locked on his role as SCIENTIST's organizer, refusing to let anything break the professional façade.

Claudine slipped quietly into the room, closing the door behind her without a sound. Claude acknowledged her with a curt nod, his mannerism polite but distant. There was a noticeable stiffness in his posture as he addressed her, a formality Lise couldn't quite place. He seemed even more aloof with his loyal courier than with his own sister. Was Claude becoming an unfeeling military man? But Claudine appeared unfazed, ignoring the chill in his demeanor with her always-ready smile.

Claude gestured for Lise to sit, the motion more of a command than a familial invitation, while he continued reading the document in his hands.

"As requested, I've arranged a W/T operator for you. Aristide is upstairs," he informed her, nodding towards the attic. "He's waiting for your messages and will start transmitting once I'm gone."

Lise understood his need for caution, but she couldn't help

feeling a pang of disappointment. She'd hoped for something more personal, something beyond the cold exchange of business. Still, she responded with a measured tone, "Thank you for arranging this, David. I know it's a roundabout way."

Claude's gaze briefly softened, though his words remained firm. "I still don't understand why you insist on working alone, Odile. You'd be more effective within a larger network. The climate is changing."

Lise recognized his concern as an attempt to protect her, but she bristled at the implication of interference—from the Firm or from her younger brother. "I do what I have to do, and you do yours," she replied, the sharpness in her voice surprising even herself. She bit her tongue, regretting the harshness that threatened to taint their limited time together.

Family, she thought with a sigh, always finds a way to bring out the best and the worst in us. But the tension eased slightly as she noticed the flicker of recognition in his eyes, a shared understanding of the familiar trap they'd fallen into. They both chuckled, the tension breaking like a thread stretched too thin.

"I know your stance, Odile," Claude conceded, his tone gentler now. "And only time will tell which approach was the wisest. We have to be more careful than ever. Since the fall of Vichy in November, the Germans have tightened their grip."

Sensing the lingering tension, Claudine intervened in a cheerful voice. "But for now, let's enjoy this moment together. Wine, anyone? I believe Yves's mother left us a meal. Let me check."

For once, brother and sister agreed, and Claudine headed to the kitchen to pour their glasses. As she left the room, Lise took a moment to study her brother more closely. He seemed more guarded than ever, the weight of his responsibilities clearly etched onto his thirty-five-year-old face.

Claudine had confided to Lise at Café Bertrand that the SCIEN-

TIST network now boasted thousands of volunteers. With an organization of that magnitude operating right under the ever-watchful eye of the Bordeaux Gestapo, it would only take one mole to bring the entire structure crashing down, leading to waves of arrests. No wonder Claude was tense.

"Christmas is in two weeks," Lise ventured, her tone hopeful. "Why don't you come to Poitiers? We could both use a bit of family time."

His expression hardened again. "I can't, Li...Odile. The work here is too all-consuming. If I leave, if only for a couple of days, I can't foresee the consequences."

'Lise' had almost slipped out unnoticed, but he corrected himself just in time. Still, she savored this slip, a small moment of authenticity in the midst of their otherwise guarded exchange. She could see that her brother—her little brother—was suffering from loneliness too, and she longed to reach out to him. But, like the stubborn boy he'd always been, he wouldn't let her in.

Claudine returned with a tray carrying three glasses and a bottle of Bordeaux wine. She had even managed to arrange bowls of bouillabaisse and a tray of crackers and Camembert cheese.

"Sorry, I overheard that last bit. Maybe I could come over for Christmas, Odile?" she said, her voice warm and soothing. But before Lise could respond, Claude interjected.

"I might need you here, Claudine," he said, his tone gruff, almost impolite.

Claudine's smile faltered slightly, but she nodded in understanding. "Of course, David. We'll see how things are closer to the date."

Lise felt another pang of disappointment but decided not to push the matter.

As they sat around the coffee table, Lise shared the progress of her ARTIST network. For once, Claude listened with interest, even seeming impressed.

"Organizing is in our blood," he remarked, subtly acknowledging that Claudine knew of their sibling relationship. "I take it your message for London isn't just about receiving new agents, but also about arming the Poitiers region?"

"Yes. So far, my task has been to welcome new agents and help them find their way to their own networks, but arming my local resisters is becoming a priority now."

"Impressive," Claude said, looking content. "And didn't you welcome our fellow Mauritian, Renaud, a couple of weeks ago? Never met the fellow, but I've heard capital things about him."

"Yes, I did. I introduced him to Alcide and Prosper in Paris. He's setting up the BRICKLAYER network in the Troyes region. Renaud has great potential."

Claude nodded. "I was pleased with the funds you secured through Alcide. Thanks for that."

"Have you been in touch with London since?" Lise asked, "Alcide relayed that the Firm was desperately awaiting a message from you."

"Yes, yes. Don't worry. Aristide is back at his post."

"I was worried," she admitted. "That's why I'm glad I can see you with my own eyes right now."

"No reason to worry on my behalf. But you be careful, especially if you rely heavily on the French. There are many traitors among them because the Gestapo pays them well."

"Anyone can be a traitor, David. I'm very aware of that."

Claudine's presence beside Lise on the couch was quietly reassuring, her fair hair catching the soft light of the lamp hanging over the coffee table. Though she remained mostly silent, her loyalty to Claude and the network was evident in her every gesture—a calm, attentive demeanor that spoke of her deep commitment. Yet, there was a hint of something else in her wide, intelligent blue eyes, something Lise couldn't quite place, an underlying tension that didn't match the sweet, almost naïve exterior Claudine usually projected.

Claude's tone, as he continued to discuss network matters, was as clipped and professional as ever, but Lise could sense an undercurrent of something deeper—an emotion he was struggling to suppress. He was the type to give orders, to maintain control, but there was a subtle shift in him whenever Claudine was near, a tension that he tried but failed to fully conceal.

This puzzled Lise. Claudine, with her warm Irish charm and natural ability to disarm those around her, should've been the last person to cause unease. She was reliable, quick, and discreet—an ideal courier. Yet, Claude seemed guarded in her presence, and that was not like him.

Lise also noticed that Claudine, who'd been so chatty and open with her at the café, was now uncharacteristically quiet, almost deferential. It was as if the vibrant woman Lise had spoken with earlier had retreated, leaving behind someone more reserved, more careful.

Claudine's contributions to the Bordeaux network were substantial, from what Lise had gathered, yet she seemed reluctant to acknowledge her role when Claude was around.

Then there were the glances. Every so often, Lise caught her brother casting a quick, almost imperceptible look in Claudine's direction. For just a fraction of a second, his stern expression would soften, betraying a connection that Lise hadn't noticed before—something beyond the usual camaraderie of wartime collaboration. It was an odd dynamic, one that seemed to hint at a deeper bond between them, though Lise couldn't yet discern what it was.

They spent the next hour discussing logistics, Claude's tone becoming more collaborative as they delved into the specifics. Lise marveled at his strategic mind, though she wished he could let his guard down, even if just for a moment.

Finally, as their visit wrapped up, Claude stood and looked down on her. "I must go but stay in touch. Keep me informed."

"I will. You do the same." Lise rose, wanting to hug him but he had turned his back on her.

"You're staying here tonight," Claudine said, grabbing Lise's hand.

Claude was already in his overcoat and heading for the door, "Six sharp tomorrow morning, Claudine."

"Yes, David."

Lise ascended the creaky steps to the attic. In the dim light, she handed her dispatches to the man codenamed Aristide. His steady eyes met hers. His antenna hung out of the open window, and it was freezing cold but his fingers in their fingerless gloves were already typing. He would urgently have to leave after the transmission, before the Germans picked up his signals.

"I'll leave your answers in the mailbox in the morning, Odile."

Lise knew all about the familiar tense vigil surrounding these messages. With a soft "thank you again," she left him and went down the steep staircase.

Claudine was waiting for her with a freshly poured glass of wine. The warmth of the room and the fire crackling in the hearth was comforting.

"I'll possibly miss you tomorrow as I'm leaving for Saint Emilion at the crack of dawn. Are you heading back to Poitiers when you have your answers?" Claudine handed her the glass.

Savoring the moment of camaraderie, Lise answered. "Yes, as soon as I have the Firm's answers. I hope to see you at Christmas, though. I'll make you coq-au-vin."

Claudine's smile was a brief flicker of light. "Sounds delicious. Can't wait and stay safe. And learn Spanish!"

"I will," Lise promised, feeling the warmth of the wine seep through her, momentarily easing the burden she carried.

Claudine's expression softened, her voice earnest. "I'll miss you,

Odile." The bond between them, forged in this war, was deeply felt by both.

Claudine, the only real friend Lise had in France, turned and walked out of the door, leaving behind a silence that was hard to bear. She listened to the light footsteps and then the closing of the backdoor, the hope for a Christmas reunion lingering in her mind.

Let Claudine come at Christmas, Lise found herself hoping, clinging to the chance of a brief respite from the relentless march of war.

28

NEW ALLIANCES

A few weeks later - Poitiers, January 1943

The frost of January clung stubbornly to the stone façades of Poitiers's buildings. An unforgiving winter had wrapped itself around France like a shroud. Christmas 1942 had come and gone, a fleeting moment of spiritual warmth in an otherwise relentless year.

Lise had allowed herself to bask in the rare comfort of the season, spending a few precious days in the company of Claudine. The young woman's lively presence, her tinkling laughter, and slightly risqué Irish jokes had offered a brief respite from the menacing shadow of Obersturmbannführer Grabowski that loomed over them from the house next door.

But now, as January unfurled in all its bleakness, that brief interlude felt distant, a warm memory quickly swallowed by the cold reality of occupied France. With the entire country under Nazi control, even the once serene rural areas were now caught in the tightening grip of tight rationing and black markets. All that was luxury went to the occupiers or was shipped off to Germany

Life, already difficult, had become a test of endurance. Yet, Lise plodded on. Her bike, her loyal companion, carried her through the frostbitten countryside, her legs pumping with a tenacity that defied the bone-deep weariness settling into her body.

Every day was a battle against fatigue, against the cold that bit at her fingers and toes, against the gnawing anxiety that tightened her chest each time she ventured out. But there was no room for self-pity or staying under the duvet. The ARTIST network needed to be built, sustained, and strengthened. Every contact, every drop, every whisper of resistance was another thread in the fragile web she wove.

Amidst the grind, Lise found solace in small victories. She was quite proficient at typing now, making it to over 140 touches per minute, her fingers flying over the keys with a precision that mirrored her strategic mind.

And now, despite the countless hours devoted to the cause, on Claudine's suggestion, she'd chosen to learn Spanish—a decision that had surprised even herself. It was an indulgence of sorts, a reminder that there was life beyond the constant vigilance, beyond the shadows of the occupation, after the war. If it ever ended.

The classroom at the *Institut des Langues de Poitiers* was a haven of sorts. Small but well-lit, it offered a rare reprieve from the harsh realities outside its walls. A weak afternoon sun filtered over the rows of wooden desks, as if giving hope with its light.

Lise sat at one of them, her exercise book open before her, diligently taking notes. The faint smell of chalk and ink reminded her of the classrooms of her youth, a sensory link to a peaceful world when all had been well.

Her Spanish instructor, Señor Martinez, was a lean, balding man whose thick accent and infectious enthusiasm for languages had quickly earned her respect. As he paced at the front of the room, conjugating verbs with a passion that bordered on the theatrical, Lise found herself momentarily lost in the rhythm of his voice, the cadence of a language that felt both foreign and familiar.

"Madame Brisse," he called out, switching to French for her benefit, "can you tell me how to say 'I will return' in Spanish?"

"Volveré," she replied with a smile. Her accent was still rough, the syllables catching awkwardly in her throat, but she was improving. The challenge of mastering a new language was a welcome distraction, a mental exercise that kept her sharp.

"Very good! And how about 'We will fight'?"

"Lucharemos," she answered, her mind briefly wandering to the real fight—the one that took place in a world where slogans like 'we will fight' could only be exchanged in whispers.

After class, as the only other two students gathered their belongings and filed out, Señor Martinez approached Lise with a curious gleam in his eye. "You have a gift for languages, Madame. Have you ever thought of using this skill for something more... significant?"

Lise smiled, a practiced gesture that didn't quite reach her eyes. "I have my own ways of using what I know, Señor Martinez. But thank you."

There was a pause, a moment where his curiosity seemed to deepen, but she held his gaze with a calm certainty that brooked no further questions. She appreciated his encouragement, but the less he knew about her true activities, the safer he would be.

This classroom, like every other aspect of her life, was a carefully constructed façade—one that she intended to keep intact. With a polite nod, she left Señor Martinez and his Spanish lessons behind, stepping back into the snow-laden January afternoon.

As she mounted her bike once more, the brief sanctuary of the Spanish class faded as quickly as it had come. There was no time to dwell on it, though. The grindstone awaited, and Lise, ever the consummate professional, continued to push on, driven by a sense of duty that far outweighed her exhaustion. And her small frame.

LATER THAT EVENING, Lise found herself in Claire Rimbaud's Café de la Paix, waiting for her next contact. Despite the shortages of everything from food to fuel to repair items, Claire had managed to keep her establishment cozy with dim lighting that shaded the worn-out fixtures and the ever-comforting smell of cooked food and draft beer.

Lise sat at her usual corner table, her back against the wall, observing the activity in the café while maintaining a low profile. Her copy of *Cuentos de la Selva* by Horacio Quiroga lay open on the table, with a round glass of Courvoisier beside it. But despite the warm atmosphere and the familiar taste of the brandy, fatigue was her constant companion that no amount of rest could alleviate.

As she watched the door open, she observed her new British contact walk in. The male agent, codenamed Gilbert, was a medium-tall man with a confident stride and an air of significance about him. His silky, dark hair was combed back, and he had the look of someone well-acquainted with danger.

Their eyes met, and he nodded subtly before making his way over to her table.

"Odile?" he asked, and as she pointed to the chair opposite her, he sat down.

"Good evening, Gilbert. Better call me Madame Brisse or Irène when in here. That's how people around Poitiers know me."

"Irène it is." They didn't shake hands.

"I trust your journey was uneventful?" Lise asked, trying to ignore the heaviness in her limbs that had settled in like an unwelcome guest.

"As uneventful as one can hope for in these times," he replied with a wry smile. "I've heard much about your work. Impressive, to say the least."

"Thank you," she said, her voice steady despite the weariness. "I'm small fish, but I understand you have some experience of your own, especially when it comes to organizing drops. I have the sites. You have the logistics and the contacts. I understand you're a flight officer by profession?"

Gilbert planted his elbows on the table and leaned in slightly, his expression serious. "Yes, I am. And due to my experience and on your request, London has tasked me with helping to coordinate drops and establishing more secure lines of communication for several networks. Your network is as crucial to our effort as all the others, Irène. Never doubt that."

Lise accepted his compliment with a ghost of a smile. "I'm in central France, so that's handy, and it's a rural area. Also, handy. I've already scouted several new locations for drops and sent them to London. We need to bring in arms, supplies, and trained agents. The people here are willing, but we lack the resources."

"That's where I come in," Gilbert affirmed. "I can arrange for the drops, but we need to ensure the security of these locations. The Germans are becoming more vigilant."

"You're telling me!" Lise took a big sip of her Courvoisier, while Sophie scooted over with another glass and the bottle to serve Gilbert.

While they continued to talk, focusing on the logistics of coordinating the drops and ensuring the safety of their operatives, an unspoken understanding developed between the two agents—a mutual respect for each other's capabilities.

Lise felt a glimmer of hope during these short days and long nights. Unlike the other agents she'd received and welcomed, Gilbert was going to assist her directly, rather than moving on to another network. Though he would also work for other networks, he would shoulder some of her responsibilities.

With help seated at her table, Lise felt even more clearly how she'd been pushing herself beyond her limits for months, and it was starting to take a toll. She made a mental note to speak with Claire before she left. Perhaps Claire, with her connections and resourcefulness, could suggest something—a remedy, perhaps, or better food to help her sleep more soundly and keep her strength up. Or she'd need to consult Doctor Giraud.

When Gilbert finally departed, Lise remained seated for a moment, staring into her half-empty glass. The adrenaline from their discussion faded, leaving her feeling drained. She needed rest, real rest, but it was a luxury she could scarcely afford.

As if aware of her inner struggle, Claire approached her table with a cup of coffee. Lise looked up, managing a tired smile.

"Claire," she began, her voice lower than usual, "do you know of anything that might help me sleep better? I've been struggling to get proper rest. And perhaps something to keep me more... fortified? The food lately, well, it's not been enough."

Claire's dark-green eyes filled with concern. "I'll see what I can do, Irène. It's not easy these days, but I have a few tricks up my sleeve. We'll get you something that'll help. You need to take care of yourself if you're going to keep this up."

Lise nodded, grateful for Claire's understanding. She couldn't tell her the Firm supplied them with amphetamines for periods like this. Until now, Lise hadn't even looked at the strip of pills in the double lining of her suitcase for fear she'd grow dependent on them.

Maybe she could consult her French helper in a roundabout way. "Thank you, Claire. It's... you know... my late husband had been prescribed some pills that... uh... perk you up extra. Do you think I should try those?"

"Claire looked doubtful. "What are they and how old are they?"

Lise hesitated, choosing her words carefully. "I'm not exactly sure. They were supposed to help him stay alert during long stretches—something to keep him going when rest wasn't an option. But they're old, and I'm not sure they're the right solution for me."

Claire nodded. "I've heard of such pills. They can be effective, but they come with risks. Dependence, for one. And they might make it even harder for you to get proper rest when you do have the chance."

"That's what I'm afraid of. I've managed so far without them, and I'm reluctant to start relying on something that could make things worse in the long run," Lise admitted.

"Let me see if I can find something else—maybe a herbal remedy or a supplement that could help without those side effects. You need real rest, not just a quick fix. And otherwise consult Doctor Giraud. He'll listen without pressing you one way or the other." Claire placed a warm hand over Lise's. "We need you healthy and fit, Irène. You know that."

WHEN LISE SLIPPED into her apartment later that evening, she felt as if some of her burden was finally shared. With allies like Gilbert to assist her and Claire's comforting advice echoing in her mind, she knew she wasn't alone in this fight. The odds might be against them, but with such support, she'd find the strength and resolve to keep going.

The next day, she resumed her Spanish lessons with Señor Martinez, grateful for the brief dream of a normal life his tutoring provided. The señor's engaging teaching style and genuine passion were infectious and Lise worked hard to tackle this new beautiful language, if only to hear him compliment her on her achievements,

achievements that had nothing to do with her clandestine activities, but were welcome, so very welcome.

"Remember, Madame Brisse," he said during one lesson, "language is a bridge. It connects people, cultures, and ideas. Never underestimate its power."

She took his words to heart, knowing that the ability to communicate effectively was a powerful weapon in her struggle. And Lise was a communicator 'pur sang.'

Language is not only a bridge, Señor Martinez, Lise thought, *it is also a shield, a way to protect the truth from the enemy for as long as we need. A language in codes.*

As she left his classroom, and braced for another snowstorm in Poitiers, Lise held onto that thought, a quiet resolve settling within her. Every small victory, every coded message sent and received, brought her one step closer to the day when the truth would no longer need to be hidden.

29

A DOUBLE LANDING

Two months later - South of Poitiers, 17 March 1943

T he winter nights in Poitiers stretched long and cold, but Lise's ARTIST network thrived in the shadows. With each passing week, her influence increased, as did the trust the Firm placed in her.

She orchestrated drops across the region, distributing weapons and supplies with a precision that left no resister empty-handed. What began as a fledgling operation had grown into a formidable force, and Lise had become the undisputed leader among her French helpers—a beacon of resolve in a land smothered by occupation.

But tonight was no ordinary night. The air hummed with anticipation in the usual silence of the countryside. South of Poitiers, a double Lysander landing was scheduled—an event as rare as it was dangerous. One plane would ferry her brother Claude and Agent Renaud back to London for consultation, while the other would deliver four new agents, including a woman codenamed Marguerite, who was set to join Prosper's network in Paris.

The opportunity to see her brother off was a rare comfort to Lise, though she didn't expect the waving off to be very personal. Just a glimpse of him would reassure her he was safe on board and on his way to England. Despite the risk, Lise had sworn to be present.

With Obersturmbannführer Grabowski conveniently out of town and his men taking their leisure in clubs and bordellos, she seized the chance to attend the landings herself.

The night was clear and frosty, the full moon casting a silvery glow over the woodlands, painting the landscape in strips of light and shadow. The scene was hauntingly beautiful, but the brightness also heightened the danger—every glint of metal, every silhouette, could stand out to prying eyes.

Lying on her stomach in the frozen grass, Lise shifted slightly as the wet ground seeped through her anorak. She turned to the figure close by. "Psst, Gilbert, everything set on your end?" Her breath formed a white plume in the icy night air.

Gilbert gave her a thumbs up, his silhouette, also flat on the ground, barely discernible in the moonlight. "Everything's ready," he whispered back, his voice carrying its usual confidence. "The pilots have their instructions, and the landing site is clear. We just need to wait for the signal."

"And you're sure we're not too exposed? The moon is so bright on this frosty, clear night."

"It's bright, alright," Gilbert agreed, "but we've accounted for that. The clearing is well-hidden from any prying eyes. And the Lysanders' bellies are painted black, as you know. We're lucky Grabowski's men are busy enjoying themselves in town."

"I hope you're right. These are two important agents we're seeing off. We can't afford anything to go wrong." The tension in Lise's chest refused to lessen.

"Every agent is important, Odile. But I understand what you mean. I know more than you think. We'll see them off safely—you have my word." Gilbert's usual bravado was tempered by a hint of empathy.

The reassurance helped, but only slightly. She turned her gaze back to the clearing, where shadows danced under the silver light of the moon.

Next to him, Lise felt the weight of responsibility for everything happening in the next hour resting on her shoulders like a sack of potatoes. This was the first major landing Gilbert had organized as her air movements officer, and while she trusted his organizational skills, a part of her still hesitated.

The new air movements officer was an enigma—a man whose charm and connections made him invaluable, yet whose true loyalties remained as vague as some of his answers. Lise's finely tuned instincts, usually so reliable in judging the trustworthiness of others, wavered around him. He was a double-edged sword, but a helper she couldn't afford to discard. Not yet.

"Stay sharp," she whispered, more to herself than to Gilbert, as they continued to watch and wait. The tension in the air thickened, and Lise knew that the success of the operation—and the survival of her brother—depended on her planning.

The stillness of the night was broken by the faint hum of approaching aircraft. Lise's heart pounded as she strained her ears to confirm the sound. Moments later, two Lysanders appeared in the night sky, their dark silhouettes descending like giant black birds into the open clearing. The engines roared as they touched down, the noise echoing through the still night.

Lise stood, her eyes scanning the scene. Her brother Claude moved quickly, his broad, tall figure a shadowy outline in the moonlight. He waved to her, a brief, silent farewell waiting for two arriving agents to disembark before boarding the first Lysander with

Renaud. Her heart ached to say goodbye properly, but there was no time. Duty called, and she had to turn her attention to the arriving agents and supplies.

The second Lysander landed smoothly, and the door swung open. Two more agents disembarked swiftly and were immediately surrounded by Lise's armed French partisans. Even the pilot in his cockpit was heavily armed.

The slim silhouette of Marguerite, emerged among the three men. Lise hurried over, helping the agents to quickly hide in the woods away from the planes and directing her men to unload the crates with supplies and arms.

The urgency of the mission left no room for personal goodbyes. Claude's plane was already up in the air. The Lysander hadn't touched ground for more than three minutes.

Marguerite, a pretty, young woman with a flair stepped in line with Lise. "Odile, it's good to finally meet you in person," she said, her voice still a bit shaky with the adrenaline of the landing.

"Likewise, Marguerite," Lise replied, shaking her hand. "Welcome back to France. My helpers will take you to your safehouse until curfew lifts. You're bound for Paris tomorrow morning, correct?"

"Yes, I am to join Marcel, who is my...uh... whom I know," Francine corrected herself, though Lise was aware the new female agent had arrived to assist her husband, codenamed Marcel, as his courier.

"Marcel is one of the W/T operators for Prosper, isn't he?" Lise smoothed over Francine's slip forgivingly. "Well, good luck, Marguerite, and take care. Paris is a dangerous milieu for people like us, as you no doubt know. But perhaps we'll meet again." With these words Lise handed her over into Renard's capable hands. The other two agents went with Gilbert.

As the young woman disappeared into the darkness with her

escorts, Lise turned her attention back to the crates of supplies that had also arrived from London. There was no time for relief, no moment to relax, to think of Claude flying away. Her mind was already spinning with the next steps, the next decisions. She couldn't afford to falter, not even for a second.

The chill of the night wrapped around her, seeping into her bones, but Lise pushed it aside. There would be time for warmth, for rest, for everything else—later. Now, there was only the mission, and the endless struggle to keep the resistance alive.

The crates were heavy, packed with much-needed arms and equipment. Lise's team worked in silence, the only sounds the crunch of boots on frozen grass and the fading hum of the departing Lysanders.

As Monsieur Gâteau, Frère Jean, and Doctor Marc Giraud secured the last of the crates in a nearby barn, Lise glanced up at the sky, now empty and silent. The planes had vanished, leaving behind their precious cargo.

Despite the biting cold, a warmth spread through her. Moments like these, despite the risks, made it all worth it.

"That's the last of them," Monsieur Giraud said, brushing hay from his hands as he joined her. "Everything's tucked away."

"Good," Lise replied with gratitude. "We've done it so fast, we're getting good at this."

"True," the doctor grinned.

Inside the barn, the team immediately began hiding the crates in the hayloft. Lise climbed the ladder first, the moonlight filtering through the wooden slats, casting a diffuse glow over the hay-covered floor. The scent of hay filled her nostrils, comforting and grounding.

As each crate was hauled up and concealed beneath layers of hay, Lise pried one open with her switchblade. The lid creaked, revealing revolvers, ammunition, detonators, forged food coupons, 'sauf conduit' permits, and French-labelled clothes. Stacks of money completed the haul.

Lise handed out the items, giving quick instructions. "Take these to the designated safe houses. Stay cautious—no unnecessary risks. We'll leave the rest of the crates here for later use."

Monsieur Gâteau nodded, his face serious as he took his share and prepared to leave.

"We'll be careful, Irène. See you on Wednesday night."

Lise still organized her Wednesday dinners at the Boulevard Solférino. Nowadays they'd turned into fully-fledged meetings.

One by one, her team slipped into the night, leaving Lise alone in the barn. She let out a slow breath, letting the events of the evening pass through her mind.

Sitting down in the hay, exhaustion tugged at her. She needed to rest for a bit. The barn was quiet now, the wind outside the only sound breaking the silence.

Lise leaned back into the hay and gave into the heaviness of her body. As it didn't make sense to risk heading back to town before curfew lifted, the thought of staying here, warm and dry, until it was safe again gave her a strange sense of calm.

The success of the operation was a victory, but the dangers never fully receded. She thought of Claude, now flying over the English Channel, and the new agents who'd joined their cause.

With her Colt ready by her side, Lise let herself drift away into a light, restless sleep, ready to face whatever challenges the dawn would bring.

30

THE BLIND DROP

Five days later, Dissay-sous-Courcillon, Sarthe Region, 22 March 1943

Another cold night's air clung to Lise like a wet jacket as she crouched in the small hut deep in the woods, her breath barely visible in the dim light of the waning gibbous moon. Another night, another drop.

But lately, a nagging thought had been creeping into her mind—was she pushing her network too far? The flurry of drops, the constant activity, the relentless demand for more agents, more supplies... it all felt like a ticking time bomb. How long before something slipped through the cracks?

Tonight, she had volunteered to assist the agent codenamed Max, head of the BUTLER network, with a large-scale drop north of Poitiers. It was supposed to be routine, but the stakes felt higher with each passing mission. The pressure was mounting, and the delicate balance she'd maintained for so long was starting to fray at the edges.

Claire and Sophie Rimbaud had insisted on joining her tonight, despite her reservations. Lise had tried to dissuade them, particularly because this was a *'parachute à l'aveugle'*—a blind drop where anything could go wrong. But the mother and daughter were as stubborn as they were brave, refusing to take no for an answer.

Now, as they sat on either side of her, their faces pale and tense in the darkness, Lise felt a twinge of unease. Was she right to bring them along? Could she still protect everyone in her care, or were the risks becoming too great?

A sudden gust of wind made the wooden planks of the hut creak, the sound jarring against the silence that was already straining Lise's nerves. They were so deep in the countryside that only the sounds of nature surrounded them, yet Lise's thoughts were consumed by the quiet. She prayed for the familiar drone of the plane engine, for the all-clear owl hoot from Max, anything to break the oppressive quiet.

"We should start hearing something now," Lise whispered, glancing at her watch. The midnight drop was meticulously scheduled, and any delay could spell disaster.

"You know what you're doing, and so does your contact man," Claire whispered back, her voice laced with the kind of certainty Lise envied. "It'll work out."

Lise wished she could share Claire's confidence, but a gnawing doubt lingered in the pit of her stomach. Something about Gilbert, who had also arranged this drop, continued to unsettle her. His restlessness, the almost-manic energy he exuded, made her wary. She couldn't shake the feeling that she was missing something crucial, that there was more to him than met the eye.

But there was no time to dwell on it now. The supplies were desperately needed, and the air movements officer was her best chance to secure them.

Lise pushed her doubts aside. The night was still young, and they had a mission to complete. But as the seconds ticked by, she couldn't help but wonder—how much longer before the delicate threads of her network began to unravel?

Finally, the faint thrum of an approaching aircraft broke the natural sounds around them. Lise listened intently as the sound grew louder. She would recognize that engine anywhere—a Westland Lysander, the same type of aircraft that had brought her to France many moons ago and taken her brother back to England just days ago. Maybe it was even the same one.

Moments later, the plane dipped low over the trees like a giant-winged bird. There were no light signals this time, just the moon and the open space. The pilot would have to guess the precise moment to order the dispatcher to release the cargo.

Before Lise could blink, the Lysander was already ascending again, disappearing over the treetops into the moonlit sky. The soft thud of crates hitting the ground followed, accompanied by the rustle of partisans waiting to move in and retrieve them.

Lise, there to lend a hand with the blind drop, waited for the signal. But when the owl-hoot didn't echo through the woods, a knot of dread tightened in her chest. "Something's wrong," she whispered.

Springing to her feet, she motioned to Claire and Sophie. "Stay behind me," Lise instructed, drawing her Colt as she moved stealthily toward the clearing.

A cry of pain, followed by a string of curse words in English, shattered the silence. Lise's heart sank as she rushed toward the commotion.

One of the agents had landed awkwardly, injuring his ankle. His face was contorted in pain as he struggled to keep silent, fully aware of the danger they all faced. Lise quickly assessed the situation, her training kicking in.

"Carry him away," she ordered one of the partisans. "Get help at the nearest farm. Quickly, but carefully."

"My ankle's broken," the agent groaned. "Damned dark!"

"Hush. And for Heaven's sake, speak French!" Lise silenced him. "You'll get us all arrested. You will be taken care of. Just keep quiet."

As they carried the injured agent away, another agent stumbled toward Lise, panic etched on his face.

"I've lost my wireless set and my suitcase!" he exclaimed. "The parachutes must have drifted off, or they're still on the plane. I need them—I'm useless without them!"

"You're Léopold, right?" Lise asked calmly, recognizing the Mauritian agent by his red hair and wiry frame.

"Yes, ma'am. I didn't expect to arrive like this. I need a torch to find my gear."

"No torch, under any circumstances," Lise said firmly. Using her field name, she added, "I'm Odile. Now let's get out of here."

"But...," Léopold began to protest.

Lise cursed silently, wondering why Max couldn't handle his agents, but he was busy directing the others. She knew she had to take control.

"We can't stay here to search," she said, her voice leaving no room for argument. "The Germans could be on our trail already. We need to move now. We'll order a new set, and you can borrow clothes until then. But first, safety."

The devastated agent nodded, finally grasping the gravity of the situation. "Thank you, Odile," he mumbled, his earlier panic subsiding in the face of her calm authority.

Together, they slipped into the cover of the trees, joining the others as they retreated toward the safety of the farm.

Claire and Sophie moved swiftly and silently, each carrying a crate to the barn where they hid the new load behind another haystack. All across France, haystacks like these were being filled with revolvers and ammunition, silently supporting the resistance.

Just as they were about to break open the crates and inspect the contents, the barn door creaked open. Gilbert entered, his expression strained. He handed Lise a letter, the paper crinkling slightly in her gloved hand.

"F-Int sent this for you," he said quietly. "A letter from your family."

F-Int was Vera's Atkins codename. And Vera had kept her word, ensuring her agents received word from their families whenever possible, despite the risks.

A surge of emotion washed over Lise as she recognized the familiar handwriting—Jean, her eldest brother, stationed in North Africa. She tucked the letter into her coat pocket, happiness spreading through her body. In this long, cold war, this was a rare drop of personal warmth.

But the moment was shattered by the sudden sweep of searchlights cutting through the darkness outside. Harsh beams danced across the fields, inching closer to the barn and shining through the cracks in the planks. Her heart raced, adrenaline surging through her veins.

"Germans," she hissed, her voice barely above a whisper. "They're coming this way."

With swift precision, Lise broke open the first crate she could reach, handing a rifle to Claire and another to Sophie. She flipped her own Colt out of her coat pocket, noting Gilbert doing the same.

The cold metal in her hand reminded her of her training. This wasn't a drill—this was real. She glanced at her fellow agent, who seemed oddly composed, almost detached. He caught her eye and gave a small nod, his expression unreadable. There was no time to ponder his aloofness or the arrival of the Germans now—they needed to act.

"We only fire if we have to," Lise whispered to Claire and Sophie.

The searchlights drew nearer, the sound of boots crunching on gravel reaching their ears. Tension filled the air, every muscle in Lise's body coiled like a spring. The barn offered little cover; they would have to move quickly if discovered.

The patrol stopped just outside the barn, their voices muffled, but sharp enough to send a shiver down Lise's spine. She held her breath, praying they would move on. But instead, the barn door swung open, and a German officer stepped inside, his flashlight piercing the darkness.

"*Wer ist hier?*" he barked, his voice commanding.

Lise's mind cleared. She calculated everything. Two of them. Young. Hesitant. It was just a patrol. They couldn't see them. *Make. Not. A. Sound.*

Time seemed to stand still.

As the officer's flashlight swept the barn, they remained as still as statues behind the hay bales, their breaths shallow and silent. The German patrol muttered among themselves, their voices resounding in the serenity of the night.

"*Ich habe ein Flugzeug gehört,*" one of them grumbled. He'd heard the Lysander.

"*Ruhe!*" the other one snapped, impatient. "We'll have another look in daylight."

For what felt like an eternity, Lise and her group waited, each second stretching into infinity. The officer's flashlight lingered on the hay bales for a moment longer before he finally stepped back.

"Let's move on," he ordered, and the other patrol reluctantly obeyed, their footsteps disappearing over the frosty ground.

Lise and her team remained motionless until the sound of their boots faded completely into the distance, followed by the engine of a car starting and disappearing into the night. Only then did Lise allow herself to let out an audible breath, the tension slowly ebbing from her body.

"*Je Vous salue Marie,*" Claire whispered, her voice trembling with relief. Hail Mary!

Gilbert looked at Lise, a faint smile on his lips. "We did it, Odile. We're safe for now." She nodded, still on edge but grateful for the narrow escape. "Let's get these crates stored away at a safer place before they come back."

They worked quickly, moving the crates to the hayloft to ensure they were well-concealed, though still reeling from the close call with the Germans. Gilbert, meanwhile, wandered off—God knew where.

As dawn approached and the world remained hushed, the three women slipped out of the barn and walked to the station to return to Poitiers. The immediate danger had passed, and they could only hope the German patrol wouldn't find any traces in daylight. And that landing spot was no longer safe.

Lise made a vow to herself: she would not attend another drop near Poitiers. She would not jeopardize her safety any further—or that of two virtuous French women—again.

31

UNEASY ALLIANCES

The next day - Poitiers, 23 March 1943

A rare moment of calm settled over Lise as she approached her apartment on the Boulevard Solférino. The nerve-wracking events of the previous night still rolled through her body, the adrenaline only slowly draining from her system. She was back in Poitiers, safe—at least for now—and not languishing in a German cell.

The near-arrest during the drop for the BUTLER network had shaken her to the core. The operation had veered too close to disaster, and she couldn't stop thinking about how easily things could have gone terribly wrong.

The fact that the commotion hadn't been near her own drop grounds was a small mercy, but it did little to soothe her frayed nerves. The thought of Claire and Sophie nearly being captured gnawed at her, a cold weight in her chest. She had promised herself that she would never put them—or herself—in such jeopardy again.

"Never again," she vowed, firmly closing the front door behind her.

The apartment was still and quiet, the silence wrapping around her like a familiar blanket. She flicked on the lamp in the sitting room, welcoming its soft peaceful glow.

Though spring was trying to take hold, the morning was dull and gray, a reflection of the exhaustion she felt deep in her bones. Her eyes were heavy after the sleepless night, but the thought of her brother's letter waiting for her offered a small comfort—a light in the darkness.

Her limbs ached from the cold and strain of the night spent in the open air. She knelt before the fireplace, striking a match to light a small fire. The coals crackled softly as the flames took hold, their warmth meager but welcome against the chill that had settled into her body.

Coals were scarce these days, and she couldn't afford the luxury of a roaring fire, no matter how much she longed for it. What she wouldn't give for a hot bath, the tub filled to the brim, the warmth enveloping her weary frame. But that was a distant dream.

Pulling her chair close to the stove, her fingers trembled slightly as she drew Jean's letter from her pocket, the envelope worn and soft from being handled so many times en route to her. The paper felt precious in her hands, as if it were made of something more than mere pulp and ink. Carefully, she unfolded it, each crease a reminder of how far it had traveled to reach her.

The words blurred before her eyes, fatigue pulling at her, but she forced herself to focus. Jean's familiar handwriting brought a wave of emotions almost too strong for her small frame—relief, love, and a deep longing for the simplicity of the past.

She hadn't realized just how much she missed her brother until that moment, with his words finally in front of her. It was like a lifeline, connecting her to the family she'd left behind, to the world outside of this war-torn existence.

The small fire took root in the hearth, thawing her chilled limbs. Lise could almost let herself relax, to believe that for just a moment, she was far from the danger and fear that stalked her every move.

The world outside felt distant, muffled by the walls around her, the roof over her head, creating a small sanctuary in the middle of her stormy life.

Cairo, 20 December 1942

Ma chère sœur,

Merry Christmas! I hope this letter finds you safe and well. Life here in North Africa is challenging, but we are holding our ground. The enemy is relentless, but so are we. And I'm grateful to be on leave in Cairo for Christmas.

Knowing that you, too, are contributing to the war effort in your unique and courageous way is a constant source of inspiration for me. And of course, our 'baby' brother, doing his bit as well. Maman and Papa can be proud of us.

Here the skies are filled with the roar of plane engines, night and day. Whereas where you are, I hope the nights are quieter. Our battles are different, but our goals are the same.

Please take care of yourself, Lise! The thought of you facing danger weighs heavily on my heart. Remember, no matter where we are, we are united by our determination and love for our country. Stay strong, ma chère sœur.

With all my love,

Ton frère dévoué.

A tear slipped down Lise's cheek as she read Jean's words. Christmas felt like a lifetime ago. His letter had traveled so far, for so long, yet it had reached her when she needed it most. It was more than just words on a page—it was a lifeline, arriving at the exact moment when her spirit had begun to falter. Jean's letter was a reminder that she was not alone, that the De Baissac family was united in their fight against tyranny, even if separated by continents and battles.

Clutching the letter to her chest, she felt a warmth spread through her, a warmth that no fire could provide. It was a warmth that came from knowing that her family was with her in spirit, that their shared love for each other and their country was what fueled their courage.

The dangers she faced daily, the close calls, the relentless fear— none of it mattered in this moment. Jean's words had brought her back to herself, reminding her of why she fought, and for whom.

The letter was a risk, she knew that. It bore her real name and details about Jean, her RAF brother stationed in North Africa. But the thought of destroying it never crossed her mind. This letter was her anchor, something to hold onto in the chaos of war. She would cherish it until this wretched conflict was over, no matter the danger.

"Thank you, Vera," she murmured, her voice thick with emotion. Vera Atkins had kept her promise. She'd said she would look after her female agents, and she'd proved true to her word.

Lise could almost see Vera's stern face before her, those sharp, intelligent eyes that seldom softened with a smile, but always glimmered with determination. Vera Atkins, their steadfast London spymistress, Buck's right hand, and the rock upon which so many of them leaned.

"When I can, I'll make sure you're not alone." Those were Vera's words, and in these brief, quiet moments, Lise felt that she wasn't. The strength she drew from Jean's letter and Vera's silent support was enough to carry her through the darkest days.

Her hands still trembled slightly as she set the letter down, her exhaustion from the night's events finally catching up with her. Her body ached, and she could feel the creeping chill of what might become the flu. She needed rest—desperately. She stood, intending to crawl into bed and steal a few precious hours of sleep before facing whatever the day would bring.

But just as she turned, a sharp knock at the door jolted her out of her reverie, snapping her back to the reality of her war-torn life. The brief respite was over, and the war had come knocking once again.

Lise froze, the cup of tea almost slipping from her grasp. Her heart pounded against her ribcage as she hastily shoved Jean's letter under the couch cushion. Scolding herself for her carelessness, she realized she hadn't closed the curtains—an oversight that left the light visible from outside. If only she had, she could have pretended not to be home. The vulnerable creature she felt herself becoming was so unlike her usual composed self. She must truly be under the weather.

Another knock, more insistent this time. She glanced at her watch. Nine o'clock.

"Coming!" she called, forcing steadiness into her voice. *"Un moment, s'il vous plaît!"*

Opening the door just a crack, she peered out into the gray morning. To her chagrin, it was Grabowski. His stern face betrayed no emotion, but his presence was an unwelcome shock. She fought to keep her displeasure from showing.

"Madame Brisse." His tone was polite but unyielding. "I hope I'm not disturbing you at an inconvenient time. May I come in?"

Despite the anxiety that created a knot in her stomach, she maintained a calm façade. "Of course, Herr Grabowski. Please, come in."

As he stepped inside, the cold from the corridor seeped into the house, following him like a shadow. In the sitting room, she gestured toward an armchair by the coffee table. "Please, sit. Would you care for a cup of tea?"

"That would be appreciated," he replied, removing his high cap and black leather gloves with deliberate precision. His boots creaked as he sat down, their noise unnervingly loud in the otherwise quiet room. So far, their interactions had been confined to his office—this visit to her home was an extra reason for concern. She could feel his hawk-like eyes scanning the room, noting every detail.

Lise busied herself with the teapot, trying to come up with conversational tracks to divert him, but the words stagnated in her brain, tangled in exhaustion and wariness. She was too tired for this charade, and the question of what the Gestapo leader wanted at this hour greatly unsettled her.

Drawing strength from the knowledge she'd successfully navigated encounters with him before, she managed a warm enough smile as she handed him his tea, her hands steady despite the storm inside her. He took a sip, his expression unreadable.

"I apologize for the early visit, Madame, but there are a few matters I wish to discuss with you." He paused, and she nodded, still smiling, though her thoughts screamed for him to get to the point so she could strategize.

"I've noticed your frequent travels and interactions with various locals. As you know, we're always on the lookout for any unusual activities."

A surge of panic shot through Lise like a poisonous narrow. *Oh no! He's seen me going out at night!*

With supernatural force she kept her face neutral, her voice even. "Of course, Herr Grabowski. I assure you, my interests are purely academic and personal."

He leaned back slightly, studying her with an intensity that made her skin prickle. "I have no reason to doubt you, Madame. But perhaps you could enlighten me about your recent activities. Any new findings in your research on Eleanor of Aquitaine?"

As he spoke, she felt the weight of his scrutiny, every word a test. *But he knows nothing. Nothing!*

Yet the look in his eyes and this sudden visit, they gnawed at her, and her mind went into overdrive. Changes had to be made—to the network, to her security, to every connection she had. Grabowski might be playing the innocent, but his instincts were sniffing out something.

WELL, so are mine!

"OH YES," she chirped, keeping her tone light. "I've recently been delving into Eleanor's influence on the Crusades and the cultural exchanges between France and the Middle East. Fascinating work, though it requires quite a bit of travel to various historical sites. And occasionally to the archives in Paris."

Grabowski seemed to perk up, his expression growing more animated. "Indeed, history is a rich tapestry. It's important to understand our past to shape our future."

Lise resisted the urge to roll her eyes. *Not that line again*, she thought. *Can you not have one original thought in your head, man?*

But she sipped her tea keeping her face straight and hoping the caffeine would steady her nerves. "Exactly. And that's what drives my research. Understanding the past also gives us insight into the present."

Now I sound like a tired record player myself, she mused, but then another thought struck her. *Maybe Grabowski isn't as clever as he wants me to believe?* The idea was intriguing—and dangerous. She'd have to probe carefully, without arousing his suspicion.

Their conversation continued, each word a careful dance. Despite her exhaustion and the ever-present chill in the room, Lise maintained her composure. She had to—any slip could herald disaster. Her brother's letter was still tucked under the cushion, a dangerous secret she could ill afford to expose.

Suddenly, Grabowski shifted in his seat, his expression softening into an almost boyish expression. "You know, Madame, given our regular encounters, perhaps we should dispense with formalities. Would you be willing to call me Friedrich?"

Lise blinked, taken aback by the suggestion. For a moment, the room seemed to close in around her. *So that's it*, she realized. *The man's just lonely*. A wave of revulsion and pity churned her stomach. *Heaven forbid, he thinks he can make a pass at me!* She forced another smile. What else could she do? "Thank you, Friedrich. And you may call me Irène."

A smile spread under his mustache, almost puppy-like in its eagerness. "Very well, Irène."

Finally, after what felt like an eternity, Friedrich finished his tea and stood. "Thank you for your time, Irène. I appreciate your cooperation." His eyes roved over the room once more, lingering on the thick curtains that hid the garden and the garden shed, as if he was searching for some hidden meaning behind them.

"Of course, Friedrich," she replied, standing as well. "If there's anything else you need, please don't hesitate to ask."

He nodded, sliding on his cap and gloves with deliberate care. "I will. Have a good day, Irène."

As the door closed behind him, Lise let out a breath she hadn't realized she was holding. The tension in her body slowly ebbed away, replaced by a bone-deep weariness. *Remain on high alert*, she reminded herself. *This man cannot be trusted.*

She retrieved Jean's letter from under the cushion and held it against her chest, her heart heavy with the burden of war. "Oh Jean," she whispered, "war is complicated. I have to ward off a Nazi, not knowing if he seeks my friendship or my arrest."

Tears welled in her eyes as she pressed a kiss to the letter before tossing it into the fire. The flames quickly consumed it, the edges curling and blackening. Grabowski was too close on her heels to keep it. But the words, Jean's words, would stay with her, a secret she would cherish in her heart.

SHE CRAWLED INTO BED, her exhaustion pulling her into a restless sleep. The fight was far from over, but for now, she could rest. For a bit. Later, she would repeat Jean's words in her head and heart. Later, she would prepare for the next challenge that awaited her. Grabowski.

32

URGENT WARNINGS

Three and a half months later - Poitiers, Early July 1943

The summer sun hung high in the sky, bathing Madame de Vigny's garden in a golden light. Lise knelt in the soft earth, her hands encased in worn garden gloves she had found in the shed, gently tending to the vibrant life growing under her care. She'd never imagined she would find solace in gardening.

Back in Mauritius and here in France, her parents had always employed gardeners; shrubbery and flowerbeds had never been of much interest to her. Yet now, with a rake, a trowel, and secateurs beside her, the act of nurturing plants had become a rare moment of peaceful activity amidst the turmoil of her resistance life.

The soil felt cool and comforting through the gloves as she worked, carefully trimming the petunias and tending to the tea roses. Their fragrant blooms filled the air, perfect and unblemished, so contrary to the world beyond this small, walled sanctuary.

Lise paused to wipe the sweat from her brow, her gaze lingering on the bees that buzzed contentedly around the buddleia and sweet peas. It was as if this corner of the world was untouched by the chaos that reigned beyond it—a place where life still thrived, despite the shackles of war.

She wasn't particularly religious, but in these moments, it felt as if a graceful hand guided the growth of these plants, allowing nature to flourish even as humanity tore itself apart. The colors were vivid, almost defiant in their beauty, and for a fleeting moment, Lise allowed herself to smile. But behind that smile, her thoughts were anything but serene.

As she continued to carefully tend to the flowers, the weight of her responsibilities as the leader of the ARTIST network pressed down on her. The news from the field was growing increasingly dire, no matter how much the Firm tried to gloss over it. More agents, more materials, were being dropped into France with every passing week, but the cost was becoming unbearable.

Lise knew better than to be lulled into a false sense of security by the summer blooms around her. Across France, SOE networks and Maquis groups were being infiltrated. Agents were disappearing, captured by the Gestapo, their fates sealed in interrogation rooms. The resistance was being squeezed, the Gestapo's grip tightening with every day.

And the news that had reached her most recently had shaken her to her core: Claude's SCIENTIST network was under severe threat, and Prosper's PHYSICIAN network in Paris was hanging by a thread.

Lise's heart ached with the knowledge that everything they'd worked for was in danger of unraveling. The garden might offer a temporary respite, but it couldn't shield her from the reality that the world she'd fought to protect was crumbling. She had to act, and soon. The safety of her comrades, her brother, and the future of the French Resistance depended on it.

As she stood, brushing the dirt from her gloves, the peaceful illusion of the garden slipped away, replaced by the urgency of decisions to be made. The sun might be shining brightly, the flowers blooming, the insects buzzing, but Lise knew grim darkness loomed on the horizon.

More bad news cast shadows over Lise's thoughts. Suzanne, the serious and experienced agent who'd welcomed Lise and Denise into France back in September '42, had been arrested in June, along with Adolphe from her reception team and two Canadian agents.

Around the same time, PHYSICIAN's organizer, Prosper, and one of his couriers, Denise, had vanished in Paris—likely taken by the Gestapo. The arrests were spreading like wildfire across France, capturing not only British agents but also the French resisters they had so carefully recruited. The walls were closing in, and a sense of doom tightened around Lise like an iron grip.

Her thoughts spiraled with concern, particularly for her brother, who'd worked closely with Prosper in Paris. The summer warmth did little to ease the chill that settled deep in Lise's heart. She tried to remain vigilant and calculating, but the arrests and disappearances gnawed at her: Was her own network still intact? For now, it appeared so, and she silently praised her decision to stay independent and away from the big cities. But for how long?

The prospect of being called back to England for safety reasons loomed over her like a dark cloud. The thought of abandoning her helpers—the people who risked everything for the cause—was almost unbearable.

The ARTIST network was just gaining momentum, and leaving now felt like a betrayal. But with the situation deteriorating, was it worth the risk to stay? Could she justify putting her team in even greater danger by remaining? The reality of the situation pressed down on her, forcing her to confront the possibility that she might have to leave them behind to protect the network as a whole.

Suddenly, the sound of hurried footsteps snapped her out of her thoughts. She looked up to see Claire rushing up the garden path, her face pale and strained.

"Irène!" Claire tried to keep her voice low, mindful of the Gestapo Headquarters next door, but panic tinged her words. "Renard and Doctor Giraud have been arrested! Grabowski's men took them this morning."

Lise's hands trembled as she dropped the pruning shears. The news struck her like a blow to the chest. "Oh no," she whispered, breathing with difficulty. "Do you know where they've been taken?"

Claire reached her, breathless and flustered. "I think they're next door, but people are saying they'll be moved to Fresnes prison. What do we do, Irène? What if they come for Sophie and me next?"

Lise steadied her breathing, forcing herself to stay calm. She rose and grabbed Claire by the shoulders. "Listen to me. Keep Sophie close. Don't let her out of your sight. Warn as many Partisans as you can but do it quietly. Tell them to cease all illegal activities immediately and wait for my instructions. We need to lay low until we understand the full extent of this breach."

Claire nodded, tears welling in her eyes. "And you?"

Though Claire was a trusted friend, she still didn't know that Irène was actually a British secret agent, not just a French resistance leader. Lise couldn't tell her that she needed to go to Bordeaux to contact her brother and inform the Firm about the collapsing SOE networks in France.

"I'll get help. Don't worry. I'll be back as soon as I can. Just lay low. Do you promise?" Her voice was firm, though the thought of traveling under Grabowski's watchful eyes made her uneasy.

"Just be careful, Irène. We can't lose you too," Claire said, gripping Lise's hand tightly.

"I'll be back before you know it. Hopefully tomorrow. Keep Sophie safe." Lise hugged her friend briefly before rushing inside to gather her things.

She packed quickly, her movements precise and practiced, her heart pounding with the urgency of the situation. There was no room for mistakes. Lives depended on her accuracy.

As Lise hurried down Boulevard Solférino towards the station, her overnight bag in hand and her Colt tucked in her belt, she remained the vigilant agent, but she felt as if falling apart. Time, the thing she needed most right now, was running out.

The boulevard was bustling with people going about their daily lives, but to Lise, every face seemed a potential threat, every shadow a lurking Gestapo agent ready to pounce. She kept her pace brisk, her senses heightened, every instinct on high alert.

As she turned a corner, her breath caught in her throat—she nearly collided with the last person she wanted to see. Herr Grabowski stood before her, his stern face an immovable mask of suspicion. His hawk-like eyes locked onto hers, probing for any sign of deceit.

"Well, well, Irène Brisse," he greeted, his tone deceptively polite but ice-cold beneath the surface. "In a hurry, I see. May I ask where you are headed?"

Lise's heart skipped a beat, a spike of fear shooting through her. She forced a smile, thinking hard for a plausible excuse. "Good afternoon, Herr Grabowski... uh... Friedrich. Yes, I'm on my way to visit a sick friend in Bordeaux. She's in desperate need of some company."

Grabowski's eyes narrowed, his gaze like a knife slicing through her words. "Is that so? It seems I've been seeing you around quite frequently with Monsieur Renard and Doctor Giraud. Your hurry doesn't involve them? I trust your intentions remain... purely personal?"

Lise's pulse quickened, but she kept her voice steady, her expression innocent. "Monsieur Renard and Doctor Giraud? I know them, of course, but what do they have to do with my need to see a friend, Friedrich?"

"They are despicable traitors to the Reich!" Grabowski spat, his voice suddenly venomous. "They've been arrested."

Lise let out a gasp, raising a hand to her mouth in feigned horror. "Oh no! I never would have guessed. They were simply assisting me with my research. That's all I knew of them."

Grabowski studied her, his gaze sharp and unyielding, the silence between them thick with tension. Lise could feel her heart pounding like a rhythmic hammer in her chest, the seconds stretching into eternity.

"I'll see what I can get out of them," Grabowski said slowly, his voice laced with menace. "I have my methods."

For a moment, Lise feared she might faint under his scrutiny, but then, to her astonishment, his expression softened.

"I believe you, Irène," he said, his tone almost gentle now. "But do be careful. These are dangerous times, and one never knows who to trust."

Lise's smile never left her face, though inside she felt her heart shatter for what awaited her friends. "Thank you for your concern, Friedrich. I will be cautious."

He stepped aside, allowing her to pass. "Safe travels, Irène. I look forward to our next conversation—perhaps about something lighter."

NEVER AGAIN, *you vile, wicked man!* she screamed inside her head.

BUT SHE NODDED and hurried on, her legs trembling with the effort to keep moving. She didn't dare look back until she reached the station. The encounter had shaken her to the core, but she couldn't afford to let it slow her down. She boarded the train just as it was about to depart, her heart still hammering in her chest.

Sinking into the seat, she closed her eyes for a brief moment, allowing herself a small measure of relief. She had made it. Escaped Grabowski's claws—for now.

But she knew the real battle was just beginning. Warning London was foremost on her mind, protecting what was left of her network and the other SOE networks.

It would be a race against the clock.

33

FINAL DEPARTURES

Six weeks later - Poitiers, 15 August 1943

T he summer heat bore down relentlessly on Poitiers as Lise paced her lavish apartment. She would leave today, abandoning the place that had been both her refuge and her headquarters for nearly a year. The weight of her decision pressed on her shoulders—leaving her friends and the remnants of her network behind. She had no idea when or if she would return to rebuild what was left of the ARTIST network.

Looking for a place that wasn't too obvious to the eye, Lise carefully hid most of her French money behind a row of books in Madame de Vigny's bookcase.

If I can't return, she thought, *Henri Gâteau can distribute it among my helpers.* The thought of leaving behind Claire, Sophie, Henri, and Marguerite Gâteau, as well as Señor Martinez, made her heart ache. And then there were Renard and Dr. Giraud, both arrested weeks ago—no word had come of their fate.

Irène Brisse would disappear from Poitiers like a thief in the night, with one thought foremost in her mind: evading the likes of Friedrich Grabowski during her escape.

Grabbing Irène Brisse's suitcase, Lise took one long, final look around the apartment before slipping out through the back door. She left the key under the doormat, as if she were simply stepping out for an afternoon stroll, rather than fleeing for her life.

She moved swiftly through the back alleys, wrapped in shadows, making her way to the station to catch the late-night train to Bordeaux. The recent news from there had been devastating—one of Claude's main locations had been raided by the Germans, leading to a wave of arrests that tore the SCIENTIST network to shreds. The call from London had been clear: return 'tout de suite.'

Upon arriving in Bordeaux without too much trouble, the scene Lise found at the safe house was far from the cold efficiency she'd expected. Claudine, usually cheerful and composed, was on the verge of breaking down in the back room, her typical warmth replaced by a barely controlled panic. Lise embraced her, bracing herself for the worst.

"What's wrong, Claudine?" Lise asked, pushing her own panic down.

"Nothing," Claudine cried, "go see David, he'll tell you."

With even more concern, Lise let Claudine slip from her arms but tried to inspect her face, which she kept hidden in her hands.

Oh no! It can't be true! Lise thought, *we have enough trouble as it is.*

Claudine, nearing forty, had confided in her months earlier she wanted a child with Claude, and he'd agreed. It had sounded clinical at the time—downright foolish, Lise had thought. How could anyone consider bringing a child into this world, especially when both parents were being hunted by the Gestapo?

But this wasn't the time to judge, and neither Claudine nor Claude had mentioned anything about a pregnancy so far. Lise swallowed her words and focused on calming the situation.

Claude stood by the window, his posture rigid, but when he turned to face Lise, she saw something in his eyes that she had never seen before: helplessness.

"David, what's going on?" she asked, her voice full of concern and urgency. "Why is Claudine in such a state? She is coming with us to London, right?"

Claude's jaw tightened. "No Odile, I've made my decision. Claudine is staying here with Roger Landes. He's a W/T operator, so there will be access to comms, and he is reliable—he'll protect her."

Lise was taken aback. Claude, always so strict with protocol, yet here he was, slipping a real name into their conversation. Something was very wrong.

"Do you mean Aristide?" She tried not to contradict him.

"Yes," Claude snapped, "that's what I just told you."

"But Claudine may be more vulnerable than you think," Lise said cautiously, choosing her words carefully. "What if she's expecting? Leaving her behind could be too dangerous."

Claude's eyes widened briefly before his expression hardened again. "Odile, that's precisely why she needs to stay. Aristide will keep her safe. And I'll be back in no time—just a quick debrief in London, and I'll return to Bordeaux on the next full moon."

Lise disagreed silently, almost certain that Claude wouldn't be able to return to Bordeaux as long as the war continued. But his determination was unshakable. "If she has to stay behind, then make sure she's well-protected. We won't forgive ourselves if anything happens to her."

Claude nodded, letting out a ragged breath. "I promise. But we need to leave now, Odile. The longer we stay, the more at risk we are."

The door creaked open, and Claudine entered, her face pale but resolute. "David, Odile... I understand why you both have to go. And

I've decided I won't fight staying. I'll be with Aristide and continue doing my part here. Come back to me soon."

"If you need a safe place, contact Henri Gâteau in Poitiers and ask to rent Madame de Vigny's apartment. Tell him Irène Brisse sent you," Lise offered.

Claudine smiled faintly. "Thank you, Odile. But you'll be back soon, won't you?"

"I will," Lise promised, though uncertainty consumed her. "Please be careful, Claudine."

Claude embraced Claudine, whispering something Lise couldn't hear. When he pulled away, the moment of tenderness passed, and he was all business again.

"Gilbert has arranged our Lysander pick-up," he said, his voice clipped. "But stay alert. I don't fully trust him."

"Neither do I," Lise replied, "but he's our best option for now."

As they prepared to leave, word came via Aristide's wireless set —Lise's ARTIST network had collapsed. The news was a blow, but it was softened by the knowledge that Claire and Sophie had been able to get away. At least for now. A small cell in Ruffec remained intact, a glimmer of hope in the encroaching darkness.

The journey to the landing field was fraught with tension and drawbacks. German patrols, a flat tire, an endless funeral hearse they couldn't pass. When they finally arrived, the field was bathed in moonlight, eerily silent except for the distant hum of the approaching Lysander.

Gilbert was there, his face smooth and unreadable as always. "Everything is ready," he said, his eyes flicking between Lise and Claude. "You'll be in London by dawn."

Lise felt a shiver of unease. Gilbert's smile was as polished as ever, but it never reached his eyes.

As they boarded the Lysander, Lise took one last look at the

French countryside, her heart heavy with sorrow and regret. But she promised herself that this wasn't the end—it was a new beginning.

Claude squeezed her hand. "We'll come back, Agent Odile. Stronger."

His words were exactly what she needed to hear. "Yes, we will, Agent David."

The plane's engines roared to life, and as they ascended into the night sky, Lise felt a strange mix of relief and resolve. They were leaving behind a land where danger lurked in every shadow, where a sinister game of Russian roulette played out with SOE agents. But Irène Brisse might be cast aside—Lise de Baissac was far from done with occupied France.

~SIL~

Marseille, September 2004

34

SHARING THE SECRET

Marseille, early September 2004

T he heat of what was shaping up to be an Indian summer poured down on Sil's back as she sat cross-legged on the cool floor of her Vieux Port apartment. Clad only in sports bra and denim shorts, her slim, brown legs were folded like a Buddha's, surrounded by a fan of letters and a weathered old suitcase. The room was silent except for the hum of the city outside her window, but Sil's mind was far from the bustling streets of Marseille.

She stared ahead, deep in thought, a shiver rippling through her despite the warmth. In her mind, she was no longer in her apartment but aboard a roaring Lysander, its engine cutting through the moonlit night as it sped over patchy French fields toward England.

The cool, collected Lise de Baissac was beside her, the weight of a collapsing network on her shoulders, yet holding herself together with a steely resolve that Sil both admired and felt within herself.

What is happening to me? she wondered, feeling the boundary between past and present blur. Sil, who prided herself on being a tough cookie—a graffiti artist with a fighter's spirit—was becoming more and more entwined with the upper-class secret agent, Lise, who was braver than she perhaps ever had realized.

Sil could see every detail as if she was living through it herself: the tension in Lise's posture, Claude's poorly masked helplessness, and Claudine's distorted, tear-streaked face. The images played out in her mind like scenes from a movie she couldn't turn off.

But this isn't a movie, Sil reminded herself, shaking her head as if to clear away the vivid pictures. *This was real, once upon a time. And now it's all in my head.*

She rose to her feet and stretched, trying to shake off the daze that had settled over her like a second mantle. Even as she moved, the images lingered, clinging to the edges of her consciousness. With another determined shake, like a dog flinging off water, she crossed the room and awoke her laptop, her fingers hovering over the keyboard. She needed to know if Lise had been wise enough to stay in England for the rest of the war.

Just as she was about to hit enter, a knock on the door startled her, pulling her abruptly back into the present. The knock was firm, bringing with it the reminder that this was 2004, not 1943, and she was Sil—an artist in Marseille, not a secret agent on the run.

But even as she turned toward the door, the echoes of Lise's world still hung in the air around her, merging the past and present in a way that was becoming impossible to ignore.

She opened the door, half expecting to come face-to-face with Obersturmbannführer Grabowski, ready to arrest her. Instead, she found herself staring into the sea-grey eyes of Justin. For a moment, she wanted to slam the door in his face, but his hand was already there, firmly holding it open.

"Miss Anderson?" Justin's expression shifted from what seemed like irritation to one of genuine concern as he took in her disheveled appearance. "Are you alright?"

"Of course, I'm alright," Sil replied, crossing her arms over her scarcely clothed torso, suddenly all too aware of her sports bra and shorts. "What do you want? The wall is fixed, and I transferred the money last week. Didn't you get it?"

"Yes, I got it. But that's not why I'm here."

They stood in silence, eyeing each other like two opponents on a battlefield. A strange tension hung between them, until a glimmer of amusement softened Justin's gaze behind his gold-rimmed spectacles. "The reason for my visit, Miss Anderson, is that I'd like to know more about your secret. If you have time."

"My secret?" Sil was still so wrapped up in Lise's world she couldn't immediately grasp what he was hinting at.

"A suitcase filled with letters from the former owner of this house?" Justin prompted, his voice gentle with a bit of a tease.

Sil frowned, the memory of her previous conversation with Justin surfacing slowly. She'd completely forgotten she'd mentioned the letters when he'd seen the suitcase during the repair work.

"Oh, that," she said, thinking fast. There was no denying it now —Justin knew. "Maybe another time. I really need to run for class."

"On a Sunday?" Justin arched a brow, his tone playfully skeptical.

"Heck, is it Sunday? Then I have an assignment to work on," Sil stammered, trying to salvage her excuse.

Justin broke into laughter, a rich, warm sound that filled the high hallway of his house. "Miss Anderson, you look like you've been camping in the woods for weeks, your room smells of decaying Thai food and... old letters, and you're dressed like you're ready to jump in the sea for a swim. And clearly, you haven't checked your calendar lately. May I inquire whether my tenant is in good health and spirits, or should I lend a hand?"

A small, involuntary moan escaped Sil's lips. "Stop it!" she protested, though she couldn't hide a smile. Justin was impossible—too amusing and way too accurate in his observations.

With a flourish, he brought an arm from behind his back and presented her with a delicious smelling bag. The aroma of buttery pastry and rich delights wafted into the apartment, making Sil's stomach growl.

"Would this give me entry to your domain? Breakfast, Madame?" Justin asked, a mischievous twinkle in his eye. "I know it's a bribe, but hey, I'm a French flatterer."

Sil hesitated, caught between the urge to resist and the undeniable allure of whatever delectable treat he'd brought. "What's in the bag?" she asked, trying to sound indifferent but failing as the smell made her mouth water.

"Just a little something from the local patisserie," Justin said with a grin. "A few croissants, some pain au chocolat, and a bit of quiche Lorraine. I thought you might need some proper sustenance after surviving on Asian rice."

Sil's resolve weakened. The thought of fresh French pastries, combined with Justin's playful charm, was too much to resist. She stepped aside, allowing him to enter. "Alright, but only because I'm starving," she said, trying to maintain a semblance of control.

"Of course," he replied, stepping into the apartment with a triumphant smile. "And maybe, while we enjoy this feast, you can tell me more about those letters."

Sil couldn't help but smirk as she closed the door behind him. She had a feeling he wasn't just here for the pastries—or even just for the letters. But for now, she decided to let herself enjoy the Sunday morning.

"I'll make coffee," she offered. From his coat pocket Justin retrieved a bottle of freshly pressed orange juice. "And two glasses."

◡

HALF AN HOUR LATER, they sat opposite each other on the floor, Sil almost purring like a well-fed cat now that her stomach was content with the carbohydrate-rich breakfast. The suitcase with Lise's letters lay between them, a relic of the past that had drawn them together in this unlikely way.

Sil cooled her face with a Chinese paper fan, her eyes drifting to Justin as he read, noting the way his perfectly shaped mouth set into a line of concentration. For once, he wasn't dressed in his usual formal suit. Instead, he wore white linen shorts that revealed tanned, muscled thighs dusted with dark, curly hair. A simple, navy t-shirt stretched over his well-defined torso, and on his feet were Nikes—no socks. Sil couldn't stop glancing at him through her lashes, pretending to focus on the laptop in her lap.

She'd handed him the first letter in which Lise rekindled her relationship with Henri Villameur and revealed she'd been a secret agent during the war. After finishing the letter, Justin looked up, pushing his glasses higher on the bridge of his nose.

"I can't make heads nor tails of what this is about just from this letter, but I can say that from a historical perspective, this is a... remarkable find. So, you're saying she explains the entire story of her secret agent adventures in the rest of these letters? But what about the replies? Are Henri's responses in there as well?"

"No, they aren't," Sil replied, her brow furrowing. "Maybe Lise only kept her own letters."

Justin shook his head thoughtfully. "That doesn't add up. As a history professor, I know a fair bit about the French Resistance during WWII. Even after the war, these people were cautious. They had to be. They'd done things—lynching Nazis, blowing up bridges —that weighed heavily on their conscience. And the SOE... there was a lot wrong with that organization. Most of their files were destroyed in a fire soon after the war ended. That probably wasn't a coincidence."

"What are you saying?" Sil frowned deeper. "Do you think these letters are fake? That makes no sense to me."

"They're real, alright, Silver..." Justin paused, his expression shifting slightly as if he had said something he hadn't meant to.

"Silver?" Sil looked puzzled. "How do you know my name?"

Justin chuckled dryly. "You *are* my tenant, Miss Silver Anderson. It was on your lease contract."

"No one calls me Silver," Sil mused, her tone more curious than accusatory. "Only my grandpa did. I'm Sil to everybody else."

There was a moment of silence before Justin replied, his voice quieter, more intimate. "I'm sorry. I shouldn't have used your first name without asking. It's just that I think of you as Silver, not as Miss or Mademoiselle Anderson. I love the name Silver. It suits you. You may call me Justin if you like, though my friends usually call me Jazz." His smile, warm and slightly mischievous, melted the last of Sil's defenses. As he made the offer, she realised she had been thinking of him as Justin for a bit now – no longer 'Mr. Bellamare, the landlord,' simply 'Justin.'

"I like Justin better," she said, a small smile playing on her lips. "So let that be our arrangement. I call you Justin, and you can call me Silver. Now, please explain your train of thought to me—why only Lise's letters are in here, Justin."

His expression shifted back to his professorial demeanor, though there was still a hint of playfulness in his eyes. "My train of thought is this... If Henri's replies aren't here, that can only mean one thing. This suitcase isn't Lise's. It's Henri's. He hid it here. Lise may never have known it existed."

"You're mistaken!" Sil cried triumphantly. "It's Lise's suitcase, alright. It has the initials I.B. I already figured out it must stand for Irène Brisse, which was Lise's alias during her mission in Poitiers."

Justin took a sip from his orange juice, his gaze never leaving Sil's. "I have no clue what you're talking about, but I'm almost certain this wasn't Lise's doing. Though I may not know about her war exploits yet, I'm pretty sure she was all about security. In 1947, no secret agent in his or her right mind would've written their memoirs or penned letters about their exploits to their lovers. No files were public then. Everything was hush-hush because of the political mess SOE had turned out to be during the war. The sacrifices made with their own agents to compete with De Gaulle's Free French and MI5—it was appalling. As you can read with your own eyes, Lise urgently asked Henri to destroy her letters. Well, apparently, he didn't."

Sil bristled at Justin's superior tone. "What about the initials on the suitcase?"

Justin's face softened into a wide smile, sweet and roguish, and for a moment, Sil's heart nearly stopped.

"Ah, you cold-blooded Brit, you know nothing of '*l'amour passionné d'un homme français.*' We Frenchmen adore our women..." he paused ever so slightly longer than necessary, glancing at her to make eye-contact, while finishing, "especially when they're strong and beautiful in equal measure." His eyes swept over Sil's posture, the admiration in his gaze unmistakable. "Love-struck Henri engraved those initials into the handle and kept her letters forever. Not a doubt in my mind."

Sil finished her orange juice and placed the glass on the table, suddenly at a loss. With herself, with her life, and with the discovery of the suitcase. But mostly with the conflicting emotions Justin stirred up inside her.

She wasn't a cold-blooded Brit—she was half Moroccan, and she'd done nothing but make a mess of her Marseille life so far. Her art wasn't taking off, and instead of exploring the city, she spent her days locked inside, lost in old letters when she should be making new friends.

The plan to roam the streets of Marseille, connect with fellow street artists, and immerse herself in her graduation year at the prestigious École des Beaux-Arts seemed to be slipping further out of reach. And then there was this man, Justin, confusing her even more.

"What is it, Silver?" his voice was gentle, with a tenderness she wasn't prepared for.

"I never meant for any of this to happen, Justin," Sil admitted, her voice wavering. "I wanted to make a clean break from my... uh... complicated life in Bristol. I need to focus on school. That's more important than these letters. You tell me what to do with the suitcase and its contents. They're yours anyway, I guess."

Justin's voice remained soft, but there was an understanding there that took her by surprise. "I knew something was off, Silver. You were so full of enthusiasm when you arrived in early August. Sure, you bristled at me, but I get it—I can be rigid at times. But then you hardly left your room. You became almost a recluse. The smell of stale food lingered in the hallway. I waited after the repairman had come, hoping you'd knock on my door. But when it became clear you wouldn't, I took the plunge. I'm glad I did."

"Lise's story has taken over my life ever since I found the letters," Sil confessed, her voice growing more animated. "As an artist, I see everything in pictures, and her writing is so vivid. It's like I'm binging a series, and I can't stop. But it's interfering with my own life. I don't know how to stop myself."

He listened intently, his gaze never leaving hers. "I'm sorry to hear that, Silver, but I do understand. I think I could become just as hooked on such a find, especially because I'd see all the historical context. How many more letters do you have left to read?"

Sil sifted through the ribbon-tied stacks. "Less than half," she said, her voice tinged with a mix of anticipation and dread. "When you knocked, I'd just finished reading about Lise's mission in

Poitiers. I think she went back to France again, but maybe not for as long."

"I'm asking," Justin said, his tone thoughtful, "because maybe it's best if you continue reading until you're done. Then you'll know what to do with the letters and what you've learned from Lise. You don't seem like someone who can do things halfway or stick to a rigid schedule of, say, one hour a day. You're a 'pur sang' artist, my dear. You need to dive deep—that's the artist's way, my dear."

For a moment, Sil wanted to argue. What did this Frenchman know about the artist's life? And calling her "my dear"—that was a bit much. But she had to admit, he was right. There was no stopping now, not halfway, not when she needed to know what had happened to Lise and her friends.

So, she nodded. "And you have to read them too. They're incredible."

"I'll catch up, my dear. No worries there. Let me take what you've already read, and then we can compare notes when I'm done."

"I... I didn't make notes," Sil said, pondering for a moment. "I made sketches."

"Of course you did," Justin said with a grin. "I foresee a big, bright mural coming from your journey through Lise's past."

"Now that's an idea I like," Sil grinned, adding with a wink, "I'll leave a tray of Thai takeout and Pepsi in front of your door every day. Just go read, Justin."

The heat of the summer evening pressed in on them, the sounds of the city creating a backdrop to their tentative truce. As they stood in the dim light, two worlds collided—one of brassy modernity and one of formal tradition—bound together by the legacy of a courageous woman from the past.

As Sil handed him the stacks she'd already read, their fingers brushed, sending a spark through her. "Thank you for trusting me with this, Silver," Justin said softly, his voice carrying that same tenderness.

She looked up at him, feeling like they were crossing a bridge to somewhere unknown. "Thank you for understanding me, just a little."

As he turned to leave, he paused at the door, glancing back with a thoughtful expression, as if waiting for something more.

"Maybe we're not so different after all," he said.

"Maybe not," she replied with a grin.

The door closed behind him, leaving her alone in the sunny Sunday afternoon, her mind buzzing with the possibilities of what lay ahead. Half of the letters were with Justin, half with her.

He'd forgotten his cap. Unable to resist, she put it on her rainbow curls, inhaling the scent of his Terre d'Hermès. She'd wear it until she saw him again.

~LISE~

England/France August 1943 - June 1944

35

A BRIEF RESPITE

London, 20 August 1943

The rain began to fall, first in soft droplets, then in a steady drizzle that polished the streets of London in a wet shine. In another time, another place, a black cab wound its way along Marylebone Road, taking the familiar turn onto Baker Street.

Lise gazed out the window, the gray sky reflecting her current state. London, drenched in rain and shrouded in mist, was a world away from the vibrant, hot summer in Poitiers. Yet here she was, physically safe, though beset with memories that had nowhere to go but whirl in her own head.

London streets are supposed to be wet, she thought, watching the city pass by, its glistening facades marked by the scars of war. Bomb craters and rubble told the story of a nation that had withstood Hitler's onslaught. The resilience of the British people was evident in every untouched building, every bustling street corner, but Lise found little comfort in the sights before her eyes.

For all the city's defiance, it was the colorless landscape rather than the vibrant toughness that matched her mood—gray, muted, and heavy with the weight of everything she'd had to leave behind.

Inside the cab, the radio played softly. Glenn Miller's suave, dusky voice filled the air with "Moonlight Serenade." The melody, with its gentle swing, soothing rhythm and reference to moonlight, took Lise back to the tense moments lying and waiting in moon-drenched French fields. She closed her eyes for a moment, letting the music wash over her, trying to fully realize she was safe now, but the tension in her chest didn't ease.

The memories kept coming, vivid and painfully real, nights in suspense, waiting in the dark, the moon casting spooky shadows as she and her helpers listened for the sound of approaching aircraft. The fields and forests bathed in silver light, black silhouettes moving swiftly and silently, unloading crates, escorting disoriented new agents. Ever more, ever faster.

Those nights, ticking with the clock of danger and shrouded in freezing cold – the cold ones stick in the memory far more securely than the balmy, summer evening ones - held an almost romantic sense of purpose. That moonlight, worshipped by lovebirds and poets alike, had been the Resistance's silent ally, their source of light and reinforcement.

None of that could Lise find in the damp streets of London; safe and dry in the black cab, she felt out of place. The pedestrians outside, huddled under umbrellas, went on their way, to a meal or a job. A red double-decker bus honked its horn impatiently as if the slow car in front of it was the enemy. A British soldier kissed his girl-friend on the corner, rather than moving stealthily through occupied France.

Oh London, if only you knew the price of freedom, Lise thought, pained by the people she'd had to leave behind. *You'd cherish it with all your heart.*

Despite the safety, despite the familiar sights and sounds of the city she'd once accepted as her second home, Lise knew her heart still beat most fervently in occupied France. The mission wasn't over —not for her.

As the cab slowed to a stop outside a nondescript building with a small plaque stating "Interservices Research Bureau"—a cover name for SOE Headquarters—Lise shook herself from her gloom. The rain had intensified, drumming hard on the cab's roof like a persistent reminder of the gravity of her upcoming debrief at HQ.

The driver glanced back at her in the rearview mirror, waiting for her to move. Lise gathered her handbag and suitcase, pressed a pound note into his hand, and stepped out into the rain, bracing herself against the downpour.

As she walked toward the entrance, her thoughts swirled with the realities she had faced in France. London might be where her passport said she belonged, but France owned her heart and soul. Her time in England was only a brief interlude—a chance to recuperate, to sleep without fear, to eat without glancing over her shoulder.

But even in this moment of supposed safety, her mind was already planning to return. When the debrief was done, her message to the Firm delivered, and the warnings they needed to hear were shared.

She entered 84 Baker Street no longer a fresh graduate; she was a hardened secret agent with eleven months in the field, about to face two office-bound managers—Buck and Vera—who, despite their best efforts, could never fully grasp what life in occupied France was truly like.

Their intentions were good, but their understanding was incomplete. They hadn't seen the networks collapsing, hadn't witnessed the arrests, the betrayals, the harrowing escapes. They hadn't felt the despair of knowing that one of SOE's most critical networks, PHYSICIAN, was in dire straits.

Claude had been called back just in time, but his SCIENTIST network was in tatters. Lise had seen the signs, the cracks forming long before London had reacted. She knew it was her responsibility to convey the gravity of the situation to Buck and Vera, to ensure that future agents were better prepared, better protected. But how could she communicate this without undermining their authority? How could she speak truth to those in power without offending the very same, who had sent her into the fray?

As she rang the bell, Lise's other hand brushed against the golden cigarette case in her pocket—a gift from Buck when she had boarded the outbound Lysander in September '42. She'd never used it, but bringing it today felt like a reminder, not just to herself, but also to Buck, of the stakes involved.

One moment in those cold, nerve-wracking hours under the moonlight, and you'd understand, she thought. But this was her reality, not his.

The porter let her into the building, and she set aside her outward appearance of gloom, adopting a neutral, professional expression as she stepped inside. Ascending briskly to Buck's office on the second floor, her calves strengthened by countless miles cycled through the French countryside, she became once more Lise de Baissac—the slight, dark-blonde, upper-class lady whose unassuming exterior belied the power and grit inherited from her Mauritian lineage.

Inside the office, the walls were lined with maps of France, marked with pins and annotated with hastily scribbled notes. Colonel Maurice Buckmaster and Flight Officer Vera Atkins stood waiting for her, their faces lighting up with relief as she entered.

"Lise!" Buck said warmly, stepping forward to shake her hand. "It's good to have you back. Safe and in one piece. And your brother too. Capital achievements by both of you. Chapeau!"

"Welcome home," Vera added, her usually stern face softened by a rare smile. For a brief moment, Lise thought Vera might embrace her, but the woman held back, opting instead for a handshake and a firm grip on her shoulder.

"Thank you, both," Lise replied, fighting to keep her emotions in check as she faced the two people who had sent her on her mission. "It's good to be back, though I would've preferred to stay."

Buck gestured to a chair. "Please, sit. We have a lot to discuss, but let's take a moment first. How are you feeling?"

Lise settled into the chair, letting out a small sigh. "Relieved, mostly. It's a different world here. People laugh, there's music... It's almost like a different war."

Vera's gaze was steady, thoughtful. "It's true. We're insulated from the worst of it here. But we do our best to understand and support the efforts in the field."

Lise nodded, her mind already calculating how she could convey her concerns. She'd seen too much, known too many who'd been taken prisoner. She couldn't let this moment pass without speaking up, without trying to prevent more lives from being lost. But she had to do it carefully, with respect for the chain of command, and with the hope that her words would make a difference.

The atmosphere remained casual at first, allowing Lise to acclimatize to her surroundings. The conversation drifted over the usual wartime topics—the weather, the latest news, the challenges of rationing—giving her a moment of respite.

But even as she sipped the real English tea Vera had poured, Lise knew these pleasantries wouldn't last long. Soon, they would delve into the critical matters that had brought her back to London.

Buck leaned forward in his chair, his expression one of genuine interest. "What was it like, Lise? Day to day?"

She paused to make sure she chose her words carefully. "Exhausting. Boring. Lonely. You're always on edge, always watching, listening. Every sound, every person could be a threat. It's not something you can easily describe. You have to keep people you like at a distance because they don't know who you really are. Protect your alias at all costs—it becomes second nature. Personally, I found the hardest part not the threat, but the loneliness. Without one's friends, one's family. Especially after something tough has happened. You have to process it all on your own. That's hard. An almost inhuman way to exist."

She hesitated before adding, with a touch of her usual optimism, "But, we've made good progress. I think we're at a tipping point in France. The defeat in 1940 crushed the country, and many chose to collaborate to survive. Now, with hardship and hunger everywhere, especially in the big cities, and the Nazis atrocities against the Jews and resisters, the mood is shifting. Germany's losses in Russia and North Africa are making even the staunchest collaborators rethink their positions. Not all of them, of course, but I've witnessed a greater dissatisfaction with Germany pressing France like a lemon with less and less juice."

"Are you saying the French are more likely to resist the German occupation?" Buck asked.

"Don't take my word on it, but I think so, yes," Lise nodded. "However, we need more trained people, more money, more arms to keep the momentum going. And, most importantly, we need better security."

She reached into her handbag and pulled out a neatly folded list, placing it in front of Buck. "I've noted down some observations and recommendations. There's been a lot of sloppiness—agents getting too casual, especially in bars and cafés. For example, they need to stay away from too much liquor. I've heard drunk agents slip back into English—an instant death sentence if overheard by the wrong person.

"And we can't afford to ignore security checks with our W/T operators. If an operator omits a security check, don't assume it's just forgetfulness. They might be trying to signal something's wrong.

These operators are the lifeblood between London and the field, and they're under immense pressure. Any deviation from protocol needs immediate attention."

Lise could feel the heat rising to her cheeks as she spoke, her passion for the subject clear. Buck and Vera listened intently, she being the only person who spoke as Buck's eyes scanned her list, while Vera took meticulous notes.

"You're absolutely right," Buck said after a moment, his tone serious. "We can't afford to be careless. The pressure on our agents, especially the W/T operators, is tremendous. Your insights are invaluable, Lise. We'll make sure they're implemented."

Vera nodded in agreement, her pen still moving swiftly across the notepad. "You've raised some critical points, Lise. The safety of our agents in the field is paramount, and we can't overlook any detail, no matter how small."

LISE HESITATED, debating whether to bring up her next concern. But her instincts told her it was too important to ignore. "There's something else… I've worked closely with Agent Gilbert, and I can't shake the feeling something's not quite right. He's efficient, resourceful, but… there's an air about him that makes me uneasy. I know it's not my place to question his loyalty, but I think it's worth taking a closer look at his credentials."

And after a brief pause, she added, "I know it may be stepping out of place, but I discussed it on the plane back with my brother. Please ask Claude's opinion on Gilbert as well."

Buck's black brows knitted together, his fingers drumming on the table. "Agent Gilbert? He's been reliable so far, but we can't afford to take any chances. I'll have his file reviewed. If necessary, we'll call him back for questioning."

Vera's expression was thoughtful as she exchanged a glance with Buck. "Thank you for bringing it to our attention."

Lise felt a sense of relief that she'd voiced her suspicions. It wasn't easy to throw mistrust on a fellow agent, certainly when he'd arranged a safe conduit back for her and Claude, but she knew her gut feeling was too strong to ignore. Yet it was a gut feeling, not based on evidence.

Buck leaned back in his chair, clearly wanting to change the topic. "You may be praising our W/T operators and organisers like Prosper and your brother, Lise, but I personally think you're the best agent we've had so far. How would you feel about using your knowledge while on leave and joining our instructor team? We need someone with your experience to train the new batches of agents, especially the women."

Lise's heart leaped at the suggestion. Hadn't she dreamed of this before? And now, here was the offer.

At first, her sole focus had been on returning to the field, but the idea of training new agents, of ensuring they were as prepared as she'd become, held a great appeal. If she could save even one life through her instructions, this part of her mission could be just as important as her work in the field.

"I'd love to," Lise beamed, conviction in her voice.

"Welcome to the team, Captain Lise de Baissac," Vera said, her smile wide as it had never been. "We're darn lucky to have you."

"Captain?" Lise gasped.

"Yes, Captain de Baissac."

36

A LEAP INTO THE UNKNOWN

Eighteen weeks later - Ringway, England, early January 1944

The past few months had swept by in a whirlwind of lectures, training sessions, and relentless drills. For Captain Lise de Baissac, now back in England for over four months, life had taken on a different rhythm—one defined by the steady march of time and the constant urgency to prepare others for the dangerous missions she knew all too well.

Despite her longing to return to France, she'd become an indispensable instructor for the SOE, pouring her wealth of experience into the next generation of agents.

Each week, she traveled between training centers in England and Scotland, sharing the hard-earned lessons from her time in the field. She taught security measures with a fierce intensity, knowing firsthand the price of carelessness.

She drilled them on shooting, the feel of a weapon becoming an extension of their hand. She emphasized the subtle art of blending into French society, where a single misstep could mean the difference between life and death.

But perhaps one of the most critical skills Lise imparted was the assembly and disassembly of the British weapons that were being dropped into France. Many of the French resisters, brave as they were, had never handled a firearm before.

The crates dropped by Lysanders and parachutes contained not only rifles and pistols, but also the weighty responsibility to arm a population that had little experience with such weapons. It was up to Lise and her fellow instructors to ensure that these new agents could teach the resisters how to use them effectively—and safely.

In her training sessions, Lise would demonstrate how to take apart a rifle, clean it, and reassemble it with precision. She insisted her trainees practice until they could do it blindfolded, knowing that in the field, they might not always have the luxury of light or time.

The clatter of metal on wood, the clicking of pieces snapping into place, became a familiar soundtrack in the training halls. Every move was practiced, rehearsed, and perfected—because out there, in occupied France, there were no dress rehearsals.

Her students were a mix of seasoned soldiers and civilians, all united by a burning desire to fight back against the Nazi occupation. Their faces reflected a range of emotions—determination, fear, excitement—as they absorbed Lise's every word, knowing that the skills they honed here could soon be tested in the most unforgiving of environments.

Some were bound for mainland Europe, others for North Africa, and now, with the war stretching its reach, some were even trained for the Far East, where the U.S. battled relentlessly against the Japanese.

Amidst the dozens of trainees, two young women had caught Lise's particular attention: Yvonne Baseden, codenamed Odette, and

Violette Szabo, codenamed Louise. It was an instructor's privilege to know their real names.

Yvonne, with her calm, composed demeanor, exuded a quiet strength that impressed Lise. There was something reassuring about Yvonne's steady gaze, her ability to remain level-headed under pressure. She showed a natural aptitude for coding, making her an ideal candidate for a W/T operator—a role that carried immense responsibility and even greater risk.

Lise knew that in the current climate, with the Gestapo's detection systems growing ever more sophisticated, a W/T operator's chances of survival were slim—six weeks at best. This knowledge drove Lise to instill every ounce of security training into Yvonne, hoping against hope that it might extend her time in the field.

Violette, on the other hand, was a different story. There was no denying her courage and skill—she was as capable as any agent Lise had trained. But Violette's vivacity, her natural glamour, and extroverted nature set her apart in a way that worried Lise.

In occupied France, blending into the background was as vital as carrying a weapon. The ability to become invisible, to move unnoticed through crowds. Lise feared Violette's vibrant personality, which shone so brightly here, might draw too much attention where it was least wanted.

As Lise watched them train, she felt she was training the best of the best, but her feelings constantly oscillated between pride and dread. These women so full of youthful life and promise were about to step into a world so dark and so ugly, while knowing the odds they faced, their fate weighed heavily on her heart.

Every night, as Lise lay in her barracks, the faces of her students haunted her dreams. The question of whether she was preparing them well enough nagged at her, even as she tried to convince herself she was doing all she could. She'd already seen that believing in certainties was foolish in occupied France.

But there was no turning back. Not for Lise, not for Yvonne, not for Violette, and not for all the others, the only way forward was the leap into the unknown—and hope that their training, their skills, and shedloads of luck would see them through.

ON A BITTER JANUARY morning at RAF Ringway near Manchester, Lise found herself standing in for the parachute instructor who was down with the flu. She was tasked with preparing Yvonne and Violette for their final jump.

Outside the hangar, the wind howled like a wild beast, tugging at their clothes and slashing at their faces with icy rain. The sky was an ominous, slate gray, heavy with the promise of a worsening storm.

Lise and the two women, burdened by the weight of their gear and parachutes, trudged through the pelting rain toward the waiting Douglas Dakota. The wind whipped relentlessly around them, and the freezing rain stung their cheeks, soaked through their clothes despite the waterproof gear. The plane's interior, though dry, was filled with the sharp smells of oil and metal, a small reprieve from the storm outside.

As always Lise enjoyed the familiar hum of the engines vibrating through the floor, the power that would soon propel them into the sky. Normally, she relished the thrill of the jump—the freedom, the acceleration, the exhilarating weightlessness as she plunged through the air. But today, the storm outside made her hesitate – was it even wise to jump today?

As the Dakota's engines roared to life, the dispatcher approached Lise, a frown on his weathered face. "Sight's very bad, Ma'am," he shouted over the noise, "and the wind's picking up fast. It's not ideal... not by a long shot, but we should be okay if you really want to do it today." His tone was anything but reassuring.

Lise hesitated, her instincts screaming this was a bad idea. The wind outside wasn't just strong—it was vicious, tearing across the landscape with the fury of a storm that had no intention of letting up. Learning to trust her gut feelings had been a hard-earned skill during her time in France, but she also knew the importance of this final jump. Yvonne and Violette needed this, as they were slated to go into the field soon.

It wasn't her call to cancel the jump, but doubt made the ride into the air feel giddy. Was it worth the risk?

She forced herself to push the thoughts aside, giving the dispatcher a thumbs up despite her misgivings. Turning to Yvonne and Violette, she yelled over the growing roar of the engines, "You know the drill! Check your equipment before you jump. Yvonne, you go first, then Violette. I'll jump last."

After taxiing down the runway and lifting into the air, the Dakota was buffeted by strong gusts, shaking as it fought against the wind. The sound of the engines now almost drowned out Lise's voice as she barked out the final instructions. "1. Chin on chest, 2. Back rounded, 3. Hands on risers, elbows forward, 4. Feet and knees together, 5. Knees slightly bent, 6. Turn off at a 45-degree angle, 7. Present the balls of your feet to the ground, 8. Go into a roll, and 9. Spill your chute by running around it or by pulling in two or three of the lines closest to the ground."

She forced a grin despite the tension in her stomach. "Make me proud!"

Yvonne gave a determined nod, her face set with steely resolve. Violette flashed a quick smile, her excitement shining through despite the storm. Lise felt a sharp pang of worry—Violette's enthusiasm, usually a strength, seemed almost reckless in this weather. But they couldn't turn back now.

The dispatcher slid open the side door of the Dakota, and a violent gust of wind blasted into the cabin, filling it with the deafening roar of the storm. Lise watched as Yvonne, her movements precise, jumped into the swirling gray below. For a moment, her figure was visible against the clouds, then she was swallowed by the storm.

Violette hesitated for the briefest second, the force of the wind pulling at her as if trying to drag her back into the plane. Then, with a flash of gusto, she leapt into the abyss. Lise watched as Violette disappeared into the storm as well, uncertain of both women's fates.

Now it was her turn. Lise steadied herself, took a deep breath, and jumped into the void. The wind yanked at her as she plunged through the sky, her focus narrowing to the task at hand—landing safely, ensuring her trainees did the same.

The descent was rapid and disorienting. Lise fought to control her parachute, steering herself toward the designated landing zone. Just as the ground rushed up to meet her, a violent gust of wind caught her parachute, spinning her off course. She tried to correct, but there was no time.

She hit the ground hard, a sharp pain exploding up her leg. The snap in her calf was unmistakable. Lise gasped, suppressing a cry of pain. For a moment, she lay still, the cold earth beneath her seeping into her bones as the reality of her injury set in. Every slight motion sent waves of agony through her body.

Her first thought was for Yvonne and Violette. *Dear God, let them have landed safely.* Gritting her teeth, Lise forced herself to sit up and examine her leg. The break was evident, the pain searing. *It's broken,* she thought grimly. *Definitely broken.*

Reaching for her emergency whistle, she blew three short bursts —the signal for help. Within minutes, the airfield official and two medics were at her side.

"Easy now," one of the medics said as they carefully lifted her onto a stretcher. "That leg is broken. We'll need to get you to a hospital."

Through the haze of pain, Lise managed a weak, "What about Yvonne and Violette?"

Just then, she saw their faces, pale and tense, emerging from the mist. Both were walking on two legs, unharmed.

"Lise, what happened?" Yvonne cried out, crouching by her side.

"Looks like I'll need some time off my feet," she quipped, trying to lighten the mood. Violette's wide eyes were filled with disbelief. "You missed the landing? How is that possible? You're such a pro."

"Not always, I'm afraid," Lise smiled faintly, "but I'm glad you're both in one piece."

The airfield official gave her a nod of respect. "You did well considering the weather, Captain de Baissac. They'll get you patched up in no time."

As they carried her toward the waiting ambulance, Lise's thoughts drifted to the past few months. Despite the injury and the throbbing pain, a sense of pride filled her. She'd trained capable agents, imparted her knowledge, and continued the fight in her own way. She knew she would return to France, but for now, she had to heal and prepare for whatever came next.

I'll be back in two full moons, ma douce France, she promised herself as the ambulance doors closed behind her.

37

SHE LANDED BY MOONLIGHT

Four months later – Flight path from England to France, 9 April,
1944

The familiar drum of the Lysander's engines resonated through the air as Lise sat in the cockpit beside Night Operations Officer Hugh Verity. It was her first time meeting the Special Duties Squadron Pilot for SOE, but she'd heard much about his 20-something record of dropping off Joes and Janes all over France.

There was always a mutual reverence and retained secrecy between the RAF pilots and the SOE agents—those who flew and those who jumped. But it was a known fact among the agents. If Verity flew you, you had a good chance of touching French soil safely.

As the Lysander he'd nicknamed 'Jiminy Cricket' climbed steadily into the night sky, Lise's thoughts drifted back to her first mission - the excitement and naiveté that had colored her journey into the heart of occupied France.

But that was in September 1942. Now, in April 1944, everything had changed. She was no longer the fresh agent eager to set up her own network, brimming with optimism. The past year and a half had hardened her, given her a clearer understanding of the stakes. She knew now that survival in this war was far from guaranteed, and the odds of making it through another mission were slimmer than ever.

As if sensing the weight of her thoughts, Hugh Verity glanced over his shoulder at her on the hard bench behind him, his youthful features catching the dim glow of the cockpit's instruments. "A penny for your thoughts, Jane," he shouted over the roar of the engine, using the generic codename that would soon be put aside for her specific codename once she landed.

Lise managed a small smile. "Just thinking about how different it all feels this time. The excitement has given way to something more... deliberate."

Verity said thoughtfully. "It's the same for us up here. The more you fly, the more you realize how much there is to lose. And how many fine pilots we've already lost."

"Yet here we are," Lise's voice held a hint of wryness. "Still doing what we do."

"That's the thing about this war," he observed. "It doesn't let you stop, even when you know better. The stakes only get higher, and so does our will to see it through."

Lise appreciated the sentiment. It resonated with her own resolve. "Thank you, Captain. I needed to hear that."

"Anytime, Jane," he said before shifting back to the focused pilot as they reached cruising altitude. "Now let's make sure you get back down in La France in one piece."

Lise turned her attention back to the dark landscape below, the familiar outline of the French coastline drawing nearer. Her heart ached for her beloved, adopted country. Both Britain and France were the countries she fought for, but this time returning was more resolve than adventure, colored by her profound awareness of the dangers ahead.

The war had intensified, and the Gestapo held the Resistance in a stranglehold. Networks had been compromised, agents captured or killed. Lise knew she couldn't set up her own network as she had before; that would be far too dangerous now.

Instead, she would join an existing network in the South—PIMENTO—though she still harbored doubts about working under someone else's command, especially in such perilous times.

The Firm had assured her, though, that PIMENTO's organiser, Alphonse, was as scrupulous with safety measures as Lise always was and that being the courier for this important, long-running network would be the best use of her qualities.

Deep in thought, Lise's mind drifted to her brother Claude, who was already back in France, this time in Normandy. They had both chosen this path, understanding the risks, but the thought of losing him—or of him losing her—was now much more real.

And then there was her friend Agent Claudine, who had stayed behind first in Bordeaux, then in Poitiers, and was now the mother to Claude's daughter.

The last message that had reached London via Agent Aristide was that Claudine had given birth in December 1943 and was heading for relative safety in Poitiers. as Lise had advised her.

Poitiers—where it had all begun for Lise. The thought of returning there filled her with pain and longing. Not being able to visit Claudine, who was family in some manner now, and inspect the remnants of the ARTIST network was one of the hardest decisions Lise had had to make. But returning to Poitiers was a risk not worth taking.

Lise reached into her coat pocket and touched the golden cigarette case Buck had given her before her first mission. It was a symbol of her connection to London, to the people who sent her into the field.

They'd made mistakes—she knew that now—but it wasn't entirely their fault. No one could have foreseen the full extent of the dangers, the treachery within their own ranks. But Lise had learned. She'd seen networks collapse, witnessed the arrests of her friends, and understood the devastating impact of small oversights. This time, she was determined to be even more cautious, to survive—not just for herself, but for the mission, for France.

She could never let her guard down. Ever. She had developed new security measures, ones she would implement rigorously. Always. She couldn't afford to trust anyone—agent or otherwise—especially now the rumors around Agent Gilbert had intensified. No one. She would tread carefully, watch her every move, question every detail. Her survival depended on it. Everywhere.

Verity glanced at her again. "Nervous?"

"Excited," she corrected, though there was an edge to her voice. "And a bit apprehensive. It's been a while, and my leg…" She trailed off, flexing her calf slightly, the memory of her broken leg still fresh.

"You'll do fine," he reassured her. "You've faced far worse."

"Probably," Lise admitted. Not completely sure.

"Well, we're almost there. I'm going to drop you off not far from Poitiers, where I understand your first mission was?"

Lise uttered a wry laugh. "Yes, but I don't think it would be wise to show my face there right now. I'd run straight into the clutches of Obersturmbannführer Grabowski, the Head of the Poitiers Gestapo. He apparently put a price on my head, that is on that of the widow Irène Brisse, though he tried to charm me with his quizzical personality when I first arrived there. Gosh, I hated the man but had to sit and drink tea with him and chat about the Crusades when I was on a crusade of sorts myself. Well, so was he, and this time he's going to lose."

"As I said, the things we do in this war..." Verity laughed with her before Lise became more serious again.

"I'll have a hard time passing by Poitiers though," she disclosed, her voice softer now. "I'm aching to know how my friends and the remnants of the network are doing. It's been very tough leaving them behind."

In particular, Lise thought of Claudine, who might be staying in Madame de Vigny's apartment in Poitiers. But she shook herself mentally. She had to stay sharp. Focus!

"You ready?" Verity's voice pulled her away from another lapse in concentration.

"Always," she replied, her voice steady despite the flutter of nerves.

The Lysander descended, skimming over the treetops before landing smoothly in a secluded field. The moonlight bathed the area in a ghostly glow, and Lise could make out the quick flashes of flashlights. For a moment, the drone of the Lysander's heavy engines became lower-pitched. Lise took a deep breath; this was it. Death or glory.

"Good folk," Verity stated, though he drew his pistol nonetheless. Lise did the same while she grabbed her suitcase with her other hand. She was now Madame Janette Bouville, another widow and with codename Marguerite.

As the plane came to a halt, Verity turned to her, flashing her his youthful smile. "Good luck, Jane. It was an honor to fly you. Make sure I can pick you up hunky-dory after you've slain the Huns."

"Thank you, Captain, I will. And thanks for the lift." She squeezed his hand briefly before making her way to the exit.

"I've got your back, Joan of Arc," he called after her.

The engines roared again, and Hugh Verity waved his long arm one last time, the pistol glinting in the moonlight. Lise took a moment to orient herself in the sudden dark that surrounded her.

Two agents emerged from the dark to take her place on the way back to England. In the shadows Lise was surprised to see one familiar face. Jacqueline, her fellow trainee, way back at Beaulieu in July 1942. The two female agents, one arriving, one leaving the field, waved and smiled at each other before Jacqueline boarded the place and the Lysander rose back up in the air.

The April night air was fresh and cool, carrying the faint scent of wood violets, cowslips and freshly ploughed soil. The chirping of crickets and the rustle of leaves in the wind told Lise she was deep in French countryside, far away from all urban sounds. This was the domain of nature, the heartbeat of rural France, and Lise felt an immediate connection to it—her soil, her land, her fight.

Moving swiftly toward the reception team at the edge of the woods, intense emotions swept through her: relief at having arrived safely, her feet touching French territory once again, and a familiar tightness in her throat as she realized the dangers ahead.

She was back where she belonged, in the thick of it, where the fight was real and the goal crystal clear. This was no longer about survival alone—it was about finishing what she had started.

She stepped out of her British shadow and embraced her French soul, the language tumbling through her mind like a welcome friend, filling her with a sense of belonging. Another De Baissac was back in France.

She observed the two figures emerging from the shadowy trees. Barely visible in the dim moonlight, their silhouettes blended in with the surrounding darkness. But she saw them alright and approached them with caution, her Colt ready at her side.

The figure who stepped forward was likely Agent Shaw, the one responsible for organizing most of the reception committees in central France these days. His face was stern, his eyes vigilant.

The other man, who remained in the shadows, had to be Agent Hector, the organizer of the STATIONER network.

"*Le vent souffle fort ce soir.*" Shaw's voice was low but clear, his tone clipped and businesslike. (The wind is strong tonight.)

"*Mais les étoiles brillent encore,*" Lise replied, meeting his gaze steadily. (But the stars still shine brightly.)

He seemed satisfied with the response. "*Bienvenue en France, Marguerite.*"

The words were polite but reserved. Lise noted the change from the early days of the war—gone was the bravado, the camaraderie that had once marked these clandestine meetings. Now, it was all about efficiency and survival. There was no time for pleasantries or the pretense of an "old boys' club" on an adventurous mission. Each agent was focused solely on doing the work and staying alive.

Lise followed them into the dark without a word, then hesitated for one second, checking herself—was she too ready to accept these men at face value? What if this was a German trap and she was being naive? But she quickly dismissed the thought.

These were the same men in the photos Vera had shown her. The passphrase had been correct. The curt, business-like reception wasn't a red flag—it was the new reality of this war. The casual camaraderie was gone, replaced by a cold, professional detachment. Words and actions were now measured with precision.

"We'll show you to your safe house for the night," Shaw informed her as soon as they were well into the woods.

"Thank you," Lise answered her tone as brisk and to the point as his. "I'll be heading for Montauban first thing in the morning. How do I get to the station?"

"You'll be picked up at 10:00am, sharp." It was the first time Hector joined in.

"Good to know." And that was all that was exchanged.

The two agents led her to a small farmhouse, secluded and seemingly abandoned. Inside, it was sparsely furnished, with only the bare essentials—also a reminder of the stripped-down, utilitarian nature of their current missions. Like the chill of the reception, such a contrast to Verity's heartwarming adieu, the safehouse only performed its function and nothing else. But Lise understood. This was the reality of the war now.

After a curt 'goodbye,' her escorts disappeared into the night again. Lise set her suitcase down by the bed, a simple cot with a thin mattress and even thinner woolen blanket. Exhausted, she lay down fully clothed, her money still strapped to her body and her weapon within arm's reach

Despite her tiredness, she couldn't catch sleep. Her mind kept nagging her with questions of the coming days. What awaited her in Montauban and Toulouse? Would she be able to work effectively with her still-healing leg? And what was the exact state of the PIMENTO network? Would the reception in Toulouse be as cold as tonight?

She forced herself to calm down and relax while she listened to the sounds of the forest filtering through the thin walls of the farmhouse.

I am in France. Tomorrow, I will go to work again.

38

UNWELCOME AND UNCERTAIN

The next morning – Montauban-Toulouse, April 10, 1944

The train ride from Ville les Ormes to Montauban was grueling, with three changes and frustratingly long stops along the way. At each halt, German soldiers stormed the compartments, their eyes cold and calculating as they demanded papers.

Lise, disguised as Madame Janette Bouville, handed over her documents with a steady hand, though her heart raced each time they scrutinized her identity. The passengers around her endured the repeated inspections with apathy, though Lise could sense their simmering irritation.

She glanced around the compartment, noting the fatigue on the faces of her fellow travelers. The rhythmic clattering of the train wheels should have been a welcome distraction, but it did little to soothe her frayed nerves.

Everything about this second mission felt different, more dangerous. She felt as if her strength was being sapped with every passing mile, and each clink of the train wheels chipped away another little bit of her sense of control over the situation.

Stay alert, stay sharp, she reminded herself, instinctively adjusting the strap of her handbag where her forged documents were stored.

Her thoughts drifted back to her new organizer, codenamed Alphonse. Vera had assured her that Alphonse was exceptional— the best of the best. At just 22, he was the youngest and longest-serving SOE agent in France, having been there since 1941.

I hope I can work with him, Lise thought, a flicker of doubt crossing her mind. She'd been warned about Alphonse's fervent socialist ideas and unorthodox methods, both of which clashed with her own values.

His insistence on recruiting only French railway personnel and factory workers, coupled with his pioneering use of abrasive grease guns to disable German railway wagons, had made him a controversial, though generally admired, figure within the SOE.

Can I be pliable enough? she wondered, not entirely confident in the answer.

The atmosphere in France had also shifted in the eight months she'd been away. The air was taut with tension, the mood grim and violent. German patrols were more aggressive, harassing people with a cruel sense of entitlement. Lise observed this firsthand as the train stopped at yet another station.

A pair of SS officers sauntered over to an elderly farmer's wife sitting across from Lise. They sneered as they toppled her basket, sending eggs and apples crashing to the floor. The woman gasped, her hands trembling as she tried to salvage what she could from the mess. Tears welled up in her eyes, the ruined produce likely her family's only source of income for the week lay smashed and bruised on the floor.

"*Warum weinst du, alte Frau?*" one of the officers taunted, his grin widening as he kicked a stray apple down the aisle. Why are you crying, old woman?

Lise bit back her anger, her fingers tightening around the spine of Stendhal's 'Le Rouge et Le Noir.' She lowered her gaze, pretending to be absorbed in the novel, though the words on the page blurred into meaningless lines. Madame Bouville, her carefully constructed alias, remained outwardly composed, but Lise seethed with indignation.

Cowards, she thought, clenching her jaw. *They only show their strength by tormenting the weak.*

The officer swaggered away, laughing with his companion, leaving the elderly woman to gather the remains of her goods. Lise desperately wanted to help, to offer some small comfort, but she knew any move could draw unwanted attention. She forced herself to stay still, to remain unseen, even as her heart ached for the injustice she couldn't alleviate.

This is what France has become, she realized with a heavy heart. *A place where cruelty goes unchecked, where the strong prey on the vulnerable.*

But it was also a place that needed her. A place where she could make a difference, even if it was just in small, invisible ways. Lise lifted her gaze from the book, waited until the Germans had disappeared before whispering under her breath to the woman across from her, "nous gagnerons." We will win.

It was all she had to offer. She would fight for those who couldn't fight back.

The countryside whizzed past in a blur of green and brown, the rolling hills and scattered farms looking eerily peaceful in a land ravished by brutal war. Montauban, a town built mainly of red brick, stood on the right bank of the river Tarn, the second eldest of Southern French bastides. But Lise wasn't here for the sightseeing.

She stepped off the train and took a deep breath. *Gosh, that was a tense trip!* She had almost forgotten what it was like to move with all her senses on high alert, missing nothing.

The familiar scent of fresh baked baguettes from a nearby bakery momentarily grounded her. She stopped to buy 'une baguette' and, sitting on a bench overlooking the river, gave herself a moment of respite.

Checking her watch, she quickly made her way to the designated meeting spot, arriving at 4 p.m. sharp, as instructed. The agent, codenamed Michel, was already there, with an attitude that was cold and unwelcoming. Lise braced herself. This was not what she had signed up for on her second mission in France—being cold-shouldered and her abilities disregarded.

Michel eyed her with suspicion from under bushy eyebrows, a burning Gitane dangling from the corner of his mouth. As she approached, he didn't offer his hand but delivered the prearranged password with a hint of reluctance in his cigarette-hoarse voice.

"*Le vent souffle fort ce matin.*" (The wind is strong this morning.)

"*Mais le soleil brille encore.*" (But the sun still shines). Lise offered a smile, hoping to break the ice. But the PIMENTO agent's expression remained stony.

"No one is expecting *you*," he stated flatly. "You're not the person we need."

Lise felt her temper flare. *So, this is that socialist attitude the PIMENTO network was known for,* she thought, frustration bubbling beneath her calm exterior. "What do you mean, no one is expecting me? London sent me here. And you came to meet me. What nonsense is this? Orders are orders."

Michel merely shrugged at her bristling, biting through his teeth, "Alphonse will be here soon. He can deal with you." He turned on his heel and walked off, whistling a tune that sounded very much like La Marseillaise—though a variation subtle enough that the Germans wouldn't pick up on it.

When Alphonse finally arrived after Lise had waited for hours, she was relieved to see the PIMENTO organizer was a completely different person from his second-in-command. Though only 22, Alphonse appeared every bit the seasoned, no-nonsense leader - someone who shared Lise's insistence on security and hard work. No gallivanting or unnecessary risks for this young organizer.

He greeted Lise warmly, a friendly smile under a small mustache on a smooth yet tired face. "Sorry I'm a bit late. Hope you had a safe arrival?" His tone was worlds apart from Michel's icy reception, and Lise's hopes lifted as she shook his hand.

"Let's head for Toulouse straight away. Can I carry your suitcase for you, Marguerite?"

"I'll be alright. Thank you, Alphonse."

"We'll go straight to 'Chez Gaston' where you can meet the rest of my team, or would you prefer to see your digs first?"

Digs, Lise mused inwardly. *That's very lower class.* But she smiled brightly, "Let's get to work, Alphonse."

During the short train journey from Montauban to Toulouse, Lise had no opportunity to ask the burning questions on her mind. But as soon as they sat in the noisy café, she fired away.

"Before I start working with you, I'd like to know why you don't communicate directly with London but instead via a contact in Switzerland?"

Brooks' lips still smiled, but his eyes hardened. "I don't see why I should explain the workings of my circuit to a newcomer, if you don't mind me saying so, Marguerite. However, since London assured me you were the right person for the job, let me explain." His tone was clipped, his words deliberate. "I take security very seriously. I even rent a place in Lyon that no one—do you hear me, no one—knows the address of. That's how I've survived."

His eyes bore into hers. "And I don't care what London orders or doesn't order from hundreds of miles away, safely ensconced in their posh, plush HQ. I don't intend to be skinned by any German." He paused, scanning their surroundings before continuing.

"Most of our SOE W/T operators are already on the radar of the German Radio Defense Corps or, worse, captured and forced to communicate with London as if still operational. I'm not taking that risk." He emptied his coffee and jammed the cup on the saucer with finality.

"That, my dear Marguerite, is why I choose to have my messages sent via a safe contact in neutral Switzerland. It may take longer to reach the Firm, and they can grumble all they want; I also may last longer this way. Satisfied?"

Lise felt a surge of frustration. *This is that socialist attitude I abhor,* she thought, but she could also see his absolute dedication to the job. There was still one other thing that gnawed at her.

"And what about your preference for working only with working class people? That's something else I've heard."

Alphonse studied her for a moment, then grimaced. "I could've seen this one coming. Because I'm from the upper classes like you, you assume we have the same outlook on life. Well, you're wrong, Madame. I work with the working classes because I believe in them. Yes, I am a socialist. Like it or not. I'm not one of those organizers who spends lavishly and still thinks I'm sitting in the benches at Oxford. This war will be won by the people, not by the ruling classes."

His voice grew sharper. "For heaven's sake, I sent Urbain away because he came here dressed like an Englishman, greeted me in English, and was smoking a pipe of aromatic tobacco unavailable in France."

Lise swallowed, biting back a retort. She knew exactly who he was talking about. She agreed with the PIMENTO organiser about not tolerating sloppy security, but why did he do everything in such a grim, restrictive way?

Before she could respond, more people joined their table, their expressions guarded and cold. The mood was set and Lise was met with more expressionless and hostile faces. It was as if they dismissed her achievements, as if she, Lise de Baissac, hadn't slept in haylofts and cycled grueling 70-mile treks to deliver a message.

I have never used my background to demand any privilege in this war, she raged silently, but the words remained unspoken.

AFTER THEIR TENSE INTRODUCTORY CONVERSATION, two days passed without any proper instructions and no further sight of Alphonse or anyone from his team. Lise became increasingly angry and frustrated. She hadn't returned to France to dilly-dally around Toulouse, feeling like a pawn in someone else's game.

Was Alphonse punishing her for being upper-class? The thought made her unhappy, but she dismissed it as beyond ridiculous. Still, the nagging suspicion lingered.

Finally, on the third day, he appeared out of nowhere, like a jack-in-the-box, and told her they were heading to Chambéry.

"I want you to meet Julien," he said, his tone brisk and matter-of-fact. "He's another leader within PIMENTO. I'll just drop you off, and he'll take it from there. I've got to run."

"Wait," Lise said, grabbing him by the sleeve before he could dash away. "I'm really frustrated. I'm not getting any jobs and feel useless this way. That's not a mood I handle well. I'm here to work. London told me I was to oversee the Lyon branch of PIMENTO. This tossing me around is a far cry from doing anything, let alone leading."

"I know, Marguerite. Julien will see to it you get a proper job. Trust me." And with that, he was gone, disappearing around the corner before she could protest further.

Lise was left waiting alone another long morning, growing increasingly tense as the hours dragged on and Julien never showed up.

By the end of the day, her patience snapped. This is absurd. She returned to Montauban and sought out Alphonse, demanding a private tête-à-tête. When she found him, she didn't hold back.

"If you don't tell me what I'm supposed to do here, I'm out," she said, her voice firm and laced with anger. "This vague runaround is unacceptable. And you, as the organizer, can't just leave me in the hands of other people. I was sent here to lead, not to be shuffled around like a parcel."

Alphonse sighed, looking weary and slightly defeated. "Julien has his methods. He's really the one you should talk to. I'm sorry he couldn't make it. We work in groups. Your role is to make rounds of the groups each week, collecting papers for Julien to send on."

Lise's frustration boiled over, her voice rising. "A postman? You brought me here to be a postman? That's not what I signed up for. I'm a seasoned agent, not an errand runner."

Alphonse seemed taken aback by her intensity. He stared at her for a moment, perhaps realizing for the first time just how mismatched their expectations were. "I understand your frustration, but this is the way our network operates. You can start in eight days with a rendezvous in Toulouse."

Wait another eight days? Was he crazy? The thought made her stomach churn. Lise could feel her control slipping away, the careful plans she'd made were rapidly unravelling after way too much waiting around. She had always been adaptable, but this...this was too much.

Without another word, she stomped out of the room, her resolve hardening with every step. *I'm going to Paris to seek help. I don't want to work for this wretched network*, she seethed internally, her decision final.

Grabbing her suitcase, she practically ran to the station, the sense of urgency driving her forward. She couldn't stay here, not like this. It was time to take matters back into her own hands, to find a mission that matched her skills and her dedication.

As she boarded the train, Lise felt completely confused. Was she doing the right thing, or should she try to talk it over with Alphonse one more time? But no, she had to let London know PIMENTO was not for her.

39

FRACTURED BENEATH A PARIS SKY

T he journey to Paris was a test of endurance and nerves. Lise found herself standing in the crowded corridor, pressed between strangers whose eyes darted anxiously as the train rattled on. Every few hours, stern-faced German soldiers swept through the cars, demanding papers with a cold efficiency that sent waves of panic through the passengers.

Lise felt the sting of each inspection getting deeper, eroding her resilience. She wore the Madame Janette Bouville identity like an armor, but in the growing chaos and tension she feared her mask would be ripped off.

The first attack came without warning—a violent jolt that sent passengers tumbling, the train grinding to a halt with a screech of metal. Lise barely had time to brace herself as the rear cars derailed, sending plumes of smoke into the blue sky of a sunny April afternoon.

She joined the mass of disoriented passengers as they were herded off the train, forced to trek across rugged terrain to the next station. Some French passengers exchanged covert glances, their eyes gleaming with a mix of fear and pride—a silent acknowledgment of the partisans' sabotage handiwork.

Lise, however, could not afford such sentiments. Every delay, every detour, tightened the noose around her neck. She pushed forward, calculating the risks of being caught with each step.

The second sabotage struck just before a tunnel, the tracks shattered by an explosive charge. This time, the passengers were marched across the countryside through a landscape that was bleak and unforgiving.

Lise's leg ached. The amount of exercise and stress was too much for her healing injury. She gritted her teeth against the pain and tried to forgive the people behind the sabotage actions. The Resistance's efforts were necessary, she knew that, but each delay increased the time it took to get to Paris.

By the third sabotage, an explosion that sent the train careening off the tracks, Lise's body was on the verge of collapse. Her legs trembled, her vision blurred from exhaustion.

By now, she had changed trains three times, each switch a harrowing ordeal, her nerves stretched to the breaking point. Sleep was a distant memory, food an impossible luxury. All she craved now was water and the solace of a bed. But there was no rest, not yet. The hardship was her crucible, the fire that would forge her resolve.

Lise de Baissac, a coveted, upper-class agent, pah! The thought was bitter. Nothing was further from the truth.

As the wreckage of the train smoldered in the distance, Lise forced one foot in front of the other. She could feel the eyes of the German soldiers on her, the suspicion lurking behind their rigid stares. But also, their fear for their own safety, and fear of the growing opposition against their presence in France.

When the last train finally pulled into Gare de Lyon in Paris, Lise felt nothing but a hollow numbness. Every muscle in her body ached, her mind was fogged with exhaustion, and the weight of the last twenty-four hours pressed down on her with a suffocating force.

Doubt absorbed her last drop of mental energy. What was she even trying to achieve here? Each decision felt like a mistake, each step forward leading to a collision into an impenetrable wall.

The level-headed secret agent Lise de Baissac was spiraling out of control, and she knew it. But she clung to the one clear thought she had left: find Maître Savy, send word to London, then drink, eat, and sleep. Maybe then she could think clearly again.

Paris, her city, had become a twisted version of itself, as well. The once-famous streets and formerly-grand avenues were now filled with gaunt, hollow-eyed Parisians who shuffled along the pavements, their gazes fixed on the ground as if hoping to find some forgotten morsel of food, some lost scrap of hope.

The Nazis were everywhere, their presence a vile stain on every corner, every café, every soul. They didn't just occupy the streets; they possessed them, draining the city of its spirit, its light.

As she limped along the pavement, her suitcase feeling heavier with every step, a young woman passed by, paused and offered a concerned look.

"Madame, do you need some help?" the woman asked, her voice soft and worried.

Lise shook her head, forcing a smile. "Non, merci. I'm quite all right."

The woman hesitated for a moment, as if sensing the lie, but moved on, leaving Lise with more determination not to draw attention to herself. Though cherishing the moment of human connection, she realized her inability to walk properly made her vulnerable and a target for the enemy.

She would not be defeated, not now. Straightening her spine, willing her throbbing leg to obey, she clutched her suitcase more firmly and set off toward the Rue d'Alger, hoping against hope Maître Savy's office was still in the same place.

But her feet betrayed her, leading her instead to the Latin Quarter, to a place she had no business going. Henri Villameur's apartment on Rue des Artistes was a remnant of her life of distant dreams.

The name of the street, very fitting for the bohemian life Henri had led before the war, now felt like a cruel joke. As she approached his street, each beat of her heart told her this would become a painful reminder of how foolish she was being. She took a risk she couldn't afford, but the longing to see him, just once more, was stronger than any logic. She needed it—needed him—like air. And to let him take care of her. Just for one brief day.

What was she thinking? What was this desperate sentimentality washing over her? This wasn't her. It couldn't be. And yet, it was. The war had stripped her bare, leaving her raw and exposed, her emotions no longer hers to control.

As she neared Henri's apartment, she knew that every step forward was a step away from reason, but she couldn't stop herself. The city, the war, the endless strain had worn her down to this—an impulsive woman driven by a need she could scarcely understand.

Then, she saw him. Henri. He emerged from the doorway, his shawl catching the wind, his dark hair tousled as she remembered, sturdy, relaxed, wide corduroy pants, a casual sweater, no hat.

Relief surged through Lise, bringing with it an ache so deep she could hardly breathe. He looked untouched by the war, as if the world hadn't crumbled around him. *Thank God*, she thought. *He is safe.* He was still the Henri she loved.

But as she watched, her relief shattered into a thousand jagged pieces. From behind him stepped a young woman, radiant with blonde curls and a bright, carefree smile. She took Henri's arm, and he gazed down at her with a warmth Lise had once believed was reserved for her alone. They walked away together, laughing, lost in their own world.

Lise staggered back, her legs threatening to give out. She reached out for the wall, struggling to breathe, to contain the tidal wave of pain crashing over her. Her heart was breaking, and all she could do was stand there, helpless and alone.

And then, unbidden, a memory surfaced. A distant evening, just before the war had torn them apart.

"I'll always be here for you, Lise," Henri had whispered in a voice full of love. And then he had kissed her. They sat together in the dim light of her apartment on the Avenue Kléber, knowing she had to leave Paris the next day. His arm had been around her, his words a balm to her fears. "No matter what happens."

She had believed him then, had clung to those words like a lifeline. But now, in the cold reality of this war-torn city, his words felt like a cruel joke, a promise broken by the harsh truth - he had lied.

Tears stung Lise's eyes, but she blinked them back. She couldn't cry, couldn't afford to let the lies of the man she thought had loved her break her. Not here, not now. Henri hadn't seen her—that was a small mercy. She had to move, to get away before she did something foolish.

With each step away from Henri and the Rue des Artistes, Lise realized how truly alone she was. Somehow, Henri's promise had kept her going through all the lonely days and nights of the war. She'd told herself, *after the war, when all is done and dusted, when I can live in Paris again.* She'd believed her own words and now that dream had burst like a fragile soap bubble, it was gone for good, that future would never materialize.

I'm not made for love, Lise thought with great sadness, *but I'm made to win this war.*

The city blurred around her, reduced to shadows and echoes as she walked away from the future life she had lost, her heart a hollow shell of what it once was.

She entered the first café she came across and ordered a cognac. Then she remembered she hadn't eaten and was close to dehydration, so she also ordered a steak and a beer. Though the steak was chewy and greasy, and the beer flat, she miraculously managed to work everything inside her exhausted body.

Staring through the dingy, sheer curtains of a rundown Paris bar, Lise fought back her tears by talking sternly to herself. This was not how a secret agent in service of SOE behaved. Shame on her. And she'd brought this heartache on herself by going to look for her former lover.

She had no right to expect him to wait for her. She had chosen her path, and he had found his. But the pain was sharp, and she had to force herself to rise from her seat, pay for her meal and not look back. Love wouldn't wait for her at the end of this war. Not anymore.

With at least a little substance in her, Lise continued to Rue d'Alger, where she should have gone in the first place. Upon reaching Maître Savy's office, she felt a slight relief to find him present. The sight of the familiar, reassuring figure of William Savy, codenamed Alcide, almost brought a new wave of tears to her eyes. But by this time, Lise was Marguerite, and she firmly pushed her private life back into the shadows where it had been for the past four years.

"You here, my dear?" Savy's dark eyes sparked with concern as he took in her disheveled appearance, the result of her long and harrowing journey.

"It's Marguerite this time, or Janette Bouville if you prefer the alias," Lise quipped, attempting to sound light-hearted, though she felt anything but.

"You don't look well. And do I smell liquor on you?" Savy's concern deepened, his gaze sharpening.

"Alcide, I'm okay, but I need your help." Lise gratefully sank into the soft armchair he pointed her to.

"In a minute. Let me get you a coffee first; it looks like you could use one. Where are you coming from? You look like a cat that's gone through the wringer."

He handed her a strong cup of black coffee with his good hand and took the armchair opposite her.

"You'll sleep in one of my places tonight. Whatever you're going to tell me, I won't let you travel any farther like this. You're a walking target for the Gestapo. Now, tell me what's up. And what's wrong with your leg? Have you been shot?"

LISE LET OUT a deep sigh of relief. How good it felt that someone, if only for a short while, took all responsibility from her shoulders.

"I broke my leg in England in January. Bad practice parachute landing. It'll be okay. I just did too much walking today." *Ha, too much indeed.*

She was tempted to tell Savy everything, also about Henri—it was right there on the tip of her tongue. They'd known each other before the war, and Savy had been aware of her relationship with Henri. Surely, he would understand the emotional turmoil she was in.

But no. She couldn't afford to let her guard down. Not now. She couldn't tell Savy she'd seen Henri, that she had foolishly sought him out and been crushed by what she found. The war had no room for personal heartbreak, and she had to stay focused on the mission.

So, she focused on the real reason she was in Paris.

"I was assigned to the PIMENTO network in Toulouse. I arrived back in France last week. But these people are intolerable, and to be honest, by now the dislike is mutual. They don't want to work with me, and I don't want to work with them. I need another network. I need to let the Firm know." The sentences came out short, as if she was out of breath.

Savy took her in, his dark brows knitted as he considered her words, his deformed arm resting in his lap. "Sounds like you've locked horns with Alphonse, so that's serious business. I'll see if I can find a W/T operator to send word to London. But it may take some time. Things are very complicated now. Everything's underground and agents are constantly on the move to avoid being caught. Where would you prefer to go?"

Lise didn't hesitate. "If I can't set up my own network anymore, I'd like to join SCIENTIST II in Normandy." Lise didn't, even between these safe walls, dare to say 'join my brother' but Savy, who was now one of the Firm's most cherished agents, knew well Claude de Baissac was the organiser of the Normandy network.

"Aha, join Denis?" he asked.

"Yes. It's the only plausible option right now. I was briefed in London that the invasion is imminent, and I know Denis is crucial to the operations there."

Savy nodded. "I'll send a message to London. Now here's the key to a safe house two streets down. Sleep there and come back tomorrow. Stay safe, Marguerite."

Leaving Savy's office with the address and the key, stepping into Paris at dusk and Lise felt new hope. It had been a great risk, coming to Paris, but perhaps it would work out after all. London would be notified.

40

DESPERATION AND RESOLVE

The next day – 13 April, 1944

L ise spent the night in the safehouse provided by Savy, a modest room with a single bed, a small table, and a chair. She'd slept fitfully, unable to shake off thoughts of her failed mission and the heartbreak of seeing Henri with another woman. She felt as blurry and non-descript as the shadows on the empty wall.

All Lise now wanted was to leave Paris as fast as her legs could carry her—anywhere else in France, as long as it meant she didn't have to return to the capital for a long time. After a quick breakfast of lukewarm coffee and stale bread – all she could find in the safehouse's sparse kitchen—she returned to Savy's office, hoping for some good news.

The weariness from the previous day's experiences still dragged her down, and her leg was still throbbing from the prior days' exertions, but she pushed through, determined to find a way to contribute to SOE in France and to erase all longings for a personal life.

"Good morning, Marguerite." The serious expression on Savy's face didn't bode well. "I managed to find a W/T operator who promised to send your message about the dissatisfaction with PIMENTO to London, but she couldn't say when - she was on the run. I'm sorry I couldn't do more for you."

Though Lise's heart sank, she approached the drawback with her usual practicality. "Well, I guess I'll have to return to Toulouse and continue working for PIMENTO until I hear otherwise."

The prospect of going back to Alphonse's network, where she was unwelcome and underutilized, wasn't a cheerful one. But Lise knew she had no other choice. She couldn't loiter in Paris. She needed to stay active, to remain in the fight against the Germans on this crucial turning point in the war.

"Can you do that, Marguerite—work under orders you disagree with?" Savy sounded unsure. He knew how strong and independent she was. For one short moment, Lise hoped he'd say she could join his WIZARD network, but she knew that was impossible. Savy worked all over France and had to hide regularly.

"Of course I can, I must." Her voice was chirpy despite the disappointment. "I'll head back to Toulouse 'tout de suite'."

"Good," in some strange way he sounded relieved. "I'll find a way to contact you, should London honor your request to join SCIENTIST II. I know you'd prefer that. Stay strong, my friend. I hope you'll feel better suited soon."

"Thank you, Alcide." And she took leave from what she expected to be the last friendly face for a while.

The outbound journey back to Toulouse was as arduous as the trip to Paris had been. The train was once again packed, and the frequent inspections by German soldiers kept Lise and everyone around her on edge. She had to change trains multiple times, enduring long waits at desolate stations. Sabotage attacks continued to plague the tracks, further delaying her journey and forcing her to walk miles along the railway lines.

When she finally arrived in Toulouse, exhausted and frustrated, she was met with the disheartening news Alphonse was not there. Lise's patience was wearing thin, and a niggling voice in her head suggested she might as well return to England, become an instructor for other agents, and leave the fieldwork behind.

No, she told herself firmly. *You belong here. You stay here until France is free. This is your fight, as much as it is theirs.*

Resolved to find Alphonse and demand they reach some sort of agreement, willingly or not, she decided to make another attempt. Ignoring the protest from her aching leg and the fatigue that followed her like a shadow, Lise traveled on to Montauban.

At a safehouse on the outskirts of Montauban, she finally found him. His expression was stern as he greeted her, the tension between them like an electric current.

"I hadn't expected you back here," Alphonse said bluntly. "I heard you went to Paris to sing your lamentations about my network. And by the way, Julien says he doesn't want to work with you anymore. He's convinced you're a double agent and has already informed London. You're not to be trusted, Marguerite."

Anger rose in Lise like a tidal wave. "That's absurd, Alphonse, and you know it!" she shouted, her voice echoing in the small room. "London will never believe I'm a double agent. They know my track record. This is utterly ridiculous! But you know what? I'm glad to be free of PIMENTO. I tried, honestly, I tried, but you're just a bunch of militant socialists unable to adapt your rigid mindsets to make use of a skilled agent. And frankly, I don't want to work with you either."

As the words left her mouth, Lise was shocked at her own

outburst. This wasn't the Lise de Baissac she knew—the woman who never lost her temper, who was sangfroid to the bone. Something had gotten under her skin, something deeper than just the rejection from PIMENTO. She was at the end of her rope, and she needed rest, desperately. But where could she find it?

Alphonse's face remained impassive as he listened to her tirade. "This is where we part ways then, Marguerite. You'll have to find another network to contribute to our cause. I wish you luck with that."

His tone was dismissive, as if he doubted anyone else would take her in. With a final, indifferent shrug, he turned his back on her, severing the last thread of camaraderie that had once existed between them.

Rage simmered inside her as Lise left the safehouse. She walked through the narrow streets of Montauban, the sounds and smells of the city swirling around her, but she was aware of nothing. Not the scent of freshly baked bread from a nearby bakery, not the acrid smoke from the factories, not the Montalbanais going about their daily lives. All she felt was the turmoil and fatigue roiling inside her.

What now?

As she sat on a bench, her eyes absently following two pigeons picking breadcrumbs from in between the cobbled stones, her mind wandered back to Mauritius.

SHE WAS TEN YEARS-OLD, sitting next to Snout's grave in her parents' lush garden, surrounded by bougainvilleas and rose-filled pergolas, the lawn as smooth as a cricket field. The sun was hot, her tears were hot, but her heart was cold. The grief of losing her little Maltese dog was unbearable.

Snout had been her constant companion since she was three years old and now she would never again caress his fluffy fur, see his funny round eyes look up at her, hear his woof-woof as he begged for a walk, a jump in the pond, or a lick of liver pâte.

The void Snout's death left felt unbearable. The tears she'd held back inside in front of the grown-ups now flowed freely, dripping onto the freshly turned earth of her pet's grave.

Buried in sorrow, she heard Claude's childish voice calling her from a distance. "Lise, come quickly! I've found a toad colony!" His voice was filled with excitement and wonder.

Wiping her tears, she felt the tug of her little brother's enthusiasm. Despite her sadness, she stood up and walked to where the sound came from. Claude was crouched by a small pond, his eyes shining with joy as he pointed to the wriggling mass of toads and their glistening eggs. His delight was infectious, and soon Lise found herself smiling, her grief momentarily forgotten in the shared discovery.

"MADAME BOUVILLE?" A tentative voice said close by. Lise shook herself from her reverie. Heavens, she'd lost her guard!

She turned to see a young girl, no older than fourteen, with wide brown eyes and a look of urgency. Lise was so confused and tired she took her for Sophie for a moment. It wasn't Sophie but someone used her alias, so she was safe.

"Madame, I have a message for you."

The girl handed her a small piece of paper.

"Thank you", she stammered as the girl took her bike and rode away.

Alcide a trouvé son frère à Paris.

ALCIDE HAS FOUND his brother in Paris.

. . .

A wave of relief washed over Lise. It was the coded message that meant her brother was waiting for her in Paris. She could join his network. Claude had really called out to her. Just as he'd saved her from succumbing to her grief all those years ago, he was calling out to her again, to help her shake off total disillusionment.

41
_____

THE SIBLINGS' PACT

Three weeks later - Normandy, May 1944

F or the past three months, thirty-seven-year-old Claude de Baissac, now codenamed Denis, had been tirelessly weaving the threads of his second SCIENTIST network from Normandy northwards. With his meticulous planning and relentless drive, he'd built up bases of support across the Mayenne, Calvados, Orne, and Eure-et-Loire departments, extending into La Manche and Eure.

He spent most of his time on the move to avoid detection by the Gestapo and placed the northern part of his network in the hands of his long-serving Lieutenant, Agent Verger, with the support of his wireless operators and fellow-Mauritian, codenamed Vladimir. A young, just-trained SOE agent codenamed Geneviève, became his own W/T operator.

Claude's work was a dangerous game of cat and mouse with the German occupiers. His life was a constant blur of coded messages, secret meetings, and narrow escapes. He moved through the shadowy landscapes of occupied France like a ghost, always one step ahead of the Gestapo. Every operation, every decision, was a calculated risk, but he knew what he was doing, and he did it magnificently.

The French Resistance fighters, the Maquis, were Claude's lifeline. Scattered across the countryside, these groups of determined men and women waited for the signal to strike. They were armed with weapons dropped from the skies, smuggled in under the cover of darkness by daring RAF pilots.

These night drops were fraught with danger; every sound could betray them, every flicker of light could be their last in the Normandy area infested with blood-thirsty Germans.

From February to April 1944, Claude grew the SCIENTIST II network to thousands of resisters. The weapons and supplies delivered to the Maquis transformed them from a ragtag band of rebels into a formidable force. They were ready to unleash chaos on the German supply lines, to blow up bridges, derail trains, and cut communication lines. They were the saboteurs pur sang, the silent warriors of the night.

"The Secret Army is so secret, I can't find it!" was one of Claude's favorite sayings.

His leadership was the glue holding the vast network together. He was a master strategist, a man who could see the entire chessboard while others focused on their next move. He set up safe houses, created secure communication lines, and trained the Maquis in the art of sabotage.

His efforts were tireless, his resolve unbreakable. He knew the actions of SCIENTIST II could well tip the balance in favor of the Allies when the day of the landings on the French coast finally arrived. And Claude knew more than others. All the hectic activity in his area gave him an inkling where the Allies would land, which added to his responsibility.

Yet, Claude was not an easy leader to follow. His insistence on absolute security and strict obedience often clashed with the Maquis' eagerness to use their newfound weapons. His demands for careful planning and timing were met with frustration from fighters eager to take immediate action against the Germans.

Knowing all too well the horrific retaliations the Germans exacted for acts of resistance, he sought to minimize these brutal reprisals whenever he could.

One evening in late April, a heated argument broke out between Claude and a group of young Maquis fighters. They had received a shipment of explosives and were eager to use them to blow up a German convoy passing through a nearby village. The enthusiasm in their eyes was met with a steely glare from Claude.

"No way. You wait until I tell you to act," he barked. "Do you want the entire village to be burned to the ground and your women and daughters raped? Use your brain if God gave you any."

A tall, fiery-haired Maquis named Raoul stepped forward, his fists clenched. "We're ready to fight, Denis! We can't just sit and wait while the Germans strut around like they own the place. They won't know it was us. We'll make it seem as if something technical went wrong."

Claude's eyes bored into Raoul's. "I said no. Didn't God give you ears either? Swallow your frustration, man, this is not a game. Every move we make must be strategic. We hit them where it hurts the most, at the *most* opportune moment. Otherwise, we risk everything. So, hold your tongue, and store these explosives where I told you to. Until I tell you where and when to use them."

The tension in the room was palpable. Frenchmen weren't good at taking orders from a Brit. But they also knew that the man they called Denis was as French as they were and knew what he was doing. As usual, Claude's volatile explosion silenced the dissent. The

Maquis fighters reluctantly agreed to follow his orders, their anger retreating to simmer just below the surface.

Claude was tired, tired and cranky. He slept in a different hayloft every night. He reeked of manure. The Maquis in his vast and fragmented territory simply had to listen, and to listen now! But darn, were they obstinate and agitated. He could do with a bit of respect and respite.

THE RESPECT and respite came in the form of Claude's older sister Lise. When she arrived in Normandy on May 5, she found her brother entrenched in his work, the weight of a difficult and multi-faceted network evident in the lines on his face and the curtness of his remarks.

"Denis, do you even take a moment to get some sleep? You're burning the candle at both ends. You won't last much longer like this." It wasn't just sisterly concern. It was a De Baissac rational observation. Claude couldn't go on like this, no matter she could see the fire in his eyes, and the determination in his actions.

He greeted her with a tight embrace and a tremor in his voice. "Marguerite, good to see you. I've been too busy to get much sleep, but your arrival may give me a moment now and then to take a short nap."

"Can we talk?" Lise asked. It was more like a command. "Alone?"

"Sure." Claude dismissed the men he had been in a meeting with and poured himself and Lise a cup of black coffee from the percolator that stood simmering on a 2-burner stove in the corner.

"Give me the details, hard and fast," Lise said as she took the seat opposite her brother at the Formica table, sipping the black liquid with relish. It was real coffee for a change.

"SCIENTIST II's main job is to scout possible large open areas where invading airborne troops can land and hold their positions, and to receive airdrops of weapons and supplies for the Resistance. But the Maquis are so eager of late, I find myself spending an increasing amount of time keeping them under control. This mission has been nothing like Bordeaux, not only in size of drops but also with waves of resistance fighters joining us."

"You think the Allies will land in Normandy then, and not further up north? I thought it would possibly be La Manche?" Lise asked as she digested her brother's words.

"No, it's likely they'll land somewhere in Normandy, but the Allied landings will be the best kept secret of the war until it happens, so even we don't have anything official and can only do what we've got to do. It would be major though, if it happened in our territory."

Lise accepted the "our" territory with grace. "So, what's your number one headache?"

Claude didn't have to think twice. "The Maquis wanting to use their new toys immediately and without stopping to think about the ramifications of brash actions."

Lise nodded. "I'm on it. Where do you want me to base myself."

"I suggest Saint-Aubin-Du-Désert in the Mayenne region. In the middle of Normandy where I can easily reach you. I'll give you the address of a safe house."

"I'm on my way there right now. And who's the Maquis leader I should have a chat with?"

"Raoul. Just ask for him discretely when you're settled."

Despite her own challenges in the past weeks and a still-aching leg, Lise herself didn't take a moment's rest. With Claude by her side, she could face whatever came their way. The Resistance was ready. SCIENTIST II was poised to strike. Lise was ready.

And with the dawn of a new day, the liberation of France would begin.

42

TAMING THE FIRE

A few days later - Saint-Aubin-du-Désert, May 1944

Once again posing as a Parisian widow, with the alias Janette Bouville, Lise settled into her new temporary home on the first floor of a house in the village of Saint-Aubin-du-Désert.

The ground floor was occupied by a bedridden, elderly lady called Madame Rousseau, whose presence provided a perfect cover for secret agent activities. Madame Rousseau rarely had visitors, and her dependence on the kind-hearted widow for small chores around the house helped cement a perfect disguise.

Lise carefully arranged her few belongings in the small apartment. Her weapons and important papers were hidden in the false bottom of her suitcase, a practice that had become second nature to her. She kept her Colt within easy reach at all times, always alert for any unexpected visitors. The presence of a group of rowdy German soldiers next door – again! - was a constant reminder of the thin line she walked between life and death.

As she unpacked, her thoughts turned to the immediate task at hand: meeting with Raoul, whom Claude had called 'a fiery-haired leader of the local Maquis.' Lise knew that gaining this man's cooperation would be crucial to the success of their operations in the region. Claude had mentioned Raoul's enthusiasm but also his recklessness. She would need to strike a balance between harnessing his energy and curbing his impulsiveness.

After ensuring everything was in place, Lise donned her deliberately-faded Parisian dress to be as nondescript and overlooked as possible, and stepped out into the warm May air of Saint-Aubin-du-Désert.

She was happy to have found an old-but-working bicycle in Madame Rousseau's backyard. Owning a bicycle these days was a cherished luxury.

As it was the lull hour after lunchtime, the village was quiet, the only sounds being the chirping of birds and the distant murmur of the river. She cycled to the small café in the next village where she'd arranged to meet Raoul, meanwhile scanning the land and its lay.

Raoul was already sitting at a corner table with a pilsner in front of him. His fiery red hair was unmistakable, and his deep-blue eyes sparkled with a mix of excitement and suspicion as he watched her approach. The red scar across his left cheek did nothing to temper his attractive, virile appearance.

The Maquis' whole attitude, upright and ferocious, had anti-German written all over him. Lise instantly understood this proud Frenchman was a walking target for the Gestapo and after his arrest it would be all too easy to bring down the entire SCIENTIST II network through him.

Raoul was the type of man who was done hiding his anger after four years of agonizing Nazi suppression and now that London had provided him the necessary weapons, he only wanted to blast his way through to the end. But for his own sake and theirs, he'd have to back off for a little while.

"Bonjour, Madame Bouville," His terse voice held a tinge of curiosity. Lise felt slightly uncomfortable under the man's gaze, which openly roamed up and down her figure. There was a glint in his eye, a womanizer's gleam that she found distasteful and entirely too forward. This was a working-class behavior she was unaccustomed to dealing with, and it threw her off balance for a moment.

Despite her discomfort, Lise maintained her composure. "Bonjour, Raoul. Thank you for meeting me."

She took the seat opposite him and crossed her feet at the ankles, folding her skirt over her knees. Raoul wasted no time. "I heard Denis sent you to take charge. Are you here to tell us what we can and cannot do? A woman, for God's sake. Is he now tied to a woman's apron strings? Bah, I'd thought better of the Major."

Lise met his gaze steadily, masking her unease and growing irritation with a businesslike expression on her face. She wouldn't fall in the same trap as her brother and fly off the handle with this packet of dynamite.

"Raoul, call me Marguerite, please. I'd rather we not start off as enemies. I am here on my own command and not that of Denis. I want to make sure the actions of everyone involved against the occupiers are strategic and effective. We have a shared goal, but we need to be smart about how we achieve it. Impulsive actions can lead to unnecessary reprisals from the Germans. Your wives, sisters, children, and elderly parents will suffer the most. And that will turn the local people against us, just when we need their support the most." Lise stressed 'us' and 'our' to make sure he understood they were on the same page.

Raoul's eyes narrowed, but his roguish smile didn't fade. "We're ready to fight, Marguerite. The Germans aren't as strong as they used to be, and the people are with us. We can't just sit and twiddle our thumbs while the Nazis continue to terrorize us. We're sick and tired of being second-rate citizens in our own country. Don't you understand that?"

"Of course, I understand your frustration," Lise said calmly. "I'm as sick and tired of this whole war as you are. But there's a bigger picture we need to consider. Every move we make must be coordinated with the overall strategy. I'm not here to take everything out of your hands, Raoul. I need you to step up as a responsible leader for all the Maquis groups in the Mayenne region. Your role is crucial in keeping them organized and under control."

Raoul leaned back, his expression softening slightly, though his gaze remained appraising. "And what exactly do you expect from me, Marguerite?" He downed his lager and waved his hand to the waiter to refill his glass.

"I'll have what he's having," Lise chimed in to the waiter. That was met with an approving grin from the handsome Frenchman.

"What I ask from you is communication with me and discipline among your men and women," Lise continued. "Make sure your Maquis follow orders and don't act on their own. We'll work together to identify the best targets and the right times to strike. Your enthusiasm is an asset, Raoul, but it needs to be channeled effectively."

As must your biological urges, Lise thought, but didn't say aloud. This man was really different from the generally intellectual and well-bred SOE agents she'd so far come across, but Raoul's rawness had an edge to it she quite liked. It made Lise only fight harder to stay in control and she never shied from a challenge to be the boss.

Raoul's demeanor shifted, his eyes flashing with defiance. "You think you can just waltz in here and start giving orders? I've been leading these men, risking my life every day. What makes you think you know better?"

Lise's patience wore thin. "Because I do know better. I've seen what happens when plans aren't coordinated, when actions aren't thought through. Villages burned, civilians slaughtered. If you care about your men and the people of this region, you'll listen to me."

Raoul slammed his fist on the table, causing heads to turn. "We're not cowards, Madame. We're fighters. And we'll fight when we see fit."

Lise leaned in, her voice low and intense. "Keep your voice down, for Heaven's sake. You twonk! Do you want to have us all arrested? Where are your brains, man? Fighting without a plan isn't bravery, it's stupidity." She spit out her words, really angry and forgetting to be diplomatic with him but keeping a low voice. When security was at risk, Lise would stop at nothing.

"You may think you're protecting your people, but you're putting them in more danger. I'm done with your recklessness. You want to lead? Then show your men and women what a true leader is. He knows when to fight and when to wait."

For a moment, the tension was palpable, the air thick with mutual hostility. Lise was already regretting her outburst, thinking she'd not come any further with this crucial pawn within SCIEN-TIST II, just like her brother before her.

So, she was surprised to finally see Raoul's shoulders sag, the lusty fire in his eyes dimming. "Fine," he muttered. "I'll do it your way. But you better prove you know what you're doing."

Lise heaved a sigh of relief, but her gaze remained steely. "I will. And so will you. We're in this together, Raoul. Let's make sure we do it right. If you can lead the men and women in the Mayenne region responsibly and effectively, I promise we will have victory on our side."

He reached out his hand and Lise took it. It was rough and warm. And she was in for another surprise. He brought her hand to his lips and, looking over their clasped hands, gave her one last roguish look.

"I like you, Marguerite. You're a firecracker."

Taking her hand back and trying not to blush, she said in a dignified manner but with a small smile, "you'd better believe it, Raoul. *Vive La France*!

43

A FRAGILE ALLIANCE

The next day - May 1944

With Raoul's cooperation secured, Lise turned her attention to another critical task: meeting and guiding Agent Geneviève. With the date of D-Day imminent, but ultimately unknown, the Firm was rushing to deploy more wireless operators to the field, but the urgency came at a cost. Barely-trained operators were being sent in, and their insufficient security preparation was a concern for Lise. Her brother had shared troubling reports on Geneviève's lack of training and general immaturity.

Sending such a young, inexperienced agent to one of the most German-infested areas of France was alarming and protecting Geneviève had now become Lise's top priority—not just for the young woman's sake, but for the safety of the entire SCIENTIST II network.

Lise had arranged to meet Geneviève in a secluded spot in St Léonard des Bois, a forested area not far from Saint-Aubin-du-

Désert. As she approached the clearing in the woods, she spotted a slight, young woman in a red polka-dot dress crouched on the moss, fidgeting nervously with her equipment.

At just twenty-three, Geneviève's smooth, youthful face was marred by a deep wrinkle in her forehead as her hands moved anxiously, almost searchingly, over the keys. The long aerial wire was tangled in bramble bushes—a mistake that would make it nearly impossible to free quickly in the event of a German patrol.

Lise observed the scene with a mix of concern and care. Despite Geneviève's dogged determination, the chaos of the entire setup was evident. She looked vulnerable, almost out of her depth, and Lise felt the weight of responsibility to help this new operator. She'd trained novice agents before, and she knew how to approach this situation with a steady, guiding hand.

"Geneviève?" Lise called out softly, her voice gentle, "it's Marguerite."

Geneviève looked up, her big blue eyes wide with relief. "Oh Marguerite, I'm so glad to see you. I've been so worried about making a mistake."

Lise smiled warmly and placed a reassuring hand on Geneviève's shoulder. "You're doing just fine, Geneviève. But we need to be extra careful. Your work is crucial in keeping our communication with London intact. We can't afford any slip-ups."

The young woman nodded vigorously, her lip glistening with a slight sheen of sweat. Lise studied her intently. Geneviève was brave and eager to learn, but her inexperience was a glaring liability. The thought of such an untrained operator handling critical communications made Lise's stomach churn. Still, she knew that Geneviève needed encouragement, not criticism.

Geneviève's voice trembled as she spoke. "I'll do my best. But it's so hard. I feel like I'm constantly on edge. I was dropped in a couple of days ago, after three failed attempts. It was a harrowing experience. When I finally landed, I was three fields away from the reception team, alone in the dark. I had no idea where my luggage was. It... it was terrible." Tears welled in her blue eyes, and she quickly blinked them away, embarrassed by her own vulnerability.

Lise's heart softened. She knew all too well the terror of a failed drop, the way it eroded an agent's confidence about her mission. But she also knew that Geneviève couldn't afford to let this experience shake her trust in herself.

"I know how tough a bad start is," Lise agreed, "but you came out in one piece. And remember, we're here to support each other. You're not alone in this, Geneviève. Stay close to me, and we'll get through this together. Your safety is my priority, and I'll make sure you have everything you need to succeed."

GENEVIÈVE LOOKED up at the older agent with gratitude, a small smile breaking through the worry on her face. Lise could see her calm words steadied the young agent's frayed nerves in a way that would benefit them all.

"Thank you, Marguerite," Geneviève whispered. "I'll do my best. I promise."

Lise squeezed her shoulder gently. "I know you will. Let's get this antenna untangled first, shall we? And then I'll show you a few tricks to make your setup faster and more secure."

As they worked together, Lise guided Geneviève with patience and care, her own spirits lifting slightly as she slipped back into her role as teacher. A fragile alliance was born between the two women —one hardened in the battle and one as new as a lamb in a spring meadow.

Lise decided it was best to keep a close watch on Geneviève, despite the considerable time it would consume. With the Germans growing more ruthless and the Allied invasion imminent, any mistake Geneviève made could lead to catastrophic consequences.

"I can't be with you around the clock," Lise admitted, "since I have to handle many of Denis' duties as well. But I'll protect you as best I can."

Geneviève revealed a more defiant side of herself, her blue eyes sparkling with brazenness. "I wasn't happy with the alias the Firm gave me," she remarked. "So, I asked Denis to make me an art student from Paris, here on holiday with relatives. People always think I'm younger than I am, so now I have new papers stating I'm still in my teens."

"Good," Lise agreed, appreciating the initiative. "If you don't feel good about your alias, it's hard to keep up the fake story. But you should've told the Firm before you went to the field. Changing your papers meant extra work for Denis and you know how busy he is."

"I tried, Marguerite!" Geneviève fumed. "But you try and tell 'F-Int' something she doesn't want to hear. She just smokes that stinking cigarette of hers and makes that dismissive gesture with her hand." Geneviève waved her hand rather arrogantly. Though Lise had a completely different impression of Vera Atkins and she thought Geneviève's remark rather rude, she let it slip by. They really needed to get moving.

"I see. Now, can I help you with this message? We really need to leave this place 'tout de suite.' You've been on the air too long."

"No, I'm done." Geneviève stood, brushing the dirt from her dotted skirt. The sunlight filtering through the leaves danced on her dark curls, highlighting her youthfulness. She seemed more at ease with Lise by her side, her earlier nerves giving way to a quiet confidence.

"For tonight, you're coming to stay with me," Lise said, helping Geneviève hoist the heavy wireless set into its unobtrusive brown leather suitcase and secure it to the back of her bike.

"Gladly," Geneviève smiled, her relief evident. "I'm not sleeping well on my own, in a different place every night."

"Tomorrow, I need to go to Paris for Denis, so you'll be on your own for the day, but I'll be back in the evening."

Geneviève's smile faded slightly at the thought of being alone again. "Do you think you could get me some new crystals for my radio set? I've asked London for a spare, but they said it could take a while."

"Sure, I'll see what I can do," Lise replied, touched by the young agent's honesty about her vulnerabilities.

As they cycled back towards Saint-Aubin-du-Désert, Lise's mind churned with the challenge of safeguarding Geneviève while managing her own demanding responsibilities.

SUDDENLY, Geneviève's voice rang out, startling Lise from her thoughts. *"Oh, bonjour! Je viens d'arriver pour mes vacances d'été!"* She shouted in an exaggeratedly cheerful tone, addressing a group of German soldiers loitering near the village entrance.

Lise's heart made a summersault. *Is the girl out of her wits?* Why did she draw attention to herself by announcing she was here on holiday? They hadn't been stopped, and Geneviève had the wireless set on the back of her bike, while Lise carried compromising materials in her pockets, along with her Colt!

The Germans, momentarily distracted by Geneviève's giddy presence, began to smile and engage her in conversation. The young operator continued to chatter animatedly, her body language relaxed and open. The soldiers laughed, clearly charmed by the young woman's friendliness. Lise forced a tight smile, her mind going in all directions with contingency plans in case things took the wrong turn.

Finally, after what felt like an eternity, Geneviève waved goodbye to the soldiers and pedaled away, catching up with Lise. As they rounded the corner, safely out of sight from the enemy, Lise's frustration boiled over.

"What were you thinking?" she hissed, her voice low but intense. "You put us both in incredible danger!"

Geneviève looked unfazed and answered calmly. "I distracted them, didn't I? Sometimes being friendly and open is the best way to avoid suspicion. They didn't even think to question us."

Lise glared at her, torn between exasperation and a reluctant admiration. "Just be more careful next time," she muttered, shaking her head. "We can't afford to take such risks." But she thought of herself in another place and time, having tea meetings with Grabowski.

When they arrived at Madame Rousseau's house, Lise was still reeling from Geneviève's nonchalance. She ushered her new responsibility inside; silently grateful they had survived the close call.

Geneviève, however, acted as if she'd accomplished a great deed. "See? No harm done," she said with a cheeky grin.

Lise sighed, shrugging her shoulders. Keeping Geneviève safe was going to be an even greater challenge than she'd anticipated. She'd thought Raoul was a packet of dynamite, but Geneviève was more like the fuse—small, seemingly harmless, but capable of igniting something far more explosive.

As she watched the young woman discarding her set and unpacking her bag, a strange mix of pride and protectiveness welled up within Lise. Despite Geneviève's reckless bravado, there was something undeniably endearing about the fearless spirit wrapped up in this small, unruly parcel of warfare dressed in a polka-dot dress.

Lise couldn't help but smile as Geneviève looked up at her with those big, beautiful eyes, brimming with innocence and mischief.

"Everything alright, Marguerite? Shall we have a real cuppa? I brought some English tea," Geneviève said, her voice filled with excitement as she held up a package of Twinings Earl Grey.

"Oh no," Lise squirmed, "that's dangerous!" But even as she protested, the thought of the smooth notes of citrus, spice, and malt teasing her palate made her mouth water.

Geneviève grinned, undeterred. "Ah, what the heck! Just this once?"

Lise hesitated for a moment, then laughed softly. "Alright, just this once."

As the kettle whistled softly in the background, the two women shared a moment of quiet rebellion, savoring the taste of home in a land far from it. Despite the danger, or perhaps because of it, the simple act of sharing a cup of tea felt like a small victory, a reminder of what they were fighting for.

44

NEW QUARTERS, OLD FOES

A few weeks later - Normandy, late May 1944

Normandy in late May 1944 was a French region teetering on the brink. The warm, sunlit days were often shattered by the menacing roar of German Messerschmitt Bf 109s and Focke-Wulf Fw 190s patroling the skies, their dark silhouettes casting ominous shadows over the fields below. The air hung heavy, not with the promise of summer rain, but with the weight of impending conflict—a storm of human design, poised to break at any moment.

The Germans, once confident occupiers, were now visibly tense, their movements frantic as they scrambled to fortify their defenses. The signs were impossible to ignore: an invasion was coming. Though they didn't know when or where, they could feel it in the very soil beneath their boots. The long-held illusion of a Norwegian invasion had evaporated, leaving the French coast as the undeniable target.

For Lise, life had become a blur of relentless activity. Each night brought the adrenaline-fueled rush of supply and arms drops, the sky above Normandy alive with the silent descent of parachutes carrying containers and crates. It was both exhausting and exhilarating, as if they were arming the entire French population, yet the sheer volume of supplies left them scrambling to find secure hiding spots.

But amidst the exhaustion and physical strain, Lise felt a profound sense of relief and happiness. After the debacle with the PIMENTO network in April, she was finally where she belonged—at the heart of the resistance, deep in the thick of it, where her skills and resolve made the most impact.

Being alongside her brother Claude, who'd now appointed her as second-in-command of the SCIENTIST II network, gave her a renewed sense of worth and confidence. Heartbreak had become a distant memory as well.

Keeping a close eye on the eager but inexperienced Geneviève was a test of Lise's patience, on top of all her other tasks. The physical toll was no less daunting—most days saw her cycling over 60 miles, delivering vital messages for Denis, her legs burning with the effort. And then there was Raoul, whose fiery temperament required constant vigilance to ensure he remained disciplined and focused.

In the short spells of rest she granted herself, the weight of her responsibilities pressed down on her like a leaden cloak, but Lise lived fully and remained unshakable, driven by the certainty the real fight for freedom was about to begin.

AFTER A LONG, clammy day running errands, Lise was relieved to finally return to her modest apartment for a much-needed rest. But as she stepped inside, her breath caught in her throat. Standing in the middle of the room was a German officer, his imposing figure almost too tall for the low-ceilinged room. The air felt heavy, charged with the overpowering heat. The officer's stern expression softened slightly as he noticed Lise's entrance.

"Rauss!" he barked. Get out.

Lise instinctively opened her mouth to protest but quickly thought better of it. Though her heart pounded, she forced herself to remain calm and look him straight in the eye.

Thank God Geneviève isn't here, shot through her. Geneviève, with her unpredictable nature, might have squeaked like a frightened mouse or flirted and joked—or worse, argued with the SS officer. Any of those reactions could have been disastrous.

This was a Hauptsturmführer, a high-ranking officer, and any argument would only escalate the situation. Did the new agents even spend hours in the Beaulieu classroom learning all the different Nazi uniforms? Lise doubted it.

"Oh," Lise exclaimed, quickly putting a hand over her mouth, feigning shock. Without missing a beat, she slipped into the role of the fragile, kind widow—a part she had perfected over her months undercover. "Has Madame Rousseau instructed you to clear me out?"

She knew full well the bedridden old lady on the ground floor was too weak to stop the Germans from taking whatever they wanted. But Lise needed to play the part, to appear innocent and harmless. The weaker, the better.

"She has no say in the matter. She can stay where she is. You are the one that has to move out. We need this apartment." The German's boots clicked sharply against the floor, signaling the finality of his decision.

Lise's mind was still assessing the situation at full speed. The flat was spartan—just two rooms, a single table, a bench, and a mattress on the floor. The walls were bare, devoid of personal touches. Everything here was designed to maintain her cover, with nothing that could tie her to the resistance. But the place had become familiar, a relatively safe place where she could get some rest. Now she had to leave it behind. *Tant pis*, she thought, but not without some bitterness.

As she began to roll up her sleeping bag, made from an agent's parachute, she glanced at the German through her eyelashes. He'd clearly been sitting on it as it wasn't as crinkled when she left that morning. What had he thought? Or had he thought nothing of it?

The material was unmistakable, its origin clear to anyone familiar with such things. Lise kept her face impassive, her movements slow and deliberate. To her immense relief, the officer seemed more preoccupied with the logistics of moving her out than with scrutinizing her belongings.

The tension in her grew as she made her way to the cupboard. Inside, hidden among the few essentials, was *Geneviève's* stash of English tea—a dangerous luxury that could easily betray her as a British agent. *Why did I let her talk me into keeping it?* She had to get rid of it. If only he would turn his back on her for a moment but no, he kept looking in her direction to see what she would do next.

Just as Lise reached for the cupboard's handle, the officer stepped forward, his eyes narrowing slightly.

"Allow me," he said, his tone more polite as he locked the cabinet securely and handed her the key. "This situation is only temporary. I apologize for the inconvenience."

Lise accepted the key with a stiff nod, her mind reeling. The officer's unexpected courtesy only heightened the surreal nature of the encounter. His scrupulous German behavior was suddenly in stark contrast to the brutality she'd come to expect from his countrymen.

"I'll wait for you to collect your belongings, Madame, before ordering my men to move in," he added, his voice oddly respectful.

Once he'd left the room, Lise quickly packed her suitcase, her hands trembling against her will. What if he had been nosier? she wondered, but she pushed the thought aside. There was no time for useless what-ifs. She'd been lucky, darn lucky. And now she needed to act, and fast.

With her suitcase in one hand and her bike in the other, she stepped out into the village square, her mind already creating a new plan.

I need to get a message to Geneviève not to return to Madame Rousseau's house, Lise thought urgently. The young operator had gone north with SCIENTIST II's other W/T operator, Vladimir, and was due back the next day. The last thing Lise needed was *Geneviève* waltzing into a room full of Germans.

Although, knowing *Geneviève*, she'd probably talk herself out of it—or worse, join them for a round of beer and cards. No, she'd charm them right out of their uniforms if she had to, Lise mused with a wry smile, but quickly pushed the thought aside. This was no time for distractions.

As Lise moved through the village, she was already on the lookout for a new temporary pied-à-terre—a safe place to regroup and continue her mission. But with every step, the stakes felt higher, the tension winding tighter like a clock about to strike midnight. Normandy was a powder keg, and she was right in the middle of it. Every house and public building teemed with Germans

One of the places where she and Raoul's Maquis had held regular meetings was an old school in the next village, now partially occupied by German soldiers. It wasn't as private as the last place, but in these times, one couldn't be too picky about where to lay one's head.

Even I can accept 'digs', Alphonse, Lise thought wryly, thinking back to PIMENTO's leader who'd scornfully called her upper-class. She'd slept in ditches and haylofts - a straw mattress on a stone floor was practically luxury living these days.

The front of the school was a hive of activity, with German voices barking orders and boots clattering on the stone floors. Lise slipped in through the back entrance, her presence barely noticed in the chaos. She found a small room at the back of the building—bare walls, the air thick with the smell of damp wood and old chalk.

It's like a twisted déjà vu, living next door to my enemies again, just like in Poitiers with Grabowski next-door. One day, after the war, I'll laugh about how I regularly shared houses with my foes, she mused as she settled into her new quarters, which were little more than a cell.

Still, despite her attempt at humor, she couldn't shake the feeling she was once again living on borrowed time. The constant German presence on the other side of the thin wall would remind her to walk on eggshells every day.

She kept her belongings packed in her suitcase as much as possible, always careful to keep her Colt within arm's reach. The room was even more spartan than Madame Rousseau's, but it would serve its purpose. As she sat on the narrow table-turned bed, her body finally demanded her attention. Suddenly, Lise was overwhelmed by an intense craving—a steak. A thick, juicy steak.

My kingdom for a steak, she giggled to herself, the absurdity of the thought in such dire times striking her as funny.

With that, she pocketed the Colt and sneaked out of the school, on a mission to find a restaurant that could satisfy her very particular—and now, very urgent—desire.

45

BAPTISM BY FIRE

A week later - Normandy, Early June 1944

The night was moonless, the sky a canvas of stars twinkling across the firmament, with the Great Bear dipping low over the French countryside. The only sounds were the distant croaks of frogs and the rustling of leaves in the gentle breeze. Suddenly, the hollow, wooden-sounding kow-kow of a cuckoo broke the silence, a subtle reminder that despite the war, it was still spring.

Lise crouched low in the bocage, the dense hedgerows providing natural cover for her and the Maquis fighters. She waited attentively for the signal for the drop. The drone of an approaching aircraft grew louder, and Lise's heart pounded in rhythm with the engines.

"Raoul, you think it's ours? I can't distinguish what engine it is," Lise whispered, her voice barely more than a breath.

Raoul, ever the fiery leader, leaned closer—too close for Lise's liking—as he whispered in her ear. "Could be. But these days, who knows? We'll find out soon enough."

Lise's nerves were stretched thin with uncertainty. Coordinating drops without the natural light of the moon was something she still had to get used to. With D-Day looming, they were receiving reinforcements almost every night across many of the drop zones on SCIENTIST II's territory.

But with the increased activity came heightened risks. The Germans were on high alert, scouring the area for any sign of nightly operations.

"Everyone in position," Raoul whispered to his fighters who were lying behind Lise and their leader on the edge of the open space. "Now!"

The Maquis fighters, well-armed and clad in camouflage, stealthily formed a circle around the clearing. Lise scanned the dark horizon, her senses heightened, ready to react at the first sign of trouble. The wrong plane, a German ambush—anything could go wrong.

On her other side, Pierre, a fighter not yet seventeen, shifted nervously. "Do you think the plane will know it's here, Marguerite?" he asked under his breath.

"Yes, they're provided with good maps and clear directions. These pilots have done this before."

Pierre tightened his grip on his rifle. "In case the Huns jump on us first, I'm ready."

"That's the spirit," Raoul murmured. "But now keep your head down and shut your trap."

The drone of the plane grew louder, closer. Lise watched it pass overhead, swiftly dropping the precious cargo into the middle of the field just beyond the hedgerows. The thud of the containers hitting the ground was almost lost in the night's silence, but to Lise, it was as loud as a cannon blast.

"Go!" Raoul hissed, and the Maquis fighters sprang into action, moving swiftly and silently to retrieve the supplies.

Lise moved with them, working as quickly as she could to clear the drop zone. The routine was well-practiced, and within minutes, the containers were secured and hidden away in the hedgerow. But the tension remained, hanging in the air like a thick fog.

Raoul turned to Lise, his expression grim. "We're cutting it close these days, Marguerite. The Germans are getting too close for comfort."

Lise wiped a bead of sweat from her brow. "I know. But we're still one step ahead. As long as we stay vigilant, we'll make it through."

Raoul's lips twitched into a brief smile. "You've got nerves of steel, Marguerite. Glad to have you with us."

She returned his smile. "Let's just hope they hold out."

As they prepared to move out, Lise glanced back at the drop zone, the tension in her chest easing slightly.

She sensed it a split second before it happened.

The tranquility of the night was shattered by the deafening roar of gunfire. Birds erupted from the treetops in a frenzy, and hares bolted across the fields in terror. A hail of bullets tore through the foliage, cutting through the darkness with lethal precision.

"Back down!" Lise cried, diving for cover, "and fight back!" Her Colt was already in hand, ready to fire.

From the shadows, German voices barked commands, and the Maquis scrambled to defend their position. Lise's hands were steady as she gripped her weapon with both hands, the cold metal her only protection against deadly stakes. She squeezed the trigger. The click of the safety, the flash of ignition, the crack of the bullet ripping through the night—all in a heartbeat. The shots rang out, echoing through the trees like a grim symphony.

The German ambush had been executed with chilling silence, waiting for the perfect moment to strike. The Maquis were caught off guard, but Lise had sensed the danger. She could see the muzzle flashes in the distance, sporadic bursts of light that revealed the chaos unfolding around her. She fired back, aiming for the shadows, her mind focused on one thing: survival.

The automatic weapons of the Maquis were a fierce counter to the Germans' Mausers. The rapid fire forced the enemy to retreat, their advance halted by the unrelenting barrage. Lise's eyes met Raoul's for a brief moment—a silent understanding passed between them. They had to hold their ground. Now.

Adrenaline surged through her veins, each heartbeat a reminder she was still alive. Despite her long service in France, Lise had never been in an open firefight with the enemy. But her training took over, her instincts honed to razor-sharp precision.

Switching to an Enfield rifle, she directed every shot with deadly accuracy, choosing each target with care. The acrid smell of gunpowder filled the air, stinging her eyes and nose, but she kept her focus, steadying herself on the damp soil beneath her.

The constant barrage of gunfire was deafening, and Lise's ears rang with the noise. Through the cacophony, she could hear the shouts of the Germans, the frantic orders among the Maquis, and the occasional scream of pain—curse words, only in German, prayers, a desperate chorus rising into the night.

Amid the chaos, Lise spotted a German soldier taking aim at Pierre. Without hesitation, she fired. The shot rang out, and the soldier crumpled to the ground, his weapon clattering beside him. The gravity of what she had done struck her for a fleeting second—a life most definitely taken—but there was no time for reflection. Only survival.

The firefight raged on, but the Maquis, fueled by determination and superior tactics, began to turn the tide. The Germans, realizing they were outmatched, started to retreat. Raoul seized the moment, leading a fierce counterattack that drove the enemy further into the darkness.

As the last echoes of gunfire faded into the night, the silence of the countryside returned, eerie in its contrast to the violence that had just erupted. Lise's breath came in ragged gasps, her body trembling as the adrenaline ebbed away. She glanced at Raoul, who nodded at her with a look of respect—his usual bravado replaced with genuine gratitude.

"We did it," he said, his voice hoarse but victorious. His kissed her cheek, the rasp of his beard oddly close.

"Th.. thank you, Mar...Marguerite," Pierre stuttered, still trembling like a reed in the wind. "I think you ... you saved my life."

Lise, herself grappling with the intensity of the battle, hands shaking, picked up the overheated and empty Colt from the moss. "You're welcome, Pierre. Any time, lad. But we need to move. They'll be back with reinforcements within the hour."

The Maquis quickly gathered their supplies, their movements swift and efficient, no one bearing a scratch. As they inched away, every step was cautious.

Arriving back near the Somme to join the other rebel groups, the events of the night hit Lise like a wave—confused victory, raw survival. She was alive, but she had taken lives.

No thinking of that. No thinking of that! she commanded herself, pushing the thoughts aside.

There would be time for reckoning later. For now, there was only the mission. The fight for France's liberation demanded everything she had to give.

As DAWN BROKE over the horizon, Lise curled up in her sleeping bag for a short nap, still trembling all over, fully understanding that this was what war was about. It was ugly, it was intense, it took too many lives. And yet, in this case, it was necessary.

~SIL~

Marseille, September 2004

46

THE LETTERS BETWEEN US

Marseille, September 2004

It had been two weeks since Sil had handed half of Lise's letters and the suitcase to Justin, and she hadn't seen a trace of him since. Whenever she rang his bell, he wasn't home. She'd left his cap hanging on the doorknob on the first floor, where it still remained every time she passed.

She wasn't pleased he was ghosting her, but more than anything, she was worried—worried he'd run off with half of her precious discovery, never mind it probably actually belonged to him as owner of the building it was found in.

But today, Sil was determined to push those worries aside. Standing on a scaffold in Cours Julien, she focused on the massive graffiti project in front of her—a mural titled "Threads of Heritage." The municipality had assigned them a wall, and Sil was finally reconnecting with the reason she had come to Marseille in the first place.

As she sprayed vibrant colors onto the wall, the intensity of the afternoon sun beat down on her back, and the buzzing atmosphere of Cours Julien—filled with artists, musicians, and curious onlookers—was invigorating.

Yet, even amidst this creative energy, Sil found her mind drifting back to Lise. The letters had been so vivid, so raw. She could almost feel the tension of that firefight in the damp Normandy night, hear the crack of gunfire and smell the acrid smoke. How had Lise survived it all? How did anyone?

Franz Ferdinand's "Take Me Out" blared over the square, pulling her out of her thoughts. Sil sang along at the top of her lungs, trying to lose herself in the music and the art.

I KNOW I won't be leaving here with you.
   I know I won't be leaving here
   I know I won't be leaving here with you
   I know I won't be leaving here with you.

"HEY, SIL, LOOKING GOOD UP THERE!" Max, one of her fellow artists who hailed from Bermuda, shouted from below.

She shouted back over the music. "Yup, Max! We're creating 'un chef-d'oeuvre,' as our professeurs would say! Let's hope they agree."

"They're out of it if they don't," German Anna remarked, stretching away from the balustrade to reach the tip of a bird of paradise's bloom.

"Most definitely," Sil agreed, working on long stripes that formed the dress of an African queen.

But even as she bantered with her friends, her thoughts kept slipping back to Lise. How strange it was to be standing in this sun-drenched square, carefree and alive, while reading about a woman who had faced death so many times, in so many ways. And she had lived here, peacefully in Marseille, for decades. In the house where Sil now lived. How strange.

As she continued to work, a sleek black Mercedes with tinted windows rolled onto the square, sticking out amid the casual and colorful chaos around it. She watched, amused, as one window lowered. She froze when she saw it was Justin, looking as out of place as his car in his formal attire.

"Silver!" he called out.

Sil felt every head turn to gaze up at her. What was he doing here? He waved at her, an almost coy smile spreading over his attractive face. "Can I have a word?"

Annoyed, Sil climbed down the scaffold. Why was he back now? She thought she heard her fellow students snicker. Of course, their curiosity was piqued—who was this guy who clearly didn't belong to their scene?

Justin leaned out of the window. "How about we go on a picnic later? There's something important we need to discuss. Come by my apartment when you are done here. Bring the letters with you."

Before Sil could respond, the window rolled up, and the Mercedes smoothly pulled away.

Max walked over, grinning. "Wow, Sil. Who's the guy in the fancy car? Didn't know you had such high-rolling friends. And why does he call you Silver? Is that part of the posh deal?"

Sil watched the car disappear around the corner, still annoyed and not understanding what he was doing to her. To disguise her insecurity, she rolled her eyes. "Heck, Max, that guy is my landlord, and he's just... he's complicated."

"Guys in suits in black Mercedes are always complicated," Max grinned, "but their bank accounts usually aren't. Maybe he can invest in us?"

"Stop it, Max. You're not funny."

Without further ado, Sil climbed the scaffold again to continue her work. She wouldn't let Justin unbalance her again. Anna nudged her playfully. "A picnic with Mr. Fancy Pants, huh? Better bring a nice blanket, and maybe leave the paint-splattered jeans at home this time."

Sil laughed nervously, taking a faulty swipe with her can that made her curse under her breath. As she corrected her mistake, she grumbled. "Yeah, yeah. It's just a picnic, Anna. To talk. About serious stuff."

Max, who'd joined them again, smirked. "Serious stuff? Sure, Sil. We believe you. Are you sure you won't rather hang out with us at Café Waaw? Might be a tad less fancy what pops from under the cork, but a lot more drôle, as the French say?"

Sil shook her head. "Despite what you guys think it's really kind of... business Justin and I have to discuss."

"Ah, you're already on first-name status? Justín, vraiment? Max grinned, pronouncing Justin's name à la French. Sil just gave Max a firm push that made him almost topple over the edge of the scaffold.

"Aggressive Brit," he grinned good-humoredly, as they all returned to their artwork,

Sil concentrated, but with a flutter of anticipation. She was angry with Justin. He would need to come up with a proper excuse for his two-week disappearing act if he wanted to get back into her good books, but despite everything... flutters.

And her new friends? She genuinely enjoyed their company. Her scene, Cours Julien, creativity, and camaraderie. It made her feel alive and part of something bigger. With Lise watching over her.

The remarks from her friends, though teasing, were filled with genuine support and curiosity.

∿

LATER THAT AFTERNOON, Sil found herself on a grassy hill overlooking the sea. Dressed in her best linen shorts and a vintage Simpson tee, she stubbornly kept on her sunglasses and had refused Justin's offer of a ride in the Mercedes. Instead, she'd raced up the hill on her second-hand Caminade bike, now cursing herself for being sweaty all over.

They weren't talking. Justin had spread out a picnic blanket in the shade of an oak tree and placed a basket with wine, fruit, and delicacies in the middle. The air was warm, and the soft hum of cicadas filled the silence as they each sat on opposite sides of the blanket.

Sil noticed he'd changed into denim shorts and a simple white tee, wearing expensive Ray-Ban aviators and canvas shoes. He looked relaxed in casual clothes, though still neat and pressed.

Justin was the first to break the silence. "I owe you an explanation for my absence. I had to go to Paris for work. It crossed my mind several times to let you know I was out of town, but I didn't have your cell phone number. And..." he hesitated, "for some reason, I held back. I'm sorry if I caused you any upset." He glanced at her, taking off his sunglasses and clipping them to the collar of his shirt. His face held the same boyish expression he'd had that afternoon in Cours Julien.

Sil shrugged, trying to appear nonchalant. "It's fine. I was just worried you'd run off with Lise's letters. They mean a lot to me."

"I know. They mean a lot to me too. I've read all the ones you gave me. They blew me away. What a woman, what an incredible woman. But before we dive into that, would you care for a glass of wine? I brought a Chardonnay, hoping you'd like white wine in this weather. I even brought a cooler."

Sil offered a small smile. "Sure. I'm not a big drinker, usually, but let me taste what you've got."

Justin uncorked the bottle and poured the golden liquid into two real glasses, not the disposable kind.

"Santé."

"Santé." Sil took a sip. It was delicious—sweet and cool, caressing her tongue.

"Before we talk about Lise, can we talk about you first? I'd like to know more about you, Silver."

Sil frowned. "What do you want to know? And will I get the chance to ask you the same questions?"

"I want to know everything about you," Justin replied with a grin. "And sure, I'll tell you what you want to know about me. But I asked first. Why not start with your family?"

Sil took a deep breath. Not her favorite topic. So, she went through it as fast as she could. "I grew up in Bristol. My mother is Moroccan, but she didn't want me. My father had an affair with her, and when I was born, he took me back to Bristol and married Ghislaine, a woman he'd known from school. I have a younger half-brother, Jeremy, who does everything right in my parents' eyes. My father is a schoolteacher, and I've always been the odd one out in the family. That's about it. What about you?"

Justin listened intently, his eyes never leaving hers through her Oxfam glasses. "Uh-huh, I'll tell you my story in a minute. Yours sounds really tough."

"It was," Sil admitted. "I left home to hang out with the Bristol gangs when I was thirteen. That's how I met Felix and started with graffiti, experimenting with drugs. And sex. School was of no importance. But my art saved me. I got better and better and finally applied for the scholarship in Marseille and got it. I cut ties with the scene back home. Now I'm here. Felix followed me, kicked that hole in the wall, but I sent him packing. You don't have to worry; he won't be back. This is my life now."

Justin's gray eyes shone with deep admiration. "That's impressive, Silver Anderson. You've certainly come a long way. You're a tough cookie and from what I've seen this afternoon, a hell of an artist."

Sil felt a warm giddiness spread through her, glad the ice between them broke faster than last time. "What about you? What's your story?"

Justin took a few moments to gather his thoughts, taking a sip of his wine. "I'm from an old Marseillaise family. I lost my mother when I was three years old, and earlier this year, I lost my father. He had several businesses here in the area, so I'm now tied up in looking after those. But my real passion is history. I'm a lecturer at the Sorbonne and usually live in Paris, but I've returned to Marseille to wrap up my father's businesses. I didn't want to move back into my parents' house, where both my parents died, so I sold the old place and bought 32 Rue Sainte a few months ago when it came on the market. I knew I wasn't going to be there much, so I decided to rent out part of it. That way the house would at least be occupied while I was gone."

He started unwrapping sandwiches from their tinfoil, looking rather lost. Sil realized Justin had made the picnic himself. She watched as his hands busied themselves, wondering what to say. He was hurting, too. Justin Bellamare, who seemed so laid-back and unflappably successful, was in pain.

"That's a lot to deal with," she said softly, "and you don't have any brothers or sisters?"

"No, my parents were only married for a couple of years when my mother got cancer."

"I'm so sorry, Justin. And here I was, thinking I'd had it hard."

"We hurt in different ways, Silver," Justin said, handing her a crab and lettuce sandwich. "But all of this has led to a chance for me to reconnect with my Marseillaise roots. And meeting you has been... unexpected and intriguing."

Though they came from different worlds, Sil felt the tension between them easing, just like when he had visited her in her room, and she'd told him about Lise's letters.

"Unexpected and intriguing, huh?" she jested. "I'll take that as a compliment. I assume there's a Mrs. Bellamare?"

Justin's eyes darkened. "There was, yes. But no longer. It didn't end with a hole in my wall like with you, but certainly with a hole in my heart. Let's leave it at that."

They ate in silence for a while, and Sil stared out over the Mediterranean. For the first time in a very long time, she felt at ease, and she suddenly realized why. The last time she'd felt this good, this appreciated, this seen had been with Grandpa Jack on the Welsh coast. A different sea, a different man, but the same total acceptance of her freaky, lovable, artistic self. No judgment.

Tears sprang into her eyes, not just because she missed her grandfather but because it was so precious to be able to be totally herself with another person.

"What is it, Silver? Something I said, ma chère?" Justin placed a warm, strong hand over her slim artist fingers. She shook her head. "I was thinking of my Grandpa Jack. I'll tell you about him one day. But not now. We have the letters to discuss."

Justin cupped her chin, took off her stubborn sunglasses, and gazed into her teary eyes. "We have all the time in the world, Silver. Lise's letters are between us. For good."

LATER THAT EVENING, Sil sat on her bed, Lise's letters spread out before her like a fan of old photographs. The sun had set, and the warm light of her bedside lamp cast a glow over her rainbow hair.

The picnic with Justin had left her feeling both lighter and more reflective—a strange combination the unruly artist in her wasn't entirely comfortable with.

She thought again about her grandfather, whose memories had brought tears to her eyes when she was overlooking the sea in Justin's presence. Grandpa Jack had been with the Welsh Fusiliers, part of the British 53rd Infantry Division, making their way through Normandy. She remembered his many stories about the invasion, always more focused on the camaraderie than the combat. Could he have passed Lise on those war-torn roads? Two different lives converging, if only for a moment?

She picked up the letter she'd been reading before Justin had re-entered her life—Lise's account of D-Day. Sil felt a familiar chill as she traced the edges of the fragile paper. It wasn't just history; it was someone's life, her life, Grandpa Jack's life. She took a deep breath before letting herself be transported back in time...

~ LISE ~

France/England June 1944 – May 1946

47

THE LONG RIDE HOME

ormandy, 6 June, 1944
The early morning sky over Normandy was a thick, oppressive gray, heavy with the threat of rain showers. The air was humid, and the wind blew in from the sea with a chill that hinted at a tempest about to unfold.

As the first light of dawn broke through the clouds, the rumble of distant thunder was soon drowned out by the roar of aircraft engines and the barrage of naval artillery.

OPERATION OVERLORD HAD BEGUN.

ON THE BEACHES, thousands of Allied troops stormed ashore, battling the fierce German defenses. Paratroopers descended from the sky, their parachutes dotting the clouds like confetti, while amphibious vehicles rumbled out of the sea.

The chaos of battle spread rapidly across the French coast, a cacophony of explosions, gunfire, and shouted orders reverberating through the air.

Men fell in the sand, in the mud, torn from tanks, and shot from the sky. Death was indiscriminate—it took them all, without regard for the color of their uniforms, their age, or their rank. But as two fell, three more clambered over the cliffs and dunes, fighting inch by blood-soaked inch to reclaim French soil.

Meanwhile, in Paris, Lise was attending a crucial meeting with fellow Resistance leaders. The city was a ticking time bomb, the air thick with anticipation and fear. News of the invasion spread quickly, rippling through the resistance like a shockwave.

Lise, along with the rest of France, had her ear glued to every radio broadcast, the static-laced words filling the room with both hope and dread.

When the announcement came—the Allied forces had landed on the beaches of Normandy—Lise felt a surge of adrenaline that left her momentarily breathless. This was it, the moment they had been waiting for. But her exhilaration was quickly tempered by the distressing reality of her situation. She was almost 150 miles away from her network, from her brother. The battle had begun and she was missing it.

Determined not to let the distance keep her from the fight, Lise knew she had to return to Normandy immediately. She needed to support the Allied forces and stand by her brother's side in this critical hour.

But the Maquis had done their sabotage jobs rather too well—the trains were no longer running, the tracks and stations blown up to cripple any German movement toward the coast. Her only option was to cycle the entire way, through a landscape crawling with angry enemies and fighting forces.

With a body driven by sheer will, Lise set out, her legs pumping furiously as she navigated the war-torn landscape. The wind whipped against her face, and the roads ahead seemed to stretch into an endless horizon of peril.

Her bad leg, thank God, had mostly healed by now but it continued to worry her whether it would play up again. The journey was grueling. She pedaled through fields scarred by craters, over hills that seemed to climb into the sky, and through forests thick with brambles and the threat of ambush.

Each revolution of her pedals brought new challenges—debris from battles long past, the distant rumble of artillery, and the ever-present risk of German patrols.

On the second day, exhaustion was setting in, but there was no time to rest. As she rounded a bend, her heart froze—a German checkpoint loomed ahead. There was no backing out now.

The soldiers eyed her with suspicion, and one stepped forward, blocking her path. His hand rested casually on the grip of his pistol, a silent threat.

"Where are you going?" he demanded in sharp German, his gaze piercing as he gripped her handlebar.

Lise called on every ounce of her training to tell her cover story with conviction. "I'm on my way to Evreux," she replied in fluent French, injecting a hint of desperation into her tone. "My sister is seriously ill. I have to get to her."

The soldier scrutinized her face, his eyes narrowing as if weighing her every word. "Why are you traveling alone? It is dangerous for a woman."

Lise forced a weak smile, slipping into the role of the fragile widow she was supposed to be. "I would rather have stayed in Paris, but my family is in dire need. My parents are elderly, and my sister is handicapped. There is no one else to assist them. Oh, why are the trains not running?" She let her voice tremble just enough to seem sincere.

"The darn French are blowing up all our locomotives and railroads, that's why," the German snapped, clearly irritated by the situation.

"I know. Isn't it horrible?" Lise lamented, inwardly cringing at the lie and praying he would let her go soon.

The soldier glanced at her bicycle, noting its worn appearance. After what felt like an eternity, he stepped aside, motioning for her to pass. "Be quick about it," he said gruffly. "And stay off the main roads. There are more patrols ahead, and it's getting more dangerous further west."

Lise nodded gratefully and cycled on while letting out a breath of relief. Though the encounter had cost her precious time, she'd made it through without even having to show her papers. She'd have to be more careful, though, scanning the road ahead for any sign of danger, the patrols dotting the landscape like anthills ready to swarm.

For three days, Lise cycled almost non-stop, pausing only briefly to rest in ditches or in abandoned barns. Parts of her body ached she didn't even know could ache, and her leg screamed with every pedal stroke. But she never gave up. Her mind was more or less blank, with just one goal. Get to Normandy. Even hunger and thirst were forgotten; this was all she had trained for, and yet, at 'le moment suprême' she wasn't there.

On the early morning of June 9, Lise finally reached the outskirts of Normandy, her clothes dirty and torn, her face smeared with grime and exhaustion.

The sight that greeted her was one of organized chaos. Claude's network was in full swing, coordinating efforts with the Allied paratroopers who had landed in the area. His men and women were executing the meticulously laid plans to disrupt German reinforcements with precision and determination.

Already, five hundred German vehicles had been put out of action with the aid of tire bursters, while the railway line between Caen and Vire was repeatedly sabotaged. All telephone lines and underground cables had been severed, crippling German communications.

The Maquis under Raoul's leadership were showing their brilliance, finally able to go footloose and fancy-free with the stockpiled ammunition and weaponry. Their actions were steeled by the presence of Allied soldiers and the knowledge that liberation was finally within reach.

Claude, satisfied his organization was fully prepared and operational, greeted Lise with urgent enthusiasm, though he took in her dishevelment with a frown on his face.

"Marguerite, you made it!" he exclaimed, embracing her briefly before turning back to the tasks at hand. "I've sent Vladimir and Verger north to work the coasts in Calvados and Manche. We will remain in the rear with Geneviève, in the Orne and Eure-et-Loir region, so we can assist the Allies from behind the German lines. I've broken down our Maquis into small groups of four to ten, because of the massive German counterattacks. They have to move swiftly and without being seen."

"What can I do?" Lise asked, her voice strong despite the fatigue that almost knocked her off her feet.

Claude took in his older sister for a moment, concern flickering in his blue eyes. "Apart from securing a wash and some clean clothes, get some rest. I expect a massive drop of sixty containers near Avenay tonight. I'd like you to oversee that. Tomorrow, you'll assist in blowing up the bridge over the Orne River near Caen."

In the face of so much action, she almost forgot her exhausting cycle trip. "I'm ready when you're ready," she replied, still a glint in a similarly blue eye.

It was as if she and her brother had been blowing up bridges and derailing trains all their lives.

If Maman could see us now, she wouldn't believe she'd given birth to the pair of us, Lise thought wryly. *En garde!*

48

THE LAST MONTHS OF PERIL

A few weeks later - Normandy, July 1944

The weeks following the D-Day landings were some of the most perilous in Lise's wartime life. As the Allies made steady progress towards Paris, the German forces grew increasingly desperate and ferocious in their retaliations.

Under Claude and Lise's leadership, SCIENTIST II Maquis relentlessly harassed the Germans across the rain-soaked fields and muddy paths of Normandy, their sabotage efforts critical in disrupting German supply lines and communications. But every victory came at great personal risk.

On this particular morning, the rain had momentarily ceased, leaving the air thick with humidity and the ground a treacherous quagmire. Lise mounted her bicycle, her clothes still damp from the previous day's downpour. As she adjusted the straps of her worn leather satchel, Geneviève approached, her youthful face grown markedly mature under the weight of being SCIENTIST's main W/T operator now.

"You ready, Geneviève?" Lise asked, as she handed her a small bundle of coded messages to transmit to London.

Geneviève nodded, tucking the bundle into her jacket. "Yes, Marguerite. I'll get these out as soon as I can find a safe spot to set up the wireless."

Lise studied the younger woman for a moment, sensing the strain that had taken its toll on both of them. The loss of Claude's former second-in-command and his loyal W/T operator, had been crushing news to the entire network. The brutal firefight near Pier-refitte-en-Cinglais in which they had been killed was a harsh reminder they could be next.

"You're doing well, Geneviève," Lise tried to take some of the strain from her shoulders. "But remember, be as quick as you can, despite being careful and precise in what you transmit. We can't afford to lose anyone else." Lise didn't add 'lose you' because Geneviève was now their only means of communication with the Firm.

The young operator managed a small smile, humming the tune of Bing Crosby's "I'll Be Home for Christmas" under her breath as she secured the wireless set in its suitcase onto the back of her bike.

The irony of the song wasn't lost on Lise; the thought of home seemed like a distant dream, a place that had become abstract and uncertain. Was it France, was it England?

As they rode through the rolling fields, their bicycles slicing through the thick mud, Lise found herself contemplating the future. The war had consumed her life for so long—four relentless years of danger, sacrifice, and loss. What would become of her when it was over?

France, the country she had fought so hard to liberate, felt both familiar and foreign. Paris, the city of her youth, was now tainted by memories she wasn't sure she could face.

"Marguerite," Geneviève interrupted her thoughts, "do you ever think about what you'll do after all this is over?"

Lise glanced at her companion. It was as if she'd read her thoughts. "Sometimes," she admitted. "But the war isn't over yet. We still have work to do."

"I know," Geneviève replied in her high voice filled with longing. "But when we can leave here, I think I'll go back to South Africa. Durban, where I was born. I'd like to settle down there, maybe start a new life away from all this."

"Durban," Lise echoed, the word heavy on her tongue. "It sounds so far away, like a world apart. Like my Mauritius."

"It is," Geneviève said with a wistful smile. "But it's home. It's where I can find peace again, I think."

"Peace," Lise repeated, as if testing the word on her lips. "Yes, that might be nice... someday."

They rode on in silence, the only sounds the rhythmic creak of their bicycles and the distant rumble of artillery. The once fertile farmland, now scarred by war, seemed to stretch endlessly before them. Lise watched as a lark soared into the sky, its song piercing the heavy air.

Oh, to be a bird, to have wings and fly away from it all, she thought wistfully, before forcing herself back to the grim reality of their situation. There was no room for melancholy—not yet.

"We need to focus," Lise said firmly, her voice breaking the stillness. "There's still a long road ahead."

Geneviève's youthful energy seemed to return as she straightened in her saddle. "Right. Let's get to it, Marguerite."

As Geneviève and Lise cycled over the muddy paths towards their new hideout, their shoes and socks splattered with mud and their blouses clinging to their backs from exertion, Lise was the first to spot them.

"Checkpoint," she gritted out through clenched teeth, her eyes narrowing at the sight ahead.

"Golly," was all Geneviève managed to reply.

The rain had ceased temporarily, but the air was still humid as the slash of a quagmire. The sentry was a tall Wehrmacht soldier, his rifle slung nonchalantly over his shoulder, yet his stance was anything but relaxed. His cold, calculating gaze locked onto them as they approached.

"Halt!" he commanded. Lise knew that look in the narrow-set eyes and it didn't bode well. She felt an urge to grab her gun as he sized them up but thought better of it. His gaze going from their face to the bulging bags strapped to their bicycles was not what she wanted to see. The other soldier stayed at some distance but followed everything with interest.

"Vos papiers," the sentry demanded in French, in a thick accent. His hand rested casually on the stock of his rifle to show the power he still had over them.

Lise, forcing herself to remain calm, handed over Madame Janette Bouville's forged papers with a steady hand, adopting the persona of the frail widow she portrayed. Beside her, Geneviève did the same, though Lise could feel her companion trembling with barely-contained anxiety.

The soldier scrutinized their documents, his eyes darting between the papers and their faces. "Where are you going?" he demanded in an unfriendly way. "It is dangerous for women to travel alone, especially now."

"We have no choice," Lise replied in fluent French, adopting her stance of helplessness that belied the fear that was creeping up. This German was not going to let them go.

"We're seeking refuge in Evreux. My sister is seriously ill, and my parents are elderly. We must help them." She prayed he wouldn't notice they were heading in the wrong direction.

The soldier's eyes narrowed further as he took a step closer, his presence looming. "Why are your bicycles so heavily laden?" He pointed to the bulging bags with a hint of suspicion.

"It is all we have left," Lise answered, forcing a weak smile. Geneviève opened her mouth as if to speak, but Lise silenced her with a sharp gesture. "We have to bring as much as we can carry. Please, we just want to reach our family."

The soldier's suspicion lingered, his gaze raking over them with an almost predatory intent. He took another step forward, his body inches from Lise's, and began to frisk her, his hands roaming over her waist, then lower, up and down her skirt, and over the bulky radio components hidden under her belt.

Lise's skin shivered under his touch, but she kept her composure, even as she went almost out of her mind. She had heard stories —horrible, violent stories—of what could happen if she were discovered. The memory of a female agent's recent brutal assault by German soldiers flashed through her mind, and she braced herself for the worst.

The soldier's hand brushed against the hidden radio components, and for a heart-stopping moment, Lise thought her fate was sealed. Her breath caught in her throat, but she forced herself to stand still, her eyes squinting in the summer light, giving nothing away. His hands moved up under her ribcage, over her hips where her gun was hidden, and down her thighs.

He must have felt something, she knew he had. The hard, unyielding shapes beneath her clothes were unmistakable.

This is it, Lise thought with a chilling calm. *I am about to be exposed.*

The soldier's touch became more invasive, more deliberate, and Lise had to fight every instinct to recoil, to scream, to run. Instead, she squirmed slightly, just enough to seem like a modest widow would, begging softly, "Please, Sir..."

Finally, after what felt like an eternity, the soldier stepped back, his expression inscrutable. "You're free to go," he said gruffly. For a moment, Lise thought she had misunderstood, but then he took another step away from her, clearing her path.

"Now go!"

Lise and Geneviève wasted no time. They jumped back onto their bikes and raced away as quickly as they dared. But just as they were a couple of yards away, Lise heard a metallic clunk. Her heart froze. Glancing down, she saw a spare radio part had fallen from her skirt onto the road. Panic surged through her veins, but with a swift, almost instinctive movement, she leaned over, scooped it up, and pocketed it without breaking her pace.

She didn't look back to check if he'd seen it. And no shot rang.

While they created an ever-larger distance between the sentry and themselves, her mind replayed the close encounter over and over. This had been too close. The closest Lise had come to arrest in all her time in France.

"We can't afford any more of these close calls," she whispered hoarsely to Geneviève, her voice trembling with the remnants of fear.

"But it went alright, didn't it?" Geneviève replied, her tone betraying a naive innocence. "I think he was actually quite good-looking... for a German."

Dear God in Heaven, was all Lise could think. *This girl trembles with fear when there's no danger, but when we're on the brink of death, she finds time for a schoolgirl crush.*

The rain began to fall again, thick drops masking their tracks as they rode on, the muddy paths and rain-soaked fields their only allies in this treacherous landscape.

It wasn't over yet.

49

STEADFAST STEEL

A few weeks later - Normandy, early August 1944

As the Americans, after weeks of grueling battles in June and July, finally seemed on the brink of breaking out of Normandy, the hopes of the French people surged. Was the liberation of France now truly within reach?

In the first week of August, however, Hitler made one last desperate stand. As the Allies gained momentum, the supply lines feeding the front lines grew longer, more stretched. So, in a last-ditch effort, he ordered his generals to sever these vital lifelines.

Despite the high German command warning the delusional Führer that the counteroffensive was doomed to fail, he wouldn't listen. The Germans struck hard at the American forces between Avranches and Mortain, right in the heart of Lise and Claude's SCIENTIST II territory.

Thanks to the Enigma decrypts, every move of the German army was anticipated. Mortain changed hands seven times within a single week of brutal, close-quarter fighting, leaving the town a blood-soaked battlefield. But the German front finally collapsed.

By August 8, the Allies were advancing in Lise's direction, and her heart swelled with gratitude and pride. The news that General Patton had taken Le Mans, and then Alençon, was greeted with triumph among the resisters. Yet Normandy was not free. The Allied plan was working, but SCIENTIST II's role in the demise of the German army was now crucial.

As the Americans closed in from the west and the Brits and Canadians pressed down from Caen, the Wehrmacht was forced into a corner, leading to their inevitable surrender in the town of Falaise.

It would now only be a matter of days before brother and sister De Baissac, shoulder-to-shoulder, would lay eyes on the American forces, while they worked around the clock to hamper the remaining German opposition.

Along the Orne River, Lise's resisters ferreted out the last German pockets. Amidst the Maquis, late-comers known as 'moth-ball men,' dressed in French uniforms that had been stored in moth-ball-filled cupboards since 1940, joined the fray, chanting, "À chacun son Allemand"—To each his own German.

In the midst of this chaotic liberation, Lise found herself constantly trying to maintain order among her fighters. As victory neared, the line between disciplined resistance and unchecked revenge grew perilously thin. It was becoming a lawless mission, fueled by hatred and a thirst for retribution.

While she couldn't prevent every atrocity, her famous sangfroid helped tone down the hottest tempers. To her followers, she was Marguerite, a force to be reckoned with, as revered as a modern-day Jeanne d'Arc.

It was during one of these intense days that Raoul, ever the passionate fighter, approached her with a broad grin plastered across his dirt-streaked face. Victory was within reach, and it showed in his giddy, almost reckless stance.

"Marguerite," he called out as they moved through the thick brush, his voice laced with an unusual lightness. "We've nearly won! Just a few more days, and it'll all be over!"

Lise listened to his enthusiasm while her own mind stayed focused on the next objective. "We're close, Raoul, but it's not over yet. We need to keep our wits."

He stepped closer, his grin widening, his eyes holding a heat that was unmistakable. "You know, once this is all done, we should celebrate. Just the two of us. I've always been drawn to your... strength."

Lise stopped in her tracks, turning to face him, her gaze locking with his. There was a part of her—buried deep beneath the layers of duty and resolve—that felt the pull of his virility, his raw, untamed energy. It stirred something in her, a reminder of her own humanity, of the desires she had long pushed aside for the greater good. But she also knew this was not the time to let those feelings take root.

"Raoul," she said in a tone that was both firm and laced with a hint of something softer, "I appreciate your... enthusiasm, truly. But this isn't the moment. We're here to fight, not to... fraternize."

The grin faded from Raoul's face, replaced by a look of chagrin. He was clearly not used to being turned down by a woman. "Of course, Marguerite. I didn't mean to overstep. It's just... well, you're impressive, that's all."

Lise allowed a small smile, letting him see she wasn't immune to his charm but that her priorities were clear. "Thank you, Raoul. But let's save the celebrations for after we've won. I'll make sure to jot down your name in my ball book." She gave him a ladylike wink.

Raoul's embarrassment was almost endearing, and Lise could see the respect in his eyes as he nodded. "Right. A waltz it is, then."

As they battled on, Lise wondered how this rugged Norman always seemed to get under her skin and reawaken a feminine side of her. Raoul was good at what he did, but so was she. And she'd keep him at an appropriate distance.

AN HOUR *later*

HOT SUMMER WEATHER had finally replaced the months of incessant rain, and Lise found herself cycling her blue bike, she'd nicknamed Blue Valkyrie, through waves of mosquitoes so thick she had to actually brush them aside. Bullet-ridden trucks and broken tanks littered the roads, rows of marching German prisoners-of-war with their hands up, and too many crosses with helmets at the top stood along the way. The chaos, the debris, the pain was spread out everywhere under the hot Normandy sun.

As she rode along the battered road, a lone German soldier suddenly stepped from behind a hedgerow bush, blocking her path.

"Halt!" he ordered, raising his rifle.

Lise straddled the frame of her bicycle, and reflexively prepared to produce her false papers, meanwhile thinking, *Do I still need to? He's the one on the run now.* But the German clearly thought he was still in charge, which led to an odd tug of war.

"*Descendez de votre vélo,*" the German ordered. Get off your bike.

Pointing his rifle at her with one hand, his other grimy hand grabbed the frame, shaking it hard and trying to make her step off. Lise knew he wanted the bike in an attempt to reach the safety of the Kitzinger Line by bike, but she was not having it. Not in this phase of the war.

No way! She held her ground with all her strength.

"What are you doing? Do you want me to call your Hauptmann?" she announced sternly, "he happens to billet next door to me." The soldier, who was a mere one-dot Leutnant, froze at the threat. Lise had guessed correctly. Even in retreat, Nazis had an instinctive reaction to ranks above them. Even firmer she added, "If you do this, I'll go straight to your boss and report you."

The German hesitated, his grip on the bicycle loosening. Lise seized the moment, yanking the bike back towards her. He stepped back and she'd won. The first open hand-to-hand battle with a German in her four years of service ended in her favor. A small victory, but still.

"*Allez!*" he barked, more to save his face than to give an actual order.

Lise didn't wait for a second invitation. She mounted her Blue Valkyrie and rode away, grinning from ear to ear.

May this be the last close call with the enemy, Lise prayed. She was quite done with these encounters. The Allies were now within earshot. Almost there! Almost.

As she cycled on through the war-torn landscape, the sounds of gunfire and exploding shells echoed through the fields. More than ever, she was thankful for her rusty, blue bicycle with its brown handlebars and its rickety luggage carrier. Her steel companion had been instrumental and served her well all the one hundred days of her second mission.

At times she'd felt the old thing was her one and only ally, constantly serving her, never giving up. Blue Valkyrie had seen her through everything, every checkpoint. It had carried all her illegal belongings and had never even complained under the weight. Two flat tires and one broken chain. That was all.

Blue Valkyrie had been more than a means of transportation; it had been her escape and her lifeline. Through nightly missions under the cloak of darkness, it had carried her swiftly past enemy lines, its creaky frame a trusted ally on countless covert operations, bearing the weight of sabotage materials and coded messages.

Each of Lise's pedal strokes had been a defiant act against the occupation, every rotation of the wheels a silent vow of resistance.

Later, when I think back about this war, Lise mused, *I will see myself cycling and cycling and cycling. All in all, I may have cycled the distance from Paris to Curepipe in this war.*

Thanks to you, Blue Valkyrie!

50

SYMBOLS AND SACRIFICE

A few weeks later - Normandy, mid-August 1944

T he arrival of the American army on August 13 marked a definitive, turning point in the war for Lise and Claude. After years of leading the ARTIST and SCIENTIST I & II networks, organizing and training thousands of French resister fighters, the brother and sister De Baissac could finally hand over the reins to the professional soldiers.

The fierce battles of Normandy were winding down, and the headquarters of the SCIENTIST II network were now securely within Allied territory. The transition from guerrilla warfare to organized military operations was still taking place amid chaotic scenes —the air thick with the dust and smoke of battle.

As soon as their terrain was declared safe, Claude and Lise retrieved their respective uniforms, which had been carefully hidden in various safe houses throughout the years. The moment Lise laid eyes on her First Aid Nursing Yeomanry uniform, a wave of emotions swept through her, nearly knocking her off her tired feet. This khaki outfit was more than just clothing; it was a symbol of her true identity, and represented the role of agent that she'd embraced for the duration of the war.

With trembling hands, she kissed the sturdy khaki fabric, her eyes welling with tears. Every thread, every stitch represented the years of sacrifice, the countless lives lost, and the strength of her spirit that had carried her through every dark and terrifying moment.

Wrenching herself out of Madame Janette Bouville's worn and faded dress, Lise put on her uniform, her heart swelling with pride. She was elated to show the world who she really was: Captain Lise de Baissac. Gone were the aliases, the code names, the fake life stories. Here she was, a proud Brit who'd defended the country of her soul, France.

The FANY uniform, though not the most fashionable, was the most beautiful battledress in Lise's eyes. The rough material, the sturdy buttons, the white blouse, the khaki tie, the weight of the jacket on her shoulders—it all felt perfect.

Even in the blistering August heat, she refused to take off the heavy jacket or her beret. She had earned the right to wear this uniform openly, and no amount of discomfort could make her relinquish it now.

Claude watched his sister emerge from the safe house, now just an ordinary French bungalow, with a warm smile, clearly equally proud as he adjusted the collar of his British Army uniform. It had been years since they could openly acknowledge who they were, and this moment felt monumental.

This was what the war had made of them, a war they'd managed to survive, with narrow escapes and a stiff portion of luck. It was surreal to wear a uniform openly in a country where, only days earlier, such an act would have brought a bullet to their heads.

"You're going to faint if you strut around like that in this heat," Claude teased gently, though his eyes, tired and with dark bags underneath, shone with triumph.

"I don't care," Lise replied, her voice barely containing her emotion. Her eyes were full of defiant delight. "I've waited so long for this moment, Claude. Aren't our uniforms a symbol of everything we've fought for?"

"They are, Lise," he agreed, kissing his sister on the cheek. "And, by the way, it's wonderful to call you by your real name again."

"Oh, Claude. We did it." Lise's voice broke as tears finally spilled over—tears of happiness, of exhaustion, and of grief for all the comrades and agents they'd lost along the way. The De Baissacs may have survived, but the cost to the SOE had been immeasurable.

At that moment, an American jeep with two soldiers in it drove by, their faces curious as they took in the sight of the brother and sister standing proudly in their uniforms. The driver braked hard, and they both leaned out, grinning.

"Hey friends, where have you two come from so suddenly?" the driver joked, pointing to their uniforms that seemed out of place amidst the rubble and ruin.

"We've dropped out of the sky," Lise shouted back with a playful smile, the irony of her statement not lost on her. Speaking English openly again was another new, exhilarating experience.

The Americans laughed and waved a 'See you later!' as they drove off in a cloud of dust. Brother and sister stood watching as the jeep disappeared out of the village. *Hey friends!* How good that had sounded.

Claude turned to his sister, his voice heavy with the weight of their shared ordeal. "How true that is. We did drop from the sky. And we always landed by moonlight."

"The liberation is here, but so are our losses. Our victory came at a high price, Claude." She knew he was thinking of Claudine as well, and of his daughter. Could she bring them up? Not now, not yet. But later, certainly. They still had work to do. Their private lives would have to wait a little longer.

ON AUGUST 15, the Nazi command ordered a full evacuation from the Normandy front, a decision that reportedly led Hitler to call it "the worst day of his life." The Allies pressed their advantage relentlessly. That same day, General Eisenhower launched his second offensive on the Côte d'Azur, the new front beginning its steady march north toward Paris.

Two days later, Claude was summoned back to England, tasked with delivering detailed reports to the Firm. He wasn't going alone. Geneviève, their loyal W/T operator, was accompanying him under her real name – Phyllis Latour.

Before Claude left, he took Lise aside, his expression more serious than ever. "We need to talk about Mary...Claudine. Her real name is Mary Herbert"

Lise was glad he brought her up himself. Claude hadn't mentioned Claudine/Mary, or his daughter, in a long time. The war had had a way of pushing personal pain to the side, but now it could no longer be ignored.

"What about her?"

He hesitated, his usual composure faltering. "I've been thinking about her and our daughter a lot lately. With the war coming to an end, I can't stop wondering if they're still out there somewhere. I need to know what happened to them. But I need to go to London. I don't know what to do."

Lise saw the vulnerability in her brother's eyes, the same eyes that had been steeled against countless dangers. "We'll find them," she promised. "Once we're completely wrapped up here, we'll go back. We'll search until we know for sure."

Claude felt visibly strengthened by her support. "Thank you, Lise. It's one of the few things that's kept me going through all of this."

Before Lise could respond, Phyllis, their ever-enthusiastic W/T operator whom everybody now called Pippa, bounded up to them with her usual energy. "Well, Major Claude, Captain Lise," she beamed, standing proudly in her newly donned navy uniform of the Women's Auxiliary Air Force, the hat slightly askew on her head. "I'm ready for a proper English tea and maybe even a scone, if we can find one!"

Claude chuckled, the tension of his discussion with Lise easing. "You've earned it, Pippa. You've been incredible."

Lise also smiled at Phyllis's innocent excitement. "Pippa dear, thank you for everything. You've been a constant source of light, even when things were darkest."

Phyllis blushed, waving her hand dismissively. "Oh, it was nothing! I mean, we did win, didn't we? That's what matters. And who knows, maybe one day we can all come back here for a holiday— under much nicer circumstances, of course!"

As Phyllis climbed into the plane, she paused and looked back at Lise with a playful grin. "Oh, and Captain Lise, I couldn't help noticing Raoul's eyes gobbling you up every time you turned your back. Now that I'm off, you'll have him all to yourself. You lucky girl!"

Lise shook her head, laughing despite herself. "Oh Pippa, you have quite the imagination. Raoul is a comrade, nothing more."

Phyllis winked. "Sure, sure. Oh, and before I forget. Remember to pack a thermos with proper English tea next time. We Brits need to keep up our standards, even in the middle of a war!"

Lise laughed out loud now. "I'll not forget the tea, Pippa. Let's hope there never will be another war. Safe travels, my dear."

She turned to Claude, who was waiting to say goodbye before it was his turn to board the plane. "Promise me you'll be careful," he urged, gripping her shoulders as if to anchor her. "You never know if there are stray pockets of Germans hiding somewhere."

"Of course, I will be careful," Lise replied, touched by his thoughtfulness. "Haven't I been careful all this time? Besides, I'll be in London soon enough. Give Buck and Vera my best."

Claude studied her, his gaze intense. "We've come too far, Lise. Don't take unnecessary risks now."

"I won't," she assured him, giving his hand a reassuring squeeze. But she knew what he meant. She would be on her own again in a country still adrift.

As the plane lifted off, Lise watched it climb into the sky, a small, silvery bird disappearing into the clouds. She felt a sudden pang of loneliness, but she quickly pushed it aside. There was still work to be done, and her time to return to London would come soon enough.

ON AUGUST 26, the bells of Notre Dame rang out to signal the long-awaited victory over Nazi Germany as De Gaulle strode down the Champs-Élysées, surrounded by throngs of jubilant Parisians. The moment was broadcast over the radio, and all of France seemed to celebrate, tricolors waving from every building, every corner.

BUT LISE'S thoughts were elsewhere.

. . .

SHE MOUNTED her loyal Blue Valkyrie, its blue frame still an enduring constant in a fast-changing world. She set off towards Pierrefitte-en-Cinglais. Her destination was somber: to visit the place where their fallen comrades, Jean Renaud-Dandicolle and Maurice Larcher, formerly codenamed René and Vladimir, had made the ultimate sacrifice.

The journey was solitary, the landscape quiet but for the rhythmic hum of her bike wheels and the distant cheers of the celebrators. When she reached the site, Lise was greeted by lush green fields surrounding the charred remains of the agents' former headquarters. The house, once alive with the sound of planning and camaraderie, was now nothing but ashes.

Lise dismounted and approached the ruins, her heart in pain. She knelt before the burnt-down structure, the memories of their shared moments flooding back—laughter, strategy, whispered conversations in the dead of night, the odd joke.

"You didn't die in vain," she whispered to the empty air, her voice catching in her throat. "We owe this victory as much to you, Jean and Maurice."

Her hands, usually so strong and steady, trembled slightly as she fashioned two simple crosses from nearby branches. With a pen, she wrote their names, "Jean Renaud-Dandicolle" and "Maurice Larcher," and planted the makeshift memorials into the ground. She knew there probably would be a real memorial for them later, but she had wanted to see the place where they'd fought to their last breath with her own eyes.

Looking around, searching for something, anything, that could stand out as a symbol. Her eyes fell on two poppies growing in the field next to the rubble that once was a house, their red petals vivid against the green backdrop.

Gently, she picked the flowers and attached the delicate stems to the crosses. "Though they may wither," she murmured, "they stand for your courage and your sacrifice."

For a long moment, she sat there on her knees, in silence, the wind whispering through the grass, carrying away the remnants of a war that had claimed too many young lives. And as the poppies swayed in the breeze, Lise allowed herself a moment of quiet grief— her own moment of remembrance.

51

FAREWELL TO THE FIELD

A few weeks later - Normandy, early September 1944

T he sun was beginning to dip behind the rolling hills of Normandy, casting shadows across the fields, as Lise sat on the doorstep of the modest bungalow where she'd been staying. The evening air was still sultry from the day's heat. This had been her home base for the final leg of the war—a place of road-mapping, reflection, and fleeting moments of rest.

Lise's thoughts were interrupted by the sound of an approaching car engine, an unusual occurrence in this part of liberated France. She rose to her feet, her curiosity piqued. As the sleek black car came to a stop, a familiar figure emerged, her crisp, navy WAAF uniform immaculate against the rustic backdrop.

Vera Atkins, the legendary intelligence officer from the Special Operations Executive, had a presence that was impossible to ignore. Of medium height, her hair and uniform impeccable and with a determined expression in the steely eyes, Vera moved with the confidence of someone who had orchestrated countless operations behind the scenes.

Lise recognized her instantly but also didn't miss the twitch around the flight officer's well-formed mouth. Vera, more even than the agents in the field, must be suffering from the huge blow SOE was dealt in France. Dozens upon dozens of agents had gone missing. The hard data had even reached Lise's ears in her sleepy village in Normandy.

"Lise, I can safely call you Lise now, can't I?" Vera called out, striding towards the door with her usual brisk efficiency. "It's so good to see you in one piece! Gosh, what a trip. I just left Paris, but I'll tell you all in a minute."

Lise stepped forward, not completely grasping how her boss had suddenly turned up on her doorstep. "Vera, you? And yes, calling me Lise is fine now. We're free here. How... what brings you here?"

Without hesitation, Vera grasped Lise's hand and gave her a quick peck on the cheek. The scent of cigarette smoke, perfume, and lipstick wafted through the air—quite an urban scent after the grime and sweat Lise had grown accustomed to.

"You and I are heading back to London tonight," Vera announced without preamble. "Your mission is over, Lise. It's time to return to the motherland."

The words hung in the air. Lise had known this day would come, but hearing it spoken so plainly felt uncomfortable. "Tonight? But there's still so much to—"

"There was no other way we could reach you now that there are no W/T operators in the area," Vera interrupted, her tone firm but understanding. "So, I decided to come and collect you myself. Flight arrangements have been made."

Lise's mind tried to process the suddenness of this announcement. The war, her mission, the people she had fought alongside— could she truly leave it all behind so quickly?

"Can I at least say goodbye to my friends... uh... my fighters here?"

"A quick goodbye, yes. But you've done more than enough, Lise. It's time to debrief and recuperate. We're going home."

Home. The word sounded strange, almost surreal. What was home now? England had been a refuge, a place of exile, and now it was calling her back. But after everything she'd seen and done, what did home really mean?

"Raoul, my most loyal local leader, was supposed to have a meeting with me just now," Lise began, still searching for a way to delay the inevitable.

VERA LAUGHED LIGHTLY. "Pippa told me Raoul's been quite the thorn in the Germans' side. And sometimes in yours."

"True," Lise agreed, her lips curving into a smile as she rolled her eyes.

As if on cue, Raoul appeared, his stride confident and his presence as commanding as ever. His face was streaked with dirt, his uniform rumpled, but his eyes gleamed with the thrill of victory. He looked every bit the rugged fighter who had led his men through the chaos of war.

"Marguerite!" he called out, his voice booming with enthusiasm. But his steps faltered as he spotted Vera. "Who's the other posh lady? Heavens, you have to introduce me to the rest of your court."

Vera rose from her chair, offering Raoul one of her rare smiles. He certainly had a way of charming the women around him, even those as composed as Vera. "Meet my boss, Flight Officer Vera Atkins," Lise introduced.

"Pleased to meet you, Raoul," Vera said in excellent French, her tone respectful yet formal. "Thank you for being such a formidable support to Lise all these months."

Raoul grinned, his eyes twinkling with mischief. "Who is Lise? Another smashing court member I haven't yet met?"

"I'm Lise," Lise replied, stepping forward. "My real name is Captain Lise de Baissac. Both Denis, who is actually my brother Claude, and I are British secret agents. We were sent by London to help the Maquis fight the Germans."

For a moment, Raoul looked puzzled, but then a slow grin spread across his face. "It crossed my mind you could be Brits. Just tiny things, but you hid that well, *Lise*. My compliments! To me, you'll always be Marguerite or Joan of Arc." He flashed his roguish smile, the one Lise had always managed to resist. "But Lise is a good name for your upper-class tea parties."

"I'll be leaving for London tonight, Raoul. Vera has come to fetch me. Will you be able to manage without me?"

"This sudden, huh? Sneaking out without saying goodbye?" Raoul's grin faltered slightly, a hint of disappointment creeping into his voice.

"I wouldn't dream of leaving without telling you, Raoul."

He took a step closer to her, as if wanting to protect her. "Ah, so the big brass is pulling you out, huh? Well, I can't say I'm not disappointed, Madame. I was still holding out for that dance, you know."

Lise chuckled, shaking her head. "You'll have to find another partner for that waltz, my friend. I'm sure you won't have to look far."

Raoul laughed, though there was a wistful note in his voice. "You're probably right. But it won't be the same. It's been an honor, Marguerite." He made a genuine bow, his playful bravado momentarily replaced by heartfelt respect.

As they stood there, the banter faded into silence. Lise was acutely aware of Vera's watchful eye, sensing the unspoken bond between the two fighters. But Lise didn't care. This was her friend, her comrade.

"Well, Marguerite," Raoul finally said, his voice only sincerity, "You've been the best woman in my life so far. I know you've protected me with your life, as I have done yours. You're the best. The absolute best."

They hugged, and Lise leaned into his warmth, his strength, his energy.

"Till we meet again, Raoul," Lise said as they let each other go. "Months like these are never forgotten, nor the people in them. I'll be back with Claude and Pippa, who you know as Geneviève."

Raoul held her gaze for a moment longer, and Lise knew they both thought of their shared experiences. "I'll hold you to that, Captain." His voice held a tinge of sadness, but mostly respect. Turning to Vera, he added with a mischievous grin, "You Brits did a darn good job. Fooling a clever fox like me."

Vera gave a small, knowing smile as Raoul tipped his imaginary cap and strode out of the bungalow with the same confidence that had always defined him. Lise watched him go, letting him go.

As the door swung shut, the reality of her departure sunk in. This long chapter of her life, one filled with danger, camaraderie, and unyielding resolve, had come to an end. And with that realization came the understanding that an unknown future awaited her.

Lise went to pack her few belongings, as Vera sat outside smoking and reading one of her eternal files.

Lise took one more look around her last safe house, her emotions a tumultuous mix of relief, sorrow, and anticipation. As she climbed into the car beside Vera, she didn't know what to feel, what to say, so she whispered, "Au revoir, ma douce France."

As the car pulled away, Lise resisted the urge to look back. She'd given every last bit of herself to the cause, now leaving nothing behind but a heartfelt, silent promise to return. The road ahead led to London but for now she allowed herself to feel the full weight of goodbye.

The landscape of Normandy blurred past her window, each passing field and village a reminder of the battles fought and the lives forever changed. That same war had taken away so much from her, but it had also given her a purpose she could never have imagined.

As the sun dipped below the horizon, Lise closed her eyes for a moment, letting the memories wash over her. The laughter of her comrades, the adrenaline of narrow escapes, the quiet moments of reflection, the pain of heartbreak and loss—all of it was a part of her now, forever etched into her soul. She had never lived more fully than in these past years.

No matter where her next road led, she knew she would carry Poitiers and Normandy, and the people she'd fought alongside, in her heart until the day she died.

52

RETURN TO A CHANGED WORLD

London, September 1944

As the plane touched down at RAF Tangmere, Lise was mostly relieved the trip was over. The flight had been relatively short, but the mental distance between France and England felt immeasurable.

She glanced at Vera beside her, whose mind was unreadable on the ever-serious face. Lise thought she looked tired, a tad more vulnerable than usual, worn down by the years of war and the recent news of their heavy losses.

The moment the plane's door opened, a brisk wind greeted them. Standing on the tarmac was Colonel Maurice Buckmaster, his posture as rigid as ever, but the tension in his face was unmistakable. As Lise approached him, she noticed how he forced a smile, though the usual twinkle in the colonel's eyes was dimmed.

"Lise," Buckmaster greeted her with a lot more emotion than she'd ever seen from him. "You've done us all proud. You're the best female agent we've had." His words were warm, but Lise could hear the strain in his voice, the weariness of a man who had sent too many brave souls into peril, now knowing many would never return.

"Thank you, Buck. I've only done my duty," Lise replied, trying to mask the exhaustion she felt deep in her bones.

"A duty worthy of an MBE," he continued. His tone was firm, but sorrow seemed to cling to every word. "You will be awarded the Member of the Order of the British Empire tomorrow."

"Oh, Buck..." Lise's voice trailed off. The honor was significant, but in that moment, it felt almost surreal. The true weight of what she had accomplished—and at what cost—had not settled in.

Her boss's eyes were soft as he grasped her hand more tightly. "You've done something extraordinary, Lise. We may never fully understand the impact of your work, but history will."

With a nod of acknowledgment, Lise allowed herself a brief moment of pride, but it was quickly overshadowed by the grim reality that awaited her outside the airport.

THE NEXT DAY

UPON ARRIVING at the SOE headquarters on Baker Street, Lise was struck by the even more somber atmosphere inside the building that never had been anything near a merry place, but now felt like a tomb. The familiar buzz of activity was muted, replaced by the quiet hum of subdued conversations and the shuffling of papers.

As she climbed the stairs to Buckmaster's office, each step felt heavier than the last. The faces of the agents she had trained, those she had worked alongside, and those she had sent into the field flashed before her eyes. The thought of who might never return plagued her, but she needed to know.

"Tomorrow", Vera had said on the plane, when Lise had asked

her to give her names. "I don't want you not to sleep tonight when you need it." Thoughtful of her, but pointless. Once Lise knew there was a list, sleep was elusive.

When Lise entered the dimly lit room, she found Buck and Vera deep in conversation. They both looked up as she stepped inside, smoothing over expressions of worry with a warm smile for her.

The maps of France on the walls, once proudly marked with active missions, now seemed to carry tiny dots of bygone times.

"Ah, Lise, there you are. So good to see a familiar face pop in here!" Buck said, rising to shake her hand. Vera quickly approached Lise and embraced her.

"It's good to be back," Lise said, though the words felt hollow. "But it's not the same, is it?"

"The long and the short of the success and failure of our missions isn't clear yet," Vera replied in a tight voice. "We're mainly busy trying to find out the fate of the agents who haven't reported in yet. When I came to pick you up, I had just returned from Paris, from our preliminary investigation. Buck and I set up shop in Hôtel Cecil in Rue St Didier, sending word around that returning agents should come to register there. Alas, only a trickle showed up. Apparently, most who didn't, perished... in Gestapo prisons or German concentration camps."

Buck's normally commanding presence was subdued, his Adam's apple bobbing as he struggled to maintain his composure. "We never knew. We never knew the Gestapo had them in their claws. So many mistakes... so many... it's unbearable."

"There's something I need to ask," Lise began in a hesitant voice. "What happened to Gilbert?"

Buck and Vera exchanged a look, one of those silent conversations Lise had seen many times between them. Finally, Buck spoke, showing frustration and regret.

"Agent Gilbert. His real name is Henri Déricourt. Well, Lise, it's now quite clear that your instincts were right about him. Déricourt was a double agent. He worked for the Germans under the code name BOE 48. We've confirmed he was feeding them information on our operations, which led to the capture and death of many of our agents."

Lise felt a shiver run through her body she couldn't suppress. She'd never completely trusted Déricourt though he'd been good to her—something about him had always felt off, too smooth, too nonchalant about the dangers they all faced. But to hear it confirmed—to know that he had betrayed them all so deeply—was still an immense shock.

"Gilbert," Lise muttered, the name almost bitter on her tongue. "I knew there was something wrong with him. And now... to know that he was responsible for so much loss..."

Vera looked grim. "Yes, Lise. You weren't the only one who had doubts, but he was too well-connected, too useful—or so we thought at the time. It's a dark chapter, one we'll be rereading and decoding for a long time."

Lise felt tremendously sad, there was no comfort in knowing she'd been right. "I suppose it's a reminder," she said quietly, "that even in this fight for freedom, there are shadows and traitors among us."

She herself had faced death countless times in the field, but she still had no idea who had been Déricourt's victims or been caught in other ways. Taking a deep breath, dreading the answer, she asked. "So, who hasn't survived that I knew?"

Vera and Buck exchanged a glance that shared the weight of their heavy knowledge. Vera spoke up, her voice trembling. "Agent Renaud - France Antelme. Agent Suzanne - Yvonne Rudellat. Agent Denise - Andrée Borrel. Agent Louise - Violette Szabo. Agent Prosper - Francis Suttill. Agent Olive - Alexandre Schwatschko. Agent Marcel - Jack Agazarian. Agent Urbain - Marcus Bloom.

Agent Vladimir - Maurice Larcher. The other Agent René - Jean-Renaud-Dandicolle. That the last two were killed, you knew of course. And many, many others. We're counting on over one hundred in France alone."

Each name was like a knife through Lise's heart. These weren't just names on a list; they were friends, comrades, people she had trusted with her life. Ten people that she knew and trusted and her life had depended on, and they were gone. "What happened to them?" she asked, though she feared the answer.

Buck's voice was solemn. "We have no confirmation, but it's likely they were captured or killed. We're working on getting records, but as most were deported to Germany, and Germany is still under fire, we have no way of knowing exactly. That's also why we still hope some may have survived. Chances are small, but chances are chances."

Lise swallowed hard, unable to process so many lost colleagues at the same time, their faces dancing before her, one by one. Why had she survived, when so many others had not? Was it sheer luck, providence?

Vera's hand on her arm brought Lise back to the present. "We'll keep searching, Lise. We won't stop until we have answers on all of them."

Lise nodded, though the acute ache in her chest remained. From somewhere she found the strength to ask the other what she hardly dared. "What about Claudine, Mary Herbert? We know she had Claude's baby in December 1943. Have you heard anything about her? Claude and I haven't."

The inevitable happened. Buck shook his head. "I'm afraid, no news of her either. I can order a plane and a service car in France for Claude, and you if you want, to go looking for Mary, as you two may have more clues where she might be, or have been."

"Thank you, Buck. We must find Mary and the baby. They are

family now. As soon as my formalities here are done, I absolutely want to return to France to find her," Lise said with conviction in her voice.

Buck managed a faint smile. "Of course. Always the righteous one. On your last mission. Thank God, we can now send you safely into France, Lise. I couldn't bear losing you as well."

Vera smiled with relief on Lise's offer to help her with the heavy work of finding an agent. "Before you head back for your last SOE mission, my dear, there's something you need to do. This afternoon, as you know, you will be awarded the Member of the Order of the British Empire. You've been invited to have tea with Queen Elizabeth and King George VI at Buckingham Palace."

"Golly," Lise chuckled, "I'm glad I can wear my FANY uniform as I haven't a presentable dress left in my wardrobe."

"One more thing before you go," Buck waved his hand. "Normally we would've asked for your reports on SCIENTIST II's mission like we did with your earlier ARTIST mission in Poitiers, but Claude has extensively briefed us on your crucial work in Normandy leading up to D-Day and afterwards. Would you be interested in what your brother told us? I have his report here on my desk."

"Depends on whether it's flattering," Lise gave him a wry smile.

"Very flattering," Buck assured and handing the widely stamped document to Vera said, "Vera, you were in charge of the women. You read it."

THE FILE IN ONE HAND, a smoldering Craven A in the other, Vera read the report:

· · ·

"OFFICIAL REPORT *by Claude de Baissac on Lise de Baissac's role within SCIENTIST II:*

Marguerite, as usual, was the most efficient assistant. She handled delicate contacts which I could not make myself, and took my place, as head of the circuit, when I was away 'en tournée'.

When in need of officers, I twice sent her to Paris, where each time she was forced to cycle through thick enemy formations. Her missions were always of a very dangerous nature, because of the difficulties of moving around, and the danger of contacting people active in the resistance, and who therefore were always under Gestapo observation, particularly in the Paris area.

On several occasions she personally took charge of the transport of Geneviève's W/T material. Once carrying plans and crystals, she was arrested and searched by the Germans and only got out of this by virtue of her incredible fortitude and strength of will to maintain her alias no matter the circumstances. Because of this, my circuit was able to keep in touch with home station at a very crucial moment."

LISE LISTENED CALMLY, her hands folded in her uniformed lap. Touched by her brother's great praise for her work. She thought for a moment and said softly.

"That's so good to hear. I was worried, you know, on my second mission, because of the fall-out I had with the PIMENTO network. But joining Claude in Normandy turned out to be absolutely the best move ever. I'm glad I did what I did, and I would do it again."

"Let's hope that isn't needed, in our lifetime or the next," Buck exclaimed with passion.

53

RECOGNITION AND RESOLVE

L ater that afternoon, Lise stood before the towering gates of Buckingham Palace. Many emotions swirled through her, predominantly pride, sorrow, and humility. It was an extraordinary honor to be invited to the palace, but the recognition was bittersweet.

She was there not just for herself, but for all those who hadn't made it—friends, comrades, and countless others who had sacrificed everything. The responsibility of being a surviving SOE agent was a mixed blessing and Lise was sure her living fellow agents felt that way, too. *Who am I that I may stand here today?*

The intricate ironwork of the palace gates, crowned with the royal crest, loomed above her like a symbol of the endurance and history of the British monarchy. As Lise adjusted her FANY uniform, she took a deep breath, stepping into the unknown pomp of the ceremony ahead.

When the gates swung open, allowing her to step through, she felt both small and significant, a single person in the grand tapestry of the war effort.

A footman in impeccable livery led her through the labyrinthine hallways of the palace. Each corridor was a journey through time, where the opulence of Buckingham Palace unfolded before her eyes.

Gilded frames encased portraits of monarchs long past, their stern gazes watching over the grandeur of the present. Crystal chandeliers cast their golden glow over the polished marble floors, and the scent of fresh flowers filled the air with a delicate fragrance.

Despite her upper-class upbringing in grand houses, and quite a few visits from lesser royals in Mauritius, Lise felt herself awed by the splendor surrounding her. This was a world far removed from the mud-soaked fields of Normandy and the tense, smoke-filled rooms where missions were planned and lives were risked.

As she entered the grand hall, she saw King George VI and Queen Elizabeth awaiting her. The room was hushed, the air thick with the gravity of the occasion. The Queen, elegant in a soft blue gown, smiled gently as Lise approached. Her eyes held a warmth that was both comforting and regal. Beside her stood King George VI, dressed in a tailored pin-striped suit that accentuated his lean frame. Though his posture was slightly stooped, his presence was commanding, and there was a quiet strength in his gaze.

Lise felt odd and slightly out of place in her stiff uniform as she approached the monarchs. This was a moment she had never anticipated during those dark days in occupied France. Hands were shaken, and Lise performed a perfect curtsy, a gesture that came to her naturally in the solemnity of the moment.

"Ah, Mademoiselle de Baissac, what a pleasure," the Queen began, her voice soft yet clear. "The King and I are delighted to make your acquaintance and hear about your recent undercover work in France."

"You've done your country an immense service," King George VI added, his voice carrying an honest tone of admiration. "I had no idea of the sacrifices you and your fellow agents have made, often at great personal risk. Prime Minister Churchill only recently detailed the exact magnitude of the Special Operations Executive to me. Mind you, I often probed him on the matter, but he always waved it aside as a minor operation. Well, clearly it wasn't."

Lise, maintaining her composure, responded with the humility that had defined her service. "It was... rather extensive," she agreed, as the memories of danger and loss flickered in her mind. "But we had great support from the French population, certainly towards the end."

"Your courage has inspired us all," the Queen said in her usual warm and friendly voice. "And it is, therefore, His Majesty's great pleasure to award you the Member of the Order of the British Empire. May I?" She rose gracefully from her seat, her silk dress rustling with her every move. She approached Lise with the MBE medal in hand.

As the Queen pinned the medal on Lise's khaki-clad chest, Lise felt overwhelmed by a pride and gratitude she didn't know she had in her. The medal was light in weight, but the significance of the honor was immense. This wasn't just a personal accolade; it was a recognition of the collective bravery and sacrifice of all those who had fought, and especially those who had fallen.

Lise felt the sting of tears in her eyes but held them back. "Thank you, Your Majesties. It's been an honor to serve."

King George VI, lighting a cigarette, added with a rare smile, "I have no doubt many medals will follow this first one, Captain de Baissac."

After the formal ceremony, Lise was led into a more intimate room for tea with the royal family. Even Princess Elizabeth, proudly wearing her ATS uniform, and young Princess Margaret were present, a pair of corgis trotting at their heels. The princesses eyed the battle-hardened secret agent with stares of curiosity and awe, so much so it almost made Lise self-conscious. That members of the royal family were staring at *her* and not the other way around!

The difference between the grandeur of the reception room and the cozy setting of the tearoom was striking. A modest fire crackled in the hearth. Even the royal family shared in the country's shortage of coals. The comforting scent of freshly brewed tea and baked tarts filled the air. They gathered around a small table adorned with delicate china, where plates of scones, clotted cream, and finger sandwiches were neatly arranged—quintessentially British.

As Lise sipped her tea, she finally felt a sense of peace and calm settle over her. The warmth, the safety, the luxury—these were all things she'd known before the war but had craved deep in her soul during those harsh years.

Nights spent in ditches, cycling through swarms of mosquitoes, enduring blistering heat and unrelenting rain, always cautious, always vigilant. The return to this world of order and beauty felt like a balm to her weary soul.

The Queen, with genuine interest, asked about Lise's experiences in France, her voice gentle yet probing. King George spoke of the resilience of the British people and the importance of remembering the sacrifices made by so many. Their words of acknowledgment for her efforts, and those of her fellow SOE agents, touched Lise deeply.

Having only recently returned from the frontlines, Lise hadn't yet fully processed the impact of her missions. But as the Monarchs praised her bravery, she began to understand that people on this side of the English Channel admired those who had 'landed by moonlight.'

"The public may never know the full extent of your bravery," the King said, "but we do. Your actions have undoubtedly hastened our victory and will be remembered in the annals of history."

"Thank you," Lise replied, feeling true gratitude on behalf of all SOE agents.

As the conversation continued, the Queen's kind eyes rested on Lise. "So, what will it be for you next?"

Lise didn't hesitate. "I must return to France at the first possible opportunity. I need to search for my future sister-in-law, who was an agent too. She disappeared without a trace nine months ago. I fear the worst, as she also had a young baby with her."

"You speak of the Irish agent, Mary Herbert?" the King inquired.

"Yes," Lise confirmed, surprised at how well-informed the King was. "My brother Claude and I will search for her in Bordeaux and Poitiers and hopefully bring them both safely back to England."

"We wish you all the luck in the world," the Queen observed with empathy.

As she left Buckingham Palace thirty minutes later, the grandeur of the ceremony and the heartfelt recognition from the King and Queen left Lise with a profound sense of wonder and lightness.

As she fingered the medal pinned to her chest, memories of her childhood flashed through her mind—especially that long-ago day when she had won a medal in a swimming competition in Curepipe.

She had worn that medal proudly, parading it around and even sleeping with it on. Now, as she held the MBE, tears welled in her eyes—not just for the honor she had received, but for the brave little girl she once was, who had gone into the lion's den and emerged victorious.

54

THE SEARCH FOR MARY

A few weeks later - Bordeaux-Poitiers, mid-September 1944

Claude and Lise set out for Bordeaux, the last known location of Mary Herbert, whom they had left behind in August 1943. It had been more than nine months since anyone had heard from her - a brief message reporting the birth of a healthy baby girl in early December.

Since then, there had been no further contact. The radio silence was troubling. Roger Landes, the former SCIENTIST I W/T operator known as Aristide, who took over the network after Claude's departure, never mentioned Mary in any of his transmissions. All information about Mary seemed to have been cut off, leaving the De Baissacs in the dark.

Lise was plagued by a constant tension. The SCIENTIST I network had collapsed entirely after Claude's narrow escape in August 1943. Landes himself had been forced to flee over the Pyrenees, and the other resisters had either gone into hiding or been arrested by the Gestapo.

The damage caused by double agent André Grandclement, who'd once been one of Claude's key assistants, had wreaked havoc within the network, with devastating consequences. Lise couldn't shake the fear of what could have happened to a vulnerable, pregnant secret agent in the midst of such chaos? The possibilities were grim.

The drive through France was tense, filled with the lingering echoes of war and the uncertainty of what they might find. The once lush and fertile French countryside was now a patchwork of ruins and recovery, a reminder of the devastation that had swept through the country not long ago.

Claude had been reluctant to go from the start. And as they drove through the war-torn landscape, his frustration began to spill out. "Lise, I want to do right by Mary, but I never was in love with her. I'll marry her if we find her so the child isn't a bastard, but I don't know if I can live with her."

Lise fumed at her brother's insensitivity. "Claude, how can you be so heartless? Mary had your child. Don't you care about them?"

Claude's hands tightened on the steering wheel. "Of course, I care! But this war... it's changed everything. I'm not the man I used to be. None of us is the same anymore."

The raw emotion in his voice took Lise by surprise. She hadn't considered her robust brother was also traumatized by the war, struggling to find his place in the peace that followed.

"I understand, Claude. We've all been through hell and back. But maybe finding Mary and the baby will help us heal."

Claude's expression softened as it often did when Lise intervened in his rigid way of thinking. "I hope you're right, Lise. I really do."

The journey continued in silence, each lost in their thoughts. They passed through villages scarred by battle, with remnants of tanks and makeshift graves marking the landscape. The scenes underpinned the cost of war and the fragile peace they now sought.

As they approached Bordeaux, Lise began to have doubts about the entire operation. What if they didn't find Mary? It could take them months, traveling wildly through France. And what if they found her, but she hadn't survived? Could they deal with that guilt?

Claude broke the silence. "Do you remember the last time we saw her? She was so full of life, so determined to make a difference."

Lise smiled sadly. "Yes, I remember. I loved it when she spoke Arabic or German. Gosh, she was a genius at languages. And she was so dedicated to the cause. Such an unlikely agent with her intellect and vivacity. I liked her from the first day we started training in Beaulieu. And she believed in you, Claude. She worked so hard for you. Oh, I can't bear the thought of not finding her, or worse..."

"I think Mary is a survivor 'pur sang.' I believe she's still around," Claude said with conviction. A conviction Lise really needed to hear.

Bordeaux was a city still reeling from the occupation, but signs of life were slowly returning. The streets, once choked with German soldiers, were now filled with the buzz of rebuilding, though the scars of war were evident everywhere.

Lise and Claude's first stop was to seek out Charles Corbin, a former police officer who'd been a part of the SCIENTIST I network and a close friend of Landes. As they approached the small, cluttered office where Corbin now worked, they were relieved to see he'd survived and was on duty again.

He greeted them with a tired smile. "David? Is that you? I didn't expect to see you here so soon after everything."

"The name is Claude, Charles. David was my code name. And this is my sister Lise. We need your help," Claude said, getting straight to the point. "We're looking for my former courier, Claudine, whose real name is Mary Herbert. Do you have any information on her whereabouts?"

Corbin shook his head with a serious expression. "I'm sorry, no. I haven't heard anything about Claudine. After Aristide left, it was chaos."

"Aristide's real name is Roger Landes. He might have surfaced under that name again after the war. We know he survived," Claude informed him.

"I know he's Roger Landes. And yes, he's alive and kicking. Dating my daughter Ginette as we speak." Corbin seemed chuffed by the news.

Claude looked surprised but smiled under his moustache. "That's great news. Capital chap, Landes. Hope to see him soon again but for now we're occupied with this search for Mary."

The police officer apologized again, "So many people went underground in that chaos, others were arrested... All the fault of that wretched traitor Grandclément. Good thing Landes sent a bullet through that swine's head. But, perhaps, I can point you to some places Claudine, or Mary as you say, might've gone."

"Please do," Lise urged. "Any lead, no matter how small, could help."

Corbin scribbled down a few addresses, handing them over with a sigh. "I'm afraid it's not much. Just places where she might have sought shelter. I wish I had more for you."

"Thank you, Charles," Claude said, taking the paper. "We'll follow up on these."

"Let me know, if you've found her."

"We will."

The next few days were spent tirelessly searching the city. They visited the addresses Corbin had provided, questioning anyone who might have crossed paths with Mary. At a small café, Lise approached an elderly woman who'd been part of the local resistance.

"Excuse me, madame," Lise began, showing her a photo of Mary. "Have you seen this woman?"

The woman squinted at the photo, shaking her head slowly. "I'm sorry, my dear. She doesn't look familiar. But then again, many came through here..."

At a crowded market, Claude approached a former contact. "We're looking for a woman named Mary Herbert, who used the name Claudine. She might have been here around December last year."

The man frowned, scratching his chin. "Herbert... Herbert... No, I can't say I remember. But Yves mentioned a British woman once. He might have known her. But Yves... he's gone missing too."

Disappointment followed them with every step. Each lead fizzled into nothing, adding to the growing weight of despair. Finally, they managed to track down a small clinic south of Bordeaux through a Françoise who'd briefly given 'the couple' a night to stay over in her house.

On Claude and Lise's puzzled looks, the elderly woman quickly added. "At least I thought they were a couple. One didn't ask too many questions during the war, you know... when involved in helping la Résistance. The woman was heavily pregnant and the man, who was short and dark-haired, addressed her as Mary Louise. They were on their way to a private nursing home in La Valence to let her give birth to her child. Could that be her?"

They thanked the woman profusely and set out to the address this first helpful contact gave them. Marie Louise was the given name of the alias that Mary Herbert had used on occasion, it could be her. In the small clinic in La Valance, looking like an ordinary house, Lise spoke to the nurse on duty, her voice filled with hope, giving her Mary's alias.

"Did a woman called Marie Louise Vernier give birth here? She would have had a baby girl last December."

The nurse ruffled through the files on her desk and nodded slowly. "Yes, she was here alright. But I see she only stayed ten days. Was paid for fully beforehand. I'm afraid she left no address behind." The nurse looked up, apologetically, "Those were secretive days, we had many half-German babies born here. You know, many single women. We did that sort of discreet work. I'm sorry."

Lise's heart sank even lower than it already was. "Thank you, nonetheless" she said and turning to Claude as they left the clinic. "It's like Mary vanished into thin air."

"We'll keep looking. We have to." Claude's voice was unexceptionally strained. "At least I now know the place where my daughter saw her first light of day."

FRUSTRATION MOUNTED. Days had turned into a week, and hope was fading faster than the light of each passing day. Lise and Claude sat in their old haunt, Café Bertrand, where they'd conducted so many secret meetings two years earlier.

The café, once the city's place-to-be for covert operations, was now alive with the sounds of freedom. The atmosphere around them was rowdy and loud, the now-liberated Bordelaises heartily joking and shouting in French. The dockworkers and seamen, who'd fiercely resisted the Nazi occupation, were celebrating, their laughter and cheers filling the air.

But the joy of Café Bertrand's clientele stood in stark contrast to the somber mood of brother and sister De Baissac.

"What if we never find her?" Claude muttered, staring glumly into his coffee.

Lise sighed, her mind searching frantically for any missed possibilities. "There's one place we haven't tried, Claude. Poitiers. I told Mary once, if she needed a safe place, to go to my old apartment there. It's a long shot, but it's all we have left."

Claude looked at her, a flicker of hope in his eyes. "Then let's go. There's nothing left for me here in Bordeaux."

Lise could sense the deeper despair that gnawed at her brother. It was more than just the search for Mary. Bordeaux held memories of the great SCIENTIST I network Claude had so painstakingly built, a network that had stretched from the Pyrenees to Brittany. Major de Baissac had led thousands of men and women into action, his strategic mind and unyielding sense of purpose making him the leader this region needed.

Even now, sitting across from Lise in their former meeting place overlooking the harbor, Claude's authority and solidity were undeniable. But beneath this outward composure, Lise could see the cracks. Her brother was at his lowest, feeling dejected and forlorn.

The spring 1943 collapse of Prosper's PHYSICIAN network, which bordered SCIENTIST I to the north and was led by Claude's friend, Francis Suttill, had also infiltrated the Bordeaux network. Many of Claude's men and women had been killed. Lise wondered if Claude carried the guilt of not taking Mary to safety with him. Was that a burden he would have to bear for the rest of his life?

"Let's go to Poitiers," Lise said, trying to inject some hope into her voice, though she knew what awaited her there was no easier than what Claude was now facing in Bordeaux.

The collapse of her own ARTIST network, tied so closely to SCIENTIST I, had forced her to leave her post virtually overnight. On the way to Poitiers, she'd have to brace herself for the ghosts she would have to confront.

The drive to Poitiers was marked by silence, each sibling lost in their own thoughts. As they approached the ancient city on the hill, the sun broke through the clouds, lighting up the facades of the age-old stone buildings.

It was an odd, indescribable experience for Lise to see those familiar steep streets and the quiet and sedateness of rural France from the front seat of a British service car.

I've cycled here so often; it hasn't changed a dime and yet it has. I have changed, she reflected, feeling how her heart fluttered as she observed her city bathing in peace as if war had never touched it. War had touched her so deeply.

"Let's head straight to my old apartment on the Boulevard Solférino," Lise managed to say, but she hardly recognized her own voice. All her emotions fought for recognition: fear, cautiousness, uncertainty, pain, grit. Mostly grit. *I can't give up.*

As they neared Madame de Vigny's house, Lise held her breath. The grey stones of the houses, her hideout and the Gestapo head-quarters, stood unchanged, side by side but the oppressive swastika flags once flapping there, were replaced by the French tricolor. One flag, a world of difference.

Lise knocked on the door of Madame de Vigny's house, wondering if the original occupant had returned from her time in North Africa. An elderly woman with a deep tan and a weathered face opened the door, her expression puzzled and cautious.

"Who are you?" the woman asked, her beady eyes scanning them from head to toe as she kept the door barely ajar.

"I rented your house during the war under the name Madame Irène Brisse with the help of your friend Monsieur Henri Gâteau," Lise explained, "but we're looking for a friend who might have stayed here after me. Her real name is Mary Herbert, but she might have used the name Madame Marie Louise Vernier. She had a baby with her. Do either of those names ring a bell?"

Madame de Vigny shook her head slowly. "No, I'm afraid not. You might try Madame Gâteau; she's still where they used to be. He's dead, you know, Henri, shot by those beasts." She inclined her head to the house next door.

Lise gasped, "Shot? Monsieur Gâteau? I know he was arress..."

Without another word, the woman closed the door—a door Lise had passed through countless times.

Lise had to steady herself for a moment against the wall of her former house. What about Claire and Sophie Rimbaud? Doctor Giraud? Renard? Oh, the ghosts of the past, she could have done well without them, but they had to find Mary.

Lise and Claude sought out Madame Gâteau, only to find her too shaken from her husband's death to be able to talk to them.

"I know no Marie Louise Vernier."

Lise thought of happier times when the kind auctioneer's wife had made Agent Renaud and her husband's favorite dish, Farci Poitevin. They'd all dove in and laughed and clinked glasses. Renaud - France Antelme - was dead as well, most likely murdered in a German concentration camp.

Lise gathered her last reserves and said to her brother, "Let's head for the Café de la Paix on the Place d'Armes." They left the service car parked and walked the last yards. Lise's legs moved with great reluctance, as if she had shackles around her ankles. And she found herself almost relieved to see the café closed, as she could not have handled more bad news that moment.

With her heart aching for Claire and Sophie, she turned to Claude. "What now, brother?"

"Let's find a hotel, get a good night's rest and continue our search tomorrow." Lise was glad her brother's brains were still working, because she was at the end of her rope.

Days of fruitless searching continued in Poitiers. Every lead seemed to fizzle out, and the city felt more like a maze of dead ends than a place of answers. But then, by chance, they met an old man who remembered seeing a woman with a baby months ago. His vague recollection led them to a small village on the outskirts of Poitiers.

The journey to the village was arduous, the roads still scarred by the war, littered with remnants of a conflict humanity was still unable to fully face or understand. When they finally arrived, they stopped to ask for directions. And luck finally seemed on their side. The woman who introduced herself as Thérèse remembered Mary, or rather Marie Louise.

"She was here during Easter," Thérèse explained. "I remember because the poor thing was desperate to find her baby. I helped her as much as I could, but she moved on after a few days. No luck. She was fiercely determined to find the little one."

Lise felt a cold wave of dread wash over her. "Find her baby? How did she lose it?"

Thérèse looked at them as though they should've known. "The Gestapo arrested her and took her baby away. She was going from one orphanage to another, searching for her child. The poor thing."

"Do you happen to know which orphanages she may have checked?" Claude asked hurriedly, wiping sweat from his brow despite the fresh fall air.

"Sure, sure. I'll write down the ones I know. Not so many here, though."

They took leave of Thérèse with her list in hand and headed for 'Le Refuge des Petits.' The anxiety in the car mounted with each passing mile. Mary had escaped from the Gestapo, but did she find her child, or did she move on, and would they ever find her or the baby?

When they reached the orphanage, the matron greeted them with cautious curiosity.

"We had a woman of that name and description here some time ago, searching for her child," she said slowly. "She found her and took her away. I believe she moved to a small house near the woods, about ten miles from here, owned by the Vaselot family."

Claude and Lise could hardly believe their luck. After so many dead ends and fading hopes, a fragile thread of possibility had led them here. They followed the matron's directions and eventually found the house, a modest dwelling nestled among the trees, hidden from the eyes of the world.

Lise's heart was hammering in her chest as they approached. Claude knocked on the door, and after a few moments, it creaked opened slightly. A wary pair of blue eyes peeked out.

"Claudine?" Lise's lips trembled as she reverted back to the name she knew from wartime.

The door swung open fully, and there stood Mary—tall, gaunt, exhausted, but unmistakenly alive. In her arms was a small child with blonde curls and wide, curious eyes, a mirror of her mother's.

"Odile! Claude!" Mary's voice, though weak, was filled with relief and disbelief. "You found us."

"Oh Mary!" Lise's voice broke as she stepped forward, enveloping her friend, her sister-in-law, in a tight embrace. Tears streamed down her cheeks, a release of all the fear and worry that had haunted her so long. "We never stopped looking. Thank God, you're safe."

Claude, usually so composed, stood helpless, his face wrenched in pain and relief as he took in the sight of his girlfriend with his child in her arms. "Mary... I'm so sorry. For everything. I'm here now, and I want to do right by you."

Mary's eyes filled with tears as she met his gaze. "Thank you, Claude. That means more than you know. This is your daughter, Claudine."

The little girl looked up at Claude, innocent curiosity in her eyes. As he gently reached out to touch her small hand, he did the right thing. He embraced her with all the tenderness of his big heart and protective body.

Lise stood a little apart, observing the scene with a quiet sadness. As she watched Claude tenderly hold his soon-to-be-wife and daughter, she felt a sense of finality wash over her. The war had taken and given. Taken their youth and their comrades. Given them this fragile moment of connection, of family.

ON NOVEMBER 11, 1944, Claude Marc Boucherville de Baissac married Mary Katherine Herbert in a quiet ceremony at Corpus Christi Church in London. It was a solemn acknowledgment of the ties that bound them, forged in the fires of war, with an understanding that doing the right thing was often complicated and never without sacrifice.

Lise stood by, knowing this was not a fairy-tale ending. Claude's marriage to Mary would be one of duty and responsibility, not of love.

As they stood together, united in their own personal way, Lise made a silent vow to herself. Whatever came next, whatever challenges lay ahead, she would face them with the same resolve that had carried her through all the long days and nights of the war.

But for now, she allowed herself to simply be present in this moment, watching her brother and his little family, and holding onto the hope that, somehow, they would all find their way to peace.

~ SIL~

Marseille
September 2004

55

THE FINAL LETTER

Marseille, late September 2004

S il's usually steady hands trembled as she unfolded the last letter from the old suitcase. The yellowed pages and faded ink were remnants of a bygone era, one from which the courage of a single woman had reached out and colored the young artist's life as nothing before.

Outside her window, the last rays of a long, hot summer blended with the vibrant hues of the approaching French fall. Yet, despite nature's beckoning, Sil needed one more hour, immersed in the final instalment of Lise's journey—a journey that had become as vital to her as her own breath.

"Mon cher Henri," it began. As Sil read on, Lise's emotions bled through the ink—raw and unfiltered. Each word echoed through time, resonating in Sil's own heart, binding her more deeply to the woman she had come to know not just through history, but through shared emotion.

She would let herself be pulled into Lise's heart and soul one more time, into her post-war world, that Sil now knew was hardly documented. All she had were Lise's own emotions, raw on the page, all the love and all the loss.

This wasn't just a document of life during war—it was a testament to love, duty, and the immense resilience one human being could muster. It was modest heroism in its purest form, the kind Sil now realized lived within her as well, waiting to be called upon.

Sil knew that what she held in her hands was more than just a letter—it was the final piece of the puzzle from the woman who never could have imagined the impact she was having on an artist's life decades later. It was Lise's last gift to her, a whispered legacy that would forever echo within the walls of the house they had shared, a place Sil now called home.

LONDON, *15 May 1947*

MON CHER HENRI,

THANK *you from the depths of my heart for your understanding and empathy regarding my "war career." Your heartfelt letters have been a balm for my soul, offering warmth and validation for what I once thought was merely my duty. I never imagined you could grasp so deeply what it was like to live as a secret agent behind enemy lines.*

THIS CORRESPONDENCE HAS BEEN MORE *than just a connection between us —it has been a lifeline, helping to mend my ravaged heart. For so long, the secrecy and the burden of my role during the war—and the silence I was forced to maintain afterward due to the Official Secrets Act—were a* heavy burden to me as the emotions and memories of what had passed still occupied such a large part of my life. Sharing that past with you has lightened the burden considerably.

I REALIZE NOW that in sharing these memories with you, I may have broken that agreement. But I trust you implicitly, Henri. Please, promise me that you will never allow these letters to see the light of day. I ask you, with all sincerity, to burn them after reading. I cannot bear the thought of compromising the safety and honor of those who served alongside me.

IT HAS TAKEN me time to gather my thoughts and the courage to write this final letter. So much has changed since we last saw each other in 1939, and even more since we began this intense correspondence four months ago.

BUT YES, my dear Henri, I would be glad to visit you in Saint Tropez this summer. There is still so much I wish to say to you in person—things too delicate for the pen.

IN MY LAST LETTER, I told you how Claude, Mary, little Claudine, and I returned to England. We are each trying, in our own ways, to rebuild our lives. Claude is learning to live in peace, Mary is embracing motherhood, and I have found a position with the French Service of the BBC. My work as a programme assistant, announcer, and translator has been fulfilling, offering a way to reconnect with my homeland, even from this distance.

LAST MAY, I had the enormous honor of participating in the Victory Parade here in London. It was the last time I wore my FANY uniform, a *day filled with both pride and melancholy. Peace—a word so fragile, yet so powerful—finally reigned over Western Europe, and by that summer, also over the Far East.*

WALKING through the jubilant streets of London, I was completely overwhelmed. The triumph of that moment was laced with the grief of knowing how many friends and comrades did not live to see this jubilation. I have lost more during the war than I ever could in the years to come —young men and women whose courage was matched only by the brutality of their deaths in the name of liberty.

OH, how I wish I could have been with you for the Liberation March through Paris on 25 August 1944. That moment, the capitulation of Nazi-Germany in France, represented everything I fought for. Though I was celebrating in Normandy on that day, the images of my fellow Parisians' joy and exultation are etched into my memory forever. Vive la France!

DESPITE THE PROFESSIONAL fulfillment I find here, my heart aches to return to France. England has been a sanctuary, a place of duty and refuge, but France is where my soul belongs. I stayed here, perhaps foolishly, because I couldn't bear the thought of living in a country where you were building your life with another woman. Fate, it seems, has an unfathomable way of intertwining our paths.

WHEN I SAW you in Paris with your then-wife in December 1942, my whole life shattered in that moment. I believed I had lost you forever. But now, knowing you are free again, it feels like life has granted us a second chance—a chance to find the happiness that was stolen from us by the war.

I NEED to be honest with you about who I have become. During the war, I was not only Lise de Baissac, the woman you once knew. I became Odile and Marguerite, a hardened secret agent for the Special Operations Executive. I fought, I sabotaged, I did things I never imagined I could do, I killed. You need to understand this part of me, Henri, so there are no illusions between us.

THE WAR CHANGED us all in ways we are only beginning to understand. I am not the same girl who loved you before the world was torn apart, but my love for you has endured through it all. I want us to meet and speak openly, to see if we can rebuild what we once had.

AT YOUR REQUEST, I will return to France. Perhaps there, in the land where our love first blossomed, we can find each other once more.

AVEC TOUT MON AMOUR,

LISE.

As SIL FOLDED the letter back into its delicate envelope, she felt torn apart, awash with emotions. Lise's words were powerful, so present, heavy with the weight of history and the unspoken hopes of a woman who had lived through the unimaginable.

Lise had found the courage to be honest about who she had become, and in doing so, she offered Sil a mirror—one that reflected the fears and desires Sil had been too afraid to confront.

Lise's love for Henri, long buried under the rubble of war and time, was not so different from what Sil felt about her own past. The way Lise spoke of a second chance, of reclaiming a love interrupted by forces beyond her control, struck a deep chord within Sil.

It made her think of Felix, of what they had shared, and of the losses that had defined her life until now—her mother, who hadn't wanted her, Grandpa Jack's death, the severed ties with her parents and brother, the drugs, the wrong choices.

But more than that, it made her think of Justin—the unexpected warmth growing between them, the way he had abruptly waltzed into her life, not to replace what was lost, but to offer something new.

Could it be that she, too, was being offered a second chance? Sil wasn't sure if it was too soon to label what she felt for Justin as love, but there certainly was something there—something both fragile and strong, like the word "peace" that Lise had so poignantly described.

Maybe it was too early to say, but perhaps, like Lise, she was standing at the edge of a new beginning, one that required her to let go of the past and embrace the future with an open heart.

She loved her course at École des Beaux Arts; it provided her with a much more comprehensive view of modern art, and her French was improving every day. She loved Marseille, and her new 'mates in the scene.' Life had smiled on Sil Anderson since she arrived in Marseille, not to mention the incredible discovery of Lise's letters.

If Lise had found a way to reconcile her past with her present, Sil needed to do the same—not just in her personal life, but in her art too.

A mural to honor Lise was already forming in Sil's colorful mind. It would not just be a tribute to Captain Lise de Baissac; it would be Sil's way of weaving their life stories together. It would be a tribute to courage, to free spirits, to the fight for freedom from oppression, and to the belief that love, in all its forms, was worth fighting for.

Lise had given her so much more than just a glimpse into the past; she had given her a map to navigate her own life. And for the first time in a long time, Sil felt ready to follow it—with all her heart.

56

AN EVENING AT JUSTIN'S

That evening, Sil found herself standing in front of Justin's apartment door, her heart fluttering with nerves she hadn't expected. The text message from him earlier that day had been simple, yet it had set her thoughts spinning.

"Want to hang out at my place tonight?
Arrive with TGV from Paris at 19:00hrs. Will
bring kebab and beer. J."

HE'D BEEN AWAY for another week, lecturing at the Sorbonne, but despite the distance, he had kept in touch, sending her funny messages and memes that made her smile at odd moments. Their budding friendship was turning out to be more delightful than she had imagined. Yet, with Justin often away in Paris, she had mostly had the house to herself—though she always felt she was sharing it with Lise.

Standing outside his door now, she realized how much she had come to look forward to these moments with him. Being in Justin's house felt comfortable, but it was Justin himself who made her feel things she wasn't sure she was prepared for. She found herself checking her unruly hair in the mirror, adjusting her unconventional clothes with an unusual attention to detail—actions that felt a bit foreign yet oddly exciting.

Tonight felt like a new step in whatever it was that was developing between them. This wasn't just a quick meeting in a café or a casual chat in her apartment, which he owned; this was his home, his personal space. She hesitated for a moment, then rang the doorbell.

The door opened almost immediately, and Justin greeted her with a warm smile that sent a small thrill through her. "Come in, Silver."

He had taken off his tie, but he was still dressed in his white shirt, the fabric clinging just enough to hint at his impressive torso. His tailored, dark-grey trousers sat perfectly on his hips, the look completed by a slim black leather Yves Saint Laurent belt.

"Sorry, no time to change, but you look delightful." He glanced appreciatively at her outfit—her mini, pleated, tartan skirt paired with a white T-shirt adorned with her own graffiti texts. For once, she had ditched her combat boots in favor of neon-pink flip-flops, adding a playful touch to her ensemble.

Sil felt a blush rise to her cheeks as she stepped inside. "Thanks." The scent of kebabs filled the air, mingling with the subtle aroma of his cologne, a mix both comforting and intoxicating.

"Make yourself at home," Justin said, closing the door behind her. "I'll grab us a couple of beers."

As she walked further into the apartment, she couldn't help but compare it to the world Lise had lived in. The sleek modernity of Justin's space, with its polished floors and minimalist design, contrasted sharply with the memories that colored her mind. Of Lise's sparse safe houses, the haylofts, the overcrowded bars to exchange messages. And yet, here she was, in a place that felt worlds apart, but was connected by the same threads of history.

Justin returned with two bottles of beer, handing one to her as they moved towards the living room. "Sorry I haven't been furbishing this new abode much. Haven't had time. It looks oddly empty, compared to my Paris flat, which is really cozy. I promise it has books and rugs and stuff," he apologized, following Sil's glance.

"I love it. You know I have a tendency for making pigsties, so your place is heaven. No papers on the floor, no trash next to the trash can, no hole in the walls,' she joked.

As they shared a laugh, Justin gestured toward the large window that dominated one wall of the living room. "Would you like to enjoy the view?"

THEY STOOD SIDE BY SIDE, looking out over the breathtaking panorama of Vieux Port. The harbor was bathed in the warm glow of the evening lights, boats gently bobbing on the water, the rhythm of city life blending beautifully with the serenity of the dark-blue sea. It was a view that never failed to stir Sil, the peaceful juxtaposition of nature and human effort.

She took a sip of her Budweiser, feeling the cool bottle in her hand and the warmth of Justin's presence beside her. She stole a glance at him, noticing how the light glinted off his glasses, softening of his features as he too took in the view. It made him seem almost celestial against the backdrop of the ancient port.

There was something about him—his intelligence, his quietly masculine kindness, the way he seemed to understand her without needing to say much—that made her want to know more, made her want to get closer to him.

Sil felt an unfamiliar but welcome sense of belonging. It was as if she was coming home after a very long time, as if the past and present were converging in this moment, not just through the shared history of Lise's letters, but in the possibility of something new, something hopeful, taking root between them.

"I'm glad you came down tonight," he said, his tone sincere. "It's been a hell of a week but it's all good now. Let's eat, drink, and be merry."

Sil hesitated, not knowing whether she should ask about his 'hell of a week' or wait for him to share more if he wanted to.

"I'm glad too. It's... nice to be here. And after reading Lise's final letter, I needed to talk to someone who understands."

Justin nodded, his expression growing serious. "Lise's story is something else, isn't it? It was part of my 'hell of a week.' I had so much on my plate but only wanted to sit crossed-legged on your faded carpet and talk about her with you. There you go. I've told you my secret."

"I brought her last letter with me. The only one you haven't read yet. I thought you might want to."

He clinked his bottle against hers with his ravishing smile. "I'd love to, but let's fill our mortal bellies first. Care to join me to the table, Mademoiselle Silver?" He playfully took her arm and escorted her to the dining room table, already set for two.

Later, they retired to his comfy leather couch but soon found themselves sliding onto the woolly rug, their backs resting against the soft leather. Sil smiled inwardly—she was pleased to discover that Justin, like her, preferred the grounding sensation of sitting on the floor. It was such an essential part of her life, a way to stay connected and present, away from the formalities of chairs and couches.

Justin carefully took Lise's final letter from her, handling it with a look of reverence. As he began to read, Sil watched him, noticing every subtle change in his expression—the way his brow furrowed, how his breath deepened or caught for a moment, the tension in his jawline, the beginnings of stubble on his cheeks.

His hands, strong and tanned with no rings to speak of, handled the delicate paper with a gentleness that struck her. He was glamorous and intellectual at the same time, a man probably a bit older than her twenty years, yet with a youthful aura she found herself mesmerized by.

They were worlds apart—different backgrounds, different lives —but it felt like there was so much to explore and experiment with together. Sil shook herself, trying to rein in her wandering thoughts. What was she thinking?

When he finished reading, his eyes sought hers, a deep understanding reflected in his gaze. "An incredible finale, Silver. Lise was larger than life, but I don't think she ever saw herself that way. She was so grounded, so unassuming, just rolling with the tides of history. "What a sacrifice. I agree with Raoul—she had that Joan of Arc stardom, combined with a beautiful simplicity."

Sil could only nod, impressed by Justin's concise description of Lise's personality. Without thinking, she inched closer to him, and he gently wrapped his arm around her, pulling her into the comforting arch of his embrace.

"I want to do her justice, Justin," she said in a low voice. "I want the world to know Lise's story, to feel what we feel when I read these letters."

"You will," Justin murmured into her rainbow curls, pulling her closer. "We will, Silver. Together."

57

THE FIRST DATE

One week later, Marseille, October 2004

Sil decided on a leather mini-skirt and a frilly white T-shirt, the best outfit she could scramble together. She applied extra kohl around her eyes and pulled her curly hair into a tight bun on top of her head. Her Roman sandals were tied securely around her tanned calves. At the last moment, she decided to remove the titanium piercing from her nose.

At precisely seven-thirty, there was a knock on her door. Justin stood in front of her, looking effortlessly elegant in a shirt with the top button open and a pair of blue jeans.

"Ready?" he asked, offering a warm smile before smirking slightly. "You look great, but where's the piercing? I was just getting used to it. You look sort of... naked without it."

"Thank you. I like being naked," she quipped, slipping her cell phone and wallet into her pocket.

"We'll go by car; it's a bit of a drive."

The sleek black Mercedes idled in front of the house, its engine purring softly. As Justin steered the almost soundless car through Marseille's busy streets, Sil tried to relax in the passenger seat, but she couldn't shake the feeling of being slightly out of her comfort zone.

"Are you taking me anywhere fancy?"

"Not too fancy. It's a friend's place. You'll like it. The food is fab, and the view is stellar."

They arrived at L'Épuisette, an upscale restaurant perched on the edge of the Mediterranean Sea. Labeled Marseille's most elegant restaurant, it indeed boasted a breathtaking sea view. The setting sun cast streaks of golden light over the waves, creating a magical pattern on the water. Inside, the restaurant exuded understated elegance, with soft lighting, damask tablecloths, silently moving waiters, and gentle background music.

The maître d'hôtel, whom Justin addressed as Paulus, greeted him with a jovial arm around his shoulder and led them to a table with a stunning view of the sea. Sil looked around, still feeling a bit like a fish out of water amidst the luxury and refinement, but Justin's attentive gestures—helping her with her chair, ensuring she was comfortable—grounded her.

Their casual conversation was soon interrupted by the arrival of their first course—an exquisite plate of bouillabaisse, the traditional Provençal fish stew. The rich, herb-filled aroma made Sil's mouth water.

After savoring her first delicious bite, Sil leaned forward, her dark, kohl-rimmed eyes sparkling with curiosity. "Apart from Lise, who was your favorite person in her letters, Justin? I'll tell you mine afterward."

He took a sip of his Bordeaux wine, pausing to gather his thoughts. "Hands down, her brother Claude. But Raoul comes in a close second. I suppose it doesn't surprise you that I'm mentioning two men?" he grinned.

"Explain yourself, Sir," Sil commanded playfully.

"Claude... I feel like I understand the man. He had an immense job to do, but it was also war, and he had his own longings. I think he really cared for Mary, and she wanted his child. I sympathize with the complexity of his situation. I actually think he and Lise were not only cut from the same cloth, but they were also alike in many ways—extraordinary leaders with a very human side. But Lise, being a woman, was the slightly stronger one. She never let her urges cloud her judgment, not even when Raoul was hitting on her. That's the strength of women. They don't lose their heads as easily."

Sil processed his words. "Interesting," she mused, focusing on her food for a moment before shooting Justin another glance. "And Raoul?"

He laughed generously. "Every man wants to be a Raoul. And only a Joan of Arc-caliber woman can resist a Raoul. Raouls were the Liam and Noel Gallaghers of their time—wild, free, and incredibly sexy and all the women want them"

Now it was Sil's turn to laugh out loud. "You wouldn't actually want to be in Oasis, would you?"

"Hell, I would," Justin grinned. "Every man wants to exude a touch of uncontrolled wildness. But most—like me—hide it under a polite layer of civilization. Think of it as having a bit of Kurt Cobain's rebellious spirit, a dash of Axl Rose's unpredictability, or even a streak of Robbie Williams' cheeky charisma, but safely tucked away."

"That's good to know," Sil observed, giggling into her napkin. "I think it's a good moment to ask your age." She made it sound snooty.

"I'm thirty, Madame Silver," he replied with a mock bow, "and pretty well preserved, if I may say so myself. Now, who's your favorite person?"

"Lise for sure. I would love to have her guts and her commitment. And I'd love to wield a handgun with such confidence and calm. But mostly, I admire how she makes me reflect on my own life. I mean, these days we never ask ourselves whether we'd defend our country. That's so not 2004. But to live a life in the service of something greater—that appeals to me. And honestly, I'd love to be a kick-ass secret agent, just like you want to be a sex-driven rockstar." As she spoke, with her chin resting on the palms of her hands, she felt Justin's eyes studying her.

"You look so darn lovely and sweet this way, Silver," Justin said, his voice sparkling. "I want to kiss you right here and now, but before that, I have to tell you—I think you're probably the same kind of daredevil Lise was."

"Oh, but I'm much more rash and impatient," Sil admitted, blushing while trying to ignore the mention of a kiss. "That's what I've been thinking about the most. How did she stay so calm? Like when she was in the room with Grabowski, sipping tea with him and chatting away. I would've pulled out that Colt and killed him on the spot. Or wrung his chicken neck with my bare hands."

"No, you wouldn't," Justin chuckled, "but I get what you mean. Lise had an extraordinary quality that few possess. She had what we French call sangfroid—a kind of cold-blooded calm. She never lost her head, even when the adrenaline must have been pumping through her veins like an avalanche."

"True," Sil nodded. "When I'm old and gray, I want to have that quality too."

"Why not now?" Justin raised an eyebrow.

Sil pondered his question for a moment. "It's just not who I am right now. I'm more of a spur-of-the-moment, feel-it-as-it-happens person. I need that for my art."

"Don't forget Lise was raised to feel on top of her game," Justin explained. "Those upper-class colonial types carried a certain—can I say—superiority? I come from a similar background, and sometimes it borders on arrogance. Lise despised the Nazis, probably looked down on them, and didn't let herself be pushed around. She never became a victim—it wasn't in her nature. Somewhere I read—was it Colonel Buckmaster?—that he called her the Queen of SOE. I think it's that: she behaved like a queen."

"Yeah, you're right," Sil replied. "And she despised Alphonse because of his socialist views, even though he was a top-notch SOE agent in his own right."

"Ok, besides Lise, who else do you admire in the letters?" Justin asked.

Sil thought for a moment. "I'd have to say Geneviève/Pippa, because she reminded me a lot of myself—clumsy, always saying the wrong things—and she intrigues me. But emotionally, I felt drawn to Claire Rimbaud. We didn't get a clear picture of her character, but I think there was a quiet force there, providing a steady background for Lise's Poitiers mission. I looked it up—Café de la Paix on Place d'Armes still exists. But she's probably long gone. Maybe Sophie, though..."

"Would you like to go and see for yourself, Silver? We could..."

At that moment, the maître d'hôtel coughed politely at their side, and they both looked up, suddenly reminded of where they were. "Would you care for the next course, Madame, Monsieur?"

"Sure, sure," Justin replied, making room for a young waiter to retrieve their bouillabaisse plates.

"What should we do with the letters and the suitcase, though?" Sil wondered aloud.

"I've thought about that too. I brought it up with colleagues in Paris—hypothetically, of course, because I didn't want to give away your discovery. We all agreed these letters have immense historical value. They should probably be handed over to any surviving family members, or if none can be found, donated to an organization like Traces of War."

"I don't think I can part with them yet." Sil's voice trembled with emotion at the thought of someone else taking possession of these deeply personal letters, or worse, that they might disappear into a stuffy archive, never to be read again.

"For now, we keep them, Sil. Don't worry. It's our secret." Justin reached across the table and squeezed her hand briefly. She wanted to kiss him so much, but she cast her eyes down to hide her desire and simply nodded. "Thank you."

Her voice still slightly shaky, she continued, "I've tried to find everything I could about Lise post-war, but there's very little. We know she married Gustave Henri Villameur in 1950 and lived in Saint-Tropez and Marseille, but beyond that, she seemed to have faded into anonymity—apart from a few interviews and mentions here and there."

"I did the same search and found the same results. Though I must say, the interviews she gave—oh-la-la, 'une grande dame' indeed! Silver-haired and sharp as a fox." Justin's face showed great admiration.

"True!" Sil's eyes suddenly flashed with indignation. "But it infuriates me that she never got more than an MBE. She should've at least been given an OBE, and her Croix de Guerre wasn't awarded until she was already 90! The SOE men and women who died in Gestapo captivity were usually more highly decorated, which is all well and good, but Lise worked in France for so long and did such instrumental work under enormous stress."

Justin smiled gently. "Perhaps she didn't care much for medals. But you're right, there's very little on Lise post-war. I asked my aunt, who lived in Marseille her whole life, and she said she'd heard about Madame Villameur's extraordinary accomplishments during the war, but it wasn't a big deal here either."

Sil sighed. "So, we'll go and see the Poitiers streets where Lise cycled? I'm most in awe of her first mission, where she did everything on her own."

Justin looked at her thoughtfully. "Yes, me too. I've been to Poitiers and the surrounding areas many times, but never with this perspective. I was there to study my specialty in history, which is... the Crusades."

Sil's mouth fell open. "What Irène Brisse was supposedly studying in and around Poitiers that kept her bumping into that awful Grabowski? All this time reading the letters, and you never said a thing!"

Justin chuckled. "I know, an odd coincidence. I think maybe it helped me feel close to Lise as well."

BY THE TIME DESSERT ARRIVED—A delicate tarte tropézienne—the connection between the unlikely couple was sealed with a promise. A promise to explore Poitiers together, to walk the same streets Lise had cycled, and to uncover more of her remarkable story.

As they left L'Épuisette, the night air was cool and refreshing. Justin took Sil's hand, a simple gesture that spoke volumes.

"Let's follow in Lise's footsteps together, Silver."

Sil smiled, her heart giddy. "Deal."

58

IN LISE'S FOOTSTEPS

One week later - Poitiers, mid-October 2004

On a sunny Saturday morning, Sil and Justin set out for the nearly 500-mile journey from Marseille to Poitiers in Justin's black Mercedes. The interior of the car was luxurious in a way Sil had never experienced—soft grey leather seats, a polished mahogany dashboard, a sunroof that opened soundlessly, and air conditioning that made not even the faintest hum.

Sitting there in her cargo pants and pink top, with cheap sunglasses perched on her nose and army boots on her feet, Sil felt like she needed time to adjust again.

This man beside her was from a different world—a world of sophistication and ease that felt foreign to her. He was almost ten years older, French to the bone, and exuded a kind of effortless elegance that made her question what she was doing here.

She was used to men—boys really—with graffiti-smeared, torn jeans, dreadlocks, or mohawks. Men who lived life with rough edges and loud opinions. Not this man, who seemed as if he had been born in a designer suit, with every hair perfectly in place. The prototype of a Mediterranean Don Juan, certainly not Silver boyfriend material.

Boyfriend, Sil? Ha! she scolded herself internally. *Never been further from it. You're here for Lise. That's all.*

But despite her self-reminders, she remained acutely aware of Justin's presence so close beside her. Every movement he made sent a spark through her, his scent—a subtle mix of cologne and something uniquely him—tickled her senses. He was such an accomplished driver, navigating the roads with the same confidence he seemed to apply to everything else in his life.

Why am I so tense now that we've left Marseille behind? she wondered. *Am I really still this insecure?*

The silence between them felt heavy, and Sil found herself wishing she could think of something to say—anything to break the ice. She even missed the playful bickering they used to share when they first met.

Sensing her tension, Justin reached over and pressed play on the car's CD player. The soulful sounds of Norah Jones's "Come Away with Me" filled the car, blending with the hum of the engine. Sil turned to the window, watching the French countryside roll by, feeling a little more at ease but still uncertain.

On the backseat, Justin's Polo Ralph Lauren overnight bag sat neatly beside her worn Nomad backpack—another contrast that only deepened her sense of unease. *Oh, Sil, what are you doing?*

After a while, Justin broke the silence. "I've found us a nice hotel in Poitiers. I booked two rooms at the Hotel Mercure Poitiers Centre. I know it well—I always stayed there when I was doing research for my thesis."

Sil was relived at his thoughtfulness. "Thank you. I appreciate that. I'll pay my part."

Justin shook his head. "I made the offer, so I'll pay. It's my treat."

Sil smiled, feeling the tension beginning to ease. "Alright, but next time, I insist."

They both laughed, the sound lightening the atmosphere. "When there is a next time, that is," Sil quickly added, but the ice had already been broken.

"I suppose you'd like to follow in Lise's footsteps to Normandy one day?" Justin suggested. "Have you ever been to the D-Day beaches?"

"Yes," Sil replied, her voice thoughtful. "My grandfather, Jack Anderson, landed there with the Royal Welsh Fusiliers. He took me to visit in 1994 for the fiftieth commemoration. I liked it, but I was only ten, so I didn't really grasp the full impact of what had happened there. To me, it was just a bunch of old men talking about the past on a strip of sandy beach. As usual I was only sketching and didn't listen much."

"Aha, so you have a personal link to World War II as well?"

"Yeah, I do. My Gramps was my everything. I wish I'd listened to him more when I had the chance." Sil felt a pang of regret that she couldn't share this newfound perspective with Grandpa Jack anymore.

"We'll go there too, Silver. To pay tribute to both Lise and your Grandpa Jack."

"Oh, Justin." Sil squeezed his arm affectionately. "Thank you."

"Anything to see you happy, ma chère." There it was again, that endearing phrase he sometimes used—ma chère. Just like Lise and her Henri. Sil adored those words.

"And you're twenty?" Justin asked, casting a sideways glance at her. His sunglasses made it difficult to read his expression.

"Nearly 21...does it show?" she quipped, trying to lighten the mood.

"No," he said with a grin. "I'll just pretend you're older and I'm younger."

"What's that supposed to mean? I know you're thirty. You're not old. Plus, who's to say I don't have an old soul and you are just incredibly immature for your age?" She gave him her challenge-me look, and he laughed, hitting the steering wheel in glee.

"I agree—inside, I'm still a testosterone-fueled teenager. Always."

"I have no clue what you're talking about," she replied casually, though her heart skipped a beat.

Justin smirked, and then, in a playful tone, he sang, "You and me, babe, how about it?" It was a line from Dire Straits' Romeo and Juliet—one of Sil's absolute favorites.

"Those are Juliet's words, not Romeo's," she retorted, her lips curving into a smile.

"True," he admitted. "So, I'll leave it to you, Juliet."

"Heavens, what a responsibility," she teased, feeling the last remnants of tension between them dissolve.

The rest of the journey passed in easy conversation. They talked about Sil's progress at art school and Justin's recent return to lecturing in Paris. They giggled, sang along to Dire Straits together, and, before long, the Mercedes had become one of Sil's favorite places on earth. She realized she wouldn't mind if the drive went on for days.

WHEN THEY ARRIVED in Poitiers toward the end of the afternoon, the city on the hill greeted them with its blend of medieval and modern architecture. Steep and narrow cobblestone streets wound through the city, flanked by historic buildings with wrought-iron balconies and colorful shutters. Churches everywhere.

Just as Lise had described, Sil thought.

Justin knew his way around and drove straight to the Hotel Mercure Poitiers Centre. After checking in and leaving their belongings, they set out to explore the city. The sun was setting, casting shadows across the streets as they made their way to Avenue Solférino. The address where Lise once lived was now a modern apartment block, no visible sign of the rich history that had once unfolded there.

From there, they strolled to the Place d'Armes, where the Café de la Paix still stood on the corner. The facade was a blend of old-world charm and rustic elegance. The two-story building had wrought-iron balconies on the first floor, each draped with vibrant flower boxes overflowing with late summer geraniums and petunias.

A large, hand-painted sign hung above the entrance, its letters weathered but still legible, inviting passersby to step inside. The café's large windows were framed with wooden shutters, painted in a cheerful shade of blue, through which the warm glow of the interior lights spilled.

Tables and chairs, reminiscent of classic Parisian style, were arranged outside under striped parasols, offering a shaded spot to enjoy a coffee or pastis while watching the world go by.

"This is it. It's open." Sil felt a thrill of excitement. "The last time Lise came here in search of Mary Herbert in 1944, it was closed. It's good to see new people have taken over."

"They probably have no idea their café was once a famous rendezvous spot for secret agents and resistance fighters during the war," Justin observed.

"Let's check it out." Sil pushed open the glass door with its brass handles.

The café's interior was timeless, typical of rural France. The walls were adorned with vintage photographs and memorabilia, telling stories of the café's rich history. Bronze chandeliers cast their light over the polished wooden tables and comfortable, well-worn, leather chairs.

A large, ornate mirror behind the counter reflected the café's inner activity. The counter itself was a polished oak bar, lined with a display of fresh pastries and an assortment of spirits. Shelves stacked with old books and ceramic coffee mugs added to the homey feel.

The floor was a mosaic of patterned tiles, leading to a corner with a grand piano, suggesting that live music was a common evening delight. Each table held a small vase of fresh flowers.

The patrons, a mix of regulars and tourists, sat peacefully side by side, their conversations filling the space, competing with the tones of country music in the background. The overall effect was one of warmth and nostalgia, a place where history and everyday life never clashed.

An elderly woman with stylish grey hair stood behind the counter, her cornflower blue eyes sharp and curious. She wore a flowery dress with an apron over it, and a pair of reading spectacles hung on a string around her neck.

Sil and Justin approached the counter and took seats on two empty bar stools. "What can I serve you?" the matron asked, taking in the newcomers with interest.

She's special, Sil thought, not quite knowing why. The whole café felt special—as if she'd been here before.

"Two coffees and two of these delicious-looking pastries," Justin ordered, taking the lead while Sil gratefully let him. She was too awestruck to speak, overwhelmed by the significance of being in Lise's café.

"*Excusez-moi, Madame*," Justin asked as she brought them their order. "Do you by any chance know if this café was owned by Madame Claire Rimbaud during World War II?"

The woman's hands trembled slightly as she set down the tray.

Her eyes narrowed with a glint of suspicion. "Why do you want to know that?"

Justin spoke gently. "We're following in the footsteps of Lise de Baissac, a British secret agent who frequented this café. She worked here under the alias of Madame Irène Brisse, a widow from Paris. We're trying to learn more about her and those who helped her."

The woman's expression immediately softened, and she swallowed hard.

"I am Sophie Rimbaud, now Madame Gâteau. Claire Rimbaud was my mother."

59

CONVERSATION WITH A RESISTER

Sil's eyes widened in astonishment. "Then you must be the young teenage girl who helped Lise!"

Sophie smiled wistfully. "Yes, I was. But how do you know that? And who are you?"

"Oh, I'm sorry," Sil exclaimed, her excitement bubbling over. "I'm Sil Anderson, and this is Justin Bellamare. We're from Marseille. Justin recently bought the house where Lise used to live on Vieux Port, and I rent rooms there. When I moved in two months ago, I found a suitcase filled with Lise's letters. She wrote them to Henri Villameur after the war, when she was still in London. He later became her husband."

Sil was so overwhelmed by the coincidence that she found herself babbling, but Sophie seemed to follow her story with interest. Justin stepped in, placing his leather briefcase on the counter.

"Silver was kind enough to copy every letter in which your mother and you were mentioned," Justin explained, retrieving a folder from the briefcase and handing it to Sophie. "We hoped to find someone in your family to share them with."

Sophie accepted the folder with a look of surprise. "Heavens," she murmured. "I never knew."

"No one did," Sil added softly. "The suitcase was hidden behind a wall."

Sophie glanced at the folder, then set it aside gently. "I'll read it later. Thank you so much." She gestured to the wall behind them. "Look behind you."

Sil and Justin turned to see a wall adorned with photographs of SOE agents who had once visited Café de la Paix, all thanks to Lise.

At the center was a photograph of Lise in her FANY uniform, her florid signature scrawled beneath it. Sil recognized several faces from her research: France Antelme, Mary Herbert, Claude de Baissac, Francine Agazarian, Andrée Borrel, and Francis Suttill. But it was the photograph of a smiling woman with an open face, wavy hair, and light eyes that caught Sil's attention.

"That was my mother, Claire," Sophie said softly. "She was arrested by Grabowski in September 1943 and executed a month later. Renaud and Doctor Giraud suffered the same fate. I was taken, just in time, to a farmer family outside Poitiers and survived. It was a good thing Aunt Lise returned to London when she did."

Sil felt a lump form in her throat as she absorbed Sophie's words. She reached out to touch the edge of the photograph, as if connecting with the past through the image of Claire Rimbaud.

"I'm so sorry, Madame Gâteau. I can't imagine what it must have been like," Sil whispered. "Your mother was incredibly brave."

Sophie nodded, her eyes misting over. "She was. And so were all of them. It's important that their stories are remembered, that their sacrifices are not forgotten."

Justin placed a comforting hand on Sil's shoulder. "That's why we're here—to honor their memories and to ensure their stories live on."

Sophie voice was full of gratitude as she said. "Thank you. It means more than you know."

The three of them stood in silence for a moment, surrounded by the echoes of history, each lost in their own thoughts. The café, with its warm and nostalgic atmosphere, seemed to hold the spirits of those who had once walked its floors, reminding them that the past was never truly gone—it lived on in the memories of those who cared to remember.

"So, you kept in touch with Lise after the war?" Justin asked, piecing together the information Sophie had shared.

"Oh yes, many times. I'll tell you all about it but let me show you something first."

Sophie led them to a small round table in the corner, facing the door. A discreet plaque on the table read, "*SOE agent Captain Lise de Baissac used this table during WW2.*" Sil and Justin were visibly impressed.

"Jean, take over the counter," Sophie called to her middle-aged son, who promptly complied.

As they settled at Lise's table, Sophie began sharing her memories. "This was where Aunt Lise would sit, often with Renaud and Doctor Giraud. They planned so many missions right here. New agents that arrived were also brought here. My mother was incredibly brave. It was very dangerous for a café owner to be a meeting point, but she didn't care. She wanted the Nazis out. They all became very close. Aunt Lise always looked out for us."

Sil leaned in, captivated. "What was your Aunt Lise, as you call her so endearingly, like? I mean, in person."

Sophie's eyes twinkled with nostalgia. "She was extraordinary. Strong, intelligent, and always so composed. Even when things got dangerous, she never lost her cool. She had a way of making you feel safe, even in the worst situations."

Justin listened intently. "And after the war? What happened then?"

"Uncle Henri loved her so much," Sophie continued. "He went from being a penniless artist to a successful interior decorator, furnishing homes of the wealthy, including one of Onassis's ships. They were very happy, but they never had children. After the war, they often visited Poitiers, and me."

Sophie paused, looking wistful. "The people of Poitiers were completely shocked to find out Madame Irène Brisse was actually a British secret agent. She'd hid it so well behind her Parisian alias of a widow with interest in archaeology. She fooled us resisters, as well. We really thought she only had ties with the Resistance movement in Paris. Never in our wildest dreams we would have thought her to be British. You can call us naïve, with British agents coming and going and arms and supplies being dropped from RAF planes, but we truly had no idea something like SOE existed. How could we?"

"Amazing," Sil said with a lump in her throat. "Ever since I found the suitcase with the letters, I've lived with Lise and her missions every day. And now Justin is infected as well." She gave him a brief smile. "That's why we're here, Madame Gâteau. It's so special to talk with someone who really knew her—who really interacted with her when she was at the height of her career."

"Please just call me Sophie. Aunt Lise would have wanted that."

"Oh yes, please and we're just Sil and Justin. So, you keep referring to her as aunt?" Sil asked.

"Yes, she felt like an aunt to me. She was and always remained very dear to me. Like family. Especially because of my mother..." Sophie's voice trailed off.

Justin chimed in, "This is such a significant moment to us all. So, Sophie, I have a burning question, and I know it's probably only the worry of a historian, but I hope you can answer it."

"I'll try." Sophie smiled.

"Great. My train of thought is that the suitcase with the letters belonged to Henri. That he kept them behind that wall in their house in Marseille without Lise's knowing they still existed. She specifically asked him to destroy them for security reasons. She also was very private about her war efforts, especially after everything that came out about SOE's disasters later. She clearly never wanted to get involved in any controversies or disclose matters that were top secret. She knew she was taking a risk writing about her missions in the first place. So why do they still exist?"

Sophie thought for a moment, her elegant, gray head tilted. "I think you're right, Justin. Aunt Lise never hinted at having written about her war efforts, certainly not to me. And Uncle Henri was the sentimental one. And he doted on her every word. He may very well have told her he destroyed them, and she may have believed him. I don't know that part. I only know how private they were. She protected her own life and that of Uncle Henri like a hawk."

Justin nodded. He had his answer. That's why there were no Henri letters. Lise had kept her part of the deal and destroyed them. Thank God for Henri Villameur's sentimentality. Because of love, he'd preserved a unique insight into the life story of his very courageous spouse.

Tears glistening in Sophie's eyes. "Thank you so much for coming and for giving me copies of those letters. It's like having a piece of my mother and Aunt Lise back. After she passed this spring, it's been so silent."

Justin spoke gently. "We want to honor your Aunt Lise's legacy properly. These letters are such a testament to her bravery and the incredible risks she took."

"Yes, and the love story between her and Henri was something else. They were devoted to each other. Quite a dashing pair, even in old age."

Sil was curious. "Did you ever visit their home in Marseille or Saint-Tropez, Sophie?"

She shook her head. "No, I think that was part of their privacy. They always came here. Stayed for two days and went back. A driver brought them and picked them up. They stayed at the Hotel Mercure Poitiers Centre."

"That's where we're staying," Sil smiled.

"It's the best hotel in Poitiers, so a good choice. But they always came here for lunch and dinner. Always at this table." Sophie sighed. "I attended Aunt Lise's funeral in early May this year. It was a small gathering. She was cremated, but I don't know what happened to her ashes. They didn't have much family left. I think it was all part of her need for privacy."

Justin and Sil shared a look of understanding. "I'm so sorry," Sil said. "Thank you for everything, Sophie. We will be back to sit at your Aunt Lise's table now and then." She stood up, feeling both uncertain and unwilling to leave. Her body wanted to move, her hands itching to create. Big, bold colors exploded in her mind's eye. She saw it crystal clear and razor-sharp—Lise's legacy: The Color of Courage.

Justin rose as well and handed Sophie his business card. "Do stay in touch, Sophie, and yes, we'll be back. But we need to get some fresh air now. We've been in the car all day."

"I won't lose sight of you two," Sophie smiled, giving them a charming wink. "You remind me of Aunt Lise and Uncle Henri—so different and yet so compatible."

Outside, Sil leaned against a warm stone wall in an alley, the heat of the day still lingering against her back. A surge of emotion swelled within her, something she had never felt before. It was as if everything had finally clicked into place—courage, color, character. Lise had it all, in abundance. Now it had to become her masterpiece.

Justin stood before her and did what she had yearned for him to do ever since their first encounter on the TGV at Gare Saint-Charles. He took her in his arms, holding her tenderly yet firmly.

And in that moment, Sil knew with the same crystal clarity that painted her mural in her mind's eye—Justin Bellamare was the rock she could build on. She didn't fully understand why, but her gut told her he was the one.

"I know what I want to do with Lise's legacy," she began, "and with my life..." But before she could say more, he kissed her.

And she kissed him back. And the world whispered bliss.

60

THE COLOR OF COURAGE

Eight months later - Marseille, 11 May 2005

T he May sun shone brightly over Cours Julien, casting its warm light over the vibrant street art that radiated from the walls. A large crowd had gathered, buzzing with anticipation.

In the center of it all was a scaffold draped with a large tarp, hiding Sil's graduation piece from L'École des Beaux-Arts de Marseille.

But to Sil Anderson, this was not just any unveiling, or any school assignment, it was a celebration of Lise de Baissac's 100th birthday, a tribute to her heroine's incredible life and legacy.

Sil stood tall on the scaffold, clad in tight, black, leather trousers and a white blouse. Her short curls were dyed platinum blonde, and her piercing caught the sunlight, glinting like a jewel. The pounding of her heart, a stiff dose of nerves and pride, was so loud she was sure everyone could hear it.

But probably not. A local DJ ensured the guests were treated to a blast of hip-hop and rap music. Sil took one more glance at the mural hidden behind the cloth. She'd worked on it for so long, first on paper and then on the wall itself, and had taken all of last night to finish it.

Under the harsh glow of construction lamps and fueled by too many bottles of Pepsi, she had pushed through the night, her hands moving almost on autopilot as she brought Lise's story to life. She wanted as few people as possible to see her work in progress, preserving the mystery until the grand unveiling.

As she stood there, her eyes heavy with exhaustion, memories of her nights in Bristol flooded back. She could almost smell the metallic tang of spray paint in the cool night air, feel the rough texture of the brick walls beneath her fingers as she worked in the shadows, illegally tagging the city's forgotten corners.

Those nights had been fueled by adrenaline, the thrill of rebellion, and a desperate need to leave her mark on the world. She had often been drunk with sleep-deprivation back then too, her body pushed to its limits as she wielded her cans, creating art in secret, knowing that the morning light could reveal her work to the authorities.

Now, standing here in the daylight, she realized how much had changed—yet how much remained the same. The rebellion was still there, the drive to make a statement, but now it was focused, purposeful. She wasn't just leaving her mark on a wall; she was telling a story that needed to be told.

As fatigue weighed on her, she thought of Lise—of the countless nights the SOE agent must have spent in similar exhaustion, working under the cover of darkness, her body pushed to the edge, her mind sharp with the knowledge that a single mistake could mean death. Lise had given everything for her cause, sacrificing sleep, comfort, and safety for a greater purpose. And now, in a much smaller way, Sil felt she was doing the same.

The parallel gave her strength. She stood there, tipsy with exhaustion but filled with a sense of purpose, knowing that she had poured every ounce of herself into this mural. It was more than art; it was a tribute, a way to honor Lise's legacy by capturing all the colors of her courage, seen through Sil's eyes.

Sil straightened her tired back. Whatever the outcome, she knew she'd given everything she had. She had channeled her past, her experiences, and all the lessons she'd learned along the way into this one final piece. And in doing so, she felt connected to Lise in a way she hadn't before—as if, across time, they shared the same exhaustion, the same commitment, and the same unbreakable spirit.

Sil scanned the faces in the audience. Among them were her fiancé Justin Bellamare and Sophie Rimbaud, their supportive presence giving her strength. The Mayor of Marseille, Jean-Claude Gaudin, her teachers from l'École des Beaux-Arts, and countless spectators were also present, waiting to hear her speak.

She caught sight of Madame Fournier, her modern art teacher, standing proudly with a group of Sil's fellow students—German Anna and Max from Bermuda included. Their faces were filled with admiration and excitement, reflecting the journey they'd all shared during their time at École des Beaux-Arts.

After a signal from her, the young DJ stopped, and a moment of silence followed. Sil began, her voice clear and steady.

"Good afternoon, everyone. Thank you all for being here on this very special day. Today, we celebrate the life of an extraordinary woman who lived right here in Marseille for decades. Her full name was Lise Marie Jeanette Boucherville de Baissac, but we'll refer to her simply as Lise de Baissac. Today would have been Lise's 100th birthday, but she passed away a little over a year ago in her home at Vieux Port.

"Let me share with you who Lise was and how this WWII secret agent connects to a 21st-century graffiti artist who originally hails from Bristol.

"Lise de Baissac is more than just a name etched into the annals of history; she was a woman whose courage, resilience, and fearless spirit deserve to be known by the whole world. Born in Curepipe, Mauritius, in 1905, she moved to Paris at age 14 with her family. With both British and French heritage, Lise eventually became one of the most remarkable agents of the Special Operations Executive during World War II. Her bravery in occupied France is truly inspiring, and I deeply believe that everyone can learn something from her actions. She was one of the first women to be dropped into France and served during two long, grueling missions.

"Lise operated under various aliases. Her code names were Odile and Marguerite; her aliases, Madame Irène Brisse and Madame Janette Bouville—both times posing as a widowed Parisian lady seeking a more tranquil life in the countryside. As Odile, Lise organized her own network in the Poitiers area, and later as Marguerite she was second-in-command to her brother's network in Normandy and played a crucial role in the Allied success of D-Day by hampering the German advance.

"Though raised in an upper-class environment, Lise chose a path that required her to sabotage German operations, gather critical intelligence, and inspire countless others to resist Nazi tyranny. Her daily protection was a loaded Colt, a switchblade hidden in her sleeve, and a cyanide pill in her purse. Between her two missions in France, Lise served as an instructor for other secret agents in Britain, teaching them everything from parachute jumping to the silent dispatching of a German sentry.

"Standing at 5'4", with a slender build and prematurely graying hair as she approached forty, Lise was nothing like the Hollywood portrayals of female action heroes—don't picture Angelina Jolie as Lara Croft. Lise was the real deal, a modern Joan of Arc.

"So, what's my connection to this incredible woman? When I moved into Lise's house at Vieux Port last August, I stumbled upon a hidden treasure: Lise's letters, tucked away in an old suitcase behind a wall. These letters, written after the war to her beloved Henri Villameur, offered a glimpse into Lise's life beyond her heroic deeds —a life filled with love, longing, and an unshakable sense of duty.

"Though Lise had asked Henri to destroy them, he apparently couldn't bring himself to do it. Instead, he kept them for posterity— for me, for us—allowing us to connect with her in a deeply personal way."

"In creating this mural as my graduation assignment for l'École des Beaux-Arts, I've made an attempt to capture the essence of Lise's life journey—her adventures, her tribulations, and her triumphs. So please, see this mural is not just a piece of art; it's meant to be a living portrayal of Lise's life, depicted through snapshots of Curepipe, London, Paris, Marseille, parachutes symbolizing her daring drops into France, and quotes from her letters that reveal the heart and soul of this incredible woman.

"Lise's story is one of enduring inspiration. It reminds us that ordinary people can do extraordinary things when driven by courage and a sense of justice. Her legacy teaches us the importance of standing up for what is right, even in the face of overwhelming odds. It is a lesson that is timeless and universal.

"Today, as I unveil this mural, we honor Lise's legacy and acknowledge the profound impact she'd had on history and on all of us here. The peace we currently live in here in Western Europe. I truly hope that this mural will keep Lise's memory alive for generations to come.

"All that remains for me is to thank Lise de Baissac. For how she enriched my life and taught me love, respect and endurance. May her memory live on in the hearts of the Marseillais forever more."

Sil stopped talking, her eyes scanning the crowd. She saw moist eyes, smiles, and nods of agreement. She looked over at Mayor Gaudin, who clapped approvingly, then at her teachers, who beamed with pride. Finally, she glanced at Justin and Sophie, who gave her encouraging smiles. Madame Fournier caught her eye, mouthing the words "bravo," and Sil felt a wave of gratitude for the support and mentorship that had guided her to this moment.

"Without further ado, let me unveil the 'Color of Courage'."

With a firm tug, Sil pulled the tarp away, revealing the mural in all its glory. The wall painting was a vivid tapestry of Lise's life, each section capturing an essence of her earthly journey. Her portrait, bold and dignified, in its FANY uniform, looked out over the crowd on Cours Julien in between scenes of her daring missions and heart-felt moments.

Applause erupted, and Sil had to grab the scaffold for stability or a moment. She felt weak and strong at the same time. All the emotions Lise had felt in her moments of intense danger and triumph. A true hero wasn't only strength, she was human.

As the applause died down, Sil clambered down the scaffold on wobbly legs but with her heart full. Art was her first love and Justin was her second. As he and Sophie approached her, she couldn't hold out any longer and burst into joyful tears.

"You did it, Sil," Justin beamed, pulling her into a tight embrace.

"We did it," Sil whispered, her voice choking as she grabbed Sophie's hand.

"Aunt Lise would've been so proud of you. You've honored her memory beautifully. Sil is almost Lise spelled backward."

"It is," Sil nodded. "I've thought of that coincidence myself at times. Though Justin calls me Silver, like my grandfather did."

Mayor Gaudin approached, shaking Sil's hand firmly. "A remark-able tribute, Mademoiselle Anderson. Through your work, I'm really learning to appreciate the art form graffiti offers us. Marseille is proud to have an artist of your caliber in our midst."

"Thank you, Mayor Gaudin, I'm so pleased to hear that. And my work is not done here yet," she added jokingly.

"I hope not, Mademoiselle."

German Anna and Max from Bermuda waved enthusiastically from the sidelines, their faces glowing with pride. Madame Fournier gave her a thumbs-up, surrounded by her fellow students who had cheered the loudest during the unveiling.

From the ground, Sil glanced up at her newest work, and for the first time, she allowed herself to truly see it. It was good—no, it was strong. The tiny imperfections she'd once obsessed over faded into insignificance. This was more than just a mural; it was a testament to how far she'd come. She had grown as an artist, pushing beyond the boundaries of the illegal paint-spraying girl who once roamed the back alleys of Bristol.

Now, she stood here, not just as a street artist, but as a modern artist in her own right. She'd earned her place in this world, just as Lise had earned her MBE.

Justin stepped up beside her, his hand lacing in hers. "It's incredible, Silver, a masterpiece. You've done something truly special."

She squeezed his hand, feeling the warmth of his support. And as they stood there together, under the Marseille sun, Sil knew this was only the beginning.

EPILOGUE
THE ULTIMATE REWARD IS LOVE

One year later - Marseille, 11 May 2006

The following spring, on a similarly bright and sunny day, Sil Anderson stood once more in the heart of Marseille's Vieux Port, the historic harbor alive with the same energy that had witnessed centuries of stories unfold.

But this time, it was not for an unveiling of her art. Today, after a year marked by profound reconnections, personal growth, and the blossoming of her career, Sil was about to embark on a new chapter. Today was her wedding day.

As she stood there, the sun warming her skin and the soft breeze playing with her natural, dark curls, Sil reflected on how much had changed since she first collided with Justin Bellamare on the TGV in Gare Saint-Charles in Marseille.

What had started as a journey to escape her past, morphed into one of discovering Lise's past, and now had led her to a future she had never imagined. Over the past year, her work had been featured in two prominent art galleries in Marseille—*Galerie du Port* and *L'Atelier des Muses*—earning her critical acclaim.

Now, with an invitation to exhibit at *Galerie Montparnasse* in Paris, thanks to Justin's connections, and another from *The Vanguard Gallery* in New York, her art was poised to reach new audiences across the globe.

The Vieux Port, with its blend of old and new, seemed the perfect place for this moment—a place where past met present, just as her own story intertwined with the legacy of Lise de Baissac.

Sil, dressed in a simple yet elegant strapless white dress that highlighted her natural tanned beauty, stood radiant under the Mediterranean sun. Her dark curls framed her face, and her brown eyes sparkled with a mixture of joy and serenity as she gazed into Justin's eyes.

Justin, looking effortlessly sophisticated in a tailored suit, held her hands tightly, his expression filled with love and admiration. They'd already weathered so much together—discovering Lise's legacy, restoring his historic home, and bridging their two worlds into one shared vision for the future.

And perhaps most importantly, they had managed to glue the fractured pieces of Sil's Bristol family together again.

Sil's journey to this moment had not been easy. The distance between her and her family had once felt insurmountable, the result of years of misunderstandings, lost connections, and personal struggles. But with Justin by her side, she had found the strength to reach out to them, to confront the pain that had kept them apart, and to begin the slow, delicate work of rebuilding those bonds.

Her father, Martin, had always been a steadfast presence in her life, but they had drifted apart as Sil pursued her own path, often in ways that clashed with the values he had hoped to instill.

It was through her discovery of Lise's letters, and the deep conversations that followed with Justin, that Sil realized the importance of reconnecting with her roots. She had reached out to her father, opening up in ways she never had before, and to her relief, he had welcomed her back with open arms.

Ghislaine, her stepmother, had once seemed a distant figure, her larger-than-life personality a complete contrast to Sil's more rebellious spirit. Yet, as they began to spend more time together, Sil found an unexpected ally in Ghislaine—someone who, despite their differences, genuinely cared for her and wanted to see her happy.

And Jeremy, her younger brother, had grown into a thoughtful, studious teenager, eager to bridge the gap that had formed between them during the years of silence.

As Sil stood there, in the garden of the home she and Justin had made their own, she felt a deep sense of healing. This wedding was not just a union between her and Justin; it was a symbol of the healing that had taken place within her family, the mending of relationships she'd once feared were lost forever.

Before the ceremony began, Sil turned to her father, who was standing nearby. "Dad," she said softly, "I'm so glad you're here."

Martin smiled warmly, placing a hand on her shoulder. "I wouldn't miss it for the world, Sil. I'm proud of the woman you've become. You've brought us all back together. And my dear father would've said, *"Ah lass, you've got the fight in you, and I'm proud to see it."*

Sil felt a swell of emotion, and she squeezed her father's hand. "Thank you, Daddy, and yes, I wished Grandpa Jack could've been here with us tonight. He would have been overjoyed we'd patched up our differences and made things right. He was such a family man."

"He's looking over us all, Sil," her father added pensively. And Sil nodded. It was as if she could hear Grandpa Jack's booming voice sounding over the guests. *"You're shining bright, superstar! Keep shining!"* And she smiled wistfully.

Ghislaine, who'd overheard, stepped forward, her elaborate hat tilting as she moved. "You've brought so much light into our lives, Sil. I've always wanted to be closer to you, and now, well, I think we're finally there."

Sil nodded, feeling tears prick at the corners of her eyes. "We are, Ghislaine. We really are."

Jeremy, quiet and thoughtful as ever, added, "You know, I always looked up to you, Sil. Even when we weren't talking much. I'm glad we're family again."

"Me too, Jeremy," Sil replied, pulling him into a hug.

As she and Justin exchanged vows, the connection between them felt unbreakable—not just a promise for today, but a lifelong commitment to each other's dreams and to the legacy they were building together.

Justin's voice was steady but full of emotion as he vowed, "I promise to cherish you, to stand by your side, and to always be your rock. Together, we will create our own legacy."

Sil, her voice clear and full of conviction, replied, "I promise to love you, support you, and walk with you through all the days of our lives."

In the front row, Sil's father looked on with pride. "That's my girl," he whispered to Ghislaine, who nodded, her eyes shining.

Sophie, seated with her son Jean, caught Sil's eye and gave her an encouraging smile. "Aunt Lise would be so proud of you," she mouthed.

Sil returned the smile, feeling a deep connection to the past, present, and future all at once. This was where she belonged.

On Justin's side, a group of his close friends from Paris, many of whom he had met through his years of lecturing at the Sorbonne, had made the journey to Marseille. They stood out in their smart attire, their camaraderie and easy banter adding to the joyous atmosphere.

As the ceremony came to a close, one of Justin's friends, Philippe, a fellow historian with a dry wit, leaned over to another guest and whispered with a grin, "I give it six months before Jazz is asking for her to paint the walls of the Sorbonne."

His companion chuckled, nodding. "At least she'll add some color to the old place."

Their light-hearted exchange only added to the warmth of the day, as laughter rippled through the small crowd.

Justin caught Sil's eye and winked, clearly aware of the jokes being made at his expense. She responded with a playful roll of her eyes, squeezing his hand to show she was in on the fun.

After the ceremony, the guests slowly made their way inside, toasting to the newlyweds as they returned to their home—Lise's former house in Vieux Port. The house, once the refuge of a hero, now began a new chapter with Sil and Justin, becoming a sanctuary of love, art, and history.

As Sil led her father and Ghislaine on a small tour of the house, she explained the significance of each room, every detail lovingly restored or reimagined to preserve the house's character while making it uniquely theirs.

The walls were alive with Sil's vibrant, eclectic art—bold murals that echoed her journey from Bristol to Marseille, and smaller, intimate pieces inspired by her time with Justin and the letters they'd uncovered.

"This is incredible, Sil," Martin remarked, running his hand along the frame of one of her paintings. "You've turned this house into a living gallery."

Ghislaine nodded, clearly impressed. "It's like stepping into your mind, darling. It's full of life."

As the sun dipped below the horizon, the colors of the sunset painting the sky, Sil and Justin stood together, hand in hand, ready to face the future. Their journey had been one of discovery, healing, and love—a journey that was far from over.

And as they looked out over the city, they knew that whatever came next, they would face it together.

They went to the living room, where a small corner was dedicated to Lise de Baissac. Framed letters, photographs, and mementos told the incredible story of the woman who had once walked these very halls. Justin gently touched the edge of a frame of the pre-war painting Henri had made of his young Lise.

"She's still here with us," he said quietly, as Sil slipped her hand into his. "We've made sure of that."

Sophie, standing nearby, nodded with a smile. "I feel Aunt Lise in every room. Her stately, snow-white presence—the Queen of SOE."

After a lush meal, the guests began to bid the new couple goodbye, leaving Sil and Justin to share a quiet moment together on the balcony. The city of Marseille spread out before them, alive with the energy and promise of the future.

"Justin," Sil began, while a warm feeling spread through her entire body. "I can't believe how far we've come. From that first day on the train to this... it feels like a dream."

Justin wrapped his arms around her, pulling her close. "It's real, Silver. And it's just the beginning. We've got so much more 'us' ahead of us."

Sil kissed him, her heart full. "Speaking of what's ahead... I've been thinking about our honeymoon. You know, bare legs and kisses between the sheets."

Justin's eyes twinkled with amusement. "I thought you might think of that. Well, I happen to have those same inklings. How do... uh... the pristine beaches of Mauritius sound to you?"

Sil looked up at him, her eyes brimming with yes! "Mauritius? Oh Jazz! That's perfect. We can explore where Lise spent her childhood... and maybe discover a new part of her story."

Justin just held her closer. "Exactly. And discover more of us, *Sil*. If you start calling me Jazz like my buddies do, I'll have to revert to Sil with the nose piercing and rainbow hair! But in all seriousness, I want us to start our married life by continuing what we've already begun—honoring the past, but also creating something entirely our own."

He kissed her with a passion that sent all the colors of Sil's world flying.

THANK YOU FOR READING *The Color of Courage*! I hope you've enjoyed Sil's and Lise's stories in the first *Timeless Agents* book!

NOW JOIN SIL AND JUSTIN ON THEIR HONEYMOON to Mauritius, Lise's birthplace. Adventure, history, and the tropics await!

Join my Newsletter here to continue the journey! If you're already a subscriber, don't worry—our system recognizes you, and you'll still have access to these bonus chapters. Happy reading!

https://www.hannahbyron.com/bonus-tcoc

AUTHOR'S NOTE

'The Color of Courage' is a work of fiction inspired by true events and real people. To create a compelling story that intertwines the lives of Lise de Baissac and Sil Anderson, I have added various elements and made certain choices where historical records are either sparse or contradictory.

My portrayal of Lise de Baissac is a blend of fiction and research, reflecting my interpretation of her, rather than an accurate historical account. Those accounts have already been written!

Telling Lise de Baissac's story presented certain challenges, as her life before and after World War II is scarcely documented. Her wartime missions, although significant, often contain conflicting accounts. The following is a clarification of where I deviated from history, presented in the order events take place in the book.

AGENTS' Names

Lise likely did not know the real names of other agents during her training and missions. In a few instances I provided her with that knowledge, but tried to stay true to her reality of only knowing most of her resistance colleagues by codenames.

Irène Brisse

There is some inconsistency on how historians refer to Lise de Baissac's first alias. It is spelled both as Irène Brisse and Irène Brisée. I've chosen for the first as that was the most commonly used one.

Letters to Gustave Henri Villameur

The letters Lise wrote to Henri Villameur are a fictional device used to frame the story. There is no historical evidence that such letters ever existed.

The Montdidiers in Cannes

Lise stayed with friends in Cannes for a couple of months, uncertain about her next steps. The names of these friends are unknown, so the Montdidiers are fictional.

Letter in Her Bag

The letter Lise finds from Henri Villameur while en route to visit her brother Claude in prison in Barcelona is a fictional creation.

SELWYN Jepson

There are different descriptions of the detective-writer turned interviewer of SOE candidates. Some describe him as soft-spoken and kind, others as a fierce interrogator. There are also different descriptions of Jepson's physique in the sources I investigated. And some argue he used an alias himself. I've opted for the fierce interrogator under his own name and will stick with that in the entire series.

ARRIVAL IN POITIERS

Historically, Lise stayed with the Gâteaus for two months before moving into Madame de Vigny's apartment. In the book, I chose to depict her as independent from the start.

CLAIRE AND SOPHIE RIMBAUD

These characters are fictional. While Lise had a teenage helper in the ARTIST network, her real name remains unknown. Lise did, however, use the Café de la Paix as a meeting point.

VISIT TO WILLIAM SAVY in Paris

The visit between Lise and France Antelme (codenamed Renaud) took place in January 1943, not December 1942 as depicted in the book.

Letter from Brother Jean

The letter Lise receives from her brother is entirely fictional.

Friedrich Grabowski

The name Friedrich is invented, as I could not find the first name of the Head of the Poitiers Gestapo. Additionally, there is no evidence linking Grabowski to the collapse of Lise's network and the arrest of her associates.

Agent Gilbert

There is no historical evidence that Lise doubted Agent Gilbert (real name Henri Déricourt) or informed Buckmaster and Vera of her suspicions. The full extent of Déricourt's betrayal became known after the war, though various agents tried to warn London he was also working for the Germans. No action was taken, though he was called back to London once to be questioned but then returned.

Hugh Verity Flying Lise to France

This scene is fictional. Verity was a Special Duties Flight Officer who flew SOE agents to France 20 times in his Lysander, nicknamed 'Jiminy Cricket.' His last flight to France was in November 1943. Some sources state he flew Lise and Andrée on their flight in September 1942, so there is some truth in the matter.

PIMENTO NETWORK

While Lise likely used different aliases and codenames during her short span with the Anthony Brooks network, I could not verify them and thus used the same names as she later used during her time with SCIENTIST II.

CONTACT IN PARIS

William Savy as Lise's contact in Paris when she wants to change networks is fictionalized for narrative purposes.

VISIT TO HENRI Villameur's House

Lise's visit to Henri Villameur's house and seeing him with his new wife is fictional. There is no evidence of them being in touch during the war. Henri Villameur did briefly marry someone else and sought Lise's reconnection after his divorce.

MAURITIUS FLASHBACKS

The flashbacks to Lise's childhood in Mauritius are entirely fictional.

MAQUIS LEADER RAOUL

While it is historically correct that Lise took charge of the Maquis for her brother during her time with SCIENTIST II, the character Raoul is fictional.

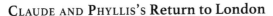

Claude and Phyllis's Return to London

The scenario in which Claude takes Agent Geneviève back to London in August 1944 is invented.

There are plenty of other scenes in *The Color of Courage* where I took liberty with history but in my opinion, they need no further mention as my book is, as stated before, **not** a biography. Yet, I hope with all my heart that I've done Lise and all the other agents mentioned credit with my words.

The sections devoted to Sil Anderson and her journey into the footsteps of Lise the Baissac are fictional. This structure allowed me to explore Lise's life through the eyes a modern-day character, offering a unique perspective on her legacy.

Thank you for reading 'The Color of Courage'.
Hannah Byron

WHO IS HANNAH BYRON?

I'm Hannah Byron, and I've been telling stories since I could hold a pen, though I never dared to dream anyone would actually want to read them. Born in Paris in the mid-1950s to a British mum and a Dutch dad, I grew up with strong ties to three countries that continue to inspire my work—France, the UK, and Holland. It's no surprise that most of my novels are set right here in Western Europe, where history and culture run deep.

For decades, I balanced life as a mother, a university professor and a translator, but now I'm a full-time author, and it feels like I've finally come home. My first dip into the publishing world came in 2010, but life threw me a curveball in 2014 when I lost my brave daughter after a battle with cancer. That devastating loss, followed by a few more rough years, made me step away from writing.

By 2019, I was ready to pick up the pieces. Armed with determination—and my big-girl pants—I dove back in, this time with a clear vision of what I wanted to write: stories of resistance women and romance set during WWII. Maybe not the most commercial choice for an independent author, but one I'm deeply passionate about. These women's courage and resilience are endlessly fascinating to me, and they inspire everything I write.

These days, life is smiling again. My eldest son is part of my business (you can thank him for this lovely website!), and my youngest son is a proud dad to my adorable granddaughter, with another little one on the way. Being a granny is absolutely wonderful—I'm loving every moment of it.

So, grab a cup of tea (or something stronger!) and dive into my world of WWII heroines and timeless love stories. I hope you find as much joy in reading them as I do in writing them.

WHAT TO READ NEXT?

Why not start with <u>In Picardy's Fields</u> ?
And then read all the other 7 books in *The Resistance Girl Series.*

And I'll be adding more and more books to the *Timeless Agents Series* so stay tuned.

I also write the occasional Victorian Mystery under the pen name Hannah Ivory but I've been neglecting *The Imogene Lynch Series* a bit lately.

Please subscribe to my newsletter to get the latest updates here and get *The Partisan Fighter* for free.
https://www.hannahbyron.com/newsletter

Conclave
Trans Lives Matter
True Detective - Jody Foster
Masters of the Air
Baby Reindeer
Amelia Perez
Hacks

Made in the USA
Las Vegas, NV
05 February 2025

17573952R00273